SECRETS
of the
TUDOR
COURT

SECRETS
of the
TUDOR
COURT

D. L. BOGDAN

KENSINGTON BOOKS
www.kensingtonbooks.com

KENSINGTON BOOKS are published by

Kensington Publishing Corp.
119 West 40th Street
New York, NY 10018

All Kensington titles, imprints, and distributed lines are available at special quantity discounts for bulk purchases for sales promotion, premiums, fund-raising, educational, or institutional use.

Special book excerpts or customized printings can also be created to fit specific needs. For details, write or phone the office of the Kensington Special Sales Manager: Kensington Publishing Corp., 119 West 40th Street, New York, NY 10018. Attn. Special Sales Department. Phone: 1-800-221-2647.

ISBN-13: 978-0-7582-4199-3
ISBN-10: 0-7582-4199-2

First Kensington Trade Paperback Printing: May 2010
10 9 8 7 6 5 4 3 2

Printed in the United States of America

To my grandfather, for giving me a love of storytelling;
for my father, for giving me a love of words;
and for my mother, for giving me a love of reading

Acknowledgments

I would first like to thank my agent, Elizabeth Pomada, for all of her hard work in making my lifelong dream a reality. I'd also like to thank my editor, John Scognamiglio, of Kensington Publishing, for taking a chance on me and patiently guiding me through this amazing process. My gratitude also goes to the fine people at the British Archives in Kew for scoping out all of the obscure information on the Third Duke of Norfolk and his family, along with every library I've ever entered (University of Wisconsin-Madison, McMillan Memorial Library, and the Marshfield Public Library in particular). I am continually thrilled by the interlibrary loan system! My acknowledgments would not be complete if I did not recognize the people who have supported me throughout this long journey: my mother, Cindy Bogdan, who *always* took time to let me read my latest scene to her on the phone; Candy Baer, Cathy Renner, Crystal Johnston, Mark Scarborough, the Barton family, the Brand family, Dr. Jeff Kleiman, Dr. Katie Kalish, Teresa Carlson, Victoria Fletcher Schultz, and everyone else who believed in me along the way. Last but not least, I want to thank Dr. David Head, author of the biography *The Ebbs and Flows of Fortune: The Life of Thomas Howard, Third Duke of Norfolk*. Without his work and valuable insights along the way, I would never have been able to entertain you with the Howards' incredible story.

❧ PROLOGUE ❧

An Entrance

Elizabeth Stafford Howard, spring 1519

He is pulling my hair—it is going to be torn from my scalp, I am sure of it. I struggle and fight against him. The pains grip my womb. I cup my rounded belly with one hand and claw my husband's wrist with the other.

"Let me go!" I cry. "Please! The baby is coming! You're going to hurt the baby!"

He says nothing but continues to pull me off the bed by my hair. It hurts . . . oh, it hurts. To my horror I see the glint of his dagger as he removes it from its sheath. He lowers it in one wild gesture, striking my head near where he is pulling my hair. I am unsure of his aims. Is he going to chop my hair off? Is he going to chop *me* up?

"Stop . . ." I beg as he continues to drag me about the house in front of cold-eyed servants who do not interfere with his "discipline."

At long last he drops me on the cold stone floor in front of my bedchamber. The pains are coming closer together. I am writhing in agony. The wound on my head is bleeding. Warm red liquid runs down my face into my eyes.

He walks away.

When his footfalls can no longer be heard a servant comes forward to help me to my bed. It is safe now, I suppose. The midwife, cowering in a corner, inches forward.

"What on God's earth could you have done to warrant that man's displeasure?" she asks in her country accent as she wipes clean my face and attends to the dagger wound.

I look at her in despair. "I don't know," I tell her honestly. "I never know."

And this is how my child enters this world. I name her Mary, after the Blessed Virgin. Perhaps so named, God will show her more favor than He has condescended to show me.

❧ 1 ❧

Doll's Eyes

Mary Howard, 1522

They tell me my father is a great man and I must be his pretty little lady. I must behave myself and stay clean. I wonder what it is to be a great man. I know that he is a favored servant of His Majesty King Henry VIII, and he is a very brave knight. I try to picture him. Is he tall? Is he handsome? I cannot remember. He is not home very much. I cling to my brother Henry's hand and await my lord, who is to see us and comment on our progress. Our progress on what, I do not know. On being people, I suppose.

My sister, Catherine—she is a bigger girl than me and quite haughty—stands beside Henry. My other brother Thomas is at the end, shuffling from foot to foot. We are a pretty row of little soldiers.

When he appears in the nursery with Mother, another foreign figure to our nursery, he reviews us all. He ruffles Thomas's blond hair and shakes Henry's outstretched hand. He compliments my sister on her smart dress.

He regards me a long moment. "Mary," he says, as though it is a new sound to his ears. "How old are you now?"

"I am three," I tell him proudly.

He *is* a great man. I can tell. He is so stately and composed, like a living portrait.

"Three," he says. "And what do you know at this great age of three?"

I think about this. I am not sure how to answer his query. Do I tell him about my letters and numbers, my colors and shapes? What does he want to know? I tell him what I am most proud of.

"I never have any accidents anymore—not in three whole months. Nurse says I will have a pretty new gown." I look up at him, beaming.

He grimaces at this. I do not think my answer pleases him. His lips twitch a moment as he stoops down, picking me up and carrying me to the window. "I shall tell you what is most important, what you should know at this great age of three," he says, bouncing me a bit on his hip. "You are a Howard." He looks into my face. "You are a *Howard*. You belong to the greatest family in the land."

I am held by his gaze; his eyes are black, deep as a starless night. They are eyes that command attention. I am captivated and frightened at once.

I wrap my arms about his neck, pressing my cheek to his, hoping to endear myself to those black orbs that remind me so much of my doll's eyes in their—what is the word? Lifelessness.

"Remember it," he says. "Always remember it."

"I shall," I whisper in earnest.

❧ 2 ❧

Awakening

1530

My father grips my shoulders and I gaze up at his narrow face, now creased in a rare smile. His exacting eyes crinkle at the corners. My lips lift in shy response. He is kneeling before me, his knee caught on the frothy pink lace of my gown.

"A little small for your age, but you'll do," he intones in a voice like sustained thunder. He places a silver circlet inlaid with seed pearls on my head. I reach up to finger the delicate headpiece, in awe. This is my first gift from the Duke of Norfolk. In fact, this is the first time he has sought me out for conversation since I was a wee girl.

He rises and the abrupt movement of his knee parting company with my gown rocks me off balance. I look up. He is a thin man, which gives him the appearance of being tall. His eyes are cold again, his smile converted to a grim line slashed across his face. For a long moment he gazes upon me with eyes that are hard and inscrutable. His hands are locked behind his back. He circles me.

"You examine her like a horse at the fair," my mother comments.

"And so she is," he snaps. Mother shrinks back. She bows her head and places a curled hand against her cheek, though he did not strike her. She does this every time he speaks to her, as though soothing the sting of a future blow in advance.

I am too fascinated by my gift to pay attention to their exchange. By now I have removed the little circlet and am ogling the pearls, hoping to capture my parents' attention once more. Their visits to Kenninghall are too rare. "Is it real?" I ask. At eleven I am already learning to appreciate the measure of good jewels.

"Silly question—of course it's real!" he cries, patting my shoulder.

I clutch it to my chest and scrunch up my shoulders, smiling.

"Ah, a true Howard girl." He laughs. "Can't resist a shiny bauble. Go now, off with you!"

I run down the rush-strewn hallway, anticipating my maid's expression when she beholds the finery my father bestowed upon me. What will Bess make of the gift? I am stopped short, however, by the sound of raised voices. I slow my feet and turn, straining my ears.

"It's no place for her," Mother is saying. "I wish you would rethink it."

"She is needed at court," he says. Court? My heart leaps. Dare I hope? "Mary must be in the foreground, not wasting away out here," he adds.

"She's much younger than the other girls," Mother tells him. "I didn't become a lady-in-waiting to Queen Catherine till I was about thirteen."

"Are you so daft that you think I would expect her to be a lady-in-waiting—to *this* queen?" His tone is mocking. It grates on my ears. I creep closer toward their voices. "She will be a member of her cousin's increasing household." His voice takes on a softer note. "And she will accompany us whenever we visit young Fitzroy so she can see her brother Henry. She'll love it."

Henry! Oh, but I *would* love it! Mother would be a fool to disallow it! But how can she disallow anything? No one opposes the duke, not even those who want to. He is Norfolk, the premier duke of all England. He is Good King Harry's foremost military commander, the best soldier and most courageous sailor. He holds a string of impressive titles: lord high admiral, lieutenant of Ireland from 1520 to 1522, and lord high treasurer. How many battles has he, a man I cannot even refer to in my own head as anything but Norfolk, won for our sovereign?

Would he let the words of my little mother thwart his plans when the whole of England trembles in awe at his very name? I should think not! My heart swells with pride that I should be sired by such a man.

I smile, anticipating his next words with glee.

"I'll be damned if you bring her now, at this time, so she can be influenced by yet another great whore!" Mother cries. I am shocked by this. Not so much by the profanity; my mother is not known for a sweet tongue. It is that she says so to him, this man whom I have been taught to hold in reverent wonder.

I am drawn from my reflections by the sound of a thump and a series of hard pummels against the surface of what I assume to be his chest. There is a bit more scuffling, followed by an abrupt silence. I creep toward the door, hiding in the shadows. I lean against the stone wall, sweating, my heart pounding. The wall is cool, refreshing against my skin, and I press my cheek to it. With care, I peer around the doorway to see that my father has Mother's wrists pinned above her head and is holding her against the wall.

"Now hear this," he seethes. "I do not need *your* permission for anything. She will accompany us where I see fit, and it is most prudent that she be present at court now."

" 'Most prudent,' " Mother mocks, craning her neck forward and attempting to bite Norfolk's long Romanesque nose. He manages to evade the small catlike teeth. "I know what you're about, Thomas Howard. You're scheming again. Isn't it enough to have your precious niece Miss Anne Boleyn dangling under the king's nose like so much fresh meat—now you're to bring little Mary? To what purpose? Who is she to be dangled before? There's none higher than the king."

Norfolk tightens his grip on her dainty white wrists, using them as leverage to pull her forward then slam her against the wall. I can but imagine the pain my mother feels as her back meets with the stone behind the tapestry. I bite my lip and begin to tremble. This is why her little hand curls against her face when he speaks. If I encounter such a man in my husband, I shall never speak against him, I vow.

Mother goes limp but is held up despite it. Her smile oozes with contempt. "Perhaps it is better if you do take her, dangle her before whom you must, rather than operate like my father and take her away from the man she truly loves, in favor of someone like you."

"Ah, yes, the Ralph Neville saga again," Norfolk says in a tone that suggests the tedium of the topic. He lowers her wrists and pins them behind her back, pulling her close to him. He speaks as though reciting lines from a play. "Ralph Neville, your dearest love. And yet what are the Nevilles to the Howards? The blood of kings runs through my veins, treasured wife." This he says with the utmost sarcasm. "Have you so soon forgotten your predecessor?"

"Have *you* forgotten that I am the daughter of the Duke of Buckingham, not one of your common whores? I bear as much if not more royal blood than your scurvy lot!" Mother cries, but her face still bears that wicked smile. Both are smiling, in fact, and I find this to be a most disturbing discourse. I am unsure as to whether they are enjoying their little banter. "And I haven't forgotten my 'predecessor,' " she goes on, her tone biting. "I haven't forgotten that your marriage to Lady Anne Plantagenet was steeped in poverty and that you lived off the pity of relatives. I haven't forgotten that all that royal blood combined couldn't sustain any of your offspring past age eleven, and it certainly couldn't sustain your 'princess'!"

Norfolk shakes her till her teeth chatter. I hear them click together like dice cast against the floor. "Venomous little bitch!"

Mother does not stop. Her voice is uneven as he jars her. "Royal blood is as red as everyone else's and spills even easier."

In one quick movement, Norfolk whirls her around so her back is to him as she kicks and writhes against him. He pulls her to the sedan. I stand stunned. I want to cry but cannot. I just watch, fascinated. As wiry as he is, he has the strength to hold her arms behind her with one hand and maneuver her over his knee. He hikes up her skirts and strikes her across the bottom like a naughty child.

My face burns in shame as I listen to the resounding crack of skin striking skin.

What inspires the most fear in me is that Norfolk's face bears so little expression given the severity of his actions. No anger, no malice. No remorse.

When he finishes he pushes her onto the floor in a crumpled heap. She struggles into a sitting position. Norfolk has turned his back on her and folded his arms across his chest, drawing in a deep breath. *Well done,* his bearing suggests. I shudder. Mother crawls forward. To my complete amazement she wraps her arms about his leg and rests her head against his thigh. They remain like this a long moment before my father reaches down and pushes back her hood to ruffle her wavy brown hair. Like a dog, I think, my stomach churning in revulsion.

She raises her head to him, smirking. "When shall we tell Lady Mary?"

"I knew you would see it my way, Elizabeth." Norfolk's tone is quite pleasant.

I turn around and lean against the wall a moment for support. Tears flood my eyes. The circlet is clammy in my cold hands. It is all right, then, what just happened? Is it some game between them? I take in a few shuddering breaths. I should not be so upset. I have much to look forward to now, it seems. Whatever occurs between my parents is best left to them. This may be how all couples relate. Should this be the case, I shall pray fervently that I am admitted into a convent. But one does not have babies in a convent! I begin to wring my hands in panic.

"My lady?" a gentle voice queries. Hands white as lilies rest upon my shoulders, and I see through a veil of tears the sweet face of my favorite maid. Her wide-set brown eyes are filled with familiar tenderness. "What is it, lamb?"

I attempt to still my trembling lip. "I . . . I do believe I'm going to court," I say, not wishing to confide the disturbing scene between my parents to Bess.

Her full, rosy lips curve into a radiant smile. "But that's wonderful!" she cries, guiding me down the hall into the nursery, where we sit on the settee. She produces a lacy handkerchief and dabs my eyes. Her other hand seizes mine and strokes my thumb in an absent fashion.

"It is wonderful," I agree, but the words are empty. I am nervous. I need to do something. I take the handkerchief. I am far too grown-up to allow her to continue blotting my tears away, and it will occupy my fidgety hands. As I bring it to my face I find the monogram, embroidered in the lovely shade of Tudor green. "T H," I say. The corner of my mouth curves into a teasing smile. "Now, what lad would have given you this, Bessie Holland?" I reach out and tug one of her white-blond ringlets.

She flushes bright crimson and lowers her eyes. Such a demure creature, I think to myself. She is everything I want to be.

" 'Tis nothing," she says, snatching it from me.

"But, Bess, it's so romantic! You must tell me!" I cry, taking her hands. "Is he very handsome? And kind?" I add. After what I just witnessed it is now vital that he be kind to my gentle Bess.

Bess offers a slow nod. "Yes," she says at length. "He is kind to me." She rises and begins to stroll about the nursery, picking up knickknacks and setting them down in a distracted manner. I admire how her voluptuous figure swaggers a bit as she walks. "I shall miss you, my lady." Her voice is wistful. "Now it will just be little Thomas, and he'll be sent away soon enough for his education. What fine ladies and gentlemen I have attended these past years! And think—soon you shall be among the finest."

"I can hardly wait to see what the ladies of the court are wearing," I muse, perked up by the thought of glittering jewels and cloth of gold.

Bess's tone grows quiet. "Take care around Anne. I used to attend her before coming here. She is the loveliest of women, but her mind is . . . unquiet."

"I don't remember her. I have not seen her since I was a child."

Bess laughs and I gather it is because she still considers me a child. I puff out my chest in indignation, imagining the breasts that will soon erupt from the flat landscape of my girlhood. I break into giggles.

"She is much favored by the king." Bess sits down again. Her eyes are alight with intrigue. "You know that she usurped her sister's place in that—"

The door bursts open, interrupting her tale, and I am disappointed. I want so much to learn of this world I am about to enter and know I cannot ask anything of my father.

"Mary." It is Norfolk himself. He offers a smile as he enters. "We will be leaving for court directly. Why don't you see to the packing of your things? Just a few things, mind you. I shall have new gowns ordered upon our arrival."

"Can Bess come?" I ask, clinging to her hand.

He bows his head, clearing his throat. "No, not just now."

I pout a moment before seizing Bess's hands and kissing her cheeks. I exit but do not run this time. Something keeps me rooted in place outside the door and I wonder if this is my fate, camping outside of doors, listening to things I do not want to hear, for surely what I am hearing now is out of a dream.

Sweet murmurs assault my ears. Yes, *assault*, because they are not exchanged between those who should utter them. I turn. My father has Bess's head cupped between his hands. She is smiling up at him with the unadulterated adoration of a love-starved child. He gathers her in his arms, kissing her with the same fierce passion he used in striking my mother. When they part they are breathless. They lean back on the settee and I watch his hand snake down her stomacher.

T. H. Thomas Howard. So the handkerchief she offered me was his. On what occasion had he lent it to her? Had she been crying over her undesirable role as mistress? Had she been demanding that he rid himself of my mother to set her, wicked Bessie Holland, in her place? I picture the whole scene, my cheeks hot with rage. My father wrapping his arms around Bess and consoling her, promising her the world if she'd only be patient a little while longer. He gives her his handkerchief and she clutches it to her ample bosom just to lure his eyes to that ripe spot wherein beats her sinful little heart. Oh, the seducer!

Bile rises in my throat as I quit the mental imagery. A firm hand grips my shoulder. How is it he can move so swiftly and silently, I think as I squeeze my eyes shut against whatever is to come. But when I open them it is into my mother's face I look.

"So. Now you see," she says in her low voice. There are no tears in her eyes. She is a strong little woman, her angular jaw set in a line of determination, her challenging gaze stormy blue. She is not like Bess—soft, round Bess—who is made of honey and cream. Mother cannot afford to be honey and cream. She is fighting, always fighting. Now I know what she is fighting for.

"Yes," I say with profound sadness. "Now I see."

"You will be careful at this court of Henry, the Eighth of That Name." I nod at the gravity of this formal order. "You must know that when you are there you will not see His Grace your father very much at all, and I will be busy attending Her Majesty. Be quiet. Watch and learn. Never tattle on anyone else, no matter how tempted you are by the promises of others. Be still. Keep your own counsel. Self-preservation, Mary, is of the utmost importance at this court."

"Yes, Mother." My throat contracts with tears. I want her to enfold me in her arms the way Bess does when I am sad or frightened. But I am angry at Bess and remind myself to admire my mother's cool sense of control rather than long for the embrace of that vile betrayer.

Mother nods to me. I nod back. We part company.

This is how true ladies conduct their business.

I am leaving. Bess catches me before I descend to the great hall. Sensing my coldness, her soft eyes make their appeal. She clings to my hands as if she does not know of her transgression. I snatch them from hers and scowl. Her face registers her sorrow as she seizes my wrists.

"My lady." Her voice is almost a whimper, stirring my heart. "Your father is a powerful man. We can only all of us do his bidding. My family . . . they depend on His Grace." Tears stream down her cheeks with abandon. "I . . . I have no choice, my lady."

I blink several times to keep fresh tears at bay. "Such topics are not suitable for my ears," I say, thinking myself to be quite dignified, but feeling a fraud. I disengage myself and turn around to go meet my parents.

"Mary!" Bess cries.

The unchecked agony of her voice causes me to stop.

"I love you like my own," she says, her milky voice edged with desperation.

I burst into tears and run to her, flinging myself into her arms. "Oh, Bess, dearest Bess," I sob. I forget the coolness of my mother and the wantonness of Bess's actions. All I know is I am in the arms of the one person I have trusted to love me without reserve— my Bess. I cannot fault her for anything now, nor can I blame my father for loving her. My sense of right and wrong has been thwarted. I do not know what game I have been thrust into. I have yet to ascertain the character of the players.

I only know that I am one of them. My mother's words ring in my ears. *Self-preservation, Mary . . .*

With effort I extract myself from Bess's embrace and know that as I leave her I am leaving all vestiges of childhood behind me.

❧ 3 ❧

Farewell to Kenninghall

I ride away with my father's armed retinue, watching my childhood home become a small black speck on the horizon. Mother
rides in a covered litter with the curtains drawn. I asked to sit beside her but was refused, as she prefers her privacy.

"Soon you will not see it at all," Norfolk says in reference to
Kenninghall as he sidles up beside me. He looks formidable on his
black charger, though in lieu of armor he wears the fine furs and
velvets of a much-favored courtier. The heavy cloak envelops his
slight personage and he appears more solid. He holds the reigns
with one slim-fingered hand while the other rests on the hilt of his
sword.

"Stop looking back," he tells me. "Howards do not ever look
back; we press onward. No matter the circumstances. Onward."
He gestures for me to look ahead and I do, taking in the fields that
surround us; they are barren and gray. Winter is pondering its arrival. It teases us with a scattering of snowflakes now and then. I
shiver. I wish we were traveling in the spring when the landscape
has more to offer.

So far what is ahead looks bleak. I am at once clutched in anxiety's sadistic fist. What if I do not fit in at court? What if no one
likes me? Kenninghall may not have been an exciting place, but

along with Tendring and Hunsdon—my other childhood homes—it was familiar. I had my lessons. I played with my brother and Bess. Now I am plunging into a life alien to me. My father is foreign to me. I have only seen him a handful of times. I want to impress him; I want him to be proud of me. Yet he frightens me. His brutality toward Mother, his tenderness toward Bess . . . I cover my mouth to stifle a sob.

"Are you ill, Mary?" Norfolk asks.

"No, my lord," I say quickly. I avert my head. I do not want him to see my tears.

"You have not been made accustomed to long rides," he comments. "You must be tired. Come." In one effortless movement he leans down and scoops me right off my saddle, setting me in front of him. I stiffen, unsure of how to conduct myself. He is my father, but he is also the intimidating soldier-duke. He is the man who beat my mother and made love to my maid in the same afternoon. But he is also the man we are taught to worship and long for.

I lean back, giving in to the need to rest against something. His chest is warm; I feel his beating heart against my back. I look down at his hand, a hand of such perfection it could have been the model for a statue, with its strong tapering fingers and subtle blue veins snaking like rivers beneath his tanned skin. It is the hand of a scholar and soldier. The thought sobers me. This hand is capable of much cruelty.

Now it rests about my waist, quite nonthreatening. In a moment forged out of the desperate need for reassurance, I reach out and take it in my own.

"I am so glad to be with you, Father," I tell him, and in that moment I am filled with the utmost sincerity.

He pauses. "I have been shown your embroidery. Quite fine," he says. "And I am told you have a nice ear for the virginals and dance prettily. At court you shall learn all the new dances. It is vital that you study all the womanly arts, Mary. It is also important to keep up with your education. It pleases me to learn that you are a good reader and know your letters."

"In English and Latin, sir," I brag, trying to mask my hurt that he has not yet told me he is glad to be in my company. Perhaps, because he is first a soldier, he does not know how to return a compliment.

"The most important thing to remember, Mary, is to keep your cousin Anne happy. Serve her, please her, whatever she wants. She is favored by the king and our family's hopes lie with her," he goes on to advise. "But as high as Anne is raised, never forget who the head of this family is. Never forget who your first allegiance is with; that it is your goodly and Christian duty to obey your father always. Swear to me, Mary. Swear to me your obedience and fidelity in all things."

"I swear," I say, unnerved by the intensity of his tone.

"Good," he says. "Very good."

He squeezes my hand.

I shall be everything he wants, I think to myself. I shall work very hard so that someday he will look at me and say *Mary, I am so glad to be with you.*

❧ 4 ❧

London!

How is it I, little Mary Howard, can be so fortunate as to enter this fairest of cities? My heart is swollen with joy as I behold all the sights and smells of this magical place. It is so very *big!* Tears sting my eyes as I behold beggars on the street, but my eyes are filled with as much excitement as compassion when they are drawn to the fine ladies and gentlemen that stroll the market, many of whom I have been assured are mere servants from the palace. If the servants are garbed in such finery, then how must it be for the true set!

Most of the streets are dirt but some are cobbled, and I love the sound of our horses' hooves as they strike against them. I ride my own pony now, sitting straight and proud. Some of the fishwives and other ladies of the market shout blessings out to me and I imagine that this is how the Princess Mary must feel when she travels about in the open.

I firmly believe that God chose England as the spot to place His most beautiful river, the Thames. In its shimmering waters float barges and little rowboats. I squirm in delight, longing to be a part of it. Ahead I can see London Bridge and the approaching Tower, where all the fair kings and queens stay upon their coronations.

"It's not all a tale from faeries' lips," one of Norfolk's pages tells me. He is young; not much older than my brother Henry. I estimate him to be about fourteen. "See that river? Every day they pull hundreds of bodies out of it. And the pretty Tower? Below it are some of the most gruesome dungeons ever constructed. They torture people on the rack and—"

"Enough!" I cry, urging my pony forward. I refuse to think of anything unpleasant as I make my debut into London.

But somehow the day is a little less sunny, the river a little less sparkly.

And the Tower is a lot darker.

Westminster is a bustling palace! There are people everywhere. Up and down the halls rush servants and heads of state, foreign dignitaries, and courtiers more beautiful in person than I could ever have imagined. As we walk down the halls, I note that my father is greeted with a mixture of aloofness and what I would call sugared kindness. He greets them all the same; with no expression and a grunt of acknowledgment.

I have to refrain from skipping. Norfolk walks with a brusque, determined step and I am all but running to keep up as it is. My face aches from smiling as I take in all the beauty around me.

"Don't be a fool, Mary," Norfolk says *sotto voce* when he catches my expression of bewildered joy. "You haven't just stepped out of a stable. Behave as though you're accustomed to some level of refinement."

I sober immediately, swallowing tears. He is right, I remind myself. I must do the family proud. It would not do my father much credit to appear ignorant before the court.

As we walk we encounter an older woman accompanied by a small entourage of ladies. She wears a somber blue gown and a long mantilla over her graying auburn hair. Her blue eyes are soft and distant. She clutches a rosary in her thin hand and every step she takes seems laden with weariness.

My father sweeps into a low, graceful bow. "Your Grace," he says in a gentle voice.

I sink into a deep curtsy before Queen Catherine of Aragon.

"Returned from your business?" the queen asks. Her voice is

low and sweet—motherly. I imagine it would be very nice to sit at her feet while she reads.

"Yes," Norfolk answers. His face is wrought with tenderness. His hand twitches at his side. He wants to reach out to her, I deduce.

"Who is this little creature?" she asks, and a wistful smile plays upon her thin lips.

She lifts my chin with two velvet fingertips. I manage to lower my eyes in respect.

"May I present my daughter, Mary," Norfolk answers.

"Ah, so you have brought another Howard girl to court," she tells my father. She removes her hand from my chin. "To ensure we do not run out?"

Norfolk does not answer.

The queen emits a small, mirthless laugh. "I must attend Mass now. Do you and your little girl wish to accompany me, my lord duke?" She does not wait for him to respond. "No, I suppose not. Attending Mass with the queen has grown quite out of fashion of late, I think."

She moves on and my mother joins her small assemblage of ladies. Norfolk bows, holding the position until she has long since passed.

When he rights himself his eyes are shimmering with unshed tears.

I avert my head, realizing with a pang that while my father is avowed to Mother and enthralled with Bess, it is Queen Catherine of Aragon he respects.

It is an esteem I, too, hope to earn.

❧ 5 ❧

Anne

She is surrounded by adoring courtiers. The ladies flutter about in their bright dresses like so many butterflies, squawking like chicks in a pen. Her apartments are grand and alive with music and poetry. So much is going on that I do not know where to look.

And then my eyes behold her.

She is not beautiful, not to those who define such as light and golden. She is breathtaking. Dark, with skin like a gypsy, her obsidian eyes are luminous and lively, her lush black hair long and glossy, worn parted down the middle and flowing down her back beneath her stunning French hood. She wears a dress of fine green velvet with the most resplendent sleeves I've ever seen. Resting at the base of her swanlike throat is a pendant of an intricate *B* for Boleyn.

She is tilting back her stunning head now, laughing at something one of her many male courtiers said when we walked in. She turns white at the sight of my father, her laughter catching in her throat.

"I decided to bring your cousin Mary back with me," he says. "She will serve you." He glances about the room and shakes his head. "I will have speech with you later."

With that he quits the room and I am alone, with no instruction. I have no idea when I will see him again, where I am to sleep, who is to look after me. I draw in a deep breath. I must press onward. I am a Howard.

I urge myself toward my cousin and curtsy. "It will be my pleasure to serve you, Mistress Anne," I say.

Anne laughs. She reaches out a hand and seizes my chin. Her touch is not as gentle as the queen's.

"You have a big nose like your father," she says in a slightly French-accented voice.

At once tears fill my eyes. This is the last thing I expect to hear. On instinct my hand flies up to cover the offensive appendage, though all my life I have been unaware of its effect. It is all I can do to keep from sobbing out loud. I blink. I must think. I must win her favor.

I lower my hand and smile. "Were it only like yours, my lady," I say. "Perhaps you can show me how to make the best of this unfortunate circumstance?"

Anne ponders me a moment, then bursts into laughter. There is something about it, an edge that makes it less joy-filled than nervous. *Immoderate.*

"You shall sleep with the other maidens," she says, putting to rest one of my anxieties. "You'll find yourself in good company. Our cousin Madge Shelton is with us, and here is my sister, Mary Carey."

She gestures to a curvaceous blonde who reminds me of my Bess. I smile at her. I remember that Bess told me she had once been the king's mistress. Through servants' gossip I heard that her two children are his bastards. She is very beautiful; soft and round to her sister's willowy delicacy. It is easy, however, to see how one could be attracted to both of them.

Mary Carey approaches me and takes my hand. "We'll take good care of you here," she assures me, and my stomach settles a bit upon hearing the soothing sincerity of her tone.

"But we must figure out a way to differentiate between all the Marys," Anne comments. "Is it the only name in England?" She rises, flinging her grand hair over her shoulder. "My sister shall be big Mary and you shall be little Mary."

"What about Princess Mary?" I ask.

Anne's face darkens and I curse myself for mentioning the princess's name. I have so much to learn about this court and I just cannot take it in fast enough!

Anne bats her eyes and adopts a playful expression. "Ugly Mary."

The room erupts into titters of girlish laughter and I stifle the guilt that churns in my gut as I imagine Princess Mary, rumored to be plain and studious, alone and unloved in her own father's court.

But I am sworn to the Howards. I am sworn to the preserving of Anne's happiness. It is not for me to fret over the princess.

Yet late that night, after I am settled into bed with my cousin Madge, I find myself mumbling a prayer for her.

No one should ever be without a friend in the world.

It does not take long to realize that there exist two courts here. One small faction remains faithful to Queen Catherine and the other—the younger, more flighty set—flocks to my lady Anne, the star ascendant. I am caught up in all the excitement. There is nothing but merriment when around Anne. We recite poetry and sing, her favorite musician, Mark Smeaton, accompanying us on his lute, playing with slim deft fingers. We playact together, rehearsing masques we will perform for the king.

The king! What a dazzling figure! He is so big and charming one cannot help but be rendered speechless in his majestic presence. One afternoon while we are readying ourselves for a picnic in the gardens, he struts into Anne's apartments with the confidence and beauty of a peacock, decked out in his finest velvet and ermine.

As he enters I am brushing my lady's hair, as she prefers my hand to her sister's when they are in disagreement, which is often.

"And how now, Brownie?" he asks her.

She laughs at the endearment and shoos me away. I manage to put the brush down but am too awed by His Grace to move, so stand transfixed.

"Who's this little beauty?" he asks, directing his gaze at me.

"Surely Your Grace met my cousin Mary, Uncle Thomas's daughter." Anne's voice is flat.

"No, we would remember encountering such a fair child," he says, stroking his tawny beard.

While it is true I have seen the king from afar at meals and entertainments since coming to court, and even bear some vague childhood memories of him, I have never been formally introduced.

He reaches out and places a bejeweled hand on my head. "Bless you, little one," he says. "How do you find our court?"

"It is the most splendid place in all the world, Sire," I say, breathless.

He laughs, a robust sound as mighty as he is. "You see? From the mouths of babes! May you always find happiness here, young Mary."

I am delighted by the encounter. He is so strong and cheerful I allow myself to imagine being held against his doublet, snuggled up safe and warm in my sovereign's arms. I wonder if his relationship with Princess Mary is affectionate.

His relationship with Anne certainly is. Now he is kissing her hand, turning it palm up to devour her little wrist. She pulls back. It is her bad hand, the one with the nub of a sixth finger on it, a very subtle deformity she hides well.

It withdraws into her voluminous sleeve. She distracts him from the gesture by fluttering her thick dark lashes at him. "And to what do we owe the honor of this impromptu visit, Your Majesty?"

"We would like to present you with a gift," he says, his crisp blue eyes sparkling. He turns his attention to the mass of courtiers eavesdropping. "Ladies and gentlemen, why don't you prepare for the gardens? We will join you shortly."

We have no choice but to do as we are told.

Madge Shelton is now my best friend at court. She is not altogether attractive, but is spirited and full of a vibrancy that creates an aura of beauty that deceives the untrained eye. She and I stand in our maidens' chamber gossiping over His Majesty's "gift."

"No diamonds or rubies for Anne," Madge says, laughing. "But Wolsey's own Hampton Court!"

I bow my head a moment. "I can't help but feel sorry for the Cardinal . . ."

"Shhh!" Madge puts her finger to my lips. "Don't say such things. We aren't permitted opinions. He failed in granting an annulment and proving the invalidity of the king's marriage, so suffered the price—confiscated lands and a confiscated title. He's the archbishop of York now, remember?"

"But he was so close with the king," I continue in genuine puzzlement. "It's frightening to think one he loved like a brother can be thrown down so fast. And so far."

"This is strange to you?" Madge's tone is incredulous. She is a true Howard, I think. There is a hardness in her voice that echoes of my father. "Haven't you observed how he treats his once-beloved wife? How many tales have we grown up listening to, of the king's love-madness for Queen Catherine—that once, before his affairs and neglect ruined her, she was the loveliest princess in Christendom? Still he manages to throw her aside. Strange, Mary?"

"Now we are ruled by two queens," I am compelled to say. I tremble at the thought, not because I am afraid but because it is so odd.

"Not for long," says Madge. "Not now that Mistress Anne is granted Hampton Court!"

We burst into another fit of giggling, all pondering dissipated. It is all such a game to us, two girls barely out of the nursery, still naïve enough to enjoy the intrigues of the court.

"Will we all move, then?" I ask.

"I imagine the Anne faction will relocate to the palace. It sounds as though His Majesty plans on making it the new London residence," says the all-knowing Madge.

"How terribly exciting!" I breathe.

"Oh, Mary, you're such a little girl," Madge scoffs, but there is no malice behind it and I respond with a smirk. "Do you think old Wolsey left all his red fabric behind?" she adds.

"Why?" I ask.

"To swathe the halls of Hampton Court, of course!"

I laugh in approval, remembering the very rotund Cardinal Wolsey.

Still, the laughter is a little forced. I do believe even cynical Madge seems to pity King Henry's poor discarded adviser, and it takes away from the excitement of our move.

A little.

I am tired. I am so caught up in this faerie world that I do not sleep at night. I toss and turn, anticipating what wonders will await me the next day. What games will we play? What songs will we sing?

We await our move to Hampton Court. We gossip in voices that ring out like the tinkling of little chimes. We drink wine. Anne thinks it's funny to see my face get flushed.

We all congregate at supper and I can't keep my eyes open. My father sits far out of my reach with the other members of the council. As Mother predicted I do not see her, but I catch glimpses of the duke at court. We do not speak, not until he lays a hand on my shoulder in the hall on the way back from an evening's entertainments, pulling me aside.

I am thrilled to be acknowledged. "How now, Father?" I ask with a cheery smile. It is Anne's smile. I practice it whenever I'm alone.

"Wipe that stupid grin off your face. You look like a harlot," says Norfolk. He grips my shoulder and guides me down the hall toward his apartments.

He takes me to his privy chamber and sits behind his austere mahogany desk, folding his hands before him and regarding me, one eye squinting, as though I am a diamond he is examining for flaws. "How is Anne?" he asks after a long pause.

"I think she is well, sir," I say.

"Has she slept with the king?"

I am shocked at the question. My face burns and I bow my head.

"Don't play innocent. I know how maidens talk." He has not raised his handsome voice; it is thin and impatient but not loud.

I still cannot look at him. "She does not speak of that," I say.

"Don't you *listen*, fool?" he demands, slamming his hand on the desk. "Do you think you're here for your own entertainment? Do you realize your task in this? You are to be my ears, Mary. I depend on you to report to me all that is said and done in those chambers."

"What am I to do if she does . . . if she is . . ." I cannot say it. I don't even know what it really means.

"Nothing," he says. "It is not your place to advise her, not that she'd take it from the likes of you as it is. You are my ears, Mary, that is all. I will expect a nightly report from this day hence. It seems she is weakening under his pressure. No doubt with Hampton Court now dangling before her, she feels secure in her position and thinks she'd have nothing to lose by giving in. Fools, all of them." The fist on the desk clenches and my eyes are drawn to it. A melding of perfection and anger. "She is difficult to manage," he says now, more to himself. "It would have made life easier if he'd have settled for that dolt of a sister of hers; she's already proven her capacity for childbearing." He shakes his head, then returns his black eyes, eyes that are much like our Anne's, to me. "It is vital that Anne understands the king's fickle nature; that he tires of his playthings once he has them."

I do not know how to respond to this monologue so remain silent, wondering if he will dismiss me.

"Do you understand, Mary?" he asks, leaning back in his chair.

I nod. "Yes, my lord. I understand."

"Go on, now. It's late," he says. "To bed with you."

I turn to leave, but he raps his hand on the desk. I turn.

Without raising his head he says, "News from Sir Edward Stanley." My brother-in-law? What news could there be of him? Was my sister with child? My heart leaps at the thought of being an aunt. "Seems your sister Catherine passed from the plague."

I am dizzy. My head tingles. Catherine . . . my fair sister, Catherine, newly married. She was going to have a happy life; a quiet country life with many children. She was so gentle and sweet . . . Catherine. How could he tell me like this? How could he just sit there and mention my sister's death with the same dismissive tone he'd describe a failed crop or broken axle?

I approach the desk, trying to remind myself that he is a soldier. It is not in a soldier's nature to show emotion; they see death all the time. Should they cry, I imagine their tears would never stop.

Rounding the desk I inch closer to where he sits. He has not raised his head. He is looking through some documents. Letters from Stanley? From behind I wrap my arms about his shoulders in a feeble embrace, leaning my head against his cheek. He stiffens, every muscle growing taught beneath my touch. I drop my arms and bow my head, tears burning my eyes.

"Will we go to her interment?" I ask hopefully.

"Of course not," he answers, his tone gruff. "It's foolhardy to go where the plague has been."

For a moment I just stand before him, helpless. There's so much I want to say but cannot articulate. "Should we say a prayer for her?" I ask at last, my voice small.

He sets the document on the desk, facing me at last. "Prayers never brought any of my other children back. I don't expect it will work for her. Off with you now."

I turn once more.

"Mary." His voice is low.

I do not face him this time. I do not want him to see the tears paving cool trails down my cheeks.

"Your hair is your finest feature," he says, reaching out to finger a tress of my thick, honey-blond mane, which falls unbound to my waist in keeping with the fashion of unmarried maids. "See that you brush it every night," he instructs. "A hundred strokes."

"Yes, my lord," I answer as I quit the room.

In the maidens' chamber my tears cannot be hidden. I walk in with my face covered. I do not want to see the other girls. I want to be alone; I want to think about Catherine, about her sweet, lilting voice, her delicate features, her patient smile. She was everyone's perfect lady, far more suited to court life than I could ever be. Perhaps it is better this way; court life seems every bit as deadly as plague, and uglier, too. Catherine was too pure for it. She was elegant, charming, composed. She was to be a country wife . . . oh, how I cried when she left. How I longed to accompany her. Waiting on her would have been far more gratifying than service to any queen.

Swirling unbidden through my mind is a memory, far more like a dream to me now. My head is tilted up toward her. She crowns me with a garland of flowers. I close my eyes. I can almost feel the flowers about my head. I take in their sweetness, the warmth of the sun on my face, and the love of my sister Catherine. The queens of Kenninghall, Bess had called us. How ill-fated is our reign.

At once Anne's voice hisses into my reverie. "Where were you, little Mary? Reporting my behavior to your father, little spy that you are! Do not think I don't know what you're about, little innocent!"

I cry harder, great gulping sobs as I throw myself on the bed I share with Madge, burying my face in my pillows.

"Little Mary . . . ?" Anne's voice bears a gentler note. "Mary, what is it?" The mattress sinks down with her weight as she leans over me and touches my shoulder.

"My sister," I sob. "My dear sister Catherine . . . she's dead of the plague."

At once Anne is moved to tears, gathering me in her thin arms with a fierceness that almost frightens me. She rocks back and forth with a franticness that is not soothing, but I applaud her efforts just the same.

"Damn bloody plague," she seethes. "Why is it all so unfair? Why do we have so little control?"

It is a question that I realize has very little to do with the loss of my sister, but it doesn't matter. I allow Anne and the other girls to soothe my tears and offer their sympathies. I soak up their embraces, wondering why it is only during tragedies that people are driven to physical demonstrations of love.

That night Madge tries to distract me from my grief by telling me stories of King Arthur.

All I can think of is my father as he imparts the news of Catherine's death.

He did not even look up.

* * *

Because my mother has not condescended to talk to me since my arrival at court, I write her a little note and send it by messenger to her chambers.

> *My dearest Mother,*
> *I am so aggrieved by my sister's passing that the joy of court life has been sucked out of me. Filling my mind are memories of us as children, writing poems and singing songs, picking out the names of our future children. Life was simple then. Why does it all change?*
> *All my sympathies are with you, Mother. I cannot imagine what it would be like to lose a child. I pray for you every night and hope you are finding comfort in the Lord.*
> *Your loving daughter,*
> *Mary*

> *Daughter,*
> *The Lord giveth and the Lord taketh away. We have no control over our fate. We can only press on. We are Howards.*
> *Bless you,*
> *Mother*

> *Dearest little Mary,*
> *My heart breaks for you. I know how close you and Catherine were, growing up. How well do I remember all of your childhood antics! You were such beautiful sisters. She was fair and good and sweet. I pray for her soul and for you as you grieve. Remember, my dear little love, that God is merciful and kind. His ways are mysterious and beyond our understanding. Now Catherine celebrates with the angels and knows no*

suffering. Her good soul is put to much better use than it could have ever been down here. May she watch over all of us.

I hope you are well and that you are making many friends at court. I hope to see you soon and that all is well between us.

With much love,
Your Bess

In the maidens' chamber, I clutch Bess's letter to my breast. I have read it over and over and it is stained with my tears. Bess knew us best. She loves us best. But thinking of Bess only makes me sadder, so I tuck the letter in my little silver keepsake casket along with the one from my mother, a letter I have read only once.

Mary Carey tells me she lost her husband to the sweating sickness. Many other girls come forward and confide of their losses, how one parent or sibling perished to the plague and other terrible things.

I feel less alone but the sadness remains. There is so much unresolved. If I had only been allowed to see her interred, perhaps there would be more closure. It would seem real. As it is, it's still as though she is off in the country, married to Lord Derby.

Norfolk never mentions her name again. He does not say much of anything during my nightly reports, which consist of nothing since Anne is careful with her words. I tell him she knows why I am there.

"Of course she does—she's not a complete idiot," he says. "May you serve as a reminder." He pauses. "She spends quite a bit of time with her brother George, does she not?"

I nod, smiling at the thought of her handsome brother, who is the picture perfect courtier. "He's very fine," I tell him.

"See to it that they aren't alone too often," Norfolk instructs.

"They're not alone," I say in confusion. "Mary Carey's with them most of the time."

"The court is talking," he tells me, but I have that feeling I often get when he's speaking; that the words are never directed at me. "Jane Parker's jealousy is . . . twisted." He refers to George Boleyn's wife, an anxious sort of woman who seems just the sort to be "twisted," always lurking about in doorways, or hovering just beyond a circle of friends in the hopes of attaining some juicy piece of gossip. Mary Carey warned me of her before, saying that her mind was poisoned with all manner of perverted ideas. Despite my curiosity I never pressed her for particulars. There was more than enough perversion at court without becoming preoccupied with hers.

"How?" I ask, overcome with curiosity.

"None of your concern," Norfolk snaps. "Just see to it the three Boleyns are accompanied as often as possible."

"But what if they don't want me along?"

"You go with them anyway," he says with an impatient wave of his hand. "Children are annoying creatures, immune to subtlety." He leans forward and meets my eyes. "In other words, Mary: be yourself."

I am struck as dumb as he thinks I am. At once every condescending word and derisive jibe he ever directed toward me is brought to mind, constricting my heart as though it were clutched in his perfect fist. Tears burn my eyes, but it would humiliate me further to let them fall in front of him. I must hide them from him, as I always do. I draw in a breath. This talk of siblings brings Catherine to mind, and an image of my brother Henry soon follows.

"Are we to see Henry soon, Father?"

"Henry who?"

I can't fault him for this. Everyone is named Henry.

"Howard—Surrey, of course!" I say with a giggle, wondering if there is anything under God's sun I can do to make this man smile.

"Oh, him." He rifles through more documents. "Your brother's at Windsor Palace keeping company with Henry Fitzroy, King Henry's boy." His eyes grow distant. "Fitzroy . . . His mother was a clever one. To think of all little Bessie Blount became . . . mistress of a monarch, the mother of the king's son, a son showered with grand titles." He offers a slight laugh. "But not quite grand enough. No, Bessie Blount went as far as she could go with what she had. But our Anne shall go even farther. No bastard children for her . . ."

I am only half listening. In truth I could not care less about King Henry's boy or fair Bessie Blount at this point. My heart surges with hope as I anticipate a visit with my beloved brother.

"Can we go to him?" I ask. "Please?"

He pauses. My heart races. Surely this means he is considering. "I'm sure he'll be at the next court function. Off with you now. Remember what I told you."

"Yes, my lord," I say in disgruntled tones as I quit the room. My heart aches for something familiar. I long for my brother's laugh— he could make light of anything with his jokes and easy nature. I long for my sister, forever lost to me. She, with her perfect grasp on a world I do not seem to belong to, would know how to advise me. In her I could confide of my awkwardness, my fear, and my desire to be the lady she was with such effortlessness.

I long for the mother I never had, a woman so lost in her own pain that it has ruined her for any of her children.

I long for Bess, for her reassurance, her ample bosom to snuggle in, her simple, uncomplicated company.

When I return to the maidens' chamber I remove her letter from the little casket.

I read it again and again and again.

As Norfolk predicted, I do see my brother at a court function; a joust. How to describe tournaments! The shining knights, the beautiful ladies, some with tokens for their bonnie lads about to take the field. Anne gives the king her handkerchief.

Queen Catherine clutches hers in her lap, twisting it with nervous fingers.

"Will you give your scarf to anyone, little Mary?" Anne asks with a wink of her obsidian eye.

"Perish the thought!" says her brother George, always cheerful. "She's far too young and sweet to be sullied by love!"

"Why, does love sully us?" Anne asks with the coquettish grin that I practice so hard to achieve. "I think I have fared quite well!"

Ripples of laughter surround me and I allow myself a giggle. It is the first time I have felt any semblance of mirth since hearing of my Catherine's death.

"Well, love has sullied me," says George with an affectionate glance at his sister. "Your father picked me quite a bride, young Mary," he tells me. Then to the rest of the assemblage he adds, "Wouldn't everyone agree that my Jane is in possession of many charms?"

The ladies burst into laughter. Indeed, we could barely escape the sour-faced maid with her wicked tongue and, from what I've heard, vicious mind. In a way I feel sorry for her. It is as though she is always on the outside, circling Anne's exclusive set, her eyes filled with a strange contemptuous longing.

George's comment causes more laughter and he tips back his dark head to join in before riding off to enter the lists.

I scan the jousters, excitement bubbling in my chest. I see a familiar head bobbing among the crowd, its owner's expression faraway. Dreamy. It is a sweet face. I leap up from my seat and run toward the yard.

"Henry Howard!" I cry out, waving my arms. "Henry, Lord Surrey!"

He turns his head, jarred from his reverie, and begins to run toward me. "Look at this!" He takes my hands and covers them with kisses. "Mary, dearest little girl."

Tears spring to my eyes. "Oh, Henry . . ." There is so much I want to say. About this weird place, about Catherine, about Norfolk. I cannot articulate it, though, so stand before him, smiling.

"What's this?" Henry asks, wiping a stray tear from my cheek. "No tears, Mary. We Howards are at the top of the world right now!"

"Are you competing today, Henry?" I ask.

"No, not me," he tells me, his long face drawn up into a smile. He is a younger version of Norfolk, his nose straight and Roman, his hooded eyes drooping slightly at the sides. Only he laughs. "Harry and I are just here to observe today, though he is itching to compete."

It is only at this moment that I realize my brother isn't alone.

Beside him stands a boy about my age, with bright strawberry blond hair and energetic blue eyes. His complexion is rosy, his gentle smile is ready; he is also the picture of his father, King Henry VIII.

I curtsy. "Hello, my lord duke."

"Such formality for your old playmate?" he asks with a giggle that betrays his youth.

It is true I have hazy memories of playing at Windsor Palace with my brother and young Harry; since my father was the boy's governor we were often in his company. But to me this seems like ages ago and the memories, like most from the dreamy days of childhood, are but distant echoes of a faerie song; one is not quite sure if it was ever real.

I blush. "Only showing the proper deference for the Duke of Richmond and Somerset, Earl of Nottingham, and Knight of the Garter," I say, but my voice bears the slightest edge of teasing.

He reaches out a hand to tap my upper arm. "Plain Harry to you," he says. "We should show her the puppies."

"Puppies?" I squeal.

"You like puppies?" Harry asks. "They're in the stables—oh, they're mongrels, not proper hunting dogs at all, but they're—they're, well, they're rather cute." He seems embarrassed to say the word *cute*, as though it is not masculine to perceive things thus.

"Oh, yes, do bring me to them!" I cry, and the three of us take to the stables. I do not think of the other girls I have left behind in the stands. I am with my brother at last. I am with people who do not seem so complicated.

We reach the stables where are housed some of the finest horses in England, each brushed till its coat gleams. In the corner of an empty stall is a bitch with her five pups. She is adorable. Her pups are little balls of gray, blue merle, caramel, and white fur; their ears cannot decide if they will be floppy or pointed, so compromise at somewhere in between.

I kneel in the hay, not caring about the state of my dress. Both Henrys kneel beside me.

"Do you think she'll let us pet them?"

"I should say," says Harry with the authoritative tone of an expert. "Do you think so, Surrey?"

My brother nods and I reach out a tentative hand, first to the mother, whose elongated snout I stroke while cooing soft endearments about her ability to breed. Once I am certain she is comfortable with me I reach out to pet one of her pups; the fur is silky soft under my hand and I purr with pleasure. I gather the little creature against my breast.

"It's so dear," I say, kissing its downy head. "Oh, if holding a pup is this wonderful imagine how grand it will be to hold my own babies!" I breathe before I can help myself.

Neither boy says anything; I imagine they don't fantasize about holding babies very often.

"Do you want to keep it, Mary?" Harry asks.

I glow at the prospect. "Do you think it's ready? I couldn't bear the thought of separating it from its mother too early."

"It's fine," reassures my brother, whom I decide to refer to as Surrey as well, just to differentiate him from all the other Henrys running about court.

I meet the gaze of the mother, as though seeking a glint of permission in the great brown orbs. I wonder what it is like to have a child taken away. Nobles give their children up for fostering most of the time and do not see their children but for a handful of times a year. Some don't see their children for years at a time.

If I take this pup, its mother will never see it again.

Something about the thought brings a lump to my throat. I blink back tears.

"Mary . . ." My brother rubs my shoulder. "Don't you want the nice pup Harry's offered?"

I nod. "Oh, yes, to be sure. But to separate it from the mother . . ."

"Mary's so sensitive!" Surrey laughs. "You have a poet's heart—like me." He wraps his arm about my shoulders and kisses my cheek.

"Do you want it or not?" Harry asks, but his tone is good-natured. "I have a mind to withdraw the offer—you know it will fare much better with you than out here."

This is true enough. I pat the mother's head in a gesture of gratitude, then rise with the pup in my arms. "Thank you, Harry."

He offers a courtly bow and I return a curtsy. We erupt into laughter at our sport as we return to the tiltyard to watch the jousting.

As I reach the stands to show the girls my new pup I see Anne watching me, a grin of amusement lifting the corner of her pretty mouth.

It is a perfect day; the sun shines off the armor of the knights and I am blinded at times as they ride past. We are treated to a superb show of sportsmanship and my throat is raw from screaming for the various champions.

King Henry takes the day, of course. Madge Shelton whispers to me that everyone lets him win else the consequences are dire. I giggle before I can help myself. He is a spoiled child! Yet I suppose he did not choose to be. He is a king and kings were first princes, spoiled and petted just for the sake of being born to the right folk.

He wouldn't even have become king had his sickly brother Arthur not passed on. In fact, he would not have married Catherine of Aragon, Arthur's own widow, at enormous inconvenience to a great many people, including the Church he rails against now, had it not been for that fact.

Yes, King Henry is very accustomed to getting what he wants. So accustomed that he does not even know there is another way to live. That is why he raises friends up only to cast them down at a whim, because no one has curbed him thus far. He will keep pushing and testing his limits and still he will not be curbed.

I wonder if his son, so close to being a prince himself, will take after him. I squeeze the puppy to my chest. I hope not.

That night as I report to Norfolk I am ecstatic. It has been a wonderful day, a day etched in memory and emblazoned in my heart. It is a day of innocence and perfection that will sustain me through the days that follow.

I am playing a prank on Norfolk tonight. The day and company of my brother have put me in a mischievous mood. I dress in my nightgown and wrap, concealing the puppy within as I bounce into his chambers.

"Wasn't it a wonderful day, Father?" I ask, beaming as I clutch my wrap tight about the warm, wriggling pup.

He says nothing. He looks down at the eternal display of papers scattered across his desk.

I tell him the things I imagine he wants to hear, verbatim conversations that have no consequence or relevance that I can see, but are the best I can come up with.

"I think Anne is smart, Father," I venture.

At this he looks up. "As smart as a woman can be, I suppose," he says. "But she is greedy and headstrong. That same temper that so charms His Majesty now could someday prove her ruin."

I shudder at the words. I do not like to hear anything bad said against my mistress, for I consider Anne more my mistress than Queen Catherine for all my interactions with the latter. I decide now is the perfect time to unleash my little joke. Norfolk seems in as good a humor as possible for him, so it may as well be now.

I clutch my wrap around me and double over. "Oh, Father, I have the worst stomach pains. Perhaps something disagreed with me today!"

"Go to bed," he says in his taciturn manner.

At once I open my wrap and out springs my new puppy. He runs around the room to investigate everything.

"Isn't he wonderful?" My cheeks hurt from smiling. "Harry Fitzroy gave him to me so I call him Fitz, after him."

"Sounds like a seizure," says Norfolk as he watches the dog relieve himself on the leg of his desk. After a slight pause he asks, "Are you a complete idiot?"

I gather the pup in my arms, chastising it in gentle tones. I do not respond to Norfolk's query, as I am not quite sure. I may be a complete idiot. I did think it would be funny to see a dog jump out of my robes, but Anne has told me countless times that my sense of humor is rather quaint. God knows Will Somers, the king's fool, could make me laugh till I begged him to cease in his antics for the pangs in my sides, and his sense of humor is none too sophisticated.

"I'm sorry, Father," I say as I right myself. I bow my head.

"Clean it up," he orders.

"Do you have some rags . . . ?"

"Use your wrap, foolish girl," he says. "You want a dog, you deal with its unpleasantness with the accoutrements at your present dispensation."

I am horrified at this. Not only because I have to sacrifice my favorite red velvet wrap from Mary Carey, but because I will have to walk through the halls of the palace in nothing but my nightclothes, and though I am still considered a child, I feel too old to prance about thus.

After a moment of staring at my father without effect, I remove my wrap and wipe up the offensive reminder of my puppy's less attractive habits. I call for a ewer filled with rose water to make certain the scent does not remain behind. The servant who brings it casts a strange look at my father and I am both angered and embarrassed. I do not want anyone looking down at him for my foolishness, nor do I want anyone seeing me stooped to this level of humility.

"You'll have to varnish the leg if any is stripped off," Norfolk says.

I nod, praying this isn't the case. I right myself, shivering. His rooms are cold.

"So you were with your brother today," Norfolk says in a lighter voice, as though nothing had happened. "Did he tell you he is betrothed?"

"Betrothed?" I am aghast. Henry married? "To who?"

"Anne had hoped to the Princess Mary, but that is not to be," he continues with a slight scowl. "Which is for the best. We do not want to be accused of placing ourselves too close to the throne. As it is . . ." He cuts himself short. There is no doubt he is thinking of Anne. "It is Lady Frances de Vere, the Earl of Oxford's daughter. They will not marry for quite some time, but the suit is a good one."

"Yes," I say for lack of anything else. I cannot imagine Henry married. This means I am not far behind. A thrill of excitement surges through me. "I wish it were me," I blurt.

"Getting married? Whatever for?" Norfolk's tone leaves its monotony to become incredulous. "Marriage is a tedious thing."

"Maybe not for everyone," I tell him, stroking my pup's silky ear. "I heard that the king's own sister has married for love before."

"And has been repaid by nothing but misery for it," Norfolk says. "One doesn't marry for love, Mary. One marries for advantage. There are only two kinds of people in this world: the advantaged and the disadvantaged. Everything you do, every choice you make, is to ensure that you remain in the former group. Getting caught up in love and lust and such nonsense are distractions the advantaged cannot afford if they want to retain their position."

"But King Henry loves Anne," I say in a small voice.

Norfolk is silent a long moment. "Go to bed, Mary." I turn and trudge out, carrying my soiled wrap balled up under one arm and my puppy wriggling under the other. "And don't bring that *creature* in here again," he adds.

I keep my head down as I walk through the halls, hoping not to run into anyone I know. All I want to do is snuggle under the covers with my new puppy, who is worthy of being called more than a *creature*. I want to think about love and marriage and my brother Surrey.

I want to believe that love can exist, even for the advantaged.

Time does not pass at court as it would in what I now refer to as "the outside world." Out there, time ebbs and flows like the tides—it surges, it slows. Here it is always surging, forging ahead, constant. If you slow your pace you are drowned. I am caught up, carried along by the current of the other ladies, of Anne, of my father.

We go on progress to visit the many great castles and palaces in the realm. We go on hunts. We have masques, and King Henry leaps out at us in disguise. Norfolk instructs Anne that she is under no circumstances to ever admit that she knows it is Henry—he loves believing he is fooling everyone. I laugh, but I think it is a little ridiculous. How could a grown man, and one as distinctive in manner and height as he, ever believe he can be shrouded in anonymity? I decide that he needs to believe it the way I need to believe in the faerie folk and love matches: anything to take you away.

Poor old Cardinal Wolsey, whose obesity and pomposity had been the source of much amusement, dies that November. He keeled over on the road on his progress to London for his execution for treason, so I felt a little better. I am certain he would rather have died on the road than by the axe. I can only imagine how many times it would have taken to strike through that thick neck. I cringe at the thought.

Anne cheers when she hears the news. "Rid of the old fool at last!" she cries.

At my obvious puzzlement regarding her joy over what I consider tragic and pathetic, Madge Shelton, ever the informer, pulls me aside.

"He was one of the parties responsible for breaking her betrothal to Lord Henry Percy," she explains.

"She was betrothed?" I ask, incredulous. Betrothal was as good as marriage; many took to the pleasures of the bed as soon as their troth was pledged.

Madge nods, eager to be the deliverer of this gossip. "How could you not know? Your father helped dispel the match with the zeal he'd exert in putting down a Scottish rebellion!" She shrugs then. "But I forget how young you are. You were at Kenninghall when all that happened." She casts a sidelong look at our tempestuous cousin. "But our Anne never forgot Wolsey's part in it all, and some think it was her more than anyone who pushed the king to have Wolsey executed. I think King Henry was just as content to have him left where he was."

My heart sinks to hear such news of my pretty cousin. I am too young to understand what heartbreak does to a person, how it embitters and twists them. I can only think with sympathy of poor fat Wolsey, dying on a muddy road.

"It's a good thing he passed," Anne herself chimes in from where she sits at the window seat of her grand apartments. She had been tuning her lute, but we should have known she didn't care a fig whether it was in tune; she was too attuned to our conversation. "That man was after the pope's tiara and nothing more. He would have tried to hold us back as long as he lived."

I shudder at the venom in her tone.

"And as far as Henry Percy is concerned, I'd prefer if you did not mention his name again!" she cries. "Let him rot in misery up in Northumberland with his pasty-faced wife." She tosses back her head and laughs, that chilling, immoderate laughter that causes me to avert my head as though I am witnessing someone's private insanity. She glares at Madge and me with wild eyes. "I am assured he is miserable," she says, breathless. "Which serves him well. He was weak and God curse weak men!"

That curse must not be entirely sincere, I think to myself. She must prefer her current Henry to be weak, else she wouldn't have been able to manipulate him into authorizing the execution of Wolsey. Wisely, I do not give voice to this theory.

Time, that raging river, keeps surging. Thomas More, another close friend of the king and a man quite unyielding in his convictions, becomes lord chancellor. My gut immediately lurches with fear for the quiet man; friends this close to the king do not seem to fare well.

In 1531 Parliament makes King Henry supreme head of the Church of England; now we are an island in more ways than geography. We are like a separate entity. We are accused of Lutheranism, but that is not the king's intent. He wishes to uphold Catholic ideology: he just does not want to acknowledge papal authority. He truly believes it is his divine right to rule over Church and state. I wonder if this is so. All my life I have been told that the king's authority is second to God, but there is something about His Majesty . . . something that does not seem altogether godlike to me. I dare think that neither he nor the pope is fit to assume such a heady role. But I never say so; the consequences of such opinions are grave.

That year two people are banished from court. The first is my mother, a figure I saw so rarely she may as well have not been there to begin with. Her crime was offending Anne by playing go-between for Queen Catherine and her ambassador, Eustace Chapuys, hiding messages in baskets of oranges. The king, displeased that Mother caused such a ruckus, sends her home to Kenninghall.

She does not say good-bye to me. Though I did not see but glimpses of her at most, the thought of being left completely alone, with none but my father as the guiding force in my life, is a daunting one. And Mother's crime . . . could it really have deserved expulsion from the life she so loved? Now what would become of her? She is as devoted to Queen Catherine as I am to Anne. To be deprived of the one person she believes in more than anything would be the worst kind of punishment—and Mother knows enough of that simply by being wed to Norfolk.

I find to my surprise that I will miss her. Or, at least, the idea of her.

The second person to be banished is Queen Catherine herself. In July she is exiled to the North. The Anne faction celebrates and the palace is aswarm with youth and vigor.

"No more do we have to see *her* haunting the halls with her rosary and hair shirt!" Anne says in triumph. We are assembled in Norfolk's privy chamber. Gathered about are Mary Carey, George Boleyn, and their parents, my uncle Thomas, and aunt Elizabeth.

"We are so close!" Anne cries out. "Almost five years I've been waiting . . ."

"Do you listen, Anne?" Norfolk hisses from across the table. "The pope has granted nothing—we are but a tiny step toward getting what we want. Dowager Princess Catherine has a great deal of support in the North; she could still win. As far as the king is concerned—"He folds his hands and cocks his head, eyeing Anne as carefully as he eyes me during my nightly reports. I am grateful that I am not the only one to be examined so critically. "He could have an attack of his infamous 'conscience' and take her back in less than a fortnight. Which means it is vital that you stay the course." He tilts a brow.

Anne scowls at him and folds her arms across her chest. "You think you know what's best—"

In a movement so swift it is almost over before it begins Norfolk is on his feet, slamming his fist on the table with a resounding *thump*. "I don't *think*. I *know*. And if you know what's good for you, you will listen." His voice is never raised, not even a note. Perhaps it would be less frightening if it were not so controlled. It would make him more real.

He sits back down and eyes Mary Carey. "You're still instructing her on how best to keep him . . . intrigued?"

A smile plays on George's mouth. Apparently he has been privy to these discussions and perhaps shared some knowledge of his own.

"Yes, of course," says the much more agreeable Mary. A slight flush colors her cheeks and Norfolk waves a hand.

"Don't play the modest spring maiden to me," he says. "We all know well what you are."

Mary Carey bows her head. I want to reach out to her but do not dare. I remain silent, taking everything in with a racing heart. I am ashamed of my fear and bow my own head.

"Never forget the people's reaction to you, Anne," Norfolk continues. " 'We want no Nan Bullen.' " He lets the words of the rioting peasants fill her ears. She covers them and squeezes her eyes shut.

"We were on the barge," she whispers, reliving her ordeal. "The poxy fishwives called it out from shore . . ." She shakes her head as though trying to banish the disturbing images. "And they mobbed me." Tears gather at the corners of her black eyes. She blinks. George wraps a protective arm about her shoulders, drawing her close. The movement creates a pang of longing for my own brother.

"You have to try to endear yourself to them, Anne," Norfolk says. "You have to make them love you and long for you as their queen. The king may weaken under the rejection of his subjects—he may decide you're not worth all this bother with the pope and Catherine of Aragon's supporters. Supporters like Charles of Spain."

"He wants an heir," Anne says, her voice taut with determination. "I can give him what he most desires. No one will deter him."

"Everyone can deter him," Norfolk argues. "Who do you think you are? You're the lady of the moment. Even should this succeed you will only be useful to him till he gets his heir. And then? Then it is a mistress."

"Not with me," Anne says with a proud but joyless smile. "He'd never dare."

"Oh, wouldn't he? He dared with Catherine," says the duke.

"He didn't love Catherine."

"He loved her dearly." My father's voice bears an edge of danger in it, and I find my fingernails are digging into my palms, sharp as a cat's claws.

"Anne, you are always dispensable, remember that. If you don't believe it, take a look at your own sister." He indicates poor Mary Carey with a careless nod.

Anne draws in a breath. "It doesn't matter," she says with a shrug of one shoulder. I know it is a false sentiment. Anne is all about Anne; even I can perceive that. She will not take kindly to rivals. "*I* will be queen, won't I?"

"If you play this right," Norfolk says. "Which means you listen to me. Do you understand, girl?"

Anne draws her expression into one of serene dignity, offering him the slightest of nods. I call this her "queen's face." I practice this one when I'm alone, along with her smiles and looks of surprise and coquettish anger. To me she is the quintessence of charm and cultivation.

We are dismissed and prepare to go to supper, but Anne remains a moment, standing in front of my father with her small shoulders squared, a hint of a smile on her face.

"You are an old son of a bitch, Thomas Howard," she says.

I am awed by the words. I expect my father to strike her for her insolence but instead, after the briefest of pauses, he says with a small smile of his own, "As are you, Anne." He pats her elbow as he guides her from the room. "Take it as a compliment."

Anne's laughter peals forth as she quits the room.

I don't know why, but I am jealous. Certainly not at the exchange of insults. Perhaps it is of the familiarity, the fact that they can vex each other and still retain some strange favor with one another. Of course Anne is very useful to my father . . .

I sigh, chastising myself for these uncharitable thoughts as I, too, quit the room, trying to chase away the feeling that I really am not useful at all.

I have mixed feelings. I begin to suspect that I am not on the right side. I think of the queen not as the princess dowager, as we are told to refer to Catherine of Aragon now, but as the queen—the sad, gentle queen who greeted me at Westminster when I first arrived. Now she is alone in her northern castle, suffering as it seems her fate to do. She is denied almost everything and retains the smallest of courts; a handful of loyal maids whose devotion I applaud. She is further punished for her stubbornness by being kept separated from her daughter, who is also in exile until she agrees to sign a document acknowledging the invalidity of her mother and father's marriage and thus naming herself a bastard.

I am expected to make merry at the expense of such misery. I am not to express even the smallest amount of sympathy for the dethroned monarch or her poor rejected daughter. I am to celebrate the victory of the Howards.

Our victory seems so precarious. What is viewed as triumph one day can be looked upon as tragedy the next; everyone's fate depends on the fluctuating moods of the increasingly cantankerous king.

"And what would you do if you were Queen Catherine?" asks Madge Shelton one night as we draw the covers over us. My dog, Fitz, sleeps between us; he is spoiled and content, innocent of treachery or plotting.

I do not answer right away. The queen has no friends here, and it would do me no good to offer sympathy of any kind. I measure my words with care. "I would grant the king his divorce; say what needs to be said even if it isn't true, just to have peace."

"Do you think it's true? Do you think Catherine and Prince Arthur consummated their marriage?" she asks with a wicked gleam in her eye.

I shrug and turn my back to her. "Only she knows. I think it's silly, really. Jesus says if your spouse dies you are free to marry again, which means it was divinely permissible for her to marry King Henry—"

"The Church goes by the Old Testament, clinging to the claim that a man cannot marry his brother's widow," Madge reminds me.

"They should go by what Jesus says, not some nameless scribe from Leviticus." I am surprised at my passion regarding the matter. But I feel the queen has been wronged, so terribly wronged . . . I must watch my words.

"Don't say that too loud," Madge says in a conspiratorial whisper. "They'll put you in the Tower for being too sympathetic to the qu—I mean, the princess dowager."

I shiver and she rubs my shoulder.

"Don't worry, Mary." She laughs. "You're Norfolk's girl; your interests are attuned to Anne. No one could accuse you of papist sympathies." She pauses, then returns to the original topic. "I'd love to know if it were true, though—about the consummation, I mean. Wouldn't you?"

"Not really," I say, not only because it seems a sacrilege to think such about the noble Queen Catherine, but because I already know the answer. No one who behaved with as much conviction as Queen Catherine could be clinging to a lie. She is the most pious, devout woman I know, as well as the most honorable, which means it is exactly as she insists. The marriage to Arthur was not consummated; her marriage to the king is valid.

I sigh. "It doesn't matter if it is or isn't," I say. "Because the king will get what he wants in the end."

"He always does," Madge agrees with a yawn as she drifts off to sleep, leaving me to ponder these great things in a mind that, to me, feels very small.

I have become interested in writing verse. Though I do not find myself to be of any unique talent, I am compelled to scribble my little observations and feelings to give them vent. There is a solace in it, an escape. Even bliss, when the words flow right and inspiration surges through my limbs like the aftereffects of mulled wine. I even set some to music, as I am quite accomplished on the virginals and lute, but I dare not say a word about it. I can't imagine anyone wanting to hear me sing, anyway.

The only person I cannot wait to discuss my newfound passion with is my brother Surrey, who once told me I had a "poet's heart." Like him. I would be glad to be like Surrey.

This is a poetic circle, and the ladies and gentlemen often share their compositions. I do not share mine, however. I keep them to myself, in my little locked casket with the few letters and other treasures it is my privilege to hold dear.

Often I write about God, His love, His mercy and kindness—traits I feel are not exalted enough. Everyone knows about His wrath and judgment, but not many sing the praises of His gentler virtues. Anne has talked a lot in secret about the New Learning, aspects of church reform that I find myself agreeing with. Anne believes everyone should be allowed to read the English Bible that William Tyndale translated in 1525. I admit I would love to study the Bible myself, lowly girl that I may be. I would love to read the Psalms and get lost in the poetry of those so inspired by the Spirit that they commended their hearts to timeless verse.

But these are thoughts kept to myself, and when I am not writing about the Divine I write about Anne: her temper, her wit, her beauty. When I feel frivolous I pick out one handsome gentleman or another to spark my muse, careful not to assign them with a name in case my poems are ever discovered.

To keep everyone amused during these tense times while the King's Great Matter persists (his Great Matter being Anne), the other courtiers make a show of their poetry, and it is not long before Anne catches on to the fact that I am concealing my own.

Unfortunately it is in front of the king himself that she chooses to point this out. Everyone is engaged in gambling in her apartments; there's a sort of laziness about it. People are drinking and conversing idly; in a corner a young musician is playing his lute and singing in a soft, sweet voice.

As I am, for the most part, invisible at court, I do not think anyone will call attention to me, curled up in a corner near the fire writing my verse, least of all Anne herself.

"What is little Mary Howard doing over there? Has she taken in too much wine?" she asks, her tone light and musical. "Come here, little Mary, and bring whatever it is you're writing with you."

I clutch my verse to my chest, my cheeks blazing as I approach the table. I sink into a deep curtsy before the king. "Your Majesty," I whisper, ever awed by the man.

He laughs. "She's a dear lass," he says. "Do tell us what you were doing all by yourself."

"Oh, she's always by herself," Anne informs him. "Except for Madge and her little pup, our Mary is as silent as a mouse."

I stand before them, my legs shaking so hard that my knees are knocking together. I am grateful they are concealed by my voluminous blue skirt.

"Won't you read us what you were writing?" she asks. "Or is it a love letter?"

I cannot discern if Anne is being kind or if she is trying to humiliate me. Now and then when in a temper, she derives a strange pleasure from the humiliation of others. I am spared this fate most of the time because of my "mouselike" virtues, but now and then her black eyes fall upon me with a wicked glint and she sees fit to wrangle me into an oral beating that brings me to my knees. Most of the time it is over my clumsiness; if I drop something or trip over my gown (or worse, hers), it unleashes a tangent so full of venom and curses the likes of which would make sailors blush, that I do nothing but murmur a terrified apology. I am at a loss in verbal warfare, much to hers and Norfolk's advantage. And yet with Anne, whose tempers are as changeable as the weather, her vinegar can be transformed to honey in the space of seconds. I can only hope for her honeyed words now.

"Yes, little one, do read to us," says the king, and since this is as good as a command, there is nothing I can do. I must obey.

I try not to stutter or stammer, remembering who my father is and how he would be most displeased to hear if I dishonored myself before the king.

I concentrate on the parchment before me, never once meeting the eyes of my cousin or sovereign.

> *"Love she hath not served me so well,*
> *God's pleasure doth see me alone.*
> *Though all my efforts have I strained,*
> *He is here yet ever gone."*

I look up. It is a stupid poem and I am embarrassed. It is written for poor Queen Catherine, though I dare not admit that. I suppose it is for every lady who fancies herself alone; my mother, Princess Mary (I should say Lady Mary), even my own Bess Holland.

Perhaps even me.

Yet when at last I meet Anne's eyes they are lit with tears.

"So young to have a head filled with such tragedy," observes the king, but his voice is tender as he beckons me near with a hand. "You have a gift for verse, little Mary Howard."

"You are most kind, Your Majesty," I say in genuine gratitude, offering another curtsy.

Anne's manner changes abruptly. Again her eyes shine with that dangerous light. "She is a charming girl," she says with a dismissive wave of her slender hand. "It is getting rather late, isn't it, Mary? You should go bid your father good night."

Again, I dip into a curtsy. My legs hurt and I am grateful to be dismissed. Gambling bores me, to be truthful, and I am quite cautious with what money I am allowed, so do not wish to squander it foolishly.

As I quit the room the young musician who had been strumming his lute approaches me. He is a short man, but well made; lean of muscle, with fine musician's hands. He bows, and upon righting himself I am struck by his eyes. They are the most unusual strain of gray-violet, like an unquiet sea beneath the ensuing purple dawn. Never have I seen such eyes. His dark hair curls about his strong shoulders and his smile reveals straight white teeth.

"I hope I'm not being too forward, Mistress Howard, but I must tell you that I was moved by your poem," he says in a low voice boasting a Cornish accent.

My cheeks burn. I am certain he sees them reddening. I bow my head. He must be at least fifteen. I cannot believe he deigns to talk to such as me!

"Thank you, sir," I say, shuffling a little awkwardly from foot to foot.

"You *are* as humble as you appeared!" he cries then, slapping his thigh with his fine hand as though he had just won a bet. "I thought to meet you just to find that out. Most ladies of the court, you know . . . well, humility doesn't run high in noble blood."

"True enough," I admit with a little laugh before realizing I should be defending my set—a group, it is clear, to which he does not belong.

"Do you write songs as well?" he asks.

"Oh, yes!" I cry with enthusiasm, forgetting I vowed to keep it to myself. "But I couldn't play them for anyone. They're so silly and childish—"

"Oh, then I wouldn't want to hear them," he says, cocking his brow.

I screw up my face in disappointment, my heart sinking at once.

"Did you expect me to beg your favor, that my ears might be treated to something you, the composer, find unsuitable?" he asks with a warm chuckle. "Always be proud of your work, Mistress Howard. Everything in this life is an illusion; everything can be taken away. Except our talent, our intrinsic gifts from God." He shrugs. "Given, there are times we compose things that are less than worthy. What do we do with those? Scrap them. And start over. That's the best part. You can always start over."

I am touched, not only by his advice, but by the fact that he has spoken to me for more than five minutes. It is a rarity I enjoy all too infrequently.

I have no words to express this. It seems I am better at verse than real-life conversation. Instead I attempt Anne's famous court smile. "I did not have the pleasure of an introduction," I say, "though it seems you know my name."

"I am Cedric Dane," he tells me with a little flourish of a bow. "A grand nobody. But it is just as well. I think it is far less dangerous to be a nobody at this court!"

It is that, but I do not say anything lest it be overheard that I am making crude comments about our grand court. "Are you from Cornwall?" I ask, not wanting to end the conversation. My heart is racing with giddiness.

"My accent still gives me away." He laughs. "Yes, Tintagel. My father served Henry VII as one of his musicians, so our current Good King Harry was thus inclined to favor me with a post here. It is a . . . fascinating place."

"Yes," I agree. "It is that."

"Well," he says, doffing his feathered cap, "the hour is late and I believe I am keeping you from something. I do hope I can hear some of your compositions—only the best ones, of course."

"I shall make certain of it!" I promise, unsure as to whether I am being improper, but not quite caring.

I leave Anne's apartments, a thrill coursing through me. I have never experienced this. I want to spread my arms like wings and fly through the halls like one of the king's great raptors. All I want to think about is Cedric Dane; his gray-violet eyes twinkling with mirth, his slender hands, his smile. His voice, even his gentle mockery. I whisper his name to myself over and over. *Cedric. Cedric. Cedric Dane* . . . Never have I felt this way. I know what occurs between a man and a maid, and that I am expected to make a marriage soon. Somewhere in the back of my mind is the knowledge that there was talk about my betrothal to Lord Bulbeck, son of the Earl of Oxford, but whether that will ever come to fruition I have no idea. Marriage—my marriage at least—is the farthest thing from my mind. But romance . . . This court, not to mention my own father, are all shining examples that you do not need to have marriage to have romance. My heart leaps at the naughty thought, sinking just as quickly as I realize where, almost against my will, I am now headed.

My father's liveried guards stand aside, offering gentle smiles as they open the doors to his rooms.

He is not behind his desk tonight, but stands before the fire in his privy chamber, hands folded behind his back. His eyes are distant and his lips are pursed.

"It's been a lovely night, Father," I tell him. "I wish you would join us more often. I think it would do you good."

"Who are you to tell me what is good for me?" he demands in his quiet voice. Before I can answer he continues, immediately arriving to his favorite topic. "How goes it with Anne?"

"She is well," I say, though I know this isn't what he wants to hear. He wants details, details of things I do not know. It is so hot in his chambers. I wave a hand in front of my face to fan myself. My throat is dry and scratchy. I wonder if it is due in part to the nervousness of having shared my poetry.

"I do not know much else," I confess. "They are close. The king is very . . . affectionate," I say after a moment, searching for a word appropriate for describing his lecherous attempts at pawing and kissing parts of Anne that should not be kissed in public. "I suppose Mary Carey or George Boleyn can tell you more. She does not confide in me."

"Of course she doesn't," he says. His voice sounds so far away I am straining to hear him. "If you waited to extract a confidence from her you'd die of old age, with your curiosity quite unsatisfied. It's all about listening. Mary Carey is not to be trusted; when she is not resentful of Anne she is influenced by her. She does not set her sights very far." He pauses. "Though I suppose George is a little more intelligent. He has a spark of ambition in him. He wants his sister on that throne, I believe."

"Yes," I say in feeble tones. This is beyond my grasp, and I am so tired. Weakness surges through me and my limbs quiver. My heart feels as though it is beating too slowly and my head is tingling, pounding. My face flushes. My thoughts come to me sluggish and disorganized. I want to panic but cannot.

"I . . . read to the king and Anne," I say against the nausea in my throat. "A poem of mine . . . They liked it." Why this sudden weakness? I bring a hand to my forehead. I want to tear off my hood, but do not have the strength. A vision of Cedric swirls before me. I can't wait to get back to the maidens' chamber to tell Madge about him; then rethink it, as most likely she would gossip about it to Anne, who would mock me in turn.

Thoughts of my cousins and the musician are chased from my mind as I struggle to keep my balance. I want to cry out but cannot. I try to focus on my father, who is coming toward me. His mouth is moving, but I cannot hear . . .

Then there is nothing.

❧ 6 ❧

The King's Great Matter

I awaken, forcing heavy lids open to find that I am not in the maidens' chamber. I am in a great four-poster bed with a soft feather mattress that smells of lavender. There is naught but a single candle to illuminate the room. My body aches. I cannot will myself to move.

Someone in nightclothes and bare feet is kneeling by a prie-dieu, shoulders shaking.

I drift back into dreamless sleep. At intervals my eyes flutter open to find the figure still there, like a wraith, back turned to me, head bent in prayer. I do not know how long it is like this. Sometimes I think I hear muffled voices. Other times I feel a cool cloth swabbing my forehead.

Strength ebbs back into me, reluctant and sluggish in my veins. I open my eyes to see the figure by the prie-dieu rising. He turns. Norfolk. I do not know if my shock registers on my face; though my father is one of the most professed Catholics at court, I did not know he really prayed much except at Mass.

"So," he says, striding toward the bed and sitting beside me. "You've decided to join us."

I nod. I wish he didn't know I am awake. I should like to watch him pray for me more, now that I realize it is him.

"Good," he says in clipped tones. "There have been many goings-on since you've been on your little holiday. I have plans for you."

My face falls.

He reaches out as though to touch my face, then seems to think better of it and withdraws his hand. Perhaps he is afraid of contracting whatever it is I have.

It is not the plague, something that would have sent king and court into such panic that they would have retreated immediately to one of the country palaces. It is a fever; some indistinguishable imbalance of the humors that the physicians assured would resolve itself with rest.

"This is quite an active life for a child as young as she," one physician ventures. "Likely it was spurred by exhaustion."

My father says nothing and the man is dismissed. We are alone. I am sitting up now, taking in broth and bread with trembling hands.

"We are returning to Kenninghall," he says. "You will rest there while I take care of some business."

My disappointment is writ on my face, for he adds, "Look sharp, girl. We will return directly."

I do not want to tell him of the heaviness in both stomach and heart at the thought of him, my mother, and Bess Holland under the same roof again. Perhaps if I play sick enough they will be too preoccupied with me to cause much grief.

I ride in a litter to Kenninghall this time, as my health is still too fragile to sit a horse. As we depart London I draw the curtains around me. To leave the bustling court for the dark, mournful halls of home is disheartening. I wonder why Father is taking me at all. I could have been left behind in his spacious apartments to recover under the watchful care of his staff. He must have his reasons; after all, he did say he had plans for me.

At the sight of my childhood home I am stirred by a surge of strength and leap out of the litter, running into the great hall. All homesickness for court has dissipated and I can think of nothing but Bess. I want to run into her arms and tell her all I have seen and done these past two years.

I know I must refrain from such displays, however. I must not offend my lady mother.

She stands in the hall, small and square shouldered, to greet Norfolk. Her dress is a somber black velvet with a matching gable hood. A few stray curls have escaped the hood to frame her face. Again I can't help but think of how becoming she would be if she were happy.

"Back so soon, my lord?" she asks in her low, ironic tone.

Norfolk sweeps into an exaggerated bow. "My lady," he says. "Trust I would have postponed the ordeal indefinitely had I my druthers. However, given your last letter, I was compelled to rush to your side." His voice is riddled with sarcasm.

Mother scowls. "To what purpose?"

"Let us call it persuasion." The corner of his mouth lifts into a suggestion of a smile, a smile without love or joy or kindness. I shudder.

She closes her eyes, looking inward to draw from some deep strength of will, as though readying herself for a great battle. She expels a heavy sigh. "Let us sup first."

No one argues. Far better to go to war on a full belly.

We are ravenous and Mother laid out a good table. From silver plates we eat an assortment of mutton, capons, venison, hare, all in rich, delicious sauces. There are sugared fruits for dessert, cheese and bread, and delicious mulled wine.

"You're looking thin, Mary," Mother tells me.

We have not laid eyes upon each other for a year. I suppose I was hoping for some kind of change during that time, that perhaps her longing for me would inspire her to embrace me. It must be much easier asking a girl of my age to change, rather than a middle-aged woman. I decide to accept the observation as a show of her concern.

"I've been ill, my lady," I inform her.

She sips her wine. "No contagion, I hope."

I shake my head. "No, my lady. Just a fever. I was overtired." I offer a bright smile. "I'm much better now and eating such a lovely supper restores me mightily."

My father is growing impatient with the nonsensical chatter. I can tell by the way he grinds his teeth on the left side. He stares at his plate, disinterested.

"You are attending Anne's elevation to the peerage," he says in a quiet voice.

My eyes grow wide. Anne is being elevated to the peerage? Anne, a subject humbly born, with no royal blood surging through her delicate blue veins?

"If you think that I am going to lower myself to serve that whore, you are sorely mistaken." My mother's voice is also quiet but bears a bitter edge. She wipes her mouth. "I will not go anywhere near the slut. Unlike some, I stand firm in my loyalties. I do not compromise my principles for sake of pride."

Norfolk draws in a breath. "You are going. You will carry her train like a good aunt. She is to be Marquess of Pembroke. Marquess, Elizabeth! Do you realize what that means? Ladies are made marchionesses at best. A marquess is a man's title. There is only one reason she is being ennobled: to elevate her to royalty so that she may be made presentable to Europe as the king's chosen bride."

"The king already chose a bride," Mother reminds him. "He has a bride and an heir."

"I should not have to condescend to explain to you that it would mean civil war putting Mary on the throne. She is a woman. No woman is fit to rule England alone, and the Tudors' hold on the throne is too weak for her to keep it by herself." Norfolk shakes his head, exasperated.

I am trying not to look. I bow my head but observe through my lashes, hoping no one sees me, like at court.

"Codswollop," says Mother. "He has Fitzroy if he wants an heir. He even has Henry Carey if he wanted to get a little desperate. Nothing is preventing him from naming either of them. And for merit he could acknowledge Catherine Carey and God knows whatever other bastards are out there."

She has him.

"Even now an act is being considered to name Fitzroy heir, should Henry not bear any more in the future," Norfolk tells her.

"Good. Then there's no need of Anne," says Mother as though it is all decided. She breaks off a piece of bread and begins to nibble on it.

"There is need of her as long as he says there is," Norfolk says, his voice firm. I stiffen at the tone. "You still do not seem to grasp how this affects us, how this will elevate us."

"I am a duchess!" Mother cries. "I don't aspire for more!" Her eyes shine bright blue with loathing as she regards Norfolk. "When I became Catherine's lady-in-waiting all those years ago, I pledged her my loyalty. She has it still."

"And a lot of good it's done you," Norfolk interposes. "Your 'loyalty' earned you banishment and nothing more. You are not remembered with favor by anyone and you certainly are not missed. Yet you will not take the opportunity to redeem yourself with the new regime."

"Pah! 'New regime'! Really, I haven't been so amused in weeks." At once her countenance turns stony. "I tell you, Thomas Howard, I will not go. See how the court finds you when they see you dragging me, screaming obscenities and biting your wrists, at Anne's ceremony. See how dignified you'll look then." She sits straight in her chair, her gaze unwavering. "I will not go."

Norfolk turns to me. "Leave this room," he orders.

I do not hesitate. I run from the parlor, tears filling my eyes. I admit I am as much disappointed in missing my delicious supper as I am in my parents' relations. This time I do not stay to eavesdrop. I run, the sound of clattering plates and trays following me all the way to the nursery. I am hoping that what is occurring in my imagination is worse than what transpires between them now.

Bess is awaiting me there. She is as beautiful as when I left her, perhaps a little fuller of figure, but it compliments her. Her long flaxen curls fall about her shoulders uncovered, as if she were a young maiden.

"I set myself to work as soon as I heard you were coming," she says as I run in. Her smile is broad as she opens her arms.

I fall into them, unable to control my sobs. I cry for my parents, for myself, for Queen Catherine, for things I do not understand.

"No tears, lamb," she coos. "Let's celebrate your homecoming!"

"But my mother and father . . ." I whimper against her skirts. "They—"

She waves a dismissive hand. "You mustn't worry your pretty head about them. They take care of themselves."

"But why must they always be at odds?" I cry, pulling away.

Bess averts her head and I regret the question, knowing I have inadvertently put her to shame. I embrace her once more.

"Are you still hungry, my lady?" she asks then. My stomach growls loudly in response and I giggle. "We'll send for some food from the kitchens and then you will tell me everything," she says in a cheery voice as she takes my hands, drawing me to the settee. "Tell me of Lady Anne and the king and how all the ladies dress. Tell me of the food and the jousts and masques."

I am all smiles, thrilled to be the center of attention and purveyor of knowledge. The food arrives—plates of cold meat, cheese, bread, and a decanter of wine. I invite Bess to share with me but she declines.

"It wouldn't be proper, dining with my lady," she informs me.

"Nonsense," I say. "You're too humble, as though you forget you're gentry yourself. Dine with me, my Bess. You have been working so hard to make my home nice for me. You deserve fine food."

Bess smiles and takes some mutton. She chews with enthusiasm, licking her fingers soundly.

As I enjoy my supper I tell her about all the new colors that Anne has set herself to naming, the gowns she designs, the voluminous sleeves and glamorous French hoods. I brag about the food, tell her that to dine at the court of King Henry is tantamount to eating in Heaven itself. I describe the grandeur of the jousts and elegance of the masques. She is riveted, stopping me now and again to ask a question or make a comment.

"Do you have friends, Lady Mary?" she asks me. "Do you get along well with the girls? They are kind to you?"

I am so touched by her concern my throat swells with tears.

"Yes, for the most part they are kind. My cousin Anne can be . . . difficult at times." I laugh as I think of her. "But as strange as she is, I can see why the king is so taken with her. She is full of fire and life. She's very smart, much smarter than I could ever be. She talks like a scholar and argues about religion and politics like a man. She appreciates art and beauty and music. I think we shall have a most learned and cultivated court under her rule."

"You think it will happen, then?" Bess asks.

I nod. "It is almost a certainty. She is being elevated to the peerage."

Bess's eyes widen and she covers her mouth with her hand as though stifling a gasp.

"She is to be Marquess of Pembroke," I go on to say. "It is unprecedented."

"Then I suppose everyone will be happy—at least the king and Lady Anne and His Grace your father," Bess comments.

"They will be indeed," I say, but my voice is void of the triumph I should feel for my family. "Still, I worry about the people's response to her. They have been so cruel." I relay the incident on the barge and the jeering cry, " 'We want no Nan Bullen.' "

Bess says nothing and I realize I have again made her uncomfortable in her position.

I squeeze her hands and continue. "Imagine how it must be for them," I say. "Anne and the king can't control their love for one another. I know a lot of people have been hurt." I think of the Princess Mary and Queen Catherine. I think of poor, dead Cardinal Wolsey. I think of Thomas More, who I have heard, was at last allowed to resign his post as lord chancellor, to be replaced by Thomas Audley. How my father lamented over that appointment! He claimed chest pains, but all knew he was wrestling with his religious convictions and the rightness of King Henry's increasing denial of papal authority. "But I wonder, had they a real choice in the matter, would they have stayed this course? The king is a victim of his passions—he has very little self-control. And Anne—well, she must love him, too. I can't imagine all the trouble they have gone to being for nothing. It must be due to their great love."

Bess looks at me, her liquid brown eyes filled with an emotion akin to pity. She reaches out, cupping my cheek in her hand.

"You are a good girl, Mary," she tells me. "Stay that way."

I nod with a small smile. At once our heads turn toward the door as we hear footfalls approaching.

"It is His Grace," says Bess. Her tone registers something between panic and anticipation; her eyes reflect both fear and expectation. She rises. "I must go, my lady."

"I'll look forward to seeing you more on the morrow, Bess," I tell her.

She throws me a kiss and exits. I hear her and my father exchange a few words outside my door.

"Damn stubborn woman is what she is," Norfolk is saying. "We will see if tonight's exertions have brought about a change of heart."

Bess says nothing. I realize I am not breathing. I wonder what he meant by "tonight's exertions." Part of me wants to run to my mother to check on her welfare, but I daren't.

"Come, now, Mistress Holland," Norfolk says in a tone I never hear used; it is almost solicitous. Almost loving. "Let us to bed."

My heart sinks. I do not want to hear that.

I return to my lavish supper set on my little table. My room is so spacious, the furniture and tapestries so vibrant with beauty.

But I am alone and do not appreciate the food anymore, nor the surroundings. I take to my bed, escaping my loneliness the only way I know how, through sleep.

In the morning I am summoned to Mother's chambers. I make certain to appear neat and proper, my hair brushed, my hood straight, my face and hands clean. I enter her rooms hoping we might break our fast together, but am surprised to find her propped up in bed. I have never seen my mother in her nightdress before—when I was little I believed she was born clothed. Yet now she is clad in a simple ivory nightgown with ruffles at the neck and wrists, appearing childlike in her large four-poster.

I curtsy. "Good morning, my lady."

She nods in greeting, regarding me with a stern countenance. With a thin hand she beckons me toward her. As I approach I note that her eyes are surrounded by puffy purple shadows. Looking closer, I realize they are not shadows but bruises. My heart begins to pound as I realize what last night's "exertions" must have been for her.

"You are growing up at this court of Henry VIII," she says.

"Yes, my lady," I answer.

"You are attractive enough." She reaches up to tuck a curl that strayed from her ruffled night cap behind her ear. As her sleeve slips down her arm I see her thin wrist is also encircled with dark bruises, imprints of my father's fingers.

"Thank you, my lady," I say, trying to fight off tears as I regard her condition. What else did he do to her?

"Things are happening," she says. "Great changes, as well you know. Many will be asked to compromise their beliefs, abandon their principles. Whatever you hold sacred, Mary, whatever you believe in your heart, keep it there. Keep your own counsel. Tell them what they want to hear, believe what they want you to believe, and keep your opinions to yourself. Do you understand?"

I nod, frightened.

To my surprise tears fill her eyes. "It is too late for me." She shrugs, bringing one thin finger to tap her chin in a nervous gesture. "I cannot stray from my convictions. If you had known Her Majesty . . ." She shakes her head. "She inspires devotion. But devotion is becoming rather passé in this day and age." She sighs. "Yet I remain so at great expense. It does not matter. I must cling to something."

I reach out and take her hand. "You have me, my lady. Always."

At this a tear spills onto her fair cheek. Frustrated, she shakes her head and wipes it away. "No. I never had any of my children. Perhaps that is where peasants are most fortunate. They keep their children; ours are sent away as chattel to be bartered for political gain. But such is our lot, I suppose. No, I do not have you, Mary. Not now, not ever."

I blink away tears at the reality of the thought. I recall my father's words about the advantaged, how sentiment cannot be considered if one wishes to keep one's position. I begin to wonder if any position, no matter how exalted, is worth such emotional sacrifice.

"I'm so sorry about Catherine," I tell her. "Both Catherines. My sister and Her Majesty."

Mother averts her eyes.

"I met Her Majesty. She was most kind to me," I say. "Oh, my lady, if only things were different."

"Don't waste time wishing for things you can never have." Her voice is firm. "Life is short enough as it is. Not one moment should be spent in regret." She covers her face with her hands an instant before going on. When she pulls them away she clenches them in impatience. "You will carry your cousin the whore's train at her ceremony. I will not be attending."

"But, my lady, what of Father?" I begin to tremble. "What will he . . . ?"

"What can he do to me?" she finishes. "Nothing. There is nothing he can say or do to break me, Mary. See this?" With effort she rises from the bed, pulling up her nightdress. I am ashamed at her nakedness; I almost turn but cannot. I am riveted by the bruises that mark her slim frame. She drops the gown, covering herself once more. "It is just a body, a shell. It means nothing to me. He can do as he pleases to it—but all is transient, temporary. I will suffer as God wills it and look forward to the freedom Heaven will surely afford me."

"My lady!" I cry in despair. I want to embrace her, but am afraid of hurting her. There are so many bruises. Never have I seen such blatant cruelty. I begin to cry.

"Don't cry for me, Mary," Mother says, settling under the covers once more. "Cry for yourself, for the lot we must suffer as women, as God's cursed creatures."

"Surely we aren't cursed," I say. "God does love us, doesn't He?"

Mother purses her lips. Her eyes are dry. "He tolerates us because we serve a purpose—rather like your father," she adds with a sound that could be called a laugh.

This makes me want to wail in despair, but I refrain, drying my eyes in the attempt to achieve a semblance of dignity. If God tolerates us, that means He doesn't have to like us. It means we are just short of a mistake in His eyes. Oh, that can't be . . . that can't be. Mother's bitterness over her own pitiful lot has caused this view toward God. Doesn't Her Majesty, the most devout woman in Christendom, see God as a loving benefactor of mercy? If she can harbor such regard for the Lord then so must I, for she is as justified in her sufferings as my mother.

We return to court and I am filled with relief. As soon as I am able, I escape Norfolk and return to the maidens' chamber. Everyone is in a frenzy of gossip. Trunks are being packed, servants are running everywhere.

No one notices I have returned; indeed, they may not have realized I was ever gone. For a moment I stand a silent observer until Madge Shelton approaches me, taking my hand.

"I thought you had abandoned us," she says in her light voice. "Are you well?" Her eyes are lit with genuine concern.

I nod. "Much better, thank you."

She beams. "Are you excited about France?"

"France?"

She regards me as though I had emerged from the tomb. "Of course, France! We are going to accompany the king and Anne after her elevation to the peerage, to meet the king of France and his dazzlingly naughty court!"

"Madge!" I cry in delighted anticipation. "No one told me! When do we go?"

"October," she said. "So you best pick your gowns out now. We are. Oh, I can't wait! Mistress Anne is in a huff. She is determined to be accepted by King François—I think she feels that if he openly embraces her she'll be—"

"Validated?"

We turn at the cool voice. It is Anne herself, regarding us with furrowed black brows and narrowed eyes. "Gossiping about me, Mary Howard, and you have not yet condescended to greet me?"

I curtsy. "My profound apologies, Mistress Anne. I am so happy to see you."

"Ha!" Anne waves me off with a hand and sits on my bed. "I suppose it's true enough." Whether she refers to needing validation or my happiness in her presence, I am unsure. Her face softens. "I have to be accepted in Europe—they must realize I am meant to be queen of England. Once they see me with His Majesty, once they come to know my mind, there will no longer be any doubt which woman is most fit to be by King Henry's side."

I say nothing. Something about Anne frightens me. Her eyes glow with a light akin to madness. She is fidgety, unsure of what to do with her hands. Her laugh is painful; forced and edgy. Joyless. I realize as I regard her that I am looking at a nervous wreck.

"So, little Mary is carrying my robes of state," she says, her eyes fixing on mine. "Such a little thing you are. You had better not trip and make a fool of yourself." With this she rises and ruffles my hair. "Glad to have you back," she says as she exits to a flock of curtsying ladies.

My cheeks burn but I do not cry. I imagine she must be under so much pressure. It would be hard to be nice all the time.

My father is also quite direct in his instruction.

"Do anything stupid and childish and I will make certain you are sent to Scotland to marry a barbarian," he tells me.

I stifle a gasp of fear. Somewhere inside I know this could be his form of jesting, but as I recall my mother's bruises I decide it may be an error in judgment to laugh.

"You will stand straight, like this." He rises from the chair behind his desk and grabs my shoulders, pushing them back as he straightens my posture, something I admit is one of my less attractive attributes. As I am usually hunched over a book or my writing, slouching has become habitual. Norfolk places his left palm on the small of my back and his right on my abdomen. "When you stand straight you draw your stomach inward toward your spine." He stands back to regard me. "And head up." He tilts my chin up with his fingers. "Proud, like a Howard girl should be. You belong to the greatest family in England. Act like it. My God, girl, who taught you to stand?" He scowls. "Now walk."

"Walk, Father?"

"You aren't deaf, are you?" he asks, as though this would be the ultimate inconvenience to him. "Yes, walk the length of this room, to the door, then back to me."

I do so, shaky and self-conscious.

"Where did you learn that?" He doesn't wait for an answer—to my good fortune, as I had none that would please him, since the only person I ever tried emulating in gait was Bess Holland. "Take slow, measured steps, toes pointed straight ahead of you. You want to glide, you want to float. You aren't off laboring in the fields. You are a lady. Now. Walk."

I walk, trying to emulate as he envisaged, but he stops me.

"Apparently you do have some sort of hearing issue," he tells me. "Do it again, and this time do it *right*."

I try again. Again he stops me. "Mary, would you like to be replaced? Is this role too much for you? Perhaps Jane Parker would be happy to—"

"No!" I cry, daring to interrupt him as I envision my sour-faced cousin Jane, wife of cheerful George Boleyn, taking my rightful place in the ceremony. "No, please. It is an honor to carry my lady's robes. Please don't take it away from me."

"If the honor is denied you, it is no fault of mine," Norfolk says. "Now. Walk. One hundred times back and forth, from me to the door. A thousand if need be. You will walk until you walk like the lady I am raising you to be."

So I walk. I walk and walk. The sun sets. The night drags on. The sun rises. My legs are heavy and my feet ache.

"Stop," he says. "That is passable."

I cease walking and stand, numb.

"Now about your hair," he says. "It's one thing to wear it down your back if you take care of it, but if it continues appearing as though you've stood the length of a windstorm, I will not allow you to wear it unbound. Who brushes your hair?"

"No one, really," I say. "Sometimes we brush each other's hair or a servant will, but everyone is so busy—"

"Come here," he says, sitting behind his desk once more. I realize for the first time that he has been standing the entire night as well. I wish he would offer me a chair. He doesn't. He calls for a brush with hard bristles. Once it is produced, he gestures for me to come to him, then removes my hood and turns me around. With hard, relentless strokes he brushes through my thick golden hair, pausing to detangle snarls without care of the fact that I feel my scalp is being torn from my skull.

"This is a mess," he says, using his fingers to detangle some of the snarls. "You are not the comeliest creature—take pride in your redeeming features." When he can't detangle certain stubborn snarls, he pulls at them so hard that they come out in clumps that he drops to the floor beside me. My scalp aches. Each hair seems to have its own individual complaint.

At last—between the pain in my legs, feet, and head—I begin to cry.

"Stop it this instant," he commands. Immediately it is as though some force has pulled my tears inward, sucking them inside my eyes. My head feels full. My body feels full, full of tears and anguish I dare not expose.

The ordeal takes an hour. When he is finished he puts down the brush and smoothes my hair with his hands. "It glows with a fire from within." He turns me around to face him. "When you come tonight we shall do it again."

"Which part?" I ask, dread pooling in my gut.

"All of it," he says. "You should be flattered that I condescend to such matters, but as no one else seems to be able to fill the capacity, including yourself, I shall have to. I can't abide you running about court like a peasant."

"I am . . . most humbled and grateful, sir," I tell him, longing to douse my head in hot water to assuage the pain.

"You are dismissed."

I curtsy and quit the room, knowing that with the demands of the day I will have no opportunity for rest, and praying he will not keep me up the entire night again.

There must be some way to find peace.

As I trudge toward Anne's apartments I hear someone whisper my name. At first I think my overtiredness is causing delusions, but when it persists I turn my head to find the musician Cedric Dane peering out from a doorway.

"Good morrow, Mistress Howard," he says with a smile. "How are you?"

My heart is racing. I pray my cheeks are not flushed. "Master Dane, a pleasure to see you. I am well, thank you."

"Can you spare a moment?" he asks.

I know I should attend Anne, but my feet remain rooted in place. I wrestle with my conscience but a moment, before following Cedric into a chamber where there are many various instruments: virginals, a lute, a harp.

"We practice here," Cedric tells me. "At least it resembles practice." He sits behind the virginals and begins playing effortlessly, a haunting melody that calls to mind lost love and distant dreams.

"It's lovely," I tell him. "Is it your own?"

"Yes." I admire how he does not have to look at the keys. That is something I am working on as yet. He regards me with a carefree smile. His eyes, those strange, violet-tinged eyes, sparkle. I feel a bubble of laughter catch in my chest.

"It needs a bit of work, though," he says. "I haven't any words to it yet. Tell me what you envision when you hear it."

I close my eyes, allowing the melody to envelop me. "The sea. Rolling waves, a calm blue sky . . . a ship . . . it is a lovely scene but sort of melancholy. It is good-bye. A man has left his maid . . ." I bow my head and know from the heat of my face I am flushing furiously.

"Why did you stop?" Cedric asks.

I avert my head, unable to meet his eyes. "Mayhap it is a little . . . I'm not sure . . ."

"Mistress Howard, please. Continue," he urges.

I raise my eyes to him to find his head is bowed toward the keys. His eyes are closed and he weaves subtly in time with the tune. He is a musician in complete harmony with his song.

"I—I see the maiden. She stands alone on shore, bidding her lover good-bye." I swallow. I am caught up in my scene. "Somehow she knows his voyage is perilous. She will not see him again."

"Tragic," says Cedric. "But beautiful, as tragic love tends to be. Leaves you blissfully unsatisfied, yet somehow there is a perverse pleasure in the agony of it all."

I never thought of it like that. Perhaps I have witnessed too much agony to find it pleasurable. Or I have not witnessed the right kind.

"Will you sing for me, Mistress Howard?" he asks. "Put verse to your story. Breathe life into my song."

"I can't—"

"Come now." He chuckles. "You're not afraid."

"Yes," I admit. "My voice might grate on you."

"It might," he says. "But I promise I will tell you."

I giggle. "I am not good at verse on the spot."

"Not many people are, save your brother, I hear."

"Henry?" I arch an eyebrow.

"I had the privilege of keeping company with him and the Duke of Richmond of late. Your Lord Surrey is a wonderful poet— a hot-tempered boy, but a gifted writer with a great deal of heart," he tells me.

"Boy!" I cry. "He's no older than you!"

"He's a boy," he says.

"And you're not?" I tease.

"That's for you to learn."

"Master Dane!" I cry, scandalized.

"Forgive me, Mistress Howard," he says. "I grow too comfortable in your charming company." He clears his throat and continues playing. "Now. Do enlighten me with a few verses."

I pause a long while, allowing images and words to whirl in my mind and take form. It is a creation in itself, writing verse, and I envisage the Psalmists feeling a similar exuberance when composing God's Word. I am tingling with inspiration. Slowly but in a clear, low voice, I begin.

"O happy dames . . . that may embrace the fruit of your delight." Tears fill my eyes. "Help to bewail the woeful case and eke the heavy plight . . ." I take in a breath. "Of me, that wonted to rejoice the fortune of my pleasant choice: good ladies! Help to fill my mourning voice . . ."

I trail off, unable to continue. Cedric stops playing. He is staring at me.

"Where did that come from?"

Embarrassed, I avoid his eyes. "I—I don't know."

He rises, approaching me. "You are more gifted than I could ever have imagined. You compose from your innermost being, from your soul, your heart . . . You are an artist." He reaches out and takes my hand. "Tell me you will write that down and finish it for me."

I nod.

He sits on the bench once more. "Please," he says, gesturing to the vacant space so near to him. I sit. I have never been so close to a man outside of my family before. His presence, his warmth cause me to shiver all over. Gooseflesh dots my arms and I'm grateful my sleeves cover it.

"Your voice is beautiful, fraught with emotion." At my dubious expression, he goes on. "It is not mere flattery, Mistress Howard. I don't waste my time with empty obsequiousness. I leave that to the courtiers," he adds with a wink.

"Thank you," I whisper.

"Thank you." He nods toward the keyboard. "Will you play for me as well?"

I place my hands on the smooth keys. They are at home here. I close my eyes. I find I cannot do anything but his bidding. I want to elongate this moment forever. I begin to play one of my own compositions. Unlike his bittersweet melody, mine is violent and dark, with a heavy bass hand and strong minor chords. As I play, tears gather at the corners of my eyes. When I finish I stare at my stilled hands. Blue veins are raised against the fair skin like a surging network of rivers from my efforts. My breathing comes quick and shallow.

Cedric is silent. "You have a talent." He pauses as though considering. "Where does all that darkness and passion come from? I should think a girl your age would be composing light, frilly little songs."

I bow my head. I cannot say where it comes from, only that it emerges from some depth of my soul and cannot be ignored. When my fingers touch the keyboard they are commanded by something else, something illogical and not of this world.

I say nothing. I cannot speak past my emotion.

He seems to perceive this so clears his throat, changing the subject. "Are you—are you excited about Mistress Anne's elevation ceremony?"

I nod, relieved. "I am carrying her robes," I say with pride.

"Quite an honor," he says. "Your family is steeped in honors, I think."

"Yes," I agree, then realize I should take offense. "What's wrong with that?"

"Nothing," he says. "Such is the way with the king's favorites. The blessings spill over. I'm certain Mistress Anne isn't the only one benefiting from her match."

I rise from the bench. "You mean my father?" I cry. "Every honor that is bestowed upon him is earned. He is a man to be feared by all—"

"Odd that should be the attribute you mention first," Cedric observes in soft tones. He arches a well-defined black brow. "Do you fear him, Mistress Howard?"

My words catch in my throat. I see my bruised mother. I feel the pain in my scalp. I recall the humiliation of being made to wipe my puppy's mess with my red velvet wrap. I blink back tears. "I fear him as I fear God," I say at last. "It is a fear born of respect for his greatness."

"Greatness." Cedric regards me with eyes that belong to a man much older than himself. "Can greatness be born of bloodshed and suffering, from manipulation and cruelty?"

"You go too far, Master Dane," I tell him, my heart sinking at knowing our moment of beauty has fled.

"Forgive me. I get caught up in debate for the spirit of it," he tells me. "I mean no offense against the great Lord Norfolk. I am certain he is a most loving and attentive father who will think of nothing but your happiness all of his days."

"Of course," I insist. "He always thinks of my happiness. He wants me to be a great lady. He is showing me how to walk. . . ." I cannot stop the tears from coming now. "If he didn't love me, why would he lower himself to such things?"

"Indeed," says Cedric. "God bless the man who instructs his thirteen-year-old daughter on how to walk."

"Why are you being cruel?" I demand.

"Oh, little Mistress Howard," he says, taking my hands. "I want you to know something, and please take it to heart. I am the least cruel person you will find at this court. The only words that leave my lips are honest ones. Mistress Howard," he says in a voice so gentle it wrenches my heart. "Mary. Take care of yourself. Look after your own interests first for, believe me, no one else will."

I withdraw my hands. "You forget yourself and my rank. You will neither address me informally nor lay hands on my person again," I say haughtily as I turn about in a whirl of skirts and quit the room.

But his words haunt me as I make my way to Anne's apartments. He is wrong, surely he is wrong. He is just an arrogant musician who is not nearly as mature as he thinks he is. He knows nothing of me or my father or my life.

He is wrong. I am well looked after. Norfolk does think of my best interests.

Norfolk *does* love me.

7

The Marquess of Pembroke

Though my feet ache from practicing my walk, it is well worth it when at last the day of Anne's elevation ceremony arrives. I vomited everything I ate that day, so decide against eating anything else, and Madge Shelton continually pinches my white cheeks to bring color to them.

"You mustn't worry so," she reassures me as we dress Anne for the event. "You're going to do wonderfully."

"You'd better," Anne cries as ladies flutter about her in an effort to dress her. Nothing is good enough for Anne today, and the slightest thing causes her to unleash a string of curse words I did not think ladies even knew. No one can do anything right. Her corset is not tight enough. Her sleeves are not tied right. The velvet itches. The ermine smells. Her bum roll is lopsided. Any grievances that can be aired against both her gown and attendants, are; and it is no surprise to fall under her criticism.

"All I need is you falling with my robes," she goes on in a sharp voice as her sister brushes out her long black hair. Despite her foul temper and the scowl that crinkles her forehead, she is the most alluring woman I've ever seen.

"I won't, my lady," I assure her. "I've been practicing." Indeed, the last few times I was with Norfolk he piled a few cloaks in my arms so that I would adjust to the weight of the robes.

Anne scoffs and regards her reflection in the glass as the other ladies offer their admiration.

When my father comes to escort her and the procession to the king's presence chamber, I cannot contain my trembling. This is the moment. This is what I have been practicing for.

I will be solemn and grand. I will do my lady and Norfolk proud. I carry the robes and the coronet to the presence chamber, following my lady with slow, measured steps.

Once there I behold the king in all his majesty beneath his canopy of cloth of gold. He radiates light and glory and *power*. This is a stunning personage and not one to be crossed. To think my cousin will soon be his wife. They will be a formidable couple. A sudden lightness in my heart tells me they will be a happy one as well.

I follow the standard-bearers, each carrying Anne's symbol: the falcon, a creature as exacting as she is. My father follows them. The Duke of Suffolk, Charles Brandon, a cantankerous old buzzard with an ever-present scowl, is there offering begrudging support to his brother-in-law the king.

The countesses of Sussex and Rutland help Anne to kneel on the platform, and already I am eager for the ceremony to end. I am shaking, and fear my father will notice and begin rehearsing his lecture in his head even as we speak.

I endure all the prayers uttered by the king's less-than-personable secretary, Bishop Gardiner. I am amazed the king has shown such mercy to Gardiner after his vociferous disapproval of the king's becoming head of the Church of England, but sometimes he surprises me. Instead of burning him at the stake or some such horror, he merely confiscated his home, Hanworth, and made it another gift to Anne.

I wonder fleetingly how many other bold clerics might lose their homes to Henry and his bride before his reign is out, then chastise myself for the treasonous thought.

At last the king approaches me, taking the robes and coronet. I am relieved to hand them off. He meets my eyes with his own glittering blue gaze and offers a bright smile. I smile back. Perhaps that is his way of telling me I did a good job and he is proud of me.

He wraps the robes about my lady's shoulders and, with the utmost loving care, places the coronet atop her dark head, creating her Marquess of Pembroke.

She stands beside her intended, glowing with pride and triumph. The air thrills with their happiness. The world seems full of hope and endless possibilities.

❧ 8 ❧

France

When I think that Anne cannot be defeated and is at last allowed a moment of quiet to revel in her joy, something spoils it, causing her to be up in arms all over again. The very next day we are informed that the queen of France will not come to Calais or Boulogne to meet my lady. This is a blatant demonstration of the French queen's disapproval of the match and the king's break from the Church of Rome.

Anne breaks down in a moment of fury and calls the queen as many derogatory names as she can think of on short notice, but the much-favored Master Cromwell, ever calm, reassures her that King François's sister, the queen of Navarre, will attend her instead, which does something to mollify Anne. Now she will at least be able to meet King François and make an impression upon him as future queen of England.

Later Anne decides that, though she is satisfied with the jewels she has planned for her trip, she would like to have in her possession Queen Catherine's jewels as well.

I am saddened at this. I do not understand why she would want another woman's jewels. But then she wanted another woman's husband, so I suppose the jewels are the least of it now. Such uncharitable thoughts do not become me, I think, and vow to be more compassionate toward my lady, whom I imagine is under the highest level of anxiety.

When the king tells her my father will be sent to fetch the jewels from Catherine, Anne's wild black eyes lose their glint of madness. She calms and, exhausted, sinks onto her chaise, demanding one of us to fan her. She is trembling and smiling, but tears fill her eyes.

I am starting to think it is not so great a thing to be Anne Boleyn.

It pains me to admit that the days my father is up north visiting the queen—I mean, the princess dowager—are my most peaceful. I pack my things for our trip to France. I break from the norm and write some frivolous verse, which I share with some of my friends who are writing their own. We decide we will make a little compilation of our work. I vow not to write anything in "O Happy Dames" for Cedric Dane. I will not write a thing for him ever. Indeed, I hope not to have any future run-ins with the presumptuous lad again.

My peace is short-lived, for Norfolk returns, somber and unsuccessful in his attempt. Her Highness said she would not relinquish her jewels without a direct order from King Henry.

"No matter what I told her, she would not hear," he sighs. "Strange. Was a time not too long past when she heeded my advice. Yet she clings to these ideals that are foolish and false. She lives in another time, or a time that never existed at all. Damn romantic fool." His face twists in a sort of agony. Is it the agony Cedric described to me that day—the agony a lover feels? "If she'd give in, her life and that of her daughter would be so much easier. Doesn't she want peace? She tries to avoid bloodshed, yet by remaining so obstinate she will cause it just the same," Norfolk grumbles that evening as I sit before him, giving an update.

"She loves him," I venture.

He flinches. "It is a matter of pride for the both of them. Love doesn't enter into it at all. It is about religion and power and being right. That's all it's ever about with anyone. When will you see that?" He removes his cap and runs his hand through his thick black hair. "She's not only obstinate, she's fanatical, a martyr. Nothing is more pathetic than a martyr, Mary. See to it you don't become one."

I nod, then bow my head. I don't want to discuss poor Catherine with him, so try another course. I raise my head and offer my sweetest smile. "I'm so excited to go to France, my lord."

"I suppose you are," he says idly, then meets my gaze with his impenetrable black eyes. "I expect you to conduct yourself like a lady. I know how it gets when traveling. Don't get caught up in any foolishness. You think just because you're abroad your actions have no consequences here, but they do. You have a reputation to maintain and I won't have it sullied by girlish fancies."

"Yes, my lord," I say in a small voice, shrinking in my chair.

He rises. I do the same. He has not removed his eyes from me and I shift, uncomfortable under the raptorlike gaze.

"You will be watched, Mary—don't think you won't. There is not one thing that happens at this court that escapes me." He lays a hand on my shoulder. I tremble, wondering if he knows about the time I spent with Cedric Dane. At the thought of the musician my heart bounds in an involuntary leap. Norfolk applies such pressure to my shoulder; dots of light appear before my eyes. The pain drives out any thoughts I'd been indulging in. He continues. "If I learn of any unseemly behavior on your part I will beat you within an inch of your life. Do you understand?"

I begin to tremble. Tears fill my eyes. It is the first time Norfolk has threatened me with physical violence. I know it is within his rights to discipline me as he sees fit, but I am not eager for such a demonstration.

I reach out, daring to take the hand that squeezes my shoulder with such force. "My lord . . . Father." I swallow hard. "Don't you think I'm a good girl?"

He withdraws his hand. "That remains to be seen." He nods toward the door. "Dismissed."

I curtsy, choking down tears, wondering how I can prove my worth to this formidable man.

* * *

His Majesty didn't waste any time with soft words and negotiations. He ordered from Catherine the very jewels he had bestowed upon her in the years he claimed she was his only love. Catherine relinquished them.

Anne's black eyes shine with triumph. She unpacks the diadem inlaid with sapphires and diamonds, the necklaces and eardrops, running her fingers sensually over each item as though they were the flesh of a lover.

"See?" she cries over and over. "See what my king does for *me* whom he loves?" She tips back her head and laughs that edgy laugh, her throat as long and graceful as a swan's. "There is nothing he will not do to please me."

"Unless you don't get an heir in that belly of yours," her sister teases.

Anne draws a hand back and brings it across Mary Carey's cheek in a resounding slap. Tears light Mary's eyes as she stares at her sister, scowling. As I regard her I realize, as if for the first time, how much Anne has taken from Mary; her lover, her place of high favor, and even her son. Anne has been given wardship of little Henry Carey, who is said to be another bastard of the king's, because Anne supposedly feared for the boy's moral development under Mary's care. The court gossip is that in truth Anne adopted him in case she does not produce a male heir of her own. The likelihood that Henry would name the boy his heir is very slim, and everyone knows it to be a desperate move on Anne's part. In any event, hopefully that is a plan she will not have to resort to. After all the trouble and heartache she and the king have wrought upon so many, the least they could do is produce a prince for the realm!

Mary brings her hand to her cheek and I am reminded of Mother doing the same whenever Norfolk spoke to her. Yes, there is a great deal of Howard in Anne.

For a moment the ladies are silent, until Anne adopts her lovely courtier's smile. "I'm certain that is an area my"—she cocks a sweeping black brow in mischief—"virile king and I will have very little trouble in," she says, causing many a speculative glance to be exchanged.

She has succeeded in lightening the mood, and soon everyone is back to discussing the voyage.

But Mary Carey stands in a corner, head bowed, staring at Catherine's jewels—more things that Anne has stolen.

After we ogle the jewels some more, Madge Shelton and I extricate ourselves from Anne's apartments and return to the maidens' chamber to pick out our favorite gowns for the trip.

"She's a wench, isn't she?" Madge asks as she helps me unlace my sleeves to get ready for supper.

I am surprised she offers such open criticism of our mutual relation and want to agree, but guard my tongue. One never knows from one moment to the next when another's loyalties will shift.

"I know I wouldn't have wanted Princess Catherine's jewels if I were her," Madge goes on. "I'd want my own. Really, Mary, it'd be like wanting the wedding ring of your husband's dead wife. It's sort of . . . well, rather like a circling vulture, don't you think?"

I can't help but nod at that.

As she helps ease my sleeve off she brushes against the shoulder my father had squeezed with such enthusiasm some time ago. I try to stifle a groan, but it has escaped and Madge grabs my arm, examining the bruise that has faded from onyx black to a deep purple.

"God's blood, Mary, who did this to you?" she asks, raising concerned blue eyes to me.

I withdraw my arm, smiling. "It was so silly," I tell her. "I ran into a doorway. I'm so clumsy sometimes."

Her lips twist. "Did the doorway resemble a man's hand?"

I cover my shoulder with my sleeve. I have no words. I want to defend myself, to contradict her implications, but cannot. I bow my head, blinking back tears.

"It's him, isn't it? The duke?" she wants to know. Her voice is gentle but bears an edge, the same edge Anne adopts when angry. When I say nothing she continues. "Everyone knows about him, Mary. How he treats your mother. Tales have circulated . . ."

"It isn't true," I say, knowing I must stop her. "Whatever you've heard, put it out of your head. Please, if you have any love for me, stop this and do not take part in spreading any false rumors about my honored father."

Madge's eyes fill with tears as she finishes helping me dress. "You are very loyal, Mary. May it serve you well."

I say nothing in my panic, wondering what the court whispers about my father, about my mother, about dark secrets that should never be aired.

That night I cannot contain my misery as I report to Norfolk. I tell him of Anne's triumphant exclamations when her jewels were delivered, of her slapping her sister, of her provocative comment, which he makes me recite over and over. He tilts his head this way and that as he analyzes the statement.

"She's far too confident in her own abilities," he says after a while. "Her arrogance will destroy her if she isn't careful. Damn!" He slams his fist on the desk. "If she'd heed my advice—what's the matter with you?"

He has noted my tears, which I do not keep hidden as I stand before him.

"People are talking about you," I tell him.

He offers what I describe as his almost laugh. A sound lacking in sincerity and warmth. "That's nothing new. People talk about everyone; I daresay gossip could sustain the court should our food-stuffs run out."

"They say you are cruel," I go on.

"Not the worst reputation a man can have," he says. "Better to be cruel than soft. Soft people don't get ahead in life, do they?"

He then continues about Anne, airing his complaints as though my interposition has not affected him at all, as I am sure it has not. I close my ears to his words. There is nothing that pertains to me anyway.

My hopes for the conversation die. Hopes that he would be moved to repent of his ways and perhaps offer kindness and . . . softness.

I am diverted by our departure for France. The mood is gay and there is happiness even in our frantic, last-minute preparations.

When we board the ship I am delighted to learn my brother and the Duke of Richmond are also joining us.

My brother Surrey clasps me to him when he sees me. "Look at you! Aren't you the little lady?" he cries when he sees me standing at the railing on deck. I am relishing the feeling of the crisp wind, salty with sea spray, whipping against my face, the roll of the waves beneath my feet. In its uncertainty the sea feels wonderful and dangerous and exciting.

"Oh, Henry!" I am so thrilled at his affectionate display I wrap my arms tight about his neck. "It is so wonderful to see you! These glimpses at court I have been afforded are never enough!"

He laughs his easy laugh and holds me at arm's length. "My God, you are a beauty. Has Father spoken to you about your marriage, then?"

I shake my head. I know it is inevitable and a slight thrill causes me to shiver as I entertain the thought. "Not since the plans for Bulbeck were tossed aside," I answer. It is just as well, too. Imagine how much I'd miss if I were some country lord's wife!

"Well, soon enough . . ." he says. "Lady Anne has plans for you. She and Father and—"

"Mistress Mary!"

I curtsy to the Duke of Richmond, who is running toward me, hands outstretched. I place mine in them and he rights me. At once the ship lurches forward, carried on a wave, and to my extreme embarrassment I topple over onto Fitzroy, knocking him to the ground. My brother helps us up, laughing.

My cheeks are burning. "I'm deeply sorry, my lord."

"It's Harry!" he grumbles in perfect imitation of his father. He offers a sideways grin. "That's a greeting I'll well remember!"

I bow my head, hoping my display doesn't get back to Norfolk or the king, especially the king. I don't want him to think I behaved wantonly in front of his son, illegitimate or not.

"A merry voyage this will be!" he continues. "We are invited to stay among the princes, Surrey and I, so a jolly time we shall spend with the naughty court of France!"

"How wonderful!" I cry, envying the lack of supervision at the famed French court where Lady Anne spent her own youth.

"Henry, I have so much to show you! I've written verse. I write all the time. Will you look at it?"

"Of course!" he cries, and I run to retrieve my little casket of poems, eager to show my brother, so adept at poetry himself that I am at once intimidated and thrilled that he'd deign to look at my humble works.

We find an unobtrusive little corner where I allowed my brother full access to my compositions, save the unfinished "O Happy Dames."

My brother looks them over. I am surprised at how fast he can read, for he flips through the pages almost carelessly. I am a little annoyed. I had hoped he would take his time with each phrase and offer helpful criticisms.

"You write a lot about God," he says. "About your desire to be closer to Him and understand Him more through His own Word. Do you think this is wise?"

"Why wouldn't it be?" I ask, defensive. "Who doesn't want to learn more about God?"

Surrey's face is stony. "I just think it echoes a lot of the New Learning. Steer clear of it, Mary."

At once I remember my mother's advice: *Believe what they want you to believe.* "No worries, brother. I follow my king," I say with a sweet smile.

"That's my girl," he says, chucking me under the chin. He hands my poetry to Harry Fitzroy without my permission.

"What did you think, Henry?" I ask, nodding to the poems now in the young duke's hands. He is reading them slowly. He does not flip through the pages as my brother did. I wonder what this portends. Perhaps he, too, finds some of it verging on heretical?

My brother shrugs. "Very pretty attempts, Mary. Adorable, even."

My heart sinks. I did not want my poetry to be described the way one would an endearing puppy or child.

"We must go to the king now," Surrey tells me. "We cannot be seen dallying with you too long. Come, Harry."

Harry waves my brother off. Surrey starts ahead and Harry returns my poems. "I think they're quite good—so much feeling," he tells me. He nods toward my brother, adding *sotto voce*, "Don't mind him. He's jealous of anyone who tries their hand with any success at poetry or anything else."

I smile. "Thank you, Harry."

"We'll have fun in France together, Mistress Mary," he says, tossing me a bright smile that reflects in his blue eyes as he follows my brother to join the other gentlemen.

My heart is light. Harry managed to assuage my brother's slight with his kind words.

France is going to be wonderful!

We arrive in Calais, England's last French holding, and I feel a freedom not known at home. I find myself laughing and joining in the mindless chatter as never before. The people of the town greet our procession with mixed feelings; some cheer *"Vive le roi!"* while others remain silent, guarded, unsure why they should pay homage to a king who does not speak their language altogether well or respect their long-held religious values. I do not allow myself to be vexed by those who are less than enthusiastic at our arrival, but get caught in the joy of the adventure.

I ride in a litter with Anne. She peeks out of the curtains, tossing out handfuls of coins here and there. A triumphant grin lifts the corners of her mouth. "This is the first step," she says.

Anne's mood changes abruptly, however, when we reach our quarters in the castle, where she is informed that we will not be permitted to go to Boulogne after all. The queen of Navarre has taken ill, so cannot attend Anne.

"Pah!" Anne cries, throwing herself on a chaise. "So Henry is to go dine with King François without me! All this way—for nothing!" Her little hands ball into fists, clenching the rich blue velvet of her gown.

It doesn't seem for nothing when Anne receives a beautiful diamond from King François. Her angled face softens; the storm in her obsidian eyes calms.

"Oh, Lady Anne, it is so grand!" I cry. "He must hold you in high esteem."

She casts a sideways glance at me and chuckles.

When King Henry returns from the French court he brings Anne an even bigger surprise: King François himself.

An extravagant entertainment is held for King François, with masking, dancing, and fine food. Anne glides across the floor, making the king of France another slave to her charms.

I am thrilled to be masking like a grown-up lady. I have never participated in one before. Now, swathed in gold and white, I dance before two great kings, all thoughts of Norfolk's warning that I am being watched forgotten. Norfolk is far too occupied with the kings, and I am acting under Anne's orders. Anne, our future queen. He cannot hurt me here.

Harry Fitzroy encircles my waist with his slim arm and leads me in a dance. "Who can this great lady be?" he asks.

I giggle. "I am a Muse," I say.

"A Muse with hair like flame," he says, his blue eyes boring into mine.

My cheeks grow hot. My steps falter.

"Now, who is the lady behind the masque?" he asks, pulling my wrist down to reveal my face. His smile is kind. "Mistress Mary . . ."

"Harry," I breathe. For a moment I cannot speak. At once I am struck by the boy's handsomeness, a picture of the king in his youth. His looks are enhanced by his sincerity and I am touched. I clear my throat. "Doesn't Lady Anne look beautiful tonight?"

"I cannot see her," he says. "My view is obstructed by a beauty as blinding as the sun."

I burst into laughter at this. Harry's eyes reflect genuine hurt and I am quick to cut short my giggling.

"Oh, Harry, I am sorry," I say. "It is you who has the poet's heart. Thank you for your lovely compliments."

The dance ends and Harry bows. I curtsy.

"I hope we see each other again before you leave," he says, pressing my warm hand in his cool one.

"I hope so, too, my dear lord," I say, my smile effortless and genuine.

* * *

My opportunity to see Harry comes in the form of a storm that delays our departure to England. The ladies are occupied with embroidery and reading, King Henry has whisked Anne away somewhere beyond my hearing, and I wander the halls of the castle without accompaniment, a rarity that my father would stridently disapprove of. But then Norfolk is occupied with his duties and hasn't bothered with me throughout the whole of our trip, which makes me fear him less.

I know not to go too far. I've heard tales of girls who met grave misfortune when wandering the dark halls of castles. Rapes, even murders occur. To the infinite convenience of the evildoers, there are never any witnesses.

I meet Harry, who is accompanied by my brother, some other young courtiers, and liveried attendants. He breaks into a smile when he sees me, takes off his cap and bows. His cheeks are flushed. I see the merry effects of fine French wine sparkling in his eyes.

"How now, Mary?" he asks. "You shouldn't be alone."

"I was only taking my exercise," I tell him. "I can't go outside what with this weather."

"Nonsense," Harry says with a laugh. "We're about to do just that, aren't we, lads?" There are a few grunts and laughs. "We're going to ride down to the beach and watch the storm."

"Oh, my lord, you mustn't!" I cry. "You could catch a chill and His Majesty wouldn't like it at all!"

Harry winks. "His Majesty is occupied. . . ."

My face burns. I blink several times, not knowing how to respond.

"Come with us, Mistress Mary," Harry says then.

"I can't go unaccompanied!" I laugh.

"Your brother is with you; he'll protect you." Harry laughs in turn. "Come along! If it makes you feel better, fetch some of the ladies. We'll make a party of it."

I hesitate, knowing no ladies will want to come and soil their pretty gowns. It is such an intoxicating offer, the freedom of riding in the tempest, the rain biting my cheeks . . .

"They won't," I say in defeat.

"Then you will," Harry says. "Come now. Let's ride!"

Well, my brother *is* with us after all. It isn't as though I am completely without a chaperone. And the Duke of Richmond is almost a prince. It wouldn't do to disobey him. I follow the little group to the stables, where we mount horses that Harry assures us are ours for the borrowing. There is no sidesaddle for me and I am not in a habit, so must make do with what is provided. Harry himself helps me up and I offer a pretty courtier's smile of gratitude.

The group rides through the town, the sound of the horses' hooves on wet cobbles music to my ears. The rain pelts against my face and neck and I relish in it, just as I thought I would. The wind whips my hair about my shoulders in a honeyed mane and I laugh out loud.

"What a sight you are, Mary," my brother says. I cannot discern whether he is pleased by what he sees, however.

The beast beneath me is magnificent; the feel of her muscles stretching and working invigorates me and I employ her full potential as we ride along the turbulent surf.

"It's so beautiful!" Harry cries as we bring our horses to a halt to watch the waves raging and crashing against the shore. The rain falls in a torrent; does it come from sky or sea? I tilt my head back to catch some of the drops in my open mouth. They are salty sweet on my tongue.

Harry rides closer to me. "Look, Mistress Mary! A rainbow. Do you see it? Oh, there's every color . . . red, violet, even Tudor green, I daresay!"

I scan the gray horizon where sky and sea frolic together and merge as one, coupling as I imagine the gods to do. My eyes fall upon the rainbow, a great arch across the sky. "God's promise," I say in soft tones.

"What?" Harry leans in.

His proximity startles me and I draw back with a nervous laugh. "His promise to never punish us again with a flood . . . his promise for brighter days filled with color and beauty."

Harry smiles, reaching out. I think he may touch me, but he strokes my horse's silvery mane instead. His expression is dreamy.

"Oh, Mistress Mary, such are the days we shall know." He tosses his strawberry blond head back, laughing. "Isn't it wonderful to be alive?"

My cheeks hurt from smiling. "Yes. It is wonderful to be alive."

My sopping wet gown I explain away as having been a result of my brother pulling me out into the deluge to see the magnificent rainbow. No one questions me. Everyone is caught up in the latest gossip.

"She was with him all night and the better part of this morning," Madge Shelton whispers.

"Do you think . . . ?" another speculates.

Madge smirks. "How could she not? It's been six years now . . ."

I don't want to participate in this conversation. I take off my gown and let it dry by the fire, then dress in a warm wrap and lie abed, dreaming of the storm on the beach, the rainbow, and Harry's smile.

I have never been sorrier to say good-bye to a city than I am to this fair port of Calais. My heart lurches as we traverse the channel, and I find that without Harry and my brother the crossing is dull and I am prone to retching over the side of the rail. When the captain encourages me to go down to the cabin I shake my head. I want to look at the sea. I want to remember the storm . . .

Norfolk's face is impassive when we arrive home. Dropped is the façade of amiable courtier, gone is the smiling man who eased Anne's tension by gambling with her on our trip. I expect he does not have to pretend now. He is only with me, after all.

He guides me to his apartments by the shoulder, his grip unrelenting.

Once we are alone in his privy chamber he sits behind his desk, folds his hands beneath his chin, and stares at me, saying nothing for a long moment. I am unsure if he expects me to speak first, so I smile.

"Wasn't it grand, Father?" I ask in delight. "All the food and entertainments—"

"It sounds to me as though you kept yourself entertained well enough," he says. "Riding alone with Fitzroy, for instance."

I lose expression, feeling the color drain from my cheeks. I know lying is useless. "Henry . . . Lord Surrey was with us. I wasn't alone. And there were others."

"Other men." Norfolk's voice is sharp. He rises, circling the desk to stand above my chair. At one time I might have described this as his "towering pose," but now that I am growing taller I realize Norfolk is small and slight compared to his peers. If one didn't know him one wouldn't think to be intimidated by him, based on his unassuming stature. Of course, that's if one didn't know him.

I look up at him. "We were in broad daylight, Father. It was an innocent jaunt in the rain." I find myself getting caught up in the memory. Roses bloom on my cheeks. My smile is dreamy. "It was so lovely. There was a rainbow and the waves were so tall—"

"Are you daft?" he demands in his soft voice. "Really. I need to know. Do you lack some basic element in your intellectual abilities?"

I know now there is nothing I can say to save myself.

He continues. "Mary, you are getting older. You are marriageable now. You cannot go about alone with boys whose blood runs hot in their veins. And you can't depend on your hotheaded brother to protect you. It was he who made sure the incident was reported to me!"

"Surrey?" I whisper. Tears sting my eyes. "Henry?"

"He says you are growing quite bold in your opinions and your actions," Norfolk says. "You seem to have a reformist bent to your religious convictions and you flirt openly with the gentlemen. Is it that you are inspired by your cousin Mary Carey?"

"As if Mary Carey is my only example!" I cry in a sudden rush of bravery. "I am surrounded by whores!" I add then. I clamp my mouth shut, stunned at my outburst. Before I can offer a word of apology, my cheek feels the heat of his blow. I am knocked to the ground, chair and all.

Norfolk pulls me up by the arm. I feel a slight pop in my shoulder as he jerks me to my feet. "Do you think I raised you to talk like a common barmaid and behave even worse?" He tears off his cloak in one wild movement, tossing it on a chair. "When I tell you something, Mary, I make good on it. I have never uttered an empty word in my life."

My heart pounds in sheer terror as I stare at this man who sired me, his chest heaving as he grabs my neck from behind and pushes me facedown on his desk. His voice is still calm, though his breath is short. "I warned you of this. I warned you before we left. Now you will have to be taught to heed."

With deft hands he unlaces my gown and chemise to the waist. I hear him working at his belt. Once free it whirs through the air as he brings it across my bare back. I cry out. He leans over me, clasping a hand over my mouth. I want to bite him but dare not. Maybe he will kill me. He wouldn't do that; to think so would prove me as daft as he believes. He has too much to lose, and killing one's child certainly doesn't look good. Of course he could cover it up. He is the master of plots . . . No! Oh, here it comes again. It hurts . . . Five, six, seven lashes. When will he stop?

As the belt laps across my back I wonder how I am going to hide it from Anne and the other ladies. I will not be able to dress in front of anyone. Or I will have to keep my chemise on at all times and wear it until my wounds heal over. That is what I must do. Of course they may think me priggish, but . . .

He stops at ten lashes. He is breathless but ever calm as he puts his belt back on. I lay atop the desk, weak, exhausted. Tears fall slick between my cheek and the wood surface. It feels slimy and at once I am filled with disgust.

Norfolk is busy behind me. How much time passes I do not know or care. I hear him call for a basin of hot water, a posset, and some salve. When all is delivered, set behind his door, which remains unopened until he is certain the servant has departed, he retrieves it and sits behind me.

"This should help," he says in an offhand tone as he dips a cloth in the hot water and covers the welts that have arisen like fat red snakes on my skin, pressing it carefully against my back with the same hands that just beat it. He holds the cloth in place a while, and when it cools removes it, dipping it again and repeating the process several times. I feel my shoulders shake with silent sobs. His gentleness in the wake of such violence hurts worse than any beating.

After the hot cloth is removed, he applies some salve. "There is no bleeding. You'll not have any scars."

"You think of everything," I say in bitter admiration.

He does not lash out as I expect, as I almost wish, so that he might end my pain forever and in it bring about his own demise. Again guilt surges through me. He is my father. I must honor him. I did not. I brought him shame. These are the results. Norfolk takes my hand and winds my arm about his shoulder, reminding me of the pain in my throbbing arm.

"Come, lie down," he says, bringing me to his bedchamber and helping me onto the bed where I lie facedown. "Leave the back open to let it air. Cloth will be hell when you do have to dress again." He informs me of this as though from personal experience, and for the first time I wonder how he was raised, who may have executed the same form of discipline on an innocent little boy. Who by starting a cycle of violence inadvertently gave him the right to continue it. "Drink this," he commands in his eerily gentle voice, handing me a goblet containing a hot posset. "It will help you sleep."

"Will I wake up?" I ask in a small voice.

He smiles. "Of course you'll wake up."

I squeeze back tears. I do not want to wake up.

A few hours later my eyes flutter open to the gentle shaking of my shoulder.

"Up now," Norfolk is whispering. The room is dark save one brazier. "To the maidens' chamber with you. The hour is late."

"No . . ." I murmur. I do not want to remain, but neither can I bear to face the other girls.

"Sit up!" Norfolk commands.

I struggle onto my elbow, then lean on my hand as I right myself to a sitting position. I am still too small for my feet to reach the floor, though his bed sits so high off the ground I doubt even his do. I stare at him in groggy helplessness. Everything looks so far away and distorted.

Norfolk laces up my chemise and dress. My back screams out in rebellion at being covered and I moan. Norfolk retrieves another object I dread; the hairbrush. At these ministrations I whimper. I am too tired to fear chastisement and he offers none, by God's grace. He brings the brush through my hair in swift, painful strokes, then sits behind me, drawing it into a thick plait that he arranges over my shoulder.

I begin to laugh. The sound is strange in my ears. It is the Howard laugh. A laugh void of merriment.

"What?" Norfolk asks.

"I was just thinking," I say, and wonder if it is the posset that makes me so bold. "Should your ducal responsibilities become too heady, you could consider court hairdressing."

To my surprise he chuckles, and as my laugh becomes genuine tears fill my throat and course down my cheeks. My gut twists and quakes as I pull my sobs inward.

He places my hood atop my head. "Now what have you learned, Mary?"

I lower my eyes. "I shall always obey you," I promise, swallowing my tears.

He nods. "Then there shall be no need to repeat this." He takes my hand and leads me through his presence chamber to the door. "Good night, Mary."

I dip into a stiff curtsy. My back is searing in pain. I turn and allow a guard to escort me to my chamber. I will not think of this night. I will obey. I will always obey. Then it won't happen again.

I have learned.

"Where were you?" Anne Savage, another of Anne's ladies, inquires as I trudge into the chamber and ready myself for bed. Her eyes bear a wicked glint, as though I may have gone where I'm not supposed to and she is hoping for the details.

I force a smile. "Talking to my lord father," I tell her. "We talked well into the night. It was the silliest thing," I go on, swallowing tears. "He made me tell him about everything over and over, just so he could feel like he was reliving it all."

"Funny," says Lady Savage. "I always thought your father was a severe man."

"He seems that way, I know," I tell her and am almost convinced myself. "But he is so gentle. He loves me very much."

She nods but her expression is sad.

The next morning a little silver box bearing my name is delivered to the maidens' chamber. Madge Shelton seizes it from the messenger.

" 'Mary Howard'?" She regards me in awe. "A gift for little Mary Howard?" She sits on our bed. I run to her to retrieve it, but she has opened it, pulling out a little silver ring inlaid with a fiery opal. "Look!" she cries to the other girls.

"How sweet," Anne Savage says, admiring it.

"Come now, girls, let Mary see it," Mary Carey says as she retrieves the box and ring, handing them to me, her beautiful face wrought with gentleness. " 'Tis her gift, after all."

I examine the little ring, the quintessence of daintiness. On either side of the opal the silver has been wrought into roses. I slip it over my middle finger; it is a perfect fit. I tilt my hand this way and that, admiring the colors the stone gives off as the light hits it from each new direction.

"What a fine stone!" Madge exclaims. "Such fire!"

"No," I say. "It is a rainbow. A captive rainbow."

In the bottom of the little silver jewelry box my eyes catch sight of a note. I unfold it and read the few words with care. *He who spares his rod hates his son, but he who loves him disciplines him promptly. Proverbs 13:24.* Tears fill my eyes. He loves me. He does. That is why he is so strict; he honors God's Word because he wants me to be the best I can be. Yes, that must be it. My heart lifts. I push away the cynical thought that he may just be placating me with a trinket, assuaging whatever guilt he is still capable of summoning, while buying my loyalty. Nor do I acknowledge for long the notion that by accepting this gift I make this form of discipline permissible. These are thoughts I push from my mind. I will not entertain the idea that Norfolk's gesture bears anything but the purest intentions.

I look down at my ring, the colors catching in the light; brilliant reds, oranges, yellows, greens, and purples, all shimmering against a pearly backdrop. A rainbow indeed. As God promised Noah not to punish the world with another flood, perhaps this is Norfolk's pledge to me; a rainbow to ease my sufferings, an assurance that there will be no more beatings if I heed him. If I am good.

I *will* be good, I vow. I will not contradict him. I will not be like Mother and hold true to convictions that serve me not; and if I do, at least I shall have the conscientiousness not to admit them.

As I regard my opal, my rainbow stone as I call it now, another thought strikes me: the beach with Harry Fitzroy and our rainbow, another promise of youth and beauty and brighter times to come.

I clasp my hands together and hold them to my chest, smiling. Norfolk could not have chosen a more perfect gift.

"Who is it from?" Madge inquires, cutting through my pretty thoughts.

"My lord Norfolk," I tell her. "Because he loves me so much," I add with a bright smile.

"A dear man, Uncle Thomas," says Mary Carey, her voice filled with irony.

❧ 9 ❧

Anne's Secret

So immersed am I in how to conceal my own pain that I do not realize Anne is changing. From Christmas through Epiphany, Anne moves a little slower. Though she laughs and smiles often, joking with her courtiers and ladies, keeping the atmosphere one of constant merriment, she is pale, drawn. She tires easily and naps whenever she can.

One morning I sit at her feet while she plays with my hair. She enjoys experimenting on my thick locks, as if I were a doll, but I do not mind. Her ministrations are nothing compared to Norfolk's; indeed, she is very gentle and it is soothing to feel a woman's touch. She is almost motherly, though she is only about twelve years my senior.

"You're such a pretty little girl," she says, which surprises me as I still believed she found my nose offensive. "It's that hair of yours. I will make you a good marriage; you can count on it."

"I thank you, Lady Anne," I say.

"A pity you're so small, though," she adds. "It will make child-birth difficult. You're delicate as a bird. It's from your father's side, I should think. He's such a little thing, himself."

I giggle at what Norfolk would make of her describing him thus. I imagine he would not be thrilled with the depiction.

"I am small myself, though," Anne goes on to say with a smile.

"But endowed with a woman's curves. I think I'll do just fine." At this she rubs her belly, looking down on it with an expression of sheer joy.

I turn toward her, resting my hand on her knee, smiling. "Lady Anne . . . ?"

She nods.

I throw my arms around her. "Oh, my dearest lady, I am so happy for you!"

Anne returns the embrace, laughing, then pulls away. "Thank you, my darling. You mustn't tell a soul." Her lips curve into that smile no one can imitate, least of all me. She places a tapered finger to her lips to illustrate her point. "Think, my dear little Mary. Soon you shall have a new cousin who will be the future king of England!"

I squeeze my arms about myself in delight. "Oh, Lady Anne!" I am beside myself with joy. This means that soon all this bother with the divorce from the princess dowager—Anne's pregnancy has cemented my view of Catherine as the princess dowager now—will be over, and we can celebrate the happiness of King Henry and his forever queen, Anne!

At once Anne's face darkens. She grips my upper arms tight, her nails biting into my tender flesh. "And don't say a word to your father. It's my news. I'll tell him."

"Of course, Lady Anne," I answer with wide eyes. As much as I am beholden to report to him the events of Anne's life, I cannot betray her in this. A mother, especially a queen, has the right to impart this happy news herself.

Her face softens, her smile warm and charming again. "You're a good girl," she tells me, stroking my cheek.

"I am?" I ask her, tears lighting my eyes before I can contain them.

She takes my hands. "You are. Now I want you to dress in your finest. Tonight you will accompany me and some of the other ladies to Hampton Court."

"Why?"

Her smile widens. It can never be called a grin, however. It is too well sculpted and perhaps not spontaneous enough for that description. "Another secret. The king and I are to be married tonight." She waves a hand. "You will witness it, along with Henry Norris and a handful of others."

I raise my eyebrows. "Then will it be over at last?" I dare ask. "Have you had word on the divorce?"

She shrugs. "It's as good as done; just a few more legal formalities." She clicks her tongue in disgust. "That stupid woman!" she says, shaking her head, and I assume she means Catherine of Aragon. She leans back on her chaise then, continuing. "Cranmer is still hesitating. He doesn't want to be archbishop because swearing oaths to the pope would compromise his reformist beliefs. But Henry will find a way around that." Her eyes are half-closed, as though she has just partaken of some decadent, satisfying sweetmeat. "He finds a way around everything. Soon we all will have what we want."

"I do hope so," I say with fervor.

In a burst of energy Anne sits up, waving her hands toward the door. "Out with you now! Go pick out your gown!"

"Yes, my lady!" I cry in delight as I scramble to my feet and head to the maidens' chamber, thinking how wonderful everything is turning out.

We all will have what we want, Anne said. I wonder what that means for me. As I make to my chamber I cannot help but question myself: what do I want? What would make me happy? Can Anne, this woman who seems destined to change the world, grant me happiness, too?

At Hampton Court we gather in the presence chamber. Anne is glowing in her white dress with its diamond-covered bodice and state jewels gracing her elegant throat. The priest mutters something about not being able to perform the service without a license, but the king, magnanimous in his furs and velvet, insists he has it "in safe keeping" and so the ceremony commences unhindered.

I carry my lady's long train, my heart light as I ponder her happiness. As they are joined in holy matrimony, tears stream down my cheeks. Handsome Henry Norris is compelled to lean over and squeeze my arm.

"Now, now, Mistress Mary, no tears," he says in his gentle voice. "This is a happy day."

"Oh, such a happy day," I say, swallowing the lump in my throat. I can only pray that their days will always be so happy and filled with hope.

I do not think of Catherine alone in the North, cold and underserved. I do not think of her daughter, separated from the mother she so reveres because of Anne and King Henry's selfishness. I do not think of that at all. They are the past.

This dark-haired creature before me, my cousin, is the future. The mother of a prince. The queen of England.

❧ 10 ❧

Anna Regina

Anne's happiness over her pregnancy sends her into a state of such bliss that I find myself dreaming of babies and wondering when I, too, might be able to join the elite set of women who are fortunate enough to add "mother" to their string of illustrious titles. I will not be as my mother, the long-suffering duchess who does not enjoy her children but rather pushes us away from her one by one. I will be loving and kind and make sure they remain in my household, where I will hire the finest tutors to educate them.

All this I am thinking on one lovely spring day while the courtiers play in the garden, each so young and merry and filled with hope, when Anne exclaims to her brother George, "Women crave the most unusual things when with child. I know I'm in a mood for fruit—some pears, perhaps? Can any be found?"

George tilts his dark head back and laughs, then orders some fruit to be brought to the sister he adores and fawns over. It makes me long for my own brother, and wonder if such affection will ever be exchanged between us. Before he left to serve Harry Fitzroy, my brother was nothing but funny and sweet—the family prankster, hiding frogs in our beds and mice in our shoes. But now his loyalty to Norfolk obscures everything, even his fondness for me. Unwanted bitterness churns my gut as I recall his eagerness to report to Norfolk my innocent ride on the beach with Harry. What has this world come to if one cannot rely on her own brother? I blink back tears at the thought. Surely I can trust him. Surely he was just abiding by his conscience as we all must. I can hope.

Anne's statement about her craving to her own loving and loyal brother sets the court aflame in gossip, just as she intends. Her words are repeated over and over, and in no time at all it is common knowledge that not only is Anne with child, she is also married to King Henry.

My father, though not pleased at the precise order of events (he believes in marriage before children, but then he also keeps true to his mistress, so I decide not to use him as my moral compass), is more than happy with the outcome.

The four-year trial over the validity of the king's marriage to Catherine is concluded in March, and Thomas Cranmer is invested as archbishop of Canterbury. A proxy made the oaths to the pope in Rome for him (though Cranmer still wrote a letter of protest to the swearing of them), so it wasn't really as though Cranmer was swearing allegiance to His Holiness himself, which I guess reconciled his conscience to his actions with King Henry, whom he swore his allegiance to first. Before God, before country, before anything.

I wonder at the rightness of this, but only for a moment.

On the Saturday before Easter I carry Anne's train to Mass, where she is prayed for as queen and consort for the first time in public.

She is radiant. Nothing can destroy her happiness now; nothing can stand in her way. She is married, she is pregnant, and she is *queen*.

In May, King Henry's marriage to Catherine is pronounced null and void. Thomas More, the former lord chancellor, protests this without reservation, a move I do not think to be wise at all. King Henry is too happy to think about his old friend, however, and I am glad that his words are, at least for the time being, ignored.

Pope Clement is another to object to the state of affairs, and without further ado excommunicates the king. This development doesn't upset the happy couple in the least. They are making their world, fashioning a religion that has no need of a pope or Rome, changing time-honored rules and traditions as is their wont.

I know now that Henry VIII is truly the greatest king to ever sit a throne. No one in history has ever changed so much in so short a time.

And all because of a woman. All because of Anne.

The coronation is a spectacle to behold. We are a fine procession of barges, each containing the king and queen's favorite ladies and lords, making our way from Greenwich to the Tower, then to Westminster Hall where my lady will be crowned. Her barge, once Catherine's, is beautiful and bears her falcon symbol.

We reach the Tower and I am itching to disembark. Everything is so exciting that as much as I want to enjoy the moment, I find the most pleasure in pondering events after the fact, when I can snuggle under my blankets with paper and quill, writing verse.

We are shown to the queen's apartments, which have been re-decorated on Anne's insistence and are beautiful. We will stay for two days' entertainments and ceremonies to celebrate King Henry and Anne's great triumph.

We are lavishly entertained at the feast by the finest musicians and bards. The food is rich and savory; meats so tender they fall apart on the tongue, sauces so creamy and tasty that I close my eyes in rapture that I should be treated to such a decadent display.

I am so full and lazy after eating that it is an effort to dance. I want to sit back in my chair and think about the happy day, but know it is disrespectful not to enjoy every aspect of the evening.

As I take to the floor with some of the other girls, I become conscious that I am being watched. I turn my eyes to meet those of the musician Cedric Dane. He is plucking a lute and singing, his voice melding in beautiful harmony with a small group of others as they launch into a cheerful song about marriage and love.

I avert my head, my face flushing. He is far too bold, staring at me like a peasant.

When the dance concludes I make my way through the crowd in the hopes of getting back to the high table where I can nibble on some cheese as a distraction, but Cedric catches up with me. He sweeps into a bow.

"Mistress Howard." His voice is deep, melodious as his singing. "I have not seen you about in some time. Are you well?"

"Quite," I say in short tones. I try to avoid his startling violet eyes but cannot seem to look away.

"Seems our king and queen are in a thrall of delight," he comments. "The world is theirs for the taking—his, anyway," he adds with a half smile.

"What's wrong with that?" I ask, catching the note of anxiety in his tone.

"We have given him ultimate power," Cedric tells me in a near whisper. "In acknowledging his marriage to Lady—Queen Anne and putting Catherine of Aragon aside, the country is assuring him that his every whim will be met. His actions are without precedent. Do you think anyone will dare cross him now? I cannot help but wonder if we have been wise. Have we just set a lion loose in an arena filled with lambs?"

I shudder at the analogy. "The king is wise and just. He is the next thing to God on earth," I say as I have been taught to say. "If he is a lion, he is akin to the lion in the Bible, who lies beside the lamb in peace." The words seem empty. Indeed, Cedric's points appear valid, but I do not want to believe him. "We must remember that he has acted with good reason. He needed an heir for the throne."

Cedric's eyes are downcast. "Oh, Mistress Mary, tell me you have not been convinced that those of your sex are inferior to rule?"

I am about to comment that I am not sure. I have not been told otherwise my entire life. I want to ask him how he came to adopt such liberal views. I want to ask him why he insists on challenging my thinking all the time. I want to ask him why he is so kind.

But I cannot say anything for he has lightened the topic with a bright smile. "How is your song coming along—'O Happy Dames'? I have not forgotten it."

I bow my head. "I have not worked on it. You were so rude, after all—"

"I was not rude." He laughs. "I was truthful. Someday you'll come to appreciate it. Indeed, you'll find it refreshing."

I choose not to take offense. He is too likable. I offer my courtier's smile. "Perhaps what we see is truth enough," I tell him. "Like looking at a rainbow. We know it is an illusion, but oh! how lovely it is for that brief moment of its existence."

"You must remember, Mistress Howard," says Cedric, his tone still light, "that rainbows are transparent. Storm clouds lie in wait on the other side."

Before I can respond my eyes are drawn to another in the room, whose stare bores into me like a dagger. I shiver as I meet the eyes of the Duke of Norfolk. I look down at my ring, my rainbow, a symbol of such hope for me, now clouded by Cedric's cynicism.

I curtsy. "I must go now," I say.

"I have offended you again?" he asks with a smile.

"No," I say quickly. "Not at all. But I must go. Please. Do continue to entertain us. You are very talented."

I turn away from Cedric's puzzled expression to make way for the high table, but am caught fast by my father, who grips my arm, his fingers pressing into my flesh like the talons of Anne's symbolic falcon.

"Forgetting so soon my advice?" he asks in a low, smooth voice that one would mistake as almost cheerful if one did not know his meaning.

"Of course not," I assure him. "Master Dane was only discussing some poetry he is composing for Queen Anne. He was hoping I might be coaxed into collaborating with him."

"You shouldn't involve yourself in such drivel," Norfolk cautions, loosening his grip. "Words appreciated today can be used against you tomorrow."

This is true enough, I suppose. "I hadn't thought of that," I say.

"No, of course you wouldn't," Norfolk says as he guides me to the table.

He watches me the rest of the night. My heart sinks. My stomach is upset, whether from the rich food or his stern vigilance I do not know. My only reassurance comes from the fact that at least in the Tower he cannot draw me aside to beat me.

* * *

Anne proceeds down the streets of London, though Secretary Cromwell thought this to be dangerous, since public opinion of her isn't high, to say the least, but she does not heed. She rides through the streets to show them all that she is queen. She has triumphed over Catherine. She has won Henry and the crown of England.

"I shall *make* them love me," she cried this morning. She started the day in bad spirits. I imagine she fears the crowds and what could go wrong. It does not seem an impossibility that someone would try to assassinate her. She trembled and retched, but after taking some wine calmed somewhat and allowed us to finish dressing her in her violet robes.

Now through the streets of London we ride, met by tableaux depicting amusing scenes, and choirs of little children at St. Paul's Churchyard. We wind our way through the streets to Fleet Street through Temple Bar. Up the glorious Strand then, where all the wealthy have their grand houses, to Charing Cross; past Hampton Court to Westminster Hall, where Anne is feasted again.

Life is a flurry of joyous activity. I am tired but tingling with excitement. How breathtaking it is to be young and bearing witness to such wonders! After the feast, my head groggy with wine, I fall into a blissful slumber.

The next day I again have the privilege of carrying my lady's train as Archbishop Cranmer crowns her queen of England, setting the heavy, bejeweled crown of St. Edward upon her dark head. It is so large and ostentatious that her head looks weighed down, but she holds it high, proud.

She is queen. My cousin Anne Boleyn is queen!

I think the summer of 1533 is the happiest of my life. I am surrounded by ladies to play with, and court life is like a faerie tale. Bess Holland has been added to the queen's household and I delight in her warm, soothing presence.

I have turned fourteen and am growing a little. My breasts are small and high, sufficiently filling out a bodice to offer a modest view of my décolletage. My waist is still tiny and I have nothing in the area of hips; indeed, I am between woman and child now, but I am satisfied enough with my body to find it adequate.

Norfolk has been kinder of late. Perhaps it is because of Bess; perhaps he is more unperturbed in the aftermath of Anne's victory. It does not matter from whence the kindness comes, only that it is there. No more does he quiz me on Anne's every move. No more am I expected to report verbatim conversations that always seemed so meaningless and time-consuming, not to mention hard to remember. He does expect me to tell him about arguments the queen may have, especially if they involve the king, or of any other behavioral issues that he would not approve of, but other than that his stricture has been much relaxed.

When we move to Windsor for Anne's confinement, I am called to his apartments one night. I have not seen him alone since my birthday in June, an event, like most of my birthdays, that proceeded without gifts or acknowledgment, save a little tablet from Bess, faithful Bess, which I keep in my silver casket of treasures.

I am dressed for a picnic in a white and pink gown bearing a large length of ribbon that ties under the breasts and flows behind me atop a lacy train. My kirtle is also pink, along with the undersleeves that peek out at the wrists, and I wear little pink slippers inlaid with seed pearls. My broad-brimmed bonnet is also adorned with a pink ribbon, tilted at an angle I find to be jaunty yet sweet.

"Well, if you aren't the picture of summer. Pretty as a Tudor rose," Norfolk comments as I enter his rooms. As usual they are outfitted with an austere desk and sturdy, overstuffed chair. He sits in it now, regarding me with a smile—an actual smile—on his face.

I about choke in shock, unsettled and pleased by the rare compliment. I return a smile of gratitude. "My lord."

He rises and approaches me. I begin to tremble. I do not know what he wants—if this is some new way of beginning a lecture, or worse. His pleasantness is disconcerting. I do a quick review of my recent behavior, trying to recall if I have done anything that could incur his wrath. It is so difficult to predict what will set him off. But he does nothing of the sort. To my increasing astonishment he draws me forward by the shoulders, kissing my cheeks.

When he pulls away he is still smiling.

"How would being a duchess suit you?" he asks me.

My eyes are wide. My heart is pounding. So this is it. He has chosen a husband for me. My thoughts are racing. Who? Where does he live? Will I be sent away? Will he be kind? Will I know happiness?

Noting my pallor, Norfolk strokes my cheek and continues. "You are to be married to the Duke of Richmond in November. How is that? You will be the premier duchess in England; the king—the king, Mary!—is to be your father-in-law." His eyes narrow. "And if there are no male heirs there is a possibility . . ." He trails off. To voice such thoughts aloud is treasonous. No one would want to be accused of putting oneself too close to the throne; the consequences for such an offense are almost always death.

"Harry?" I ask in awe, referring to my lord Fitzroy, not his father. "Harry . . ." Indeed, fortune could not be kinder. I can imagine Harry being the dearest of husbands. I don't care so much about the possibility of being queen, knowing it to be quite remote. I can only give thanks to God that I will marry someone as fun and nice as Harry. Already I begin making plans. I think about babies and where we will live. I know he has a residence at Sheriff Hutton. So far from court! But we will have a court of our own. I will have my own ladies, nurses for my babies, and wonderful tutors. I will read and write poetry and there will be entertainments all the time. We will talk about religion and philosophy and art. All opinions will be appreciated and welcome. None will be condemned for their beliefs.

"How generous of the queen to arrange this for me," I say, and know immediately that it is the wrong thing. Norfolk drops his hand and scowls.

"What makes you think it was Her Grace's doing?" he demands. "The king approached me back in twenty-nine, asking after you or Catherine for Lord Richmond."

"As far back as that?" I ask. No wonder a marriage to Lord Bulbeck faded to nothing. It suddenly occurs to me as strange that my fate was arranged for me without my having any knowledge of it at all. Strange and frightening. What else don't I know?

"One thing we can thank the queen for is that she convinced His Majesty to waive the dowry," Norfolk says, sitting in his chair and pouring himself a drink. "Do you know how much that saves me? He likes you, Mary. Thinks you're a . . . what the devil did he call you? A 'sweeting' or some such nonsense." He downs the glass of wine, then reaches for my hand. I take it; he presses it while pouring another glass of wine, which he hands to me. "A toast," he says, clinking glasses with mine. They are crystal, he tells me, from a place called Venice. "Fine and delicate—like you," he says, pulling me close to kiss my cheek again.

I am startled by his show of affection. As much as I have longed to be petted and coddled, Norfolk's edge is ever present. Love is doled out on his terms, to his purposes; one wrong word, one wrong move, could send me to the floor in a humiliated heap with his belt across my back.

I am not so much of a fool that I do not realize being the king's daughter-in-law is another mark of favor for my father. He stands to gain much from this most advantageous of matches. Like all thoughts of this nature, however, I force it away. I think about how the other ladies will receive the news. I think of my future—my bright, wonderful future as Lady Henry Fitzroy, Duchess of Richmond.

And I revel in Norfolk's rare demonstration. He leans back in the chair, holding my hand and admiring, I'm sure, his well-made contract. But I squeeze his hand in turn, trying to prevent the sudden onslaught of tears that threaten to spill onto my cheeks any moment. I do not want to let him go. This first show of fondness may well be his last.

❧ 11 ❧

A Royal Birth

Because I am not married I am not allowed in the birthing chamber to witness the miracle. I am just as glad not to be there. I cannot imagine staring at someone while she does something that I believe should be between her, the midwife, and God. But I know because of my high birth and the marriage I am making I, too, will be expected to give birth in front of a roomful of people.

I see where it makes sense for a queen, I suppose. Giving birth before multiple witnesses proves that the child is indeed royal—and not a monster, or dead, or changed with an imposter.

Anne went into labor in September, a month earlier than expected. The court buzzes with gossip. Everyone knows the king and queen consummated their love before their January wedding, so the turn of events is no real surprise. But everyone makes a show of concern for the "premature" birth nonetheless.

The king already has announcements drawn up. He wanted to name the prince Edward or Henry, but as Henry Fitzroy was already openly acknowledged, it seemed odd to name him the latter. Yet my father has a half brother named Thomas, so I suppose it isn't an altogether unheard-of thing to have two siblings of the same name. And in the grand scheme of things, I do not think my betrothed matters that much to King Henry. We will not be around much to be confusing anyone, should they choose the name Henry for their prince.

Norfolk is in the birthing chamber along with nearly a hundred other lords and ladies. It is quite a spectacle, the birth of a prince. I am frightened as I pace the halls. I want something to do. I want to help my lady, but know there is nothing I can do to alleviate her pain and bring about the prince any faster.

"It will be fine," a calm male voice assures me. I turn to find Cedric Dane beside me. "Her Majesty is healthy. She will bring us a nice healthy prince."

I offer a wan smile. "Do you have a big family, Master Dane?"

He nods. "I am one of fifteen—the only boy."

"So many dowries!" I cry.

"They have made good matches," says Cedric. "They are a fine batch of beauties, are my sisters," he adds with a broad smile. "Celtic to the last."

"Do they sing, too?"

"Each and every one sings like an angel and plays a variety of instruments with great skill," he tells me, his pride in his family touching. "Yet none so fine as you."

I flush in a mixture of embarrassment and pleasure. "I am to be married," I am compelled to say. "To Lord Richmond."

Cedric's face is blank. "My congratulations to you, my lady," he says with a bow. "Do you expect to be happy?"

"Oh, yes," I say with a genuine smile. "I feel it in my heart. Lord Richmond is very kind. He would never hurt me."

"Well." Cedric clears his throat. "What more can you ask for?" He turns and, without excusing himself, storms down the hallway without another word.

I am puzzled by the exchange, but do not have time to ponder it as the doors to Anne's chamber burst open.

"What is it?" I ask, but no one answers. People pass me by as I push forward, trying to seek out Norfolk.

When I find him he takes my arm and guides me away from the throng. "A girl," he says, disappointment written on his face. "All this trouble for another girl."

"She didn't mean to be born a girl," I tell him, knowing most of womankind would have chosen differently, for how little we are valued in this life.

Norfolk pushes me away, clicking his tongue in disgust. "What kind of foolishness do you speak? Do you think I'm an idiot? Please try to hold your peace around the king; I pray he doesn't see into that head of yours long enough to realize the fool he is taking into his family."

Tears fill my throat as I watch him head down the hall, his steps brisk and purposeful. I imagine he is going to cancel the elaborate jousts and banquets that were to be held in the prince's honor.

It is like that, you see. For boys there are fireworks and feasting. But girls—pitiable, unwanted girls—are welcomed with a candlelit toast, if only so the parents can drink away the pain of their new liability.

She is beautiful, our little Princess Elizabeth. There is no doubt that she is a Tudor, with her red curls and fair complexion. She is sturdy, vibrant with health, her cry lusty and demanding.

"Just like her father," Anne tells me when I am allowed to see my new cousin for the first time. "I'm not discouraged at all, Mary," she adds. "I have born him a daughter, true, but I have also proven my fertility. Sons are certain to follow."

I do not dare disagree with her. Instead I take the little princess in my arms and hold her, rocking back and forth. My heart stirs in longing.

"I hope I have a baby soon," I tell her, squeezing the princess close to my breast. She is so warm and soft; I decide I enjoy holding her even more than my dog.

Anne leans back in her bed and smiles. "You are so young. You've years yet. Take pleasure in Fitzroy first. You're fortunate not to have any pressures upon you but to enjoy life to the fullest."

"Yes, but to have a family, people to always love you—"

"Oh, little Mary." Anne leans forward to rest a hand on my knee. "You of all people should know that having a family doesn't secure you love." Her voice is thick with sadness as she reaches up to stroke my cheek.

I can say nothing to this. I look down through tears at the sleeping princess, vowing that if Anne can make the people love her, then I can make my future children love me someday, too.

"I tell you, I *will* have Lady Mary's christening gown!" Anne cries in a fury, referring to the baptismal clothes worn by King Henry's oldest child. "What's good enough for her is certainly good enough for the princess. Why shouldn't they belong to me?"

"With all due respect," my father begins in his quiet voice, "why *should* they belong to Your Grace? Don't you want your own christening gown designed for the princess?"

"You grow daft, old man," Anne seethes at my father. Already she is pacing about her apartments in fine figure, just as trim and willowy as before her pregnancy. "It isn't because they were Lady Mary's. It is to show that *I* am queen, that my word is supreme. That my orders are to be followed."

"You push too hard, Your Majesty," Norfolk tells her, impervious to the insult she threw him. "This should be a time to count your blessings and let things be."

"How dare you attempt to guide me?" she demands.

Norfolk laughs. "How dare I? You forget it was I who brought you this far."

"It was *I!*" she cries, balling her hands into fists. "*I* who caught the king's eye, *I* who kept him entranced, *I* who hold his ear above all others—"

"And all this you achieved under my instruction," Norfolk reminds her.

"Pah on your instruction!" Anne rushes toward him as though she might claw at him, then falls back, dignified and composed. "You should be bowing to me. It is through me that all your blessings flow."

"And I count each and every one," Norfolk tells her with a sardonic smile as he sweeps into an exaggerated bow. "Your Majesty, cease this fighting. Let poor Princess Catherine keep her gown; she has little other comfort."

"To think you of all people should concern yourself with a woman's comforts," Anne spits as her eyes fall upon me.

I am trying to disappear into the corner with Mary Carey. Our heads are bowed over our embroidery as she and Norfolk engage in their discourse, but through my lashes I see every expression, every nuance. I wish I were not here.

To my relief Norfolk is dismissed. He offers his queen another graceful bow and quits the room, leaving Anne to wander back and forth, muttering about the unfairness of her situation.

"Everyone's always against me," she moans as she throws herself onto her favorite chaise.

Mary Carey and I exchange a glance. Mary's smile is slightly mocking.

The princess dowager does not relent; King Henry does not force the issue. Anne is wise enough to know that, because she did not produce the son he wanted, it is best to let it go, as Norfolk advised.

The baptism is a grand affair and I carry the chrism. I am so honored that I cannot contain the tears from sliding down my cheeks. To think I am cousin to a princess!

My step-grandmother, the Dowager Duchess of Norfolk, is there and carries my new cousin to the archbishop, who cannot contain a smile of his own as he regards the robust little girl being handed to him.

He holds her aloft, then proceeds with the ceremony, baptizing the little princess before the court of merry lords and ladies, who for the occasion manage to stifle their scathing gossip about the disappointment over her sex.

The princess is taken to Greenwich. I find myself dreaming of her, wishing I could have been one of the ladies chosen to keep company with her. I long to hold her and rock her and take part in every aspect of the sweet baby's new life.

Anne professes a certain longing for her child as well, and visits when she can; but affairs of state keep her busy and, though she glows with maternal pride when near her daughter, she is the queen, after all, and queens are not allowed the same luxuries as average folk.

My hopes that I will soon be a mother are intensified as plans for my own wedding commence.

Harry has returned to court.

∾ 12 ∾

The Duchess of Richmond

I see my brother first. He is in the gardens amidst a group of ladies and other courtiers. When he sees me he draws away from them and approaches me with a broad smile. I embrace him but am wary.

"You do not know what your report to Father cost me last year," I tell him. I know he never would have said anything had he known what Norfolk's reaction was to be.

Surrey draws back, smiling. "I'm sure whatever was meted out was deserved, my sister. Our father is the greatest man alive; everything he does is to a purpose, to further the good name of the Howards."

I lose expression. Surrey's admiration for Norfolk shines radiant on his face, as though he is speaking in reference to a god, a god that to his good fortune chose to be his sire.

I swallow my despair. So I am to be alone. Surrey will never be my ally.

Before I can retort, Harry Fitzroy appears, offering a timid smile of his own. "My lady," he says with a slight bow.

We are shy now, both unsure as to how to relate, now that we are betrothed.

I curtsy. "My lord."

He exchanges a glance with my brother. Surrey shrugs and joins the other courtiers, leaving Harry and me alone but chaperoned to a degree that would satisfy Norfolk.

"Well, I'm not in the succession," Harry says—an odd way to open a conversation, but I follow it with a smile. "I don't mind really. I was considered; they even thought of marrying me off to a Spanish or French princess."

I do not like the thought of this. I bow my head. Perhaps this is his way of telling me that he does not find our suit adequate. That I am not enough for him.

"Imagine when I found out I was marrying you," he goes on. My heart is sinking. It throbs painfully in my chest. I bite back tears. He sighs. "I was so relieved." I raise my head, eyes wide in surprise. "A princess would be so far from who I am. Not just because I am a duke, but because . . ." He cocks his head, searching for the adequate description. "I imagine a princess to be full of arrogance, constantly lording her station over me. When it came to my ears that I would marry you, my little Mary Howard, it was as though God was telling me all is as it should be. We've known each other a long while—we even are tied by blood to a degree." He reaches out and presses my hand. "And you're so lovely and sweet. You'll be such a fine wife and friend to me, and a loving mother to our children." His face is flushing endearingly. He bows his head, raising his bright blue eyes. "Are—are you happy with the match? Marrying a king's bastard isn't beneath you?"

"You mustn't say such things," I tell him, pressing his thin hand in turn. "I am honored to become your wife. It is everything I could have hoped for."

Harry takes both my hands in his. "How I wish I could embrace you before everyone," he says. "But soon enough." He dares to wink. "I best get back to the lads. We'll see each other soon, Mistress Mary . . . Mary."

He doffs his cap and bows. I curtsy again, my heart full.

He wants me. Somebody wants me, little Mary Howard! We are going to have a wonderful life; I know it!

I am shown beautiful fabrics for my gown but am not allowed to design it. Norfolk takes charge of that, going over each detail with care. We argue about the sleeves. I want them to reach the floor, in the style that Anne has made famous, but he wants them to fall just below my hips.

"You're too small for those sleeves," he tells me. "You'd look like you were drowning. It would be comical."

I bite my lip, disappointed. I had so wanted some input on my gown. I do not make an issue of it, however. I am so happy that I do not want to cause anything to mar the experience. My comfort comes in the knowledge that soon Norfolk will not have any more say in anything I do. I have but to bide my time.

Norfolk has his way and the gown is not disappointing. His taste is impeccable. It is ivory lace with a cloth-of-gold kirtle and gold ribbon at the hems of the sleeves and train. The gown is covered in gold roses with a matching stomacher. My veil is pinned over my hair, which Norfolk himself has brushed to a golden sheen while I swallow tears, gritting my teeth against the pain of his ministrations, thinking how wonderful it will be to have my own servant attend me when I am wed. My veil is lace, reaching my feet, which are adorned with gold slippers.

November 26, my wedding day, has arrived. The ladies fuss over me. Margaret Douglas, the king's delightfully naughty niece, informs me of all the things that occur on the wedding night, which instead of filling me with anticipation, sends shivers of dread through me.

"But that sounds awful!" I cry as we gather in the maidens' chamber. My spirits are dampened. "Who would want to do such a thing?"

"If you want a baby, you have to do it," says Margaret. She smiles. "Besides, it isn't all bad after the first pain of it, they say. Some women love it as much as men do."

"Truly?" I ask. I am intrigued by the thought but feel too naughty entertaining such notions, so divert myself by dressing for the ceremony.

As a last touch, under my veil I add the little circlet that Norfolk presented me years ago when I first came to court. Though it is silver, no one should notice it beneath the intricate lace of the veil.

"So beautiful," Margaret Douglas coos as she arranges my veil over my shoulders. I look into her face, searching for sincerity. She is so beautiful herself, with her Tudor red hair and sparkling blue eyes, that for her to compliment me is most flattering.

"I'm scared," I say to her, clutching her hand.

"Don't be, Mary," she reassures, squeezing my hand in turn. "Just think—soon we will be cousins!"

I smile. A tickle arises in my chest—that strange feeling one gets when about to laugh.

"How is our bride?" It is Anne. She sweeps into the chambers in all her glory and I know, looking at her, that no bride can compete with her beauty.

"She's afraid, poor dear," says Madge Shelton, rubbing my arm.

Anne's face is soft. "You're going to be all right, little Mary," she tells me, taking me by the upper arms and gazing into my eyes. Hers are lit with tears. "You're going to be *happy*."

She draws me forth into an embrace and I hug her tight. "Thank you, dearest Majesty."

She pulls away and touches my chin in a gentle gesture. "I must be off. His Majesty is waiting. The ceremony is about to begin."

I am trembling now. My step-grandmother the dowager duchess has come. She is a flustered old lady, grossly overweight so that she hobbles with every step. She is quite absentminded and farts a lot, which sends the ladies into fits of giggles. I can only imagine how my father, so strict regarding behavioral proprieties, handles being in her presence. Yet he does visit her now and then, so there must be some attachment.

"A fine bride you'll make," she is saying. "Pretty little girl that you are. You're the image of your mother, you know. She was a fine lass when she was young, before she started pissing off His Grace."

I am shocked at the language and stifle a giggle. Certainly her candor helps ease my nerves. I loop my arm through hers and purse shut my twitching lips. I do not voice my other thought: what did my mother ever really do to anger Norfolk so? No, I simply take amusement in my lady duchess's bawdy talk.

We proceed to the chapel where I am met by Norfolk. Hot tears fill my eyes as I take his proffered arm. He is smiling; it even reflects in his eyes. Together we progress down the aisle. The chapel is filled with immediate friends and family. Anne and the king sit in the front, smiling and exchanging words that I imagine to be about Harry and me. Surely their happiness extends beyond our match. Marrying Harry to someone beneath his station ensures his removal from the succession, securing Anne's children their place in the royal line.

All eyes are riveted toward me. I am at once flattered by and self-conscious of the attention. I lean on Norfolk's arm, turning my eyes to look up at him as we reach the altar where waits my intended, my Harry.

He is splendid, dressed in gold and white to match my gown.

Norfolk raises my veil and kisses my cheek, then lowers it again, drawing back to be seated beside his stepmother. It is then that I notice someone is missing.

My mother. She did not approve of Anne's hand in the marital arrangements, I am told later. This prevented her from joining in my happiness. Bess is in attendance, however, and chases my disappointment away with her reassuring smile.

I look to Harry and offer a nervous half smile, which is returned with an equal amount of anxiety.

The ceremony proceeds in a blur. Our vows are exchanged and it isn't long before the rings are slipped onto each other's fingers. I hold my hand out to admire the simple gold band, my lips quivering with unshed tears.

Harry lifts my veil and brushes his lips against my cheek.

We are married. I am a wife. I am Lady Richmond.

There is feasting that night to celebrate our union; a small gathering, but I do not require more. Harry and I are seated together. I have trouble eating due to nerves, but he seems to have overcome his and is enjoying the dinner as much as his father.

"Are you happy, Mistress—I mean, Lady Mary?" Harry leans over to ask.

"So happy," I tell him. My cheeks are rosy from wine. My limbs tingle pleasantly.

After we dine there is dancing. I notice that Cedric Dane is not among the musicians this evening. Somehow I am sad not to see him strumming his lute and singing to our happiness, but the thought is a fleeting one as Harry takes me in his arms to lead me in a dance. I have never felt so sure of my steps. I am married! I am truly grown up now. I look to my husband. I long to stroke his gentle young face, kiss the soft red lips. Oh, to be so lucky!

"How now, we can't have this," says a jolly voice. A large hand falls on my shoulder and I turn to see the king. I dip into a curtsy, afraid I am about to be scolded. Perhaps His Majesty has seen the longing in my eyes and deemed it too bold?

He is laughing, however. "You'll have time enough with your bride. Give us a dance," says King Henry, taking me in his strong arms.

How can one describe dancing with a king? I am in the arms of the sovereign of England, the man who has changed the world for his bride. This man and my father-in-law are one and the same.

I offer a sweet smile. "This is the most wonderful day of my life, Your Majesty," I tell him.

"May every lass in England pray for your sweetness, Lady Mary." The king smiles, holding me tight. We circle the floor a few times before he barks, "Norfolk! Come dance with your little angel. It would please us to see a father and daughter love each other well."

Norfolk hesitates, then comes forward, encircling my waist with one arm, holding my hand with the other. Of course he is the perfect dancer. There is not one element of his life that he has not mastered. Together we glide about the floor.

He reaches up to finger the circlet about my head. "Look at this," he comments. "You still have it."

"I'd never forget it," I tell him, hoping he takes from the statement what I intend. Hoping he knows I shall never forget him and the good that is in him. I reach up and stroke his cheek. He flinches. "I shall always be your daughter, my dear lord," I tell him.

He wrinkles his nose. "Of course you will," he says as though I had just uttered something ridiculous.

The dance ends and we part. Once again I am led into a dance with Harry, my lord and husband, giving me little time to ponder Norfolk's dismissive attitude.

"You're so beautiful," Harry breathes, holding me as tight as he dares. "How wonderful our life will be. I hope to make you very happy, Mary."

"I know you will," I tell him, believing it. As I regard his gentle countenance a thought strikes me. "Harry, you will be kind to me?" I shrink back from his startled gaze. "You'll—you'll never hit me?"

He laughs as though this is the most preposterous suggestion I could have ever made. Already relief begins to surge through me. "Hit you? Why would I hit you? Never," he says, daring to reach up and cup my cheek. "Never will I lay a hand on you, sweet Mary. You have my word."

Tears fill my eyes.

"How I wish you could come with me to Sheriff Hutton," Harry is saying now.

My steps falter. "What do you mean?"

His face is drawn, sad. "You were not yet told? Your father says you can't live with me as my wife till you are older."

"What?" I ask, my voice feeling as though it is being pulled from somewhere else. "No." Tears fill my eyes. I feel my fists clench. "But I *am* old enough! So many other girls take on their . . . their marital responsibilities at my age. Often a baby comes within the year!" I feel unladylike discussing this sensitive topic with Harry, but I am burning with fury. The idea of holding off motherhood is unthinkable.

Harry rubs my back in an effort to soothe. "Talk to him. Maybe you can influence him." He smiles. "Who couldn't be influenced by you? You're so beautiful, Lady Mary. Mary. My Mary."

I want to embrace him but know it isn't proper. We take to the table again for more food and wine, but both of us are disheartened.

I cannot imagine influencing Norfolk any more than influencing the sun to shine.

*   *   *

True to Norfolk's word, I am not led to a bridal chamber but to the maidens' chamber, where I dress into a simpler gown. I am too angry to sleep. The other girls sense this and offer their sympathies.

"I can't understand why he doesn't grant you your wedding night either," says Margaret Douglas. "We were counting on you telling us everything."

"Margaret, really!" cries Madge. "Poor thing has been heartbroken tonight."

I am so angry that their words have little effect. I wind my hair about my silver circlet under my hood, as is fitting for a married lady to do, then it is off to Norfolk's apartments to use whatever influence I can in the hopes that he will grant me the life I long for.

Norfolk is abed when I come to him. He dresses hurriedly, never being the type to receive anyone in an undignified manner. He is without his cap, however, and whenever I see him thus I am always surprised at what nice hair he has—thick and black, without a fleck of gray. A shame he does not show it more often. The lack of the austere black cap makes him appear a little more human.

"I'd have thought you'd be worn out," he says by way of greeting as he allows me into his privy chamber.

"Why can't I be with Harry?" I ask, too angry for nonsensical banter. "Why are you preventing our marriage from being made true?"

He purses his lips, folding his arms across his chest and leaning on the desk. "Why should I have to explain anything to you?" He sighs. "But being that it doesn't appear you will leave anytime soon, I shall tell you: you are too young, Mary. Bearing a child at this stage in your growth wouldn't be healthy. You're too small—"

"I may always be small, and Lord knows there have been smaller women than I to give birth!" I cry. "Why did you allow me to marry at all if you didn't plan on letting me be a real wife? What is to become of me now?"

"You'll stay here and serve the queen until I deem you ready for all that marriage entails," he says in his cool voice.

Tears burn my eyes. My brow aches from furrowing it. "When will that be?"

"When I say and not before," he tells me. "Why the hurry, Mary? Are you so hot you cannot contain yourself? Do I have to worry about your virtue?"

Appalled, I can only stare at him. He has struck me to the core. "How can you not think it natural for me to imagine such things when I learn I will be married? Don't you think I've spent hours planning my new life, dreaming of babies—" I cannot go on. A lump swells painful in my throat.

"You will have babies. You have years for that," he says, echoing Anne. "Go to bed now, girl. You're overtired."

"I will not go to bed until this is resolved," I say, filled with sudden bravado. "If you do not let me go to Harry, I shall appeal to the queen."

"Do that and I will make sure you suffer for it," he tells me.

"Will you?" I cry. "How? What more can you possibly do to me? Kill me? Say I met with an unfortunate accident?" I feel a bit of my mother in me as I say the dangerous words. I cannot seem to stop myself. "You married me off, my lord. I am not beholden to you any longer. I am to honor my husband before all others. It is to him that I belong now."

Norfolk grabs my shoulders, shaking me till my teeth chatter. "Don't get high-minded with me, miss! Cease this madness at once!"

"No!" I cry, pulling away from him. I remove my silver circlet, throwing it to the floor; it lands at his feet with a delicate clatter. He stares at it, his expression changing from annoyed to almost surprised that I should dare demonstrate my displeasure. He stoops down to retrieve it.

"You cannot escape who you are," he says in calm tones. "You are a Howard first, do you hear me? First, last, and always."

My control is ebbing away like the receding tide. I am sobbing with abandon. "I curse the day God chose for me to be born a Howard!"

This is too much for Norfolk. He hauls off and with a closed fist strikes my temple, knocking me off balance. I trip on the hem of my gown, falling toward the desk. From somewhere I hear a loud crack, my head meeting with the hard wood surface . . .

The world is black.

I am revived by my throbbing head. Something is caught in my throat. I am gagging. I roll onto my side and retch. Hands are on my shoulders.

"Mary . . ."

I cannot rise. I lie on the floor, my eyes fluttering. I cannot draw anything into focus. I must not pick up my head. It is fractured, I know; part of it will remain behind if I attempt to raise it. I cannot speak. I slither my hand across the floor, not knowing what I am reaching for. Perhaps I just want to see if my arm will obey me.

"Mary!" Norfolk's voice, panicked.

I moan. I cannot answer him. What were we even talking about? What happened?

I am married, I know that much. Momentary bliss. I danced with Harry and the king. And my father. And then . . . then . . .

He cut it short. The dance, my happiness, now perhaps my life.

I cannot will my eyes to stay open. It is a strain to hold any image captive. There is too much pain to cry, too much pain to put effort into anything besides breathing. I do not move. I am still.

Norfolk eases his arm about my back, drawing me into a sitting position. I whimper again, my head lolling against his shoulder, my mouth held agape. If I hold it thus it seems to ease the pain in my temple. I do not look to find reason in this. I only know it alleviates the pain somewhat and that is enough.

Norfolk rises, pulling me up with him. I have no strength. I will fall to the ground if he does not hold me up. He sits me in his chair, then disappears a moment, returning with a ewer of bitingly cold water. He kneels beside me, winding a cloth about his slim hand and placing it at my temple. I draw in a quick breath. I still cannot focus. I squint in a vain attempt to bring definition to his blurry features.

"To the maidens' chamber with you now," he says. "You'll have a good sleep and everything will look better in the morning. You'll see reason then."

He holds the cool cloth to my temple a while longer before lowering his arm and helping me to my feet. I wobble, then sink back into the chair. My head is swimming. Bile rises in my throat. I begin to gag again. Norfolk holds the basin before me and I retch till there is nothing left but to heave brokenly.

"God," mutters Norfolk, his voice thick with disgust.

I lean back in the chair, weakened by the exertions. My gut aches. I close my eyes and relax my jaw. If only the pain would go away. . . .

"Are you quite finished?" he asks, setting the basin down and nudging it away from him with his foot.

I offer a feeble nod.

"All right, then. Let's get you back," he says, assisting me to my feet, looping my arm through his.

He escorts me to the maidens' chamber.

We do not speak of Harry or my dashed hopes ever again.

My wedding night is spent with a throbbing head that I claim is due to taking in too much wine. The knot that has formed at my temple I cover with a creative sweep of my hair.

I sleep beside Margaret Douglas instead of my husband.

I look at my rainbow ring, at last able to focus on something. But it holds no hope for me now. No longer am I able to push aside the dark thoughts that for so long danced at the fringes of my consciousness. Now they stalk me like ravenous devils, waiting to devour me. I must not let them. I must find something to hold on to.

I think about the future. It is still possible. I will prove my maturity to Norfolk. I will show I am ready to be a wife and mother, and God willing he will send me to Harry all the sooner, where my life might begin anew.

There *is* hope. As long as I am alive, there is hope.

The next day I receive two gifts: from my husband a beautiful gold comb wrought in the shape of a butterfly, with mother-of-pearl wings and emerald antennae, which I immediately place in my hair; the second is a collar of pearls from Norfolk.

The ladies fuss over them. Margaret Douglas clasps the pearls about my neck; they are cold against my skin.

I am still dizzy and ask Margaret if I might lean on her as we go to Mass.

"Too much wine last night?" she asks with a wink.

I nod, forcing a laugh.

We enter the chapel where I see Harry, who offers a bright smile.

"Any luck, my lady?" he asks before the service begins.

I shake my head. Tears fill my eyes; even they aggravate the pain in my head.

Harry squeezes my hand. " 'Tis all right, Mary. We'll be together soon enough. And maybe he's right. I couldn't bear it should anything happen to you if . . ." He flushes.

I bow my head. Part of me was hoping he'd appeal to his father, who would command Norfolk to allow me to live in my rightful household. His easy acceptance of the situation saddens me.

I draw in a breath. "Thank you for the comb, my lord."

"You like it, truly?" he asks.

I nod, my smile genuine. "I will wear it every day until we are allowed to be together. Then you shall remove it yourself."

Harry laughs. "I shall await that day with great eagerness!"

He takes leave of me then, returning to his attendants.

I return to the other ladies.

And so our lives shall be lived out as such. In separate circles, separate beds.

I bow my head and pray that the time might pass, that I might grow older and take my proper place beside my lord husband.

God honors my prayers with the passage of time. Court life is so busy that I haven't much opportunity to miss Harry, though I am coming to realize it isn't Harry I miss so much—I do not know him so very well, after all—as the idea of a life and babies of my own.

I take delight in Princess Elizabeth. Anne brings me with her whenever she visits the tawny-haired cherub and I love playing with her. Her hands and feet are so tiny! I love to marvel at the dimples that serve as knuckles and kiss her smooth chubby cheeks.

I never speak to Anne about my longing to leave court and set up my own house, nor does she bring it up. I imagine she believes it is my wish as much as Norfolk's that I remain in her service. No doubt serving a queen is the highest of privileges, one I do not take for granted, but . . .

One day as I coo over the little princess, Anne rises from her window seat, her manner distracted. She is fidgety today.

"They still don't like me, Lady Mary," she tells me, looking out the window as though a stream of belligerent citizens will crash through it at any moment. "I had hoped with the birth of the princess, with the proof of my fertility . . ." She sits back down, pursing her lips.

I rush to her side, daring to reach out and take her hand.

She bows her head, gripping her stomach. "It doesn't matter. This next one will be a prince, I'm certain."

"Oh, Your Majesty!" I cry, a stab of pain and delight piercing through me at once. "I'm sure you're right."

"And if it's not," she goes on, her voice bearing that Howard edge, "the king is busy creating the Act of Succession. None but *my* children can ever sit the throne of England."

"A wise move," I say, thinking of the former Princess Mary, wondering what she will make of the act.

"Pray for me, Lady Mary," Anne says, reaching out to cup my cheek. I flinch. Even all these months later, contact with the right side of my face causes stabbing pain in my temple. "Pray that I deliver England of a son."

"With all my heart, dearest Majesty," I tell her through my pain.

I cast my eyes down at the princess, whose own gaze is as dark and alert as her mother's.

How wretched it is to be born the wrong sex, I think, stroking the silky red curls.

As Anne's pregnancy advances so does the progress of the Act of Succession, which is passed on March 23, 1534. Elated, Anne dances about her apartments, whirling about with one lady or another until, exhausted, she sits back on her chaise and encourages us to continue the merriment. That same day the pope declares that King Henry's marriage to Catherine of Aragon remains, as it has always been in Rome's eyes, valid.

Anne scoffs at this, then proceeds to discuss her ideas about church reform. She believes in simpler things; less grandeur in the chapel, humbler priests with better intentions than those who take indulgences to fatten their own pockets, profiting from the so-called expiation of others' sins. "How can they intervene on our behalf, anyway?" she asks. "One should not need a confessional to make their world right with God." She even dares to admit that women should be allowed to study the scriptures to come to a better understanding of God's Word. I agree with her with a whole heart and enjoy the lively conversations she holds about the topic.

Yet the day is so merry that we don't discuss such heady issues as reform in too much detail. Musicians have been called, led by Anne's favorite, the talented Mark Smeaton, and they erupt into tunes that call the freshness of spring to mind.

Cedric Dane is among them. He offers a slight smile as he is tuning his lute. "Lady Richmond," he says in greeting. The name still rings foreign in my ears and I stifle the urge to look about to see if it is indeed me he is addressing. "Still haven't joined your husband? I'd have thought you'd be eager to start your life as a bride."

Frustrated that he is this perceptive, I avert my head. "I am obligated first to my queen."

He nods. When I meet his gaze again I find no mockery there.

"And have you done any more writing?" he asks.

"Not recently," I tell him. "Though some of the ladies and I have put together quite a collection." I smile at the thought of it. "It was a delightful way to pass the time."

"I shall be practicing tonight," he goes on to say. "I have been working on a new composition on the virginals. I'd love for you to hear it. . . . I shall be there late into the evening if you—"

"Master Dane, you must cease trying to seek me out," I tell him in firm tones. "It is inappropriate for one of my station to associate with you."

I break away from him then, stunned by my harshness. I swallow a painful lump in my throat as I rejoin my circle, never feeling quite so isolated as I do in this crowd.

That night in the maidens' chamber we are readying for bed when a servant informs us that Norfolk is waiting outside.

I begin to shake. Has he discovered me conversing with Cedric? Oh, God . . .

But no. It is to Madge Shelton that he wishes to speak. Relieved but puzzled, I watch my cousin saunter outside. I hear a happy exchange outside the door.

"How now, Uncle Thomas!" she cries in her bubbly voice.

"Ah, the delightful Madge," I hear my father say with a chuckle. "Come share a cordial with me. I do not think I have taken the proper time in acquainting myself with you."

I draw the coverlet over my shoulders and roll on my side, confused.

When Madge returns I am fraught with curiosity. Reading it, she climbs under the covers, her smile broad.

"The king is feeling a little restless," she whispers. "Uncle Thomas is hoping I can . . . divert him."

"But His Majesty loves Anne!" I whisper back, shocked the king would go to all this trouble only to take on another mistress.

"That may be so, but love certainly doesn't equal faithfulness for Henry VIII," Madge goes on in smug tones. It is easy to see her task excites her, even when she wrinkles her nose and adds, "Though it will be ghastly. His Majesty has become quite portly this past year." She draws in a breath and squares her shoulders in a perfect imitation of Anne. "But I can give him what he needs for the duration of her pregnancy and keep his eyes from straying toward other factions—the Seymours, for instance."

I see my father's strategy at once. "Best to keep it all in the family, I suppose," I admit, knowing that the acceptance of such behavior indeed makes me a Howard.

Knowing it is all a game to Norfolk. He will move us about the playing field as is his wont; we are inanimate, no better than wood or pewter. We do not feel or think or dream.

We only have this name, this Howard name, and that is the most important thing, a name that cannot be touched, smelled, or tasted. A mere sound and assortment of letters that mean, in God's grand scheme, nothing.

Who will remember the Howards, really?

Knowing that Madge is the new bait for the king keeps me awake. My stomach hurts. My legs are restless and twitch under the covers. Madge kicks me and mumbles for me to settle down. I decide the best course is to get up. I don't know what to do with myself. I try to embroider, to no avail, pricking my fingers and growing more agitated with each passing second.

It is easy for me to leave the maidens' chamber. Everyone knows of my frequent visits to Norfolk, so my whereabouts are not questioned. I dress in a light pink gown and plait my hair—ensuring that my father will not look upon my mane and decide to bring the dreaded brush through it—then wrap about my shoulders a soft white cloak to ward off the chill damp of evening.

I do not know what I will say to him, but will endeavor to do what I can to help Anne. She deserves better treatment than this. She is our queen and possibly carrying a prince; how could anyone so flagrantly disrespect her? I do not blame Madge. She is flirtatious, bred for such intrigues; she is also following my father's orders. Very few dare cross Norfolk.

As I make my way down the hall I hear the sound of virginals; it is a bittersweet melody. I am not conscious of following the sound until I am standing outside the door of the musicians' informal practice room. I hear nothing but the music. There is no male chatter; no one is pausing to say "wait," the all-time favorite phrase of musicians the world over while figuring out chords and the like.

I know who is behind the door; I remember his invitation. In my mind's eye I see him sitting there, eyes closed, weaving in time to the music, his slender fingers upon the keys, bringing them to their full potential. I cannot help myself. I push open the door.

He is as I envisaged. I enter. I know I should not be here. I should either go to Norfolk or back to the maidens' chamber. I should go anywhere but here.

But I do not go. I remain, transfixed by his song.

"Well, at least you can't accuse me of seeking you out," says Cedric without opening his eyes.

"I heard the racket," I say in my haughtiest tones, "and wondered who would be so rude as to play at such a late hour."

"The door was quite closed. And the court keeps late hours, my lady," Cedric returns. His hands fall silent on the keys. The room is too quiet now. Our voices echo against the stone walls. He is smiling, a brilliant mocking smile that fills me with a strange ecstasy.

"So the music is a 'racket,' eh?" he asks, rising and approaching me. "Then I shall cease with that composition so as not to offend your fair ears."

I laugh. "I wouldn't say it was a complete racket. . . ." I say by way of apology. My face is flushing. There is no escaping it. I do not bow my head because it would only draw more attention to it. "Do not cease the composition. Who is it for?"

"A lady," he confesses. He stands before me now. I tremble at his nearness. He is by far the most handsome man at court; even more handsome than my cousin George Boleyn or the poet Thomas Wyatt.

"Who?" I ask, my voice breathy and tremulous.

"My betrothed," he answers.

My heart sinks. Betrothed? Cedric? I curse myself. Why shouldn't he be betrothed? I am married, to the king's son, no less. I am almost a princess. And I love my Harry. He is my husband; it is my duty to be his loving little wife, even if I never see him.

I offer a frosty smile. "My congratulations to you, Master Dane," I tell him. "Might I inquire as to the identity of your future bride?"

He laughs. "She isn't gentry, so I suppose it does not matter to the likes of you."

I am hurt at this, even though I know it is true. What gives us the right, I ask myself, to look down on those more humble? Are they not the ones who will inherit this earth? Perhaps it is far more of a blessing to be humble than noble.

"You mustn't say that," I tell him, feeling thoroughly wretched.

"It is a fact," he says. "In any event, her name is Helen Duncan."

"A Scot?"

"Half a Scot," he says with a chuckle. "Does it make a difference? Her family has lived in England these past hundred years. Their ties to Scotland are quite severed, I believe."

Unexplained tears fill my throat. I swallow them. "I wish you much happiness. Will you remain in the king's service then?"

"Yes," he says. "For some reason His Majesty likes me, so I shall stay on. He has given me a little home in London as a wedding present."

"How generous," I comment. "Your betrothed . . . is she very lovely?"

"Quite lovely," he says. "A hard worker. Very real."

I do not understand the last attribute. Real. What is it to be real? Perhaps he does not think those of us in this glittering world of the court live in reality. Then where do we live? I am filled with panic at the thought that I am missing out on something crucial and unattainable.

"I'm sorry you scoff upon our world," I say in a huff. "I'm sorry you do not think us real enough for you."

Cedric takes my hands. His are large and warm. I do not withdraw. I do not want to withdraw, even in my annoyance.

"No, I do not think you're real enough," he tells me, his tone heated, "but you could be. If you were not so afraid of the beautiful, strong-willed woman you are inside."

I want to retort but find he is drawing me toward him. His lips are on mine, his arms enfolding me to his broad chest. I embrace him in turn, yielding to his soft, warm kiss. Thoughts run wild as stags through my head, wicked thoughts. I think of what lovers do, of what I am told they do. Of what my body yearns to do.

I think of Harry. Of the kisses I am not allowed to exchange with him, my lawful husband.

I pull away, breathless. He still holds me. We regard each other in a moment of mingled shock and longing. My hands rest flat on his chest. I do not want to leave this embrace. But I cannot stay. He is not mine. He can never be mine.

What do I tell him now? Do I thank him for awakening my youthful passion, or curse him for it?

I reach up, cupping his face between my hands. "I cannot see you alone again," I whisper.

He nods in understanding.

Tears burn my eyes. "May your marriage bring you much joy," I say as we disengage.

His Adam's apple bobs several times. He averts his head. He takes my hands. "Good-bye, Mistress How—Lady Richmond."

He drops my hands and turns away.

I quit the room, strangled by a sob.

That night I ponder the kiss. I relive the moist warmth of his lips pressed to mine. I chase away the guilt even as I try to chase away the rising passion.

I do not see Norfolk that night but confront him the next. "Confront" is probably too strong a word for what passes between us, as indeed it is a fool who seeks to confront Norfolk.

"I did not send for you," he says in greeting as I enter his rooms.

I try to stay calm. "My lord, I know you are wise and good," I begin.

"Oh, God," he interjects, his tone thick with annoyance. "What is it? Out with it. I've no time for meaningless flattery."

"My lady Madge Shelton," I confess. "I do not think—"

"No, Mary, you do not think," he tells me, his tone firm. He approaches me. His face is inches from mine. I shrink back in terror. "*I* do the thinking. While we are on the topic, I should inform you that not only do you not think, you do not question, or criticize. You say, 'yes, my lord' or 'how may I best serve you, my lord?' Do you understand?"

I have stepped a few feet out of his arm's reach to better my chances of eluding him should he feel the urge to physically illustrate this point. I am nodding. "Yes, my lord. I understand."

I leave in a hurry.

I failed. I cannot intercede for my cousin.

At once there are very few things that seem fair in this life.

* * *

Madge serves as a good distraction, keeping the king's eye on the Howards, with her swaggering walk, rippling laugh, and quick wit. Together they go hunting and hawking; under Norfolk's instruction she is everything a king's mistress should be. But Anne is quick to protest the plot, and despite Norfolk's impatient explanation of its logic, lets everyone know where she stands, including His Majesty.

"I will not have it!" she cries to the king, clutching her rounded belly as though to remind everyone that she could be the mother to a prince and should not be crossed. "I will not have you parading about with your whores while I suffer for the sake of carrying on your line! How dare you flaunt that slut where I can see her?"

"A fine day it is when you call your cousin a slut after you yourself used to play cards with Catherine while we were in the midst of our divorce!" King Henry returns in his thundering tone.

I am frightened and cower in the corner while this transpires.

"You will not see her," Anne seethes. "Or I swear I will not come to you as your wife again."

The room is stunned silent. How can one pretend to be busy in the face of this display?

"You would not dare," says the king. "You are my subject, madam. You are at my command, just as any dairy maid or soldier or anyone else is."

"I will!" Anne cries in desperation. Her black eyes are wide. Her breath comes quick. A sheen of sweat glistens on her forehead. Her hands are clenched at her sides. "I swear I will!" She dissolves into tears. Her eyes are lit with a genuine sense of betrayal. "Oh, Your Majesty, how could you? After all we've been through, how could you?"

King Henry cannot resist her tears. Indeed, I do not think many can. I want to run to her and wipe them away myself.

"Now, now, sweetheart, you know it is meaningless," he tells her in a rich, soothing tone. "I have no great designs on Madge Shelton." He approaches Anne and takes her in his arms. "I love no one but you. Always."

"Promise?" Anne asks in a small voice as she tips her lovely head up to regard him.

"On my crown, I promise," he answers, kissing her cherry red lips.

When she pulls away her eyes are dry, her smile is bright.

I am relieved. The king will stray no more. Anne will receive the respect she is due.

I return to Kenninghall with Norfolk and Surrey for a brief visit. I am thrilled that we shall all be together as a family. Perhaps my brother's presence will ease the tension in the house. In the very least, his eyes might be opened to the nature of our parents' relations, dimming Norfolk's halo.

It is not to be. Apparently Norfolk has Surrey's complete adulation. Surrey offers Mother a cool greeting of acknowledgment, yet fawns over Bess Holland whenever she is present. Fortunately for her sake as much as Mother's, she has remained at court for this trip.

Surrey takes the opportunity to go hawking, leaving me to take supper alone with Norfolk and Mother, an affair that is accompanied by its usual strain.

Mother's jaw is set as she sips her wine, her eyes fixed on Norfolk as he picks at his beef.

"I want you to leave Mistress Holland," she says, lingering over the word *mistress.*

I almost choke on my bread. I bow my head, applauding her bravery and fearing for her at once. The words that she has longed to speak are out at last; they cannot be retracted.

This is not going to be good.

"Really?" Norfolk's tone oozes with disdainful mockery.

"I cannot have this anymore. It's her or me," she says.

"All right, then," he says, his tone calm. He addresses two portly female servants. "Take her."

Mother is seized. I begin to tremble. My stomach churns and lurches. My mouth is dry. Mother's eyes are wide and search mine out.

"Go, Mary," she says as a servant takes her arms and pins her to the floor. One is sitting on her chest, as though Mother is a beast that needs such rough handling in order to be mastered. Norfolk stands above her. She is coughing. Blood spews forth, flecking her lips. The most frightening thing about it, even more frightening than the spectacle itself, is that it seems practiced. *Routine.*

"You will not advise me on with whom to keep company," says Norfolk in his soft voice, regarding my mother as though she were an unsightly insect to be squashed.

I scan the room, wishing my brother would come now. Why isn't he here to see this?

"Please!" I cry, running forth to take Norfolk's arm. It is a risk, I know, but what kind of daughter can stand by and watch this transpire? Could I ever forgive myself if I just walked away?

Norfolk turns to me, his black eyes afire with the same madness Anne's adopt when she is in a temper. He draws his hand back and slaps me. It is my bad side, the side that has ached ever since he struck me on my wedding night almost a year ago. I stumble, dizzy. My vision is a blur.

"Run, Mary!" Mother cries. "Just run!"

I am a coward, I decide, for I listen to her, I run. I run from the great hall to my chambers and lock myself in. I do not want to see anyone; not Surrey, not even my poor wretched mother.

I want to disappear.

Surrey claims to have witnessed the whole thing. He came home to find Mother seated at table, listening to my father's tirade, her expression bored and "completely disrespectful," as Surrey phrased it.

He did not see her pinned down by the servants, coughing up blood, and told me I was exaggerating when I relayed the story.

"You women are so soft," he tells me. "It's natural for you to ally yourself with her; natural but not wise. Our father is the greatest man alive. The punishment he doles out is as just as God's."

I want to hit him then as I never wanted to hit anyone before. I curse his single-minded devotion even as I curse my own.

We are leaving now.

There is no one to safeguard my mother from the brutality of my father's own servants, who are well paid to demonstrate their loyalty to their master in this repulsive fashion; indeed, if I have learned anything about human nature, some may be glad to perpetuate her suffering. Norfolk has her locked away in her chambers, without clothes or jewelry or any accoutrement that could bring my poor lady comfort. I do not know how long his orders are to keep her there, and am terrified to ask.

My brother takes residence at Kenninghall, justifying Norfolk's actions with his whole heart.

Mother is eventually moved to Redbourne in Hertfordshire. I am not allowed to see her.

Norfolk and I return to court. We do not speak of Mother except for him to inform me that he is seeking a divorce.

"She is a fool, your mother," he tells me over and over. "I would give her whatever she wanted—her clothes and jewels, whatever, if she'd just grant me this one thing."

"I admit, it escapes me as well," I dare to say, but not because I sympathize with his plight. I cannot imagine why Mother would not be thrilled to sign divorce papers, freeing her of this man and giving her the life she so deserves.

Nor does it make credible her ultimatum; it is obvious when she presented Norfolk with the choice, he was to choose her. She truly did not think he would choose Bess. Perhaps it is out of a sense of revenge that she will ensure he does not have her; that, coupled with the fact that she is a staunch Catholic and supporter of Catherine. It would go against every principle she has, to grant my father a divorce when she believes that a man and woman, once joined in holy matrimony, cannot be separated except by death.

I mourn for her. I cannot believe any principle is worth staying married to my lord Norfolk.

At court I try to seek out Bess in the hopes she can bring me to a better understanding of the situation. But Bess, though never cold toward me, skillfully avoids me.

At once I decide that this is something I will never comprehend.

It is best to let it go.

*   *   *

In July Anne miscarries, bringing forth a little stillborn prince. I am shocked and saddened; she was almost seven months with child. How can it be considered a miscarriage then?

I sit at Anne's bedside at Greenwich while she rubs her newly flattened belly. She is in a state of awe.

"I do not understand it, little Mary," she tells me, tears slick on her alabaster cheeks. "How can he have been inside me, a part of me, kicking and moving, stretching, so alive and perfect, and now be just . . . gone? No more. Gone." She averts her head on the pillow and emits a strangled sob. She does not remove her hand from her belly. "Empty womb." She turns her head to face me, holding out her arms. "Empty arms." She bows her head, crushed by the tragedy. "Empty."

"Your Majesty," I croon, taking her hands. "You will have other babies. . . ." The words are as empty as her arms.

"I wanted *this* baby," Anne whimpers, rolling on her side.

I reach out to stroke her dark hair. I do not say anything.

There is nothing to say.

In September, to everyone's horror, Mary Carey announces to our immediate family that she is with child. She has married William Stafford, a man far beneath her, and will retire to the country to set up house with him.

"And good riddance to you," Anne seethes. I am saddened by the exchange. I understand that Anne's disappointment in her own childbearing situation causes jealousy, and that the sisters have always experienced a certain rivalry, but to sever their relationship like this . . .

"You will never be welcome at my court again, do you hear? You went behind our backs and acted like a common dairy maid," Anne goes on.

My father is thrilled to join in. "Let Stafford take charge of the slut; indeed that is what she has always been and always will be. You'll not see your son again, Mary, I guarantee it." Mary flinches at this. With Anne granted custody of young Henry there is no doubt that my father's words are not an empty threat. "And you will not receive a pittance from the Howards, ever. Do you understand? I wash my hands of you forever. Go."

"I will go," Mary Carey Stafford says, a smile of triumph curving her full pink lips. "I will go, and let there be no doubt that I will know more happiness, poor and banished, than any of you at this court of the damned ever will!"

"Dismissed!" Anne cries.

Mary dips into a farcical curtsy and, in a whirl of skirts, quits the room and our lives.

I ask if I might leave to take the air. Anne grants the request and as soon as I leave Anne's apartments I run through the halls to catch my cousin.

I seize her by the arm. "My lady," I say, tears clutching my throat. "You have always been kind to me. Let it be known that I think you are quite brave. I hope you know nothing but happiness."

Mary cups my face between her hands and presses her lips to my forehead. "Good-bye, my dearest. The best of luck amongst these wolves."

At once it is all I can do to stifle the urge to beg her to take me away, too, away from this court and its miseries and intrigues, away where there is none to answer to but oneself and one's own dreams.

I do not see her again.

❧ 13 ❧

Falling Stars

1535

Anne is expecting again! Her joy is muted, however. Her last experience with pregnancy makes her more cautious. Often her face is white, her eyes gleaming with tension as she notes every little thing that transpires. She consults her ladies and midwives frequently, making sure that this or that is a normal sign that the pregnancy is progressing as it should. She is assured by all that the birth of a healthy prince is imminent and she indeed has nothing to fear.

Things pass by in the normal manner, or what is normal for this court, and the holiday season is merry. There are feasting and masking and tourneys. Now and then I see my husband, Harry, but never alone. He sends me little gifts, however; handkerchiefs of the finest linens, bolts of fabric for new gowns, jewels, and trinkets.

He is as good a husband as he is allowed to be.

I spend my time writing. I compose more poetry. I sing and hone my musical abilities. I avoid Norfolk but take joy in acquainting myself with his family.

My half uncle Thomas has come to court. He is a dear man, so fine and fair it is hard to believe he is my father's brother. Perhaps he favors his mother's side of the family.

Uncle Thomas, as it seemed no one could come up with a more

original name for the poor lad, enjoys being a courtier to the fullest, but unlike most courtiers he is sweet and genuine, taking good care of the hearts in his keeping.

I find myself drawn to him. I can tell him anything and his openness with me speaks of a reciprocated connection. He confides that he has fallen in love with the beautiful Margaret Douglas, niece of King Henry.

This notion causes my heart to soar with excitement. Margaret often tells me how much she admires my uncle Thomas; she cannot talk about his looks and well-turned legs enough.

I begin to act as their messenger, which gives me quite a feeling of importance as mine is such a happy task. They exchange flowery letters and love poems. I am so caught up in the romance that I compose many a verse about the secret couple and am often sighing over their blossoming love.

I do not think, not for one moment, that I am doing anything wrong.

Thomas More and Catherine of Aragon's friend Bishop Fischer decide not to participate in the taking of any oaths that are to be sworn the country over supporting Anne's queenhood, the king's supremacy over the Church of England, and the Act of Succession.

They are tried before Secretary Cromwell—that crafty creature who makes me think of a well-oiled door, too eager to hit you in the bum when passing through it—and sentenced to death along with four other monks.

I retch when I hear of the monks' sentence: hanging, castration, and evisceration, all to be done while the poor men are still alive to appreciate the depth of their torture.

More, once so dear to His Majesty, is beheaded along with the bishop. Their heads are displayed on pikes on London Bridge as a warning to others who dare defy His Majesty.

Nightmares plague me. I see kind Master More's face being pecked at by birds, his unseeing eyes plucked out to be dropped in some faraway nest.

They went to their deaths at peace with their convictions. They would not be swayed even under the axe.

Nothing is as pathetic as a martyr, my father said.
Nor is anything as brave.

Anne gives birth to another dead little prince. This time I am
not summoned to her bedside.

She grieves alone.

My heart aches for my lady. I say nothing, however. Anne con-
ducts her life with a forced gaiety, the strain of which shows on her
drawn features and sunken cheeks. She forces herself to live beyond her exhaustion; her manner is giddy and agitated.

King Henry behaves differently after the loss of this child. He
distances himself from Anne and her charade of happiness. She is
the grand courtier once more, throwing her famous tantrums. But
instead of sparking the king's desire and capitulation as they used
to, his face darkens in resentment and annoyance.

She plays a dangerous game.

Norfolk tries to caution her. She does not heed.

"She calls me things unfit for a dog," Norfolk tells the Spanish
ambassador, Eustace Chapuys, one day.

While I'm certain they are well-deserved epithets, I agree that
Anne should follow Norfolk's advice. Now is not the time to display her renowned temper. She should be sweet and acquiescent.

For there are vultures among us.

The Seymours have begun to circle.

In September 1535 the king visited the Seymours' estate of
Savernake and met little pious Jane, a dreadfully plain and boring
girl who is the complete opposite of my vibrant cousin. Perhaps it
is for this reason alone that she sparks the king's fancy.

He begins courting her in November, making it no secret to
Anne, though she has announced that she is again with child.

Norfolk is tense over the development. The Seymours have
been our rivals for Lord knows how long, and to see them wriggle
their way into the king's favor is not a good sign.

"The last thing we want are those damn upstarts," he seethes.

I sigh. He does not profess concern for Anne's well-being at all.

By now I should expect nothing less.

* * *

Catherine of Aragon dies in early January of 1536. Lady Mary, formerly the princess, is shut away at Hatfield, made to attend her sister Elizabeth, and was never allowed to go to her mother in her final hours.

An autopsy reveals the princess dowager's blackened heart. Was she poisoned? Few express this possibility; the consequences of suggesting that foul play was involved are too dire, so we keep our thoughts to ourselves.

Those who are brave enough to voice their opinions blame everything on Anne. They also fault her for Lady Mary's ill health, and any chill my own husband, the Duke of Richmond, might take on. They even go so far as to blame failing crops, droughts, and too much rain on my lady. To the general public Anne is a witch, and the king but a helpless victim of her evil charms.

The king still makes people suffer for objecting to the marriage and voicing anything negative about his wife, but a seed has been planted. He regards her with a wary expression now.

The court is consumed with Catherine's death, but not out of grief. The king and queen arrange a celebration and dress in bright yellow costumes, dancing about, ordering feasts and the fool Will Somers to be at his finest. There is a sort of hysteria in the king's blue eyes tonight. Anne's obsidian orbs sparkle in triumph.

The display is garish. I do not think even Anne's staunchest supporters find any of this in good taste. Indeed, my father takes to his bed early tonight. I pass by his chambers to bid him good night. I took leave of the festivities early as my stomach is upset.

He is behind his desk, his chin in his hand, his mouth covered by his fingers. He is staring on some fixed point beyond the room's confines, a point in time perhaps when things were simpler.

I curtsy. "My lord. I came to say good night."

He removes his black cap and runs his hand through his hair with a heavy sigh. "I respected her," he says then. I wonder what it is to be a woman and have Norfolk's respect. It is a rare thing. Yet despite his respect for the late Catherine, he did nothing to save her. So his respect does not amount to much, I decide with a heavy heart.

"And they dance." His tone is a mingling of bitterness and horror.

I do not know how to respond. Anything I say could send him into a fury so I remain silent. I approach him, reaching out to touch his cheek. I lean down and kiss his hair. "Good night, my dear lord."

He says nothing.

I leave him to be alone with his grief, as is his wont.

January 1536

The king's greatest enemy is gone. One would think the battle is over, that now Anne can enjoy triumphant relaxation at long last. But there is no such thing.

At a joust where we pretend all is normal and right between the king and queen, His Majesty takes a fall on the tiltyard, rendering him unconscious. We watch in the stands in horror as attendants rush to his aid.

I run to seek out my husband. It is the first time I have been truly alone with him since our marriage two and a half years ago.

He takes my hands in concern. "What will we do if . . . ?"

That is the question foremost in everyone's minds over the next few hours as the king lies in the faerie country, that strange place between death and life.

His death would leave the realm to the little princess. A regent would have to rule in her stead until she achieved her majority, and only if civil war didn't erupt over the rights of Lady Mary's claim. No doubt my father and Cromwell would wrangle over their right to rule as regent . . .

And then there is Fitzroy, my Harry, who stands helpless and frightened before me now. His fear is more pure, however. He thinks of his father dying. He does not think of what it would be like should the country surprise everyone and choose *him* as heir to the throne, being that he is Henry's only acknowledged male issue.

I clutch Harry's hand. "He will be all right, Harry," I tell him in sweet tones. "His Majesty is the strongest of men. This is nothing to him." I force cheer into my tone, bringing about a small smile from my lord.

"Mary, I want you to come home with me after His Majesty recovers," says Harry. "Appeal to your father, I beg you. I want you beside me. We'll start our lives. You're sixteen now, old enough to have children. Please. See if it can be done."

Part of me wants to shout that he should appeal to Norfolk himself if he wants me beside him, but in the light of what is taking place on the tiltyard I say nothing. I stroke his cheek.

"It's what I want more than anything in the world, Harry," I tell him in honesty.

How wonderful it would be if Norfolk decided I was old enough to leave this increasingly wretched place. I want no more of it; no more plotting and intrigue and fear.

I want to be in my own home with my own husband and babies.

Much to our relief the king is revived. His leg is injured but he is expected to make a full recovery. He takes to his apartments to recuperate while Anne miscarries in her own chambers.

It is January 29, the same day Catherine of Aragon is interred.

I am at Anne's bedside this time. She lies in a state between dreams and consciousness, uttering terrible things. She talks about her brother George, how his wife Jane always tried to come between them. She talks about the Lady Mary and how she failed in winning the bastardized princess's respect. Sometimes she bursts into hysterical laughter, followed by an onslaught of gasping sobs.

I sit and cry beside her, helpless as always.

Then Anne discusses the most terrible thing of all. The baby, the baby that is said to have been born a monster, its spine exposed and its head nearly thrice the size of a human being. Already rumors are spreading that witchcraft is involved.

"He was not a demon child," she says over and over. "My little prince was not evil! I may go to Hell for my sin, but he was innocent!"

I do not know how to respond. I know not of her sin and will not pry. I only know that my cousin is a mother driven to distraction by her grief, and there is nothing anyone can do about it.

When Anne recovers consciousness she is white. Her black eyes are wide in terror. "It is over for me now, little Mary," she says. "All over."

"No, you mustn't say it," I tell her, stroking her fair cheek. "It's just the beginning. You will prevail. You always prevail."

She shakes her head.

The woman whose determination and resolve changed the course of history is defeated.

Her recovery is slow. The king, completely discouraged with Anne's inability to carry a child to term, does not go to her anymore. He has set his sights on the meek Jane Seymour.

I hate Jane. I want to slap her every time I see her. She pretends to be meek and modest, praying like a diligent little nun, and all the while she plays at the same game Anne did when King Henry was married to Catherine! She even goes so far as to copy Anne's refusal of a gift, as it might compromise her "virtue" to accept it, and she cannot submit to being a mistress, but only a wife. This was an Anne original, overseen by Norfolk, of course.

We are beside ourselves with annoyance.

"It's her brother, that upstart Edward," says Norfolk. "And that idiot Thomas. They are pushing her forth. Unfortunately she is just what the king wants right now—a little breath of fresh air after being at odds with Her Grace all the time."

I sigh in exasperation. The parallels are so unbelievable to me that voicing them would just earn me a beating, so I say nothing.

"And if that damn fool Anne doesn't start heeding my advice, there's nothing to be done but bear it," Norfolk continues. "I just do not know how to get through to her. She must submit to him, be meek—"

"She would not be herself should she behave thus," I dare to say. "She can't be someone she's not. It's not in her nature. She made it this far because of who she is, just as much as by you helping her."

Norfolk glares at me.

I sigh and dare to continue. "My lord, I do not wish to remain in her service. This place frightens me. I want to begin my life with my lord Richmond. I am old enough now, nearly seventeen. Please."

He shakes his head. "No. To leave the queen now would appear as though you were deserting her. You must remain and see this through."

"How long?" I cry. "How long before *my* life can start?"

"It's always about you, isn't it, Mary?" His lips twist in that sardonic smile that chills me to my core. He rises. "You will stay by my side until I send you away. Is that understood?"

"No!" I cry. "It is not understood! You have no real use for me! Her Majesty has no use for me! I'm just here!" I sink to my knees before him, sobbing. "Let me go—oh, I beg you, my lord, let me go! I want to be a wife! I want to have a baby!"

He pulls me to my feet, gripping my shoulders. "Now, now, this won't do. I have too much to think about for this nonsense. Go to sleep. Think of something pretty, anything you like, and I'll see that it's yours if only you leave this room."

"I only want one thing, and that's a child—you can't give me that!" I cry.

"Mary! None of that filth!" he says, pushing me away. "Go!"

I turn, quitting the room, containing my sobs until I reach the maidens' chamber where I throw myself on the bed, losing myself in the manner I always have, through sleep.

A strange escape comes in the form of sitting for Hans Holbein the Younger, the court painter, who has been commissioned to render my likeness. Norfolk chooses my gown and hood, a monstrosity bearing a ghastly feather that I detest—not the stylish French hood that Anne has made so popular.

Other than these inconveniences, I find sitting for the gentle painter a relaxing experience that gives my mind plenty of time to engage in the activity of wandering to happier places.

Holbein doesn't say much. Now and then he'll arrange my hands a certain way or remind me to bend my head. I am to look modest and prayerful; surely this is a device of my father, for Anne would have me appear strong and proud.

After the first sketch, where Holbein jots some notes about the color of my gown—a dainty yellow—he raises his head and smiles.

"You are very beautiful, Lady Richmond, if I may say so," he tells me.

"Of course you may, Master Holbein!" I cry, thrilled to be receiving a compliment from a man whose profession is to seek out beautiful things.

"My only concern is that I will never be able to capture it." He laughs. "You're rather like a rainbow, you know. Sort of translucent, something one can admire and exclaim over but never really"— he squints as though the rainbow in his mind's eye is somewhere just beyond his point of vision—"grasp."

"Thank you, Master Holbein," I tell him, taking the man's chalk-stained hands in my own and offering a gentle squeeze. "Your words touch me in a way I cannot express."

He sinks into a graceful bow and takes leave.

I will never forget him or that last day of my innocence.

Anne tries to distract herself from the king's waning affections by holding court in her usual festive manner. Like her unfortunate predecessor, however, she watches as mealymouthed little Jane Seymour collects a group of courtiers in her own vulgar fashion. Jane's mind is not possessed of the keen wit that Anne has, and her strategy, guided by her brother Edward no doubt, is to be as pious and tranquil as possible. Always she walks with her little head bowed, attending Mass at every opportunity, but making sure to be on King Henry's lap when he calls.

I am fuming. I hate her. I am not fool enough to think she is better than Anne. Anne played the same game; one could (and many do) say that she is getting only what she deserves, but the difference between Jane and Anne is that Anne—temperamental, spoiled, vain Anne—is my cousin, my family. I am sworn to her.

The king's neglect drives Anne to distraction. She throws her tantrums. There is nothing anyone can say or do about it. She sinks into deep melancholies and sobs for hours. She breaks into immoderate laughter that rings out a little too loud and a little too long. Sometimes she just sits on her chaise while Mark Smeaton, her favorite musician, flirts with her while playing his lute and sings soothing odes of adoration for his queen.

She still has her admirers. Francis Weston and Henry Norris are always about, eager to shower her with empty words of praise and adulation. Anne's responses are a little colder toward the men. They are not what she wants—who she wants. It is not wise of them to be so open in their admiration, she subtly cautions.

But no one really listens.

And then one April day Mark Smeaton is arrested.

Madge Shelton is in a frenzy of terror as she relays the details to me. "They tortured him, Mary," she says as tears stream down her cheeks. "They tortured him and made him confess . . ."

"Confess what?" I demand.

She cannot say it. She chokes on a sob.

I take her shoulders gruffly, then release her as an image of my father swims in my mind. *"Confess what?"* I cry.

"He is under suspicion of—of treason. Criminal knowledge of the queen." The words are pulled forth in a whisper. Madge's little face is white. We are in a terror.

"No . . . no . . ." I sink onto the bed, trembling. "No. Poor, dear man. They must have tortured him mightily for him to confess such lies—"

Madge is sobbing. "What will this mean for Her Majesty? What will this mean for Anne?"

I take her in my arms.

Madge is no fool.

The king has made his move. Anne's brief reign is at an end.

Hopefully the temperamental queen will cooperate better with King Henry than the last one.

Anne is summoned before the Council led by William Fitzwilliam, the royal treasurer, and my father. My father. He led the examination against my cousin, his niece. I repeat these facts to myself over and over. I wonder what he is asking her. How does he look when he speaks to her? Does he appear reluctant to execute this dubious task? Is there any gleam of sympathy to be found in those black eyes?

I soon find out.

When Anne leaves the room she eyes me. "Your father has used me. All my life I've done nothing but his bidding, and this is what it all comes to."

I cannot respond. What can I say to the truth?

We accompany her to her chambers, a court of frightened ladies, all pretending life is normal. We are always pretending. We do not talk about her examination proceedings, nor do we talk about Mark Smeaton. We embroider. We erupt into nervous giggles about nothing. We ramble about any nonsensical thing to strike our fancy, anything to distract us from these dark days.

My fingertips are bleeding from the needle pricks. It is foolhardy to try to embroider—it sits on my lap, abandoned, and I stare at nothing, trying to will myself somewhere else, anywhere but here.

And then Norfolk arrives.

His face is taut. "Come along, Your Majesty," he says, proffering his arm.

Anne answers him with a questioning arch of her exquisite black brow. "Where are you taking me, Uncle Thomas?" Her voice sounds very young.

He draws in a breath. I cannot tell if he feels sorry or not. I pray the hesitation means it is so. "The Tower," he says. "You are under arrest for high treason."

I am sobbing. I retch from sobbing. Madge is holding me, rocking gently back and forth.

"How could he?" I cry over and over. "How could he?"

She shakes her head. We are all in awe. Nothing makes sense any more.

"What about Princess Elizabeth?" I ask. "What's going to happen to the little princess?"

"Rest, Mary," Madge coos. "There's nothing you can do about anything. Rest and try not to upset yourself so much. You make yourself ill. Please. We can do nothing but ride the tide of events."

"No . . ." I sob. This answer is not good enough for me. There must be something. Surely someone will come forward to speak for Anne, someone strong and credible.

But her most credible witness is her uncle, the premier duke in the land, Thomas Howard.

And he has made it clear where he stands.

He will not see me. No doubt he knows what I will say and he does not wish to expel any needed energy in beating me, so decides the best course is avoidance. Perhaps it is better this way.

The next few days are spent in a stupor. In three days five more men are arrested for having criminal knowledge of Her Majesty. They are Sir Francis Weston; Sir William Brereton; Sir Richard Page; my brother's rival, the poet Sir Thomas Wyatt; and, worst of all—oh, the very worst of all—my dear, handsome cousin George Boleyn.

George has been accused of adultery with the queen, his own sister. His wife, the evil Jane Boleyn, is all too happy to accuse him, also claiming that Anne confided to her once in French that the king had "neither potency nor force" in the bedchamber.

My cousin, among all those other dear and pretty men, now suffers in the cold, damp cells of the Tower.

All of them are innocent. The knights, the poets, my dear George. And Anne. Always Anne.

I cannot contain my hatred for Jane Boleyn. It spills over onto my cheeks in a torrent of hot tears as I regard her now, alone in the maidens' chamber.

"She is your sister-in-law," I tell her. "Your husband's *sister.* How can you say such wickedness? How can you even *think* it?" My shoulders quake with sobs. "You and George have a child together. How can you risk George's life? How can you risk the life of the father of your child?"

Jane shakes her head. "I'm doing what I have to do," she tells me. "I have my reasons."

"What reason can possibly justify this?" I demand, lunging at her. I pin her to the wall by the shoulders, in a show of strength I do not even know I possess. "Explain, Lady Rochford! Explain these despicable actions!"

Her face lacks expression; indeed, she almost appears amused. "I would have thought you Howards coined the term 'despicable.' Let us review the definition of the word so that it is very clear to you. 'Despicable' means neglecting your wife in favor of fondling your own sister—your own sister, and any stable boy or pretty-eyed fop that comes along. 'Despicable' is conceiving a child with your sister and bringing forth a monster in the hopes of passing him off as a prince!"

I break away in horror. "Stop! You must not say it! Don't dare say it!" I recall my father's adjective for her. "You *are* twisted! Sick! You are evil. May you rot in Hell with the devils that consume you!"

Jane only laughs. "Little Mary doesn't betray the Howards. Loyal to the end, are you? Well, this is the end, Mary. This is the end of the Howards. We are going down. Nothing can save us—except perhaps betrayal. Your father is the master of that. Let him serve as an example to you."

She quits the room and I am alone, left with her words playing in my mind over and over, like a relentless melody I despise.

Norris, Weston, Brereton, and poor, tortured Mark Smeaton stand trial and are found guilty of adultery and treason—to the king's pleasure, no doubt. Their sentences are to be carried out at Tyburn, where they will be hung, eviscerated, and quartered.

My stomach is constantly upset. I cannot eat. My hair is falling out. I can pull out strands when I run my fingers through it. I wind it on top of my head in a simple chignon and try to ignore it.

The poet Wyatt and Sir Richard Page do not stand trial and remain in the Tower, to my relief. I am sure Surrey was hoping Wyatt would hang, just to have a rival poet out of the way, even though he grudgingly admires him.

On May 17, Anne and George's trials begin. The Great Hall of the Tower of London, that place I found so magnificent when first arriving here, is full of people ready for blood. Everyone believes Anne is guilty; a witch, a seductress, a creature out of Hell.

They are tried before the lord high steward.

My father.

I cannot move. I watch the unraveling of not just our dreams, but of two fragile lives, used and abused in the worst ways possible. And they are tried before family and friends. My brother—yes, Surrey is here, eager to follow in his father's footsteps—serves as earl marshal. Even Henry Percy, Anne's first love, is present, white faced and having the good grace to appear agonized. And Secretary Cromwell, once so supportive of Anne, is also here, his manner as foxy as usual.

Only one does not attend. His Majesty.

But he has better things to do: courting Jane Seymour, who has moved into the palace—indeed, into Cromwell's old apartments, which adjoin the king's rooms by secret passageway. Even now rumors are rampant that her wedding dress is being made.

Anne dismisses her charges with a cool reserve that can only come from God, for we all know this is not her nature. Each charge is listed: incest with her brother, adultery, witchcraft, plots to marry Henry Norris after the king's demise, the poisoning of Catherine of Aragon, and the attempted poisoning of Lady Mary. Through it all, her beautiful white face is an impervious mask. Her answers are brief and eloquent. There is no hysteria in her tone, no dramatic appeals for a justice she deserves. She only tells the truth: that she is not guilty, not to even one charge.

My father leads the questioning. He is uncomfortable in his role, at least. He keeps working his jaw and clearing his throat, clenching and unclenching his fists.

I am sweating profusely as I watch. I know my chemise is soaked and I probably reek, but fortunately everyone else is in a similar state. The hall is rank with humanity.

After the questioning, Anne rises. Each noble of the Council gives his verdict.

A single tear slides down Norfolk's cheek as he utters the word, "Guilty." Two sets of black eyes hold each other as he continues.

"You are to be burned here within the Tower of London, on the Green; or beheaded, at the king's pleasure."

The crowd erupts into a clamor of speculation over the unusual sentence. Never is a woman sentenced to beheading.

My brother silences the crowd with an elegant hand.

Anne is calm. She blinks several times as she addresses the crowd. "I am not afraid to die. If I am guilty as judged, then I will die as the king bids. I only regret that I have caused the death of these innocent men. I have not always borne the king the humility I owed him, but God is my witness if I have done him any other wrong."

And that is it. She is taken away.

I weep brokenly.

George's approach to his trial is almost tinged with humor. He mocks the fact that he is tried at all, and is quite crafty with legalities. He is so bold that when my father hands him a paper with an accusation too scandalous to read aloud, he does so anyway; it was the stomach turning testimony of his own wife, Jane. The hall is in an ecstasy of shock in the way spectators desire to be shocked. It is a compulsion, a strange human need, I find, to seek out the grotesque and unusual, hence the freak-show venue at country fairs.

People like to see suffering.

And so they shall.

His sentence is predictable; hanging, spared the evisceration and quartering, as he is noble.

I can only imagine what it is like to be George. No, that isn't true. I can't imagine. I cannot begin to imagine what it is like to learn I will die, betrayed by my own uncle, and not even afforded the comfort of my spouse's loving prayers.

It is a sorry state we are in.

George, my sweet cousin George, is dead.

I watch him and the other four brave souls swing from the gallows on Tower Green, the same place so many festivities have been held in years past. I will never view this as any place but one of needless slaughter.

I will never see my father-in-law the king as anything but a brutal sadist.

I am numb. I cannot even cry.

George is dead. One moment here, the next gone. My heart is wrought with agony. I am fortunate to be far enough from his widow so as not to strangle her myself, nor do I stand by Norfolk.

I stand with Surrey. We hold hands and watch the handsome courtiers die.

They say Anne lost her mind in the Tower, alternating between tears and laughter, making strange comments and the like. But this is nothing I do not expect; how can one keep one's wits in her circumstances?

She puts to rest rumors of a shattered mind on her execution day, appearing a font of calm.

A French swordsman is ordered to carry out Anne's execution. Perhaps it serves to mock her for her love of the French court and its fashions; perhaps the king is merciful, taking into consideration the swanlike throat and the accuracy needed to smite it from the body he once craved. I do not know.

It is a private execution, for the pleasure of the court. The king is not here, of course. I do not think he is very good at farewells. He did not say good-bye to Catherine or Lady Mary. He does not see the little Princess Elizabeth, God protect her.

No, there are no farewells or reprieves, even after the glimmer of hope that shone briefly when his marriage to Anne was invalidated days before. We had thought he would divorce her in the manner he had Catherine. It is not so. The end he seeks for Anne is more final.

Once the king wants you out, you're out.

In all the years I have seen Anne, I find it strange that she appears most beautiful this dark day. She wears a deep gray damask gown trimmed with fur over a scarlet kirtle, a mantle of ermine, her black hair bound beneath her French hood.

I am glad she wears the hood; she has remained true to herself.

Today I am again beside my brother Surrey. I am grateful Norfolk is not near me, but I spy him regarding his niece with tears in his eyes. I am startled at the show of emotion and wonder if the tears are for the fall of the Howards, or the fall of this wronged lady.

My husband is here, too, but we are not able to stand together for the thickness of the crowd. He is white-faced and trembling as he watches the mother of his sister meet her fate.

She stands before the courtiers, with the ladies who attended her in the Tower. Her spine is straight, her little shoulders square as she regards the assemblage. She is Norfolk's image of perfect posture.

"Good Christian people," she begins in a clear, calm voice. "I am come here to die, for according to the law and by the law I am judged to die, and therefore I will speak nothing against it. I am come here to accuse no man nor to speak anything of that whereof I am accused and condemned to die, but I pray God save the king and send him long to reign over you, for a gentler nor a more merciful prince was there never, and to me he was ever a good, a gentle, and sovereign lord. And if any person will meddle of my cause, I require them to judge the best. And thus I take my leave of the world and of you all, and I heartily desire you all to pray for me. Oh, Lord, have mercy on me. To God I commend my soul."

The executioner's eyes sparkle with tears. Anne kneels but keeps her spine straight, her head held high. In French executions there are no blocks, so she remains thus, a perfect embodiment of dignity. Her hood is removed and replaced with a blindfold.

"Where is my sword?" the executioner asks then.

Anne turns her head, distracted, and it is then that I realize the swordsman's strategy.

He did not want her to know when it was coming.

In one clean cut her head is severed from its beautiful body and she is gone. The executioner is required to hold it up before the crowd. Her lips almost appear as though they are moving.

I bury my head in Surrey's shoulder. "No!" I murmur against his chest.

He rubs my arm. "Say nothing," he orders.

I obey.

Anne's body is placed in an arrow chest, as a coffin is not provided. She is buried in an unmarked grave in the Chapel of St. Peter ad Vincula. She was twenty-nine years old.

She is gone. The vivacious, spirited, and delightfully frustrating woman is gone.

I tell myself over and over I will not see her again.

I try to believe it.

"Good-bye, Your Majesty," I whisper as the crowd disassembles. "God keep you."

❧ 14 ❧

My Harry

Harry and I are allowed to meet in the gardens the next day when Henry VIII announces his betrothal to stupid Jane Seymour. I do not voice my thoughts to Harry; he is the king's son after all, and it isn't prudent for a Howard to be too vocal at this point. Instead I clutch his hands in mine and swallow tears.

"I wanted to tell you . . ." he says with wide blue eyes, his voice a whisper. "I wanted to tell you I'm sorry for all that's happened." We seat ourselves on a bench and I try not to recall all the days spent in the gardens with Anne and her merry court. Anne and Mary Carey and George . . . how we'd play and sing and gossip. How nothing could touch us then. No! I must not think of it. I'll lose my mind if I do.

Harry shakes his head in despair. "Words seem empty," he says in helplessness. He releases my hands to rub his chest. Tears light his blue eyes; they are bright as the ocean under the afternoon sun.

"Words are empty," I tell him. "Actions give them meaning." I dare rest my head on his upper arm. No one sees us. No one cares now. The court is consumed with the scandal of Anne and George and the others; they are obsessed with the king's new love affair. We do not matter at all, and that is how I want it. I do not want to matter. It is too high a price to pay to matter to Henry VIII.

"We are almost seventeen, Harry. If I appeal to my father, will you appeal to the king?" I ask. "Will you ask him if we can now be together?"

Harry's face is white with terror. "Yes. I'll ask him soon, but, Mary . . . we may have to wait a bit."

I draw in a breath of panic. I do not want to be here. I do not want to serve that wench Jane. I do not want to be near Norfolk. I want a home and babies. I want Harry. I want not to be afraid all the time, afraid of death, afraid of the king, afraid of my father, and what seems to be my worst fear of all: transience.

Harry brings a finger to my lips. "Just a bit, Mary. Till more distance is put between us and this . . . event. After he has settled himself with Lady Jane."

I swallow my disappointment.

Harry and I say nothing more to each other. We sit side by side, trying to digest the tragedy, neither knowing how to bring comfort to the other.

The king and Jane Seymour are wed May 30, eleven days after the slaughter of my lady. She is proclaimed queen of England on June 4 and Parliament passes a new Act of Succession. Now only children of Queen Jane are to be acknowledged as lawful heirs to Henry VIII. My little princess, dearest Elizabeth, is as much a bastard in the king's eyes as her half sister, Mary. The only justice that is served is that the king meets with the willful Lady Mary at last, at Queen Jane's urging; perhaps some of their differences can be resolved now, despite the fact that Mary is a staunch Catholic and completely resolved not to acknowledge any of the king's reforms.

I bend my knee to the new queen. I have no choice. Norfolk, his mood sullen, does the same and acknowledges his rival family's rise to power with a grudging respect. He thrives off challenge. Even now I am certain he is devising ways to elevate himself in the king's favor once more. He will not be long thrown down.

He does not summon me to his apartments and I do not seek him out. I have not seen him since Anne's execution. I have not seen him alone since before her trial.

It is just as well.

I do get to see Harry more. He comes to court to pay his respects to the queen. I suppose I don't hate her so much. If she is a tool of her brother Edward Seymour, she is no different than our Anne was to Norfolk. She is encouraged to be as opposite in trait and demeanor to her predecessor as possible; indeed, she quite resembles Catherine of Aragon with her piety and devotion.

She is not what one could describe as fun, and our court is not nearly as merry, but the king still keeps his lively retinue of musicians, and Will Somers is still commanded to be at his comedic best, which he is. But I see his sober face when he thinks no one is paying note, the sadness in his eyes, the downward turn of his lips. He has known the king a long while—he could even be called his friend, after a fashion—and the events of the past nine years have taken a toll on the witty man.

Cedric Dane has been retained as well and performs at his best when called. When I am afforded a moment with him at one of the entertainments, his face is drawn with solemnity.

"You are fortunate to be married to Richmond," he tells me. "It is not a good time to be a Howard."

"I'm a Howard regardless," I respond, tears clutching my throat. "Oh, Master Dane, these days we have known . . ."

Cedric scans the room. "Best not to say anything here. Best not to say anything anywhere."

"Sometimes I feel if I don't say something I'll die," I tell him with sustained fervency.

"Turn it over to prayer, Lady Richmond," he says. "And your music. Sing. Write. 'Tis the best way to handle grief."

"Yes," I say in feeble tones. I purse my lips, regarding the king and queen from across the room. She appears completely enamored. Her dull face is turned up to his jocular one; she hangs on his every word. Yet what are her consequences if she does not? My breathing becomes shallow. My face is tingling.

"Lady Richmond?" Cedric's tone is solicitous. His violet eyes are tinged with concern.

"Please . . ." I tug at the ruff about my neck. It is strangling me like a hangman's noose. "I must excuse myself."

I cannot be here anymore.

* * *

The secret betrothal of Margaret Douglas and Uncle Thomas has been discovered. For two reasons the beautiful Margaret is sent to the Tower, the first being that those of royal blood must seek the king's permission to marry, the second being her choice of husbands. Lord Thomas is a Howard, and the king is feeling none too merciful toward anyone associating with a Howard these days. My poor uncle is accused of placing himself too close to the throne and is sentenced to death.

The king is negligent in the signing of the warrant, however, making Uncle Thomas a permanent resident of the Tower. I sob in despair and, in desperation, seek out my father.

Norfolk is quick to chastise me. "If you were involved in any way, make no mistake, you will be thrown in the Tower alongside my idiot brother and will meet the same end. And if you think I will come to your rescue, you are wrong."

"I would expect nothing less from you," I seethe. "Why wouldn't you betray a duchess? You did not hesitate to betray a queen—a queen who was your own niece!"

"You do not realize why?" Norfolk grips my shoulders. "Everything I do is for this family. Everything. But in the end it comes down to this: us or them. In the choice between Anne and myself, who did you think I would choose?" He shakes his head, frustrated at what I'm sure he believes is my naïveté. "If you think I revel in it you are mistaken. I did what had to be done and no less. I will preserve our name. But I will preserve myself first."

The words are so cold, so self-serving that I begin to tremble in terror. I sob harder, knowing it is all futile. Knowing there is nothing I can do. If I could not save my cousin, queen of this realm, how can I save my uncle, a virtual nobody?

"But they love each other," I say. "Why shouldn't they be together? Who are they hurting?"

"Love, always love with you." Norfolk waves an impatient hand. "Don't you see that isn't what this is about? He was placing himself too close to the throne. He was being an upstart."

"Aren't we the same thing?" I ask, no sarcasm implied. I am genuinely puzzled at what creates the distinction between us and Lord Thomas Howard.

I earn a slap for my confusion. Fortunately it is not the bad side of my head and I can recover my senses enough to back away from him.

"If you had a part in this, you keep it to yourself. I don't even want to know, you hear me?" He shakes his head in impatience. "Dismissed."

"Yes, my lord," I whimper as I exit, holding a hand to my swelling cheek.

My uncle is to be added to the mad king's increasing death toll. My uncle is to die, and my father expresses no grief.

No one speaks of Margaret and my uncle. They are in the Tower and that is that. The ladies occupy themselves with a quieter court life. King Henry pretends to be normal. And Harry has taken ill.

He is at St. James's Palace. I am told it is not serious and I am not to worry, but I see the lines of anxiety crinkle my father's forehead as he fetches me one sunny July afternoon.

"You are to go to Lord Richmond," he tells me. "You will be accompanied and guarded. Discuss your visit with no one."

Alarmed, I take Norfolk's arm. "Is my lord well?"

He says nothing.

At St. James's Palace I find out for myself.

Harry, my sweet, innocent Harry, is on his deathbed. His lips are blue, his face is white, and he is wracked by an agonizing cough that dots the white handkerchief he covers his mouth with in bright flecks of blood.

The guards remain at a discreet distance as I sit beside him, clutching his hand. "Oh, my dearest, why? Why didn't anyone tell me?"

"It was so sudden," he says in a thin voice, reaching up to stroke my cheek. "I didn't want to worry you. And the king . . ." He draws in a rattling breath. "He doesn't want anyone to know. I can't imagine anyone being alarmed at my passing."

There are those who suggest Harry is capable of stirring up a rebellion so that he might seize power; those who do not know my gentle husband, and enjoy spreading vicious lies. Yes, anyone who does not want the princesses to come to power would have good reason to be alarmed should anything happen to Harry.

Now is not the time to remind him of this, however. It no longer matters.

"Mary . . ." Harry reaches up, cupping my cheek. "Promise me you will not marry again."

"I'm married to you," I tell him. "There is no reason for me—"

He is seized by a fit of coughing. When he recovers himself he places a hushing finger to my lips. "Promise!" His voice is a husky whisper. "It will be difficult for a while, I know. But as the Dowager Duchess of Richmond you will be afforded the kind of life ordinary widows are not; a freedom other women cannot enjoy. I do not pretend to think that you won't fall in love, but you must not marry for it. Love, Mary, but do not wed. Neither someone of your father's choosing nor someone you have found for love, for regardless, Norfolk will see to it that your life is made a terror."

I am certain of that. But not to marry again, not to have babies . . .

"Do you realize what you are asking of me?" I breathe.

He offers an earnest nod. "Fight for your inheritance, Mary. You can have happiness, more than you know, when the fight is won."

"But I never win," I whisper brokenly, tears sliding cool trails down my cheeks.

"You will not think that way, dearest," says Harry. "You will not. You will find happiness in the smallest things: summer, picnics, flowers, rainbows—"

"Rainbows . . ."

He nods. From his wistful expression I know he is recalling our rainbow on the beach of Calais. "Yes, rainbows. And then, upon taking such pleasure in those small things, you will appreciate life's great wonders all the more."

"But what of babies, Harry?" I ask. "What of them?"

He lowers his eyes. "Have them, if it pleases you. In secret. Keep them from this life. There are ways. Mary, there is always a way to get what you want. One thing I can credit the Howards with is getting what they want. In this, you must think like a Howard."

It is futile to think of now, anyway, I surmise. Instead I am caught in the immediate. I force a smile. "Oh, Harry, you aren't leaving me. This is all silly talk." I stroke his pasty cheek. "You will come through fine. I . . . I must tell you something, my love. Father, good Lord Norfolk, has given his permission for us to be together at last. As soon as you are well we shall set up house wherever His Majesty deems fit, and we'll be so happy—"

"Promise, Mary," Harry insists, squeezing my hand.

Tears stream down my face. "I promise, my good lord."

Harry reaches up, stroking my hair. His thin hand finds the butterfly comb securing my chignon in place. He removes it, regarding the mother-of-pearl wings and emerald antennae with tears in his eyes. "You have worn it all this time?"

"Since the day you sent it to me, the day after our wedding," I tell him in truth.

He closes his eyes, smiling, his hand clenching over the little comb. "I shall take it with me," he tells me. "And place it in your hair once more when we meet again."

I swallow a sob.

A guard steps forward. "His lordship is tired. He must rest."

I rise and am escorted home.

I am not permitted to see Harry again.

It is Norfolk who tells me a week later that he is gone.

I sit in front of him, stunned. "I was not permitted to be there when he drew his last breath . . . my own husband . . ." I sink my head into my hands and sob.

"Really, Mary, you must cease in this pretense that he was your husband. It isn't as though you shared any sort of real history. You didn't live together. No children tie you," Norfolk says in cool tones.

"No, you saw to that." I raise my head. I am unable to summon any more tears. I stare at him. "But you will never tell me we were not wed. I loved Harry well for what I was allowed."

Norfolk folds his arms across his chest and grunts.

"The funeral," I begin. "Where will it be held? Where will my lord be interred?"

"It has been taken care of," Norfolk tells me.

"The arrangements or the funeral?" I cry.

"He's been interred, Mary," Norfolk says. "The king did not wish any attention to be drawn to his death." He bows his head. "A damnable job they did of it. He was to be encased in lead, but the damned servants loaded his coffin under a pile of straw and hauled him off to Thetford Priory. They'll be made to suffer for their negligence," he adds darkly.

I am trying to digest this. He has told me my husband is dead. He has told me my husband, a duke, son of a king, is buried without acknowledgment or farewell. He has described his last journey as one would the misadventures of a merchant and his sack of wares. He has told me no one attended him at his funeral, save two inept servants.

I cannot breathe. My throat is raw. Somewhere a sound is ringing in my ears. It is a moment before I realize the sound is my own screams. Norfolk takes my upper arms. He is shaking me, his black eyes wide.

"Stop!" he orders. "Stop it, do you hear!"

"Harry . . ." I sob. "I want Harry . . ." I begin to writhe against his clutches. "Take me to Harry!"

"Stop, fool. Calm yourself. Do you want the guards to hear you? Cease!" Norfolk commands, shaking me more, as though this will serve to quiet me.

I cannot stop. I am wailing. The tears I have tried to stay, for Anne and all the others that suffered under the king, are unleashed. My temple is throbbing in pain as my sorrows pour forth.

"He is evil," I sob. "He is mad! His son is dead and he does not mourn him! His daughters he turns away . . . his wives he slaughters in one way or another!" I begin to pummel Norfolk's chest with my fists. "And you! You help him! You spirit his dead son away! You help him exile his first wife, you help him murder his second . . . the Devil's right hand you are!"

Norfolk drops his arms, staring at me, his face void of expression.

I cannot slow my tears or modulate my breathing. "Oh, beat me—may you beat me to death and end my misery!" I begin to tear at my dress. "Here! I shall help you!" I bare my back and turn.

"Here!" I throw myself onto the floor, spreading my arms. I pound the floor with my fists. "Here!"

For a moment I can think of nothing to add to this tirade. My head is throbbing. I feel as though I will retch. I await his belt. It does not come. He kneels beside me, laying a hand on my back. He regards me a long moment, perhaps entertaining a punishment best suited for this show of temper. And then draws me into his arms.

Such is my state of bewildered shock I am no longer able to cry. I emit little whimpers, mewing like a sick kitten.

Norfolk begins to rock back and forth. He smoothes my hair and kisses my forehead. "We will take you home to Kenninghall," he says in the softest tones I've ever heard him use. "We will take you to Kenninghall and there you shall recover." He is still rocking me. "It is best," he says as though to himself. "You have fallen under suspicion for your involvement with Lady Margaret and Lord Thomas as it is. You will go home till it passes."

I do not care about this new piece of information, nor that his motives for sending me home have more to do with protecting himself by disassociating with me than his desire to see me recovered from my grief. I only care that he is sending me home.

"Away from this place?" I ask, my voice small. "You will take me away?"

He nods. "Yes, Mary. I will take you away."

I fall against his chest once more. I bury my face in his doublet and sob tears of relief.

Let Norfolk have King Henry VIII. I am through with him and his court.

❧ 15 ❧

The Fight

I start the journey home in a litter, so weary am I from the exertions of grief, but find creeping upon me the sensation of being trapped, so request a horse that I might ride in the open air. I chase away thoughts of Harry and me riding in Calais. I take in the warm summer air, the green fields, the flowers in bloom—all those little things Harry told me to derive my joy from. Norfolk rides beside me for a while in silence. He is unsure of me, I think. Perhaps he believes I've gone a little mad. Perhaps he is right.

At last I draw in a breath and ask in low tones, "How did you sort out the loss of your first family—Anne Plantagenet and—" I swallow a painful lump. "And all those poor children?"

He is silent a long while. "I went on. I am a Howard. That is what Howards do." He meets my eyes. "And that is what you will do. You shall see."

And so we go to Kenninghall, where I shall endeavor to do just that.

I am alone here. Both Mother and Bess are at other manors now; Mother as a prisoner of sorts, Bess as lady of the house. I am not to seek them out, Norfolk instructs before taking leave the day after our arrival. I am to stay here, he says, and manage my affairs while he tries to repair relations with the king.

And so I remain. I lie abed most of the time in the beginning. I think about Harry and Anne. The servants try to coax me into eating, but I cannot ingest anything but broth and pottage. My stomach aches. I hear them talk about me, the servants. They believe I will be dead within the year; they take bets in the kitchens.

I do not pay them any heed. Little by little my strength returns. I begin to eat a bit more.

I keep company with one of the servants' daughters, a young girl named Lily Rose. She is sweet, easy to talk to, and very interested in the New Learning. She is fearful, however, because as I was once an esteemed member of King Henry's court I might condemn her for studying the Scriptures and turn her over as a heretic for her forward thinking.

I assure her that I am so low that the king can't even condescend to grant me my rightful inheritance. The last thing I have is influence over His Majesty. I am so interested in the topic myself that it would be hypocritical to condemn her as a heretic. If she is, then, I think with a shudder, so am I.

Lily and I take to reading the Bible together. It is amazing reading it in my own language. I love to ponder Psalms and Proverbs without the bother of translating from the Latin in my head. I read the traditional stories that brought me joy as a child, stories about Noah's Ark and Jonah and the big fish. I delve into the teachings of Jesus and the meanings behind the parables. Our discussions are animated and filled with good-natured debates. We talk about the overindulgent priests of the Catholic faith, how things should be simplified, how their coffers should be emptied. As we speak of these things I recall my Anne, sitting in her luxurious apartments, sparking my interest in the topic for the first time. I blink back tears of anguish.

Despite this, the discussions, along with Lily's gentle company, prove to be my salvation. But I remember my mother's warning. I keep my faith to myself and await better times.

Perhaps I should have realized that Norfolk was not going to support me, that I am expected to run this household, pay my staff—and buy food and clothing along with the rest of life's necessities—by myself. Yet I did not. My debts accumulate. I have no concept of how to handle finances. I never had to before. I am fraught with anxiety as I try to learn. At night I lie awake and think of ways to pay the servants. I cannot dismiss them and live in a large manor by myself. And no one else is willing to take me in. Surrey is busy with his wife and children. There is no room for me in his life.

I write to Cromwell, appealing for my inheritance. But he is a busy man with much to think about. The widow of Henry Fitzroy is not a priority. I am told the king is reconsidering the validity of my marriage on the grounds that it was not consummated. My gut churns as I recall his "invalid" marriages to Catherine of Aragon and my Anne.

I write to my father. In his brief notes he tells me he is doing all he can, that I will just have to wait. But he offers no personal assistance.

And then in October begins the Pilgrimage of Grace, a revolt that started in Lincolnshire to protest the king's dissolution of the monasteries as well as his other religious reforms—the only innovations the king has made that I actually agree with, save for the inevitable bloodshed that accompanies King Henry's every move.

It becomes a widespread rebellion in the North and I fear for all those involved, for no one deserves to suffer. Norfolk is given charge of the king's forces but does not utilize them at first, hoping to coax the rebels into peace with promises of pardons if they stop the violence. I believe he sympathizes with them to a degree, being that he is a Catholic himself and does not want to resort to carnage. The rebels begin to disperse and the situation seems quite encouraging.

But in January more rebellions break out. My father does not waste any more time negotiating with anyone this time. He supervises executions in five counties, brutal murders that send me into a panic of nightmares.

All I can see is Anne's beautiful head being severed from her body, the crimson blood pouring forth from the stump of a neck. To me, all the rebels are Anne, innocent Anne. I envisage Norfolk

among them, rows and rows of Annes, watching them die and calling it a job well done.

He is rewarded richly for his work. Even his rival Cromwell
helps him acquire some of the former monastic properties. He has
redeemed himself and retained favor.

I have not.

I continue my appeals, drafting letters that all come to nothing.
No one will see me. No one will hear me. I begin to sell one jewel,
then another, then another to cover the costs that living incurs.

My brother pays a call with his wife, Frances de Vere, and I am
thrilled with the company. I give a feast in their honor and, though
it is modest, Surrey is polite enough to comment on the tenderness of the stuffed capons and creaminess of the cheese.

Surrey was alongside Norfolk in fighting against the Pilgrimage
of Grace rebels, and I am eager to hear his perspective on the
issue.

"We did what had to be done," he says of the executions. His
eyes are sad, however. He shakes his head. "No one wanted it. But
it had to stop. We have to have uniformity in religion, Mary. We
have to support the king."

"Yes," I agree with reluctance, thinking of His Majesty's unwill-
ingness to part with a few pounds to support his son's widow. "He
is making progress but it is slow. He seems torn between making
England reformist or adopting this strange hybrid of Catholicism." At Surrey's alarmed expression I add, "I am not saying we
have to be a Protestant country. But how nice it would be for Mass
to be conducted in our native tongue!" My cheeks flush in excitement.

"Mary." His expression is grave, a younger portrait of Norfolk.
"You must curb this reformist bent. You cannot afford to be viewed
as anything but compliant. Your position is precarious." He pauses.
"You . . . heard about Uncle Thomas?"

I shake my head, my heart pounding painfully against my ribs.
"Tell me."

Surrey swallows. "He is dead, Mary. Wasted away in the
Tower."

I bow my head. Uncle Thomas dead—and all for love. Poor Lady Margaret! How must she be coping with his loss? Tears pave slick trails down my cheeks. "Well," I whisper, my voice husky, "God bless him, then."

We are silent a moment. Poor Frances sits with her head bowed, picking at her food. I decide to engage her in a lighter conversation.

"And how is the baby?" I ask.

She raises her head. She is beautiful, with her delicate features, full lips, and wide brown eyes. "Our little Thomas is a delight. He is just now beginning to smile." Her face softens with the pride of motherhood, and I swallow the painful lump that rises in my throat as I recall my promise to Harry. How could he have encouraged me to have children out of wedlock? Oh, *why* did I promise him I wouldn't marry again? But he did say it would be hard for a while; he was far too honest to suggest my path would be an easy one. Though I have a long fight ahead of me, I must not lose heart. Perhaps he was right; perhaps I can know more happiness in the single estate.

I try to swallow my envy as Frances tells me about the baby and Surrey chimes in with, "Oh, it transforms everything, being a parent. Your whole perspective is altered. I know my writing has changed as a result; I feel a new depth . . ." His eyes are sparkling. I wonder if he is trying to hurt me, then dismiss the thought. Surrey is not heartless.

"Do you have any of your poetry with you?" I interpose. Suddenly I can't bear to discuss babies a moment more. I curse myself for my jealousy, but no amount of chastisement seems to dampen it.

"Here is a recent one," says Surrey, leaning back in his chair and laying his head back as he begins the recitation.

> *"The soote season, that bud and bloom forth brings,*
> *With green hath clad the hill, and eke the vale.*
> *The nightingale with feathers new she sings;*
> *The turtle to her make hath told her tale.*
> *Summer is come, for every spray now springs,*
> *The hart hath hung his old head on the pale;*

The buck in brake his winter coat he slings;
The fishes flete with new repaired scale;
The adder all her slough away she slings;
The swift swallow pursueth the flies smale;
The busy bee her honey now she mings;
Winter is worn that was the flowers bale.
And thus I see among these pleasant things
Each care decays, and yet my sorrow springs!"

I clap my hands at its completion. Frances offers her husband a proud smile.

"What do you call it?" I ask him.

" 'Description of Spring, Wherein Every Thing Renews, Save Only the Lover.' " He sits up in the chair, smiling. "And what of your work, Mary? Still attempting poetry yourself?" His eyes sparkle in mockery.

I hesitate, then laugh. "Oh, yes," I tell him, deciding not to take offense. "It is a great way to pass the time."

He nods but says nothing.

I cry when they leave.

"You mustn't worry, dear," assures Frances as she embraces me. "We'll be back time and again; this is our home, too. And soon you will be awarded that inheritance of yours and things will be set right. Be patient, love."

But they never once offer to help me.

Within a few months I learn that my brother struck a man at Hampton Court who accused him of being sympathetic to the insurgents of the Pilgrimage of Grace, and was arrested. My father's rival Cromwell, however, sees to it that he does not have to appear before the Privy Council and Surrey is sent to cool his heels at Windsor.

I curse Surrey's hot head and inability to rein in his impulses, and pray he will not end up in our late cousin's place.

I wonder if Norfolk will remember Cromwell's kindness to our family and soften toward him somewhat.

From my safe vantage at Kenninghall I am afforded a neutral view of the court and am just as glad not to be in the thick of things. I still write to Cromwell, hoping that since he was successful with my brother's case he will have some influence over mine.

But I hear nothing.

I continue my routine; my secret reformist discussions with Lily; long horseback rides through the countryside, where I visit the tenants, bringing them food and clothes sewn by my own hands, and collecting herbs and flowers from my little garden. They are peaceful days if they are poor ones.

I learn that the new queen is expecting. My heart lurches in anticipation. Will this at last be the prince His Majesty craves, or will it be another cursed princess he will soon render a bastard? I put aside my dislike for Queen Jane and pray for her with an urgency I haven't felt since Anne's last days. I fear for her. If she does not produce an heir her life is at risk, I have no doubt.

That spring I receive a note from Norfolk saying he will pay a visit. As angry as I have been at him, I am thrilled at the news. I order the slaughter of an ox and new lambs for the occasion and supervise the efforts in the kitchens to make certain everything is perfect for his visit. I sell more jewels to purchase the finest cheeses and wines. The manor is sweetened with new rushes and his rooms are cleaned top to bottom.

At the hour he is to arrive I dress in my prettiest mourning gown, allowing my hair to cascade down my back in the fashion of a maiden, as I do not need to wear it up any longer. It falls about my shoulders in a honeyed cloud.

The hours pass. He does not come. I grow worried. Where is he? Has he met with harm? Have his enemies cut him down at last? I begin to tremble as I torture myself with one tragic scenario after another.

I stroll down the drive. I stroll back. I wander the halls of the manor, drumming my chin in thought as the servants shake their heads and sigh.

At last a messenger arrives to tell me that Norfolk will not be coming. He has changed his mind. When I ask why, he shrugs.

"Just changed his mind, my lady," he says. "No real reason. Just didn't feel like making the trip, I expect."

My cheeks burn in rage. Tears fill my eyes but I blink them back. I draw in a breath as I think of the cost of this feast. "It's all right," I tell the messenger. "You will stay and be my guest. I have set a great feast."

I invite some of the tenants into the manor and tell all of the servants that they must indulge themselves tonight. They are all my guests of honor and this feast is a gesture of thanks for all of their hard work.

They are appreciative and the evening is lively, ending in singing and storytelling. Some of the tenants are gifted musicians and lead spirited country dances in which I participate, despite the fact that I should be a grave widow.

"A toast, then," says one of the servants, raising his goblet. "To Lady Richmond—a more generous duchess cannot be found!"

"God keep Her Grace!" the room choruses as goblets clink together.

Tears of delight warm my eyes. I suppose it is a success of sorts.

It is a prince! A prince at last! Little Edward is born 12 October and Norfolk has the honor of being named godfather when he is christened at Hampton Court on the fifteenth. I breathe a sigh of relief. Queen Jane is in the clear.

And then the gravest of tragedies. The bells toll a deep mourning song, a song I know all too well.

The queen I once loathed for taking my Anne's place dies of childbed fever on 24 October, twelve days after the birth of her son. She was twenty-eight years old. I cringe when I learn that wretched Jane Boleyn was at her bedside during her final hour while the king was not.

I lie abed and cry for her. She will not see her son grow up to become king. She will not watch him smile and crawl and play. She will never marvel at his little dimpled hands and feet.

Fate is not kind to the wives of Henry VIII.

* * *

In the spring of 1538 Norfolk arrives at Kenninghall, his long face bearing a bright smile that appears as awkward on him as armor on a goose.

I greet him with a smile in turn. He is my family, after all, and I cannot be uncharitable toward him. He may have news of my suit.

We sit to a very modest supper, where he leans forward and places a hand on my wrist. His black eyes are sparkling with intensity.

"I have found a husband for you," he says.

My heart begins to race. A husband? I cannot sort through these feelings. Am I excited at the prospect? Can I so quickly abandon my promise to Harry in the hopes of seizing a life of my own? My breathing is shallow.

"Wh—who?" I whisper.

"Thomas Seymour, the brother of the late queen, uncle of the future king," Norfolk answers in satisfied tones. "King Henry is enthused about the arrangement and gave his permission for you to be wed. Seymour seems pleased as well."

My pounding heart seems to have lodged itself in the base of my throat. Thomas Seymour. Yes, Father mentioned him before, but in my grief for Harry I scoffed at the suggestion. He is handsome enough but known to be quite the rake . . . No! What am I saying? I cannot be so dishonorable as to break my promise to Harry, he not even two years gone.

I shake my head. "I don't know . . ." Tears clutch my throat. "I can't. My lord, I thank you for your attention to this matter but I cannot—"

Norfolk seizes my hands. His grip is excruciatingly tight. "Mary. You must think. This match serves everyone. King Henry, for obvious reasons, is pleased. He will no longer be financially obligated to you, and you will be free of that whole situation. The Seymours and I are pleased. It is a sound alliance." I wince at the word *alliance*, though why I would ever think myself to amount to anything more than that in Norfolk's eyes, I do not know. When he sees this vein is unsuccessful he continues. "You'll be supported in the manner you should be. And you will have your babies, Mary. Isn't that what you've always wanted? Babies? Think of it."

He has me. Babies are what I want more than anything in this world. Oh, to hold a little lamb of my own . . . Tears burn my eyes as I feel my promise to Harry fading away like a rainbow in the sun.

I nod. It is not me nodding. I am powerless in the face of my greatest desire. "Yes. Yes. I will marry Tom Seymour. Let us begin the preparations for my wedding."

Norfolk slaps his hands on the table and emits his almost laugh. "Well done! Let us drink to it!"

So it is done. I am to be remarried. I have broken my promise to Harry.

I do not know what kind of person this makes me.

Arrangements commence for my wedding. My servants are in a thrill of delight. I admit to a little excitement myself as I think about the babies Tom Seymour and I will have.

I begin to plan my dress. I will have the sleeves I want this time. I will have it all this time.

"I'm so happy for you, my lady," says dear little Lily Rose. "Finally you're getting some happiness!"

A smile tugs at the corner of my lips. "I *am* happy, Mistress Lily. This is the right decision. I can feel it."

Then I receive a passionate letter from Surrey. He tells me Tom Seymour is the worst scoundrel of the entire upstart Seymour clan. He is manipulative and cruel. He even raped a girl when he was younger, he reports. I'd be a fool to marry him, a fool to give up my title. Norfolk may think the alliance is sound, but in his dotage forgets that the Seymours are the greatest enemies of the Howards. Surrey believes sidling up to them is a risk I should not take. What's more, do I really want a man such as Tom Seymour siring my children? he asks.

I read the letter again and again. Tears course icy trails down my cheeks. Could it be true that he is a rapist? Oh, God . . .

My heart is pounding. My cheeks are hot. My stomach aches. I try to think. Is Surrey cautioning me because of his devotion to me, or because of his devotion to his own self-interests? Both, most likely. Still, if he didn't care he would not have sent the warning.

He is a rapist. I repeat the vulgar word to myself. *Rapist.* Even if it is a rumor, something has to be behind it. Rumors are fed by grains of truth, after all. And yet I think of my Anne, and the vicious rumors King Henry was all too willing to perpetrate until he ended up believing them himself. Witch, whore . . . none of these things was my Anne. Could it be that Tom Seymour is in a similar situation? This court is fraught with wrongful accusations . . .

And yet I cannot shake the thought. The thought that he *might* be a rapist is enough to chill me to the core. I cannot give myself to such a man. I would never be able to think of anything else when we . . .

Then there is my forgotten promise to Harry. I squeeze my eyes shut as I recall his blood-flecked lips, his blue eyes lit with fevered urgency as he exacted my pledge. Oh, my Harry. How can I have dismissed you so easily?

I heave a deep sigh, then summon a messenger.

"Please go to the Duke of Norfolk," I instruct. "Tell him Lady Richmond has decided against the wedding to Thomas Seymour."

The messenger's eyes are wide.

I shoo him away with an impatient hand. "Yes! You heard me— the wedding is off! Go!"

When he departs I am alone, disillusioned and despairing.

I rest my head in my hands. "Forgive me, Harry," I murmur. "I was weak. . . ."

Norfolk's response is brief.

> *You are a fool. If you insist on living life the hard way,*
> *then by all means continue.*

The words do not affect me as much as a beating would, so I continue living "the hard way." As much as I long for the life of a wife and mother, I know I made the right choice. I could not have sustained living with such a rake as Tom Seymour.

I pass the summer. Her fire yields to the repose of autumn, then to winter's sleepy embrace. Christmas comes and goes. Lent begins. Spring emerges from the mist, dusting the world with dew. Flowers begin to turn their heads up to the sun and in March I learn that at last I am to receive a grant from the king.

I have survived this fight. Almost three years after my husband's passing, I am awarded my inheritance.

❧ 16 ❧

The German Bride

After being rejected by numerous European princesses—including Christina of Milan, who quipped, "Had I but two heads I would risk it, but I have only one"—the king has found a new bride in a sister of the Duke of Cleves. Cromwell urged the match, seeing the alliance with a Protestant duchy as a way to bolster England's reputation as a reformist country. Though I am unsure of her personal religious convictions, I cannot imagine being from Germany and not having a reformist bent. Anticipation stirs my heart at her possible ability to influence King Henry in church reforms.

The Duchy of Cleves is not the worst of allies. They are emerging as a rival to the Netherlands in trade, and may prove quite useful to England. Cleves stood against Charles V of Spain over some duchy called Gelderland as well as both France and the Habsburg Empire, both of whom were disgusted with King Henry's declaration of supremacy over the Church of England. It was a good move, Cromwell said, to be united with the duchy that is allied with Saxony and the league of Lutheran princes; they can prove most helpful should war break out. I see the reason behind the match; indeed it is the most political union the king has ever made. May it end in love.

When Hans Holbein returns to court with portraits of two fair

Germans, Anne and Amelia, the king chooses Anne. She is twenty-four, four years older than I. I admit the name sends a shiver of terror through me and pray she does not meet the same fate as the last wife bearing that name. At the same time I am excited at the prospect of a new queen. I hope she is everything the king wants, that she will prove her worth in childbearing, and that they will stay married forever, leaving England's heartbreaks behind.

Norfolk sends an armed retinue to escort me back to court. It seems the Howards are in favor again. I have been chosen as one of Anne's ladies-in-waiting. Though I thought the last thing I'd ever do was return to King Henry's court, I find I am bursting with anticipation at the thought of serving her. I hope she is clever and cheerful and leads her ladies in spirited discussions about religion and poetry.

I hope hers is a merry court.

It seems that the threat of war with France and Spain has passed, and the king decided against fighting Charles V for Anne of Cleves's brother, which puts to sleep the political urgency of the match. Despite this, the king goes ahead with the wedding and the couple is wed by proxy that November. We now refer to Anne of Cleves as Queen Anne and await her arrival. The weather has been dreadful in Calais, according to reports, and delays her crossing for two weeks. The king is in a fury of impatience.

On New Year's Day we wait in the queen's tent at Hampton Heath, that we might be sheltered from the elements. The court is in a thrill of excitement.

Everyone is there, including musicians to welcome Her Majesty with compositions praising her beauty, and it is among them I see Cedric Dane. He is older, filled out, and as beautiful a man as there can be. A strange warmth flows through me at the sight of him.

When he sees me he makes his way over, bowing and removing his cap. His violet eyes are sparkling. "Quite a day, is it not, Lady Richmond?"

I offer a bright smile, extending my hand. "Still at court, I see, Master Dane."

He kisses the proffered hand, sending a shiver up my arm. "Through it all, it seems." His expression grows somber. "My lady, if I never told you . . . I'm so sorry about Fitzroy."

Tears clutch my throat. I shake my head, forcing a smile. "I press on." I blink several times. "Do tell me how your wife is faring."

"Quite well," he says, a smile of pride touching his lips. "She's given me three bonny lads."

"Three!" I cry. I choke down my envy. "In so brief a time!"

"The first two came as a set," he says with a chuckle.

I laugh. "Twins! How delightful. I'm so happy for you, Master Dane."

"And you? Are you happy, my lady?" he asks, his eyes alight with genuine concern.

I avert my head. I cannot bear to look at him. "It is good to be back at court," I say.

He clears his throat. "Well. I suppose you must rejoin the ladies before you're missed. But I do hope to see you. We shall have to practice together."

I want to say "for what?" but refrain. It would be fun practicing with him for the sheer joy of his company, for whatever joy I can take in it. I offer a smile in parting and return to the queen's tent, his smile seizing my heart with joy and something else . . . that agony—that agony he described to me years ago.

Forcing him from my mind, I concentrate on my present company. There are several ladies-in-waiting. Jane Boleyn is among them and I make sure to ignore her. There are others more cheerful than Lady Jane, some of whom I have been acquainted with since my Anne's time, and I hope to win their friendship. I am relieved to see Margaret Douglas among them. In her wistfully tender expression she communicates that she is my ally. I nod to her, hoping to convey my sympathy; we have suffered much, Margaret and I.

"I hear Queen Anne is very fair, with hair as blond as corn silk," says one of the girls next to me.

I turn to regard her and my breath catches in my throat. Never have I laid eyes upon a more exquisite creature in my life. She is small and soft, her skin creamy and delicate. The sun weaves golden streaks through her lush auburn hair, which falls in waves down her back. Her wide blue eyes dance with youth and eagerness, as though bidding the world to come hither. Her gown clings to each supple curve and I imagine many a lad falling under her spell.

Her full lips curve into a smile. There is something vaguely familiar in it.

"I have just come to court for the first time. My name is Kitty . . . well, Catherine, actually, but everyone who likes me—I don't know if that's really that many people—calls me Kitty," she says, extending her slim hand.

I take it, delighted. "I'm Lady Richmond but you may call me Mary."

"Lady Richmond?" she asks, cocking her head. "Oh! Are you something terribly grand? Are you a countess or something?"

I giggle. Her blatancy is most endearing. "I am the Dowager Duchess of Richmond."

"Dowager? You're so young to be a dowager!" she exclaims. "Richmond . . . Richmond . . . why, I know who you are!" She claps her hands in delight. "Here we act as strangers and we are first cousins! You are Mary Fitzroy, are you not, formerly a Howard?"

"Always a Howard." I laugh. "How are we related?"

She offers an enthusiastic nod. "My daddy was Edmund Howard, but he died—he was quite poor. I was raised at Lambeth by my step-grandmother." She scrunches up her shoulders and giggles. "Such a naughty household that was! I suppose it is good preparation for court!" She takes my hand. "So your daddy is Uncle Thomas then?"

I nod.

"You are so lucky! He came to visit me these past few months at Lambeth and helped secure my place at court," she tells me. "He is so kind! He said I was very pretty and amusing. He bought me some new gowns."

Oh, God. What does this mean? Where does this sweet girl fit into his plans?

"How old are you, Mistress Catherine?"

"Do call me Kitty," she insists with a laugh. She grimaces. " 'Mistress Catherine' sounds like an old spinster!" She beams. "I am going to be fifteen soon. How old are you? You look terribly young, but you must not be if you've already been married and widowed."

Her refreshing candor brings nothing but a smile to my face. "I am just turned twenty."

"So you are six years older than I am? That isn't so bad," she decides. Her voice is musical and filled with vibrancy. "You are young enough to be my friend. We shall have such a merry time at court together, dear cousin!"

I wrap my arm about her shoulders and draw her near. "Indeed we shall!"

"Just get used to Wiener schnitzel!" she adds, which sends us into such a fit of giggles that Jane Boleyn sends me a wicked glance.

At last Queen Anne's golden coach arrives and she is assisted out. Kitty and I lean this way and that, trying to catch a glimpse of her.

"Ugghh, who dresses her?" Kitty asks.

Indeed, German fashions are worlds apart from ours. Her gray gown looks as square as the strange headdress she is wearing. In all she looks like a box.

"Oh, no," I whisper to my cousin. "But her hair is pretty, at least."

I wonder what the king will think of her. His obese frame is draped in his finest ermines and velvets today; jewels bedeck every fat finger. His beady eyes are narrowed at the lady who approaches him. He steps forward, takes her hand, and offers a brief kiss on her cheek.

"D'you think he likes her?" Kitty asks in hushed tones. Then she shrugs. "Not that he should set his standards too high. Look at him. He's so fat he could sink a barge!"

"Kitty!" I admonish, though I agree. "You must not say such things too loud. Such words could fall upon the wrong ears and you will find the king's court can be quite merciless."

"Oh," says Kitty, disappointed to have her observations cut short.

When it is time for her ladies to be introduced, I curtsy before the queen, studying her through my lashes. She is not a small woman to be sure, but she is fair, with sparkling blue eyes and a merry smile.

"You?" she asks, her accent decidedly German.

"I am Mary Fitzroy, Dowager Duchess of Richmond," I tell her. She nods. "Most pleased." Poor girl! I don't think she knows much more English besides that!

The ladies parade before her and the king shamelessly ogles us all.

But no one captures his attention like my cousin Kitty Howard, who dips into a perfect curtsy, giving His Majesty ample time to appreciate her perfect décolletage.

I shudder. He is the last person I would want admiring me.

The slap rings in my ears long after it has been issued. My cheek stings and I bring a hand up to it to soothe myself.

Norfolk stands before me. "That is for the Seymour debacle." Then, in a movement just as swift as the slap, he draws me forward and kisses the same cheek he struck. "And this is for what you will do to make up for it."

I begin to tremble. Now I remember perfectly why I hated serving at King Henry's court.

"I want you to make certain our little Kitty is in the king's view as often as possible. Be subtle, of course," he says.

"To what end?" I demand, pulling away from him, disgusted. "He has made a good match with the German. May they have an eternity of happiness together and many bonny princes."

"Are you insane?" Norfolk spits. "He hates the German. She repulses him. He can't even bed her, for God's sake."

I know that much. Poor Queen Anne is so naïve that she believes sleeping in the same bed together is enough to conceive a child. She is far too innocent for the likes of our lusty king.

Norfolk's expression is the quintessence of slyness. His black eyes are narrowed, his lips are twisted into that sardonic smile; he is a fox about to pounce. "I wonder, does his inability to bed his queen mean he is cursed in some way?" His tone oozes with sarcasm. "Really, Mary, it's almost too easy."

Norfolk is not a superstitious man, but he knows our king, and our king is as paranoid as they come. Norfolk knows exactly how to play this new game.

"Don't do this," I caution. "*Please* don't do this. Queen Anne is innocent, as innocent as a body can be. Let her get used to our ways. Once she learns our customs and masters the language better, they will be a happy pair. You will see . . ."

"Oh, get out of here. You vex me to no end," Norfolk says. "Just remember to do what I said. Keep that delicious little Kitty in the foreground."

I dip into an exaggerated curtsy and flee his rooms, swallowing the rising bile in my throat.

Poor Queen Anne's German attendants are sent home and she is left with us. I know I should be glad to be rid of the gossiping gaggle, but my heart churns in sympathy, for the poor queen is so far from anything familiar to her and is so obviously disliked by the king. His comments about her appearance and even their intimate bedroom habits have been spun into well-known tales.

He hates her figure and accuses her of being older than she is. Her stomach is not flat, her breasts are sagging, and her face . . . ! His words are completely lacking in human decency. But this is the man who had one of his wives beheaded, so I cannot expect more.

We try to amuse Her Majesty by teaching her English, though she has a tutor come and instruct her every day. She seems to have a marvelous affinity for it and is determined to acclimate herself to our land.

"I will be good queen, no?" she asks us with a timid smile.

I swallow my misgivings. Dashed are all hopes of illuminating conversations of religion and art. We can barely get past salutations.

"Yes, Your Majesty," I say sweetly. "Of course you will."

Jane Boleyn draws me aside. "What's this friendliness toward the German? Your father said—"

"So you're his agent, too?" I seethe. "I do not want to know. Stay away from me, Lady Rochford. I do not want to retch in the queen's apartments."

Jane Boleyn scowls and returns to her sewing.

When not fretting over poor Queen Anne's situation, I revel in a new friendship with Catherine Parr, Lady Latymer. An understated beauty, with rich auburn hair swept under her hood in a fashionable chignon and a trim figure, she is set apart from the other maids by her quiet dignity and soothing presence. Her impeccable manners and posture have even won Norfolk's admiration. Often he has pointed her out, nudging me in the ribs, saying, "Now, if you carried yourself like *her* . . ." But of all Lady Latymer's charming attributes, it is her eyes that strike me as most endearing. The soft brown orbs are filled with compassion and sincerity, inspiring a trust too rare in an environment where betrayal is as commonplace as daily prayer.

At one time Lady Latymer was considered for a position in my household as one of my ladies-in-waiting, but that never came to fruition. She is only seven years older than I and very intelligent. We are of the same mind in regard to religion and enjoy discussing it for hours on end. She is a good substitute for my Lily, whom I have been missing dreadfully.

To differentiate between all the Catherines at court, she prefers to be called Cat. It seems most appropriate, as she is far more mature than my Kitty Howard, whose nickname could not suit her better.

Cat is on her second marriage, and though she is fond of her husband, it is not the love match she had dreamed of as a girl.

"It seems the timing's always wrong," she confesses one day.

"Who would you marry if you could?" I ask her. My cheeks begin to flush as I realize the boldness of my question. "I'm sorry. I—"

"It's all right, Mary," she says, her expression dreamy. "My heart is bound to one man but belongs to another. Lord knows I am a faithful wife to my lord Latymer. But if God wills it, I should hope that one day I can marry Tom Seymour for love."

My heart leaps into my throat. Doesn't she know about the rumors? I say nothing but reach out to squeeze her hand. "I wish you nothing but happiness, Cat."

Her brown eyes grow wide. "You won't say anything? Sometimes I fear I am too trusting . . ."

I shake my head. "I promise I will say nothing, but," I add, "it is probably not so good a thing to be too trusting at this court."

She offers a grave nod. "You are very wise."

It is a wisdom too painfully gained, I fear.

❧ 17 ❧

A Rose Named Kitty

True to his implications, my father moves fast. It is not long before the Catholic faction at court seizes the opportunity to accuse the Lutheran-leaning Cromwell of pressuring His Majesty into this unfavorable alliance to suit his own interests. Now that there is no real political reason to be married to Anne of Cleves, the king is looking for a way out.

He finds it in Francis, the Duke of Lorraine, whom Anne had been engaged to in the 1530s. Close examination reveals there is no dispensation ending the betrothal. If Anne is still betrothed to Francis, she cannot legally be wed to King Henry. Low and behold, another invalid marriage!

Then there are the rumors that she unmanned him, that every day she rises from her bed *virgo intacta*. These are rumors my cousin Lady Jane Boleyn is too happy to perpetrate, giving evidence certain to damn the poor foreign girl for the crime of being untouched. Few people are willing to believe a girl so innocent that she does not know how to coax forth a king's desire. It is not a simple matter of attraction; like everything else at this court, it is made sordid and dark. Before long there is an evil whisper on the wind: she is a witch, a witch like the cursed predecessor who bore her name.

Norfolk is thrilled and I shudder in disgusted despair.

* * *

For a while the progress in the case against Queen Anne is sluggish. This gives the king ample occasion to court the young woman who has captured his fancy, a girl-child he pulls aside at every opportunity to pet and spoil and entice. She is our own Kitty Howard.

"It isn't as though I really *like* the king," Kitty confesses to me one afternoon. "But he likes me, and you can't very well reject *him*. Oh, I know he isn't the best looking." She wrinkles her button nose. "He's so old and *large!* But he buys me such pretty gifts— sweet pets and gowns and jewels! You should see the collar of table diamonds he gave me!" Her blue eyes sparkle in bewildered delight. "I've never had pretty things of my own before." She sighs. "When I think back on life before I came here—how dull it was, and how nobody ever cared for me at all except . . . well, all the wrong people—I think I must be very blessed indeed. Uncle Thomas swept down on Lambeth like—like Merlin, and plucked me from my dreary existence, dropping me down on this Camelot. He's made me a princess! And he says as long as I'm a good girl and do just what he says, the king will keep showering his favor upon me."

My heart lurches. "Kitty, you must be careful. My father—"

"Is so wonderful! He *really* loves me," Kitty interposes. At once her eyes mist over. "No one's ever really loved me before . . ." She swallows, brightening. "And I never knew my father really, so I am so happy to acquaint myself with my good uncle. For once someone cares about what happens to me! He really wants what's best for me. He says I'm a pretty little kitten and will do the Howards proud."

For my father to utilize the phrase *pretty little kitten* in any sentence causes me to shudder in disgust.

It has all happened before. My chest is tightening in dread. Now it is happening again. This king, this mad king—does Kitty have any idea of the depth of his madness?

"Kitty—" I begin.

"Oh!" she cries. "I must be off. His Majesty is expecting me. I can only imagine for what." She emits a naughty little giggle as though she knows exactly for what, rises and kisses my cheek, and in a flurry of skirts, dashes from the maidens' chamber.

I bow my head in despair.

That evening when I am shown into Norfolk's privy chamber it is no surprise to find Kitty already there. Norfolk is leaning against his desk, staring down his hawklike nose at her, in an expression of annoyance that poor Kitty does not seem to pick up on.

"I do not want to go to Norfolk House," she is saying, jutting her lower lip out into an attractive pout I am certain has been rehearsed for its endearing effectiveness. "I want to stay here at court. If I go back there I'll miss everything."

Norfolk opens his mouth, then snaps it shut. His lips twist into a forced smile. "Kitty," he says, his tone solicitous. "You must go to Norfolk House now. It is better for you while this unpleasantness with His Majesty's annulment is being sorted out. Soon enough you shall make your grand return and will head them all up. Look at the grand scheme of things, little one. His Majesty wants *you*. He is planning to marry you and make *you* queen of England." He allows the words to sink in a moment before continuing. "Now, you are going to Norfolk House and that is that. We shall not have unpleasant words, shall we? You must remember who has gotten you this far to begin with." He pauses. "Kitty, do you remember your cousin Anne—Queen Anne?"

Kitty's nod is grave. "She came to see me once when I was little. She brought me a present."

"Yes, you would recall that," says Norfolk, but the sarcasm is lost on her. He continues. "Anne was a bad girl." I cringe at the blunt description, as a vision of my Anne conjures itself before my mind's eye—radiant, her black eyes sparkling with wit and merriment. Anne . . . "That is why she is never mentioned at court; she was so wicked the king forbids it." Little Kitty's face is white. "She died by the sword, Kitty, because she did not listen to me, who had her best interests at heart just as I do yours. So you see that it is vital you listen to your uncle, d'you see?"

Kitty, so unlike her late cousin Anne when it comes to battles of wits, melts at this. Her smile is guileless. "Oh, yes, of course. I shall always listen to you, Uncle Thomas. Were it not for you putting me in His Majesty's path so often, he may not have noticed me at all."

Norfolk laughs, stepping forward and taking her pretty little hands in his. "You are a hard one to miss, my little kitten." He taps her nose with his finger. "Now. You must be off to sleep. You will leave in the morning. His Majesty plans to visit you every day, or at least as often as he can, and I'm certain he will bring many gifts for his little rose."

"His 'rose without a thorn,' " Kitty says in awe. "Can you believe he calls me that? It is quite sweet. That is what I must think of. All the sweet things. I won't think about him being so old and large. I'll think of all the grand things."

"That's right, Kitty," says Norfolk.

"And hope he will consummate the marriage in the dark!" Kitty finishes with a laugh of her own that catches Norfolk off guard.

"Er . . . yes," he says, shifting uncomfortably. "Best not suggest that to him, however, Kitty."

"Oh, of course not," she says. "Worst comes to worst, I can always close my eyes."

Norfolk is shaking his head and I am stifling laughter.

"Will you visit me at Norfolk House, too, Uncle Thomas?" she asks, laying her hand upon his doublet. She casts her eyes upon me. "And bring Mary?"

"Certainly," he says.

She wraps her arms about his neck and kisses his cheek. He returns the embrace stiffly, patting her back while trying to extract himself from her. She does not see this, however. She is the type who immerses herself in a hug, pressing herself in full to the person she embraces, as though her greatest desire is to merge with them, body, heart, and soul. Yet there is nothing sexual about it at all. She is a girl made to love and be loved.

She tilts an adoring face up to Norfolk. "I love you, Uncle Thomas," she tells him, her voice shaking with sincerity.

He draws away, clearing his throat. "Well. Yes." He shoos her away. "To bed now, Kitten. You want to be fresh and pretty for to-morrow."

She smiles, bounds over to me to kiss my cheek, then quits the room. I hear her offer a cheery exchange with the guards. There is laughter. I smile. There is laughter wherever Kitty goes.

When I am certain she is out of earshot I turn to my father. "My lord, I must entreat you."

"What now, Mary?" His voice is weary, as though the exertion of being kind to Kitty has exhausted him.

"You must promise . . ." The laughter in my throat has turned to tears. I wring my hands. "You must promise me that Kitty will never come to any harm. She is as innocent as a girl can be."

"Innocent? Kitty?" Norfolk's tone is incredulous. "Don't mis-take sheer stupidity for sheer innocence, Mary."

I sigh. "She isn't stupid; she's young. Fourteen. This is such a heady world for her. She isn't like Anne—the king may tire of her inability to match wits—"

"At this point the king does not want a girl for her intelli-gence," Norfolk tells me. "Take one good look at that imp. Would any man in his right mind want her for her wits?" He laughs. "He no longer needs late-night debates and mental stim-ulation. He wants a pretty little thing to pet and spoil. And as long as she can give him the heirs he needs, her life is assured—and I do not foresee any problems there. As you said, she's young and healthy."

"But the king . . ." I begin. I do not want to say too much for it is treason to predict the death of a king. "He is not a well man. You've seen him dragging that leg around."

Norfolk grimaces. "Indeed. Putrid rotting thing that it is. Kitty has all my sympathies there."

I sigh in frustration. "Do you suppose a man in his state can even beget heirs? Do you suppose he'll take the responsibility if he cannot?" I shake my head. "You know as well as I who will be to blame."

"Of course I do, Mary," Norfolk says. "Thank God you have de-

veloped some sense of astuteness. You may be my daughter yet."
He pauses, clasping his hands behind his back. "There are ways
around all that, anyway," he says to himself.

"What ways?" I ask, my voice rising in panic.

At once his face arranges itself into an impatient scowl. "Leave
it to me. Now go join your cousin."

"But, my lord, you haven't promised," I say in firm tones. "I
want you to promise—"

"Good night, Mary." His tone is a warning I do not heed.

"Promise me!"

He seizes my shoulders. "I said good *night*, Mary!"

I pull away. "Please . . ."

Norfolk sighs. "There is no reason to believe our Kitty should
remain anything but the king's rose. His 'rose without a thorn'—or
some such nonsense." His smile oozes with sarcasm. "There.
Does that reassure you? Go now. Go on!"

I curtsy and quit the room, my heart thumping in a fear that no
amount of reassurance can assuage.

The marriage is annulled in early July. Anne of Cleves ruled as
queen for a total of four months and no one at court saw her since
the festivities on May Day. She is said to have taken the news
quite well; so well that the king was annoyed at her eagerness to
cooperate. She signed a letter of submission, naming herself
"daughter of Cleves" and not "queen of England" and was given
Richmond Palace to reside in as the king's "dear sister." I cannot
even begin to imagine but . . .

At least she kept her head. For that the German bride is to be
congratulated. She kept not only her head but the king's favor,
even making the occasional appearance at court, where she appears happier than ever.

Our Kitty contented herself at Norfolk House during the worst
of the split, receiving lands, bolts of the finest fabrics, jewelry, and
nightly visits from His Majesty. Whenever I visit her she delights
in showing me her newest gown or bauble.

"It's not so bad, really," she tells me one day, her tone strained in an effort to convince herself. "Really. All I have to do is have a baby. That's not too much to ask."

I do not draw to her attention the pallor of her cheeks or trembling limbs. I nod and compliment her beautiful gowns and exclaim over her newest piece of jewelry.

"These were Jane Seymour's," she tells me. "Her very own jewels. Fancy that they're in a Howard's hands now!"

I emit a soft laugh. "Yes. Fancy that."

Of course the king needs someone to blame for the Anne of Cleves debacle. In this my father seizes the opportunity to shift all responsibility onto the shoulders of the too-Lutheran, newly titled Earl of Essex, Thomas Cromwell. His archenemy. Anti-Lutheran sentiments are running high, but for Norfolk religion has nothing to do with it. Cromwell is a rival to be removed and it is as simple as that. For this crime he deserves to die. Forgotten are Cromwell's interventions on behalf of my brother, and his appeals for my inheritance. Norfolk wants to be rid of him and rid of him he will be.

So, without ever suspecting a thing, Cromwell is stripped of his titles and honors and thrown into the Tower, arrested for high treason. An act of attainder is passed against him, which in essence means that he will die without trial.

He is beheaded on July 28, Kitty's wedding day.

"It's so very strange," says Kitty as we are dressing her. "I never thought Cromwell to be so bad a man." She pauses, cocking her head as she ponders her tiny pearl-encrusted slipper. "He was the king's dearest friend for so long." She shudders.

"Best not to think about it, my lady," advises Jane Boleyn.

"Yes," I say. "Listen to Lady Rochford. She knows all about how to put beheadings behind her."

Jane shoots me a scathing look and I smile.

The wedding is not filled with the same pageantry some of His Majesty's former brides have been afforded, but there is a grand breakfast. Kitty, now Queen Catherine, is by far the most beautiful bride I have ever beheld. In a display that churns the stomach, the king's hands are all over her. She does not shoo him away, of course. She knows better than that.

Under the advisement of Norfolk, Kitty chooses her ladies-in-waiting. Jane Boleyn is appointed chief lady of the bedchamber. I am in shock. Jane's smile is triumphant as she fusses over Kitty, who is so easily won that she has no idea of Jane's duplicitous nature.

Kitty is generous to her past acquaintances from Lambeth, girls she shared chambers with, and grants them all one position or another. I know as I watch them, these greedy mongrels, that no one comes here out of loyalty to the little queen. They come as vultures, circling, ugly things beneath all their finery, waiting to take Kitty for all she is worth.

But these girls are around Kitty's age and they play together and dance about Hampton Court, making merry, giggling and teasing, and no one seems a happier queen than Catherine Howard.

" 'No other will but his,' " she tells me one night, her smile bright. She is in her big bed of state, the bed that once belonged to Anne of Cleves, her sumptuous covers drawn up to her shoulders. "That means I am the king's obedient little miss. How do you like that? It's my motto. It's a good motto, don't you think? Except it does echo Jane Seymour's 'Bound to serve and obey,' but I suppose everyone's forgotten her by now, except for that she is little Prince Edward's mother." She scoots up against her pillows. "Strange to think I am stepmother to people almost as old as I am. Lady Mary is older! Fancy that!" She shrugs. "Queen Anne—Anne of Cleves, I mean—adores the children. She sees them whenever she can—except Mary, since she's out of favor again, her being such a papist and all." She sighs. "I suppose it will be very hard trying to be stepmother to her. I hope not to see her very much. Once I give the king babies of our own I imagine he'll forget all about them." She considers. "Except Lady Elizabeth. We cannot forget her. She is our cousin, after all, and it would be good to see her restored to favor."

I nod, my eyes misting over at the thought of the abandoned little princess. "Indeed it would."

Kitty sits up, drawing her knees to her chest and hugging them, her adorable face scrunched up in delight. "Do you want to know a secret?"

I'm not sure. "Yes," I answer, as I'm certain there is no getting around it.

"I may be with child even as we speak," she says. "It is early, however, and I have never really been—well, on course, but there is a good chance."

I take her slim hands in mine. "Oh, Your dearest Majesty, I pray it is so." As I look into her sweet face I recall a similar confidence exchanged between Anne Boleyn and me so many years ago . . . I blink away the memory.

"You never had a child, did you, Mary?" Kitty asks me.

I shake my head, my throat constricting with painful tears.

"But you were my age when you married the duke, were you not?" she asks.

I nod. "I was not allowed to be with him," I tell her. "My father . . . he would not permit it."

She reaches out and strokes my cheek. "How dreadful for you." Once again she favors me with her bright smile. "I shall help find you a husband if you wish it."

I shake my head. "My fondest wish is to remain here and serve you, Your Majesty," I tell her. *And keep you safe,* I add to myself.

"Then serve me you shall," she says. "And be richly rewarded! Can you believe I'm saying that? 'Richly rewarded'? I have the power to reward people! Isn't that something?"

I nod. "Yes, Your sweet Majesty. It is really something."

At once the king enters, the stench of his ulcerated leg causing my stomach to turn. I dip into a low curtsy.

"Lady Richmond!" he exclaims as though there's never been a quarrel between us. "How now?"

"I am quite well, Sire," I answer, keeping my head bowed so he cannot see me swallowing the urge to gag. I cannot imagine how Kitty stands night after night of his intimate company.

He chucks my chin. "Well, good night to you, then."

"Good night, Sire."

I hurry from the room before I retch in revulsion.

* * *

To my delight I meet Hans Holbein, the court painter, again, in Norfolk's apartments, when he is commissioned to render his likeness.

He bows, offering a bright smile. "My lady Richmond," he says. "You know I have an unfinished sketch of you somewhere. We shall dig it out and finish it one of these days."

"I would be most honored," I tell him, flattered the artist should remember drawing someone as insignificant as I am, when some of the greatest nobles and heads of state in the world have sat before him.

Norfolk is thrilled to be sitting for him, or standing as the case is. He dresses in his finest ermines, piling clothes onto his slim frame so that he appears sturdy and broad of chest. He carries his staffs of office as lord treasurer and earl marshal, wearing his heavy garter chain about his shoulders and consummate black cap that hides his nice hair—but I suppose that's his affair. As it is, I am stifling laughter beholding him standing before the artist like an overstuffed doll about to topple over for the weight of his clothing. The only indication of his true bone structure is his hands, his handsome hands that clutch his staffs with such pride.

He stands for what seems like hours, not moving a muscle, and I can't help but marvel at his discipline. When Holbein finishes with the rudimentary sketching, Norfolk leaps down from his platform to admire the drawing.

"What do you think, Mary?" he asks me, his voice as excited as a child's. "Do you like it? Do I look good?"

It is the strangest question I've ever heard coming from someone who could never include vanity in his long list of negative personality traits.

"It's a very handsome rendering, Father," I tell him, rubbing his arm. "You make quite a royal personage."

He wraps his arm about my waist, drawing me as close as his ermine cloak allows. "I think so, too," he says. Then to Holbein, "Well done, Master Holbein. I like what I see so far."

Master Holbein bows again and my father toddles out of the

room; so heavy are his robes of state that he doesn't realize the comical effect his walk has on us. Upon his exit we burst into controlled giggles, hoping he does not overhear us.

"Well, my lady, what do you really think?" Holbein asks as we stand before the portrait in its most nascent state.

"It is his likeness," I tell him. I can't say it is handsome; if Norfolk was ever a good-looking man it was too long ago for me to recall. "His clothes are beautiful. And one cannot tell how big they are on him in the drawing."

"Yes, I modified it a little," Holbein says, swallowing a chuckle. He squints an eye as he examines his work. "There's something about him . . . something I tried to capture . . . I do not know. Would I offend you if I asked your opinion about something, Lady Richmond?"

"Of course not," I tell him, interested to know what he is thinking.

He pauses. "Have I captured . . . well, have I captured your father's expression? I mean, when you look at him do you see that— that sort of . . . how do I put this without sounding offensive—"

"Please, you must not worry about offending me," I assure him. "What is it, Master Holbein?"

"His lifelessness," he says. "Have I captured his lifelessness?"

I behold the portrait once more, staring past the beautiful robes of state, the ermine, and the gold. I look into my father's face. A memory stirs. He is holding me. I am very little, looking into his eyes, those hard black eyes . . . I shudder.

"Yes, Master Holbein," I tell him with certainty. "You have captured his lifelessness."

Never have I heard a more apt description of my father.

The court is merry again. Kitty sees to it. Though it is not a philosophical court, it is filled with young people whose only desire is to have fun. I am caught up in it, just as I was when my Anne was in power.

The only intellectual stimulus comes from Cat Parr, and together we have many a long discussion on church reform and the

Bible. I enjoy her calm presence immensely. She is neither the prettiest nor liveliest of women, but when I am around her I feel a measure of comfort foreign to me. She is a friend I can confide all to; unlike most of the set she is not a gossip, waiting for the next morsel of wicked news to be thrown to her like a ravenous dog. She is very unhurried, thinks everything through, and, despite the love she confesses for Tom Seymour, is very devoted to her aged and ailing husband, John Neville.

There are many cliques at court. It is no surprise that because I am all of twenty-one I am excluded from the younger girls who surround Kitty like drones to their queen. I am content to keep company with Cat—and Margaret Douglas, who fancies Kitty's brother Charles.

There is not a soul at court besides perhaps Kitty herself whom I pity more than Margaret. It seems she is fated to fall in love with all the wrong men. For her daring to give her heart to Charles Howard she is sent to Syon Abbey to repent. Charles removes to France, where he dies unmarried and brokenhearted.

The scandal delights the court, who prey on such things, and I am short a dear friend, a friend I have considered kin since my marriage to Harry Fitzroy. Kitty is glad to have Margaret gone and I can see why. Margaret is a blood royal, and made no secret of her annoyance with my frivolous cousin.

With Margaret's disgrace to keep the court's tongues wagging, no one sees Kitty's eyes sparkle as they behold a young gentleman of the king's privy chamber, her cousin Thomas Culpepper.

Though Kitty has not become pregnant yet, she has managed to survive almost one year of marriage to the king.

"He loves me so much, the silly old man, that I don't think he even cares just yet if I even have a child," says Kitty in the spring of 1541, laughing. We are sitting in the gardens and she is picking the petals off of a pink rose, rubbing them between her fingers before letting them drop to the ground. "He is a dear; his greatest pleasure in life is to see me happy." She leans her head on her knees. "And I don't think he loves me like a wife—not to say that he doesn't lust after my body and all that—but when I think of it really . . . really I think he loves me like I'm his own little girl. Is that strange?"

There is nothing stranger, but I do not say so. "I think older men often are given to such fancies," I say instead. "Just be wary, Your Majesty."

She nods. "Oh, yes. I am quite careful in all I do. Your cousin Lady Jane is most good to me and always watches out for me. As long as His Majesty is happy, as long as he thinks me his faithful little rose—well, there is nothing to worry about, is there?"

I do not want to entertain Kitty's inferences. Why would she be worried, why must she be careful, if she is the king's faithful little rose? And what does vicious Jane Boleyn have to do with anything?

I shudder. "Your Majesty, may I beg your leave? I am not feeling so well."

"Of course, Mary. Do feel better. There is to be dancing later."

I nod as I curtsy, then leave her to a group of adoring courtiers as I seek out the one man who can answer my questions.

"Mary, you can't be this ignorant," Norfolk says when I confront him in his chambers. He is rubbing his forehead and squinting at some documents. "Tell me you're not this ignorant. You know as well as I do that His Majesty is too sick to beget any more children. So it is up to Kitty to find another to"—he arches a brow and smiles—"fill that place."

I draw in a breath. "Culpepper."

Norfolk shrugs. "Really, I don't care if it's the stable boy so long as he gets a babe on her."

"And Lady Jane?" My voice is shaking. "Lady Jane cares nothing for her, you must know that. She is in this for her own gain. She's always been in it for her gain. That's why she betrayed Anne and George, so she could have everything—the lands, the titles . . ." Tears stream unchecked down my cheeks. "My lord, please. Don't encourage this."

"I don't encourage anything," he says. "I don't discourage anything. Lady Jane, on the other hand, is most eager to act as go-between—run a note here, a note there, 'Stand outside the door a while, Lady Jane, while we . . .' " He chuckles. "She probably has a stiff neck from peeping in the keyhole."

"And the queen? Does no one care about what could happen to her?" I whisper in terror. "Does no one care about *her?*"

Norfolk stares at me. "In fact, I was going to summon you, Mary. I need your help in this. Our little kitten could use more alibis."

I shake my head. "No. I will have nothing to do with it. I would rather die."

"We are all going to die, Mary," he says, and I swear for a moment his face has contorted into that of the Devil himself. I draw back in horror. Am I losing my mind? "It is just a matter of when and how." He returns to the original topic. "You would be doing a royal service, unbeknownst to His Majesty, of course."

I shake my head. "No. No. I will have no part in this. This, whatever comes of it, is yours and Lady Jane's responsibility."

Norfolk rises and lunges at me, gripping my shoulder. Like all his movements, it is so sudden it captures my breath. He backs me up against the wall. "Do you think I am *asking* for your help? Do you think when I talk to you I'm just making suggestions? When I tell you something I expect my will to be done. You *will* help me, Mary, and your cousins."

"Like we helped Anne?" I cry. "Look where our help got her!"

Norfolk's hand has seized my throat. I begin to sputter and cough. This is the end . . . he has chosen my death. He will explain it away. Tomorrow I will be lying in a pile of straw in a wagon somewhere while he attends to matters of state. He will keep scheming and plotting and I will be dead . . .

His hand is tightening about my neck. Little specks of light dance before my eyes. I begin to ponder necks. Mine is small like Anne's, so delicate, in fact, that it is easy for Norfolk to grasp the whole of it in one slender hand. My face is hot. I cannot breathe . . .

Tears are streaming down my cheeks. I cannot choke; I cannot gasp.

At once Norfolk's face goes slack. His eyes are wide. He slides his hand from my neck to my heaving chest.

"Mary . . . ?" he asks in a low voice.

I begin to sputter and cough. "Wh . . . why?" I gasp, taking in a deep breath. "Why?"

Norfolk has backed away from me. He is staring down at his hand. It is trembling. He returns stricken black eyes to me. "Mary . . ."

I am rubbing my neck. "Oh, my lord. For God's sake, why didn't you just end it?"

Tears light his eyes. "Mary!" He reaches for me.

I turn on my heel and run.

I am blind as I weave my way through the halls. I want to make it back to the maidens' chamber and find some semblance of peace. As I am running I meet with the obstacle of a man's chest. Arms encircle me. I am gasping and sobbing with abandon.

"Lady Richmond?" a voice entreats in soothing tones. "Lady Richmond, what is it, dear heart?"

I pull away, meeting the violet eyes of Cedric Dane. "M—Master Dane—"

"Lady Richmond, please, collect yourself," he urges, his voice soft. "What is it? Tell me."

I shake my head, still rubbing my throat as I look here and there for my father's guards.

"Come," he says. "To the practice room. We will have privacy there."

I allow him to take my elbow and guide me to the chamber, where he bolts the door. We sit on the bench behind the virginals. He takes my hands and I do not fight him.

"My lady, what is causing such distress?" he asks, as though to a very small child. The sweetness in his tone causes me to cry harder. "Please. You can trust me. Let me help you."

"No one can help me," I sob. "No one could help her. And now . . . now . . ." I envision Kitty's sweet face alight with her girlish infatuation. Despair grips my heart in a chokehold more successful than Norfolk's. "God save the queen," I say at last.

"Lady Richmond." He is stroking the backs of my hands with a strange mixture of urgency and gentleness. "Please . . ." His voice is a husky whisper. "Let me in."

I shake my head with vehemence. "No! No! You do not want to be let into this. Once you are in you cannot get out, you cannot escape. You are trapped, forever trapped—"

He reaches out and cups my cheek. I lean into his hand, allowing my tears to mingle with his soft warm skin.

"Shall I call a doctor?" he asks. "Are you quite well?"

"I do not know," I tell him in honesty, for I do not know. Was I ever sane? Was I ever allowed a glimpse of sanity? I meet his eyes, my lips twisting into a grim smile. "There is no cure for what ails me, Master Dane." I begin to rub my aching throat, inadvertently drawing his eyes to it.

"Your neck!" he cries, reaching out to trace it. I flinch. "Lady Richmond, there are marks—bruises. Were you accosted? Who did this to you? Who hurt you?"

I shake my head. How can I explain this one away? I shake my head again. "It's no good, Master Dane. It's no good." I laugh, a hysterical sound that rings of Anne's edgy giggle.

It seems Cedric knows continuing in this vein will prove fruitless, so diverts me by placing his slim-fingered hands on the keyboard and playing a soothing melody. He swallows several times. "I wrote this for my Helen," he tells me as I collect myself.

"She must love it," I told him, sniffling.

He stops playing. "She did." His voice catches in his throat. "Lady Richmond . . . my lady wife . . . she has passed on."

Fresh tears sting my eyes. "No! Oh, Master Dane, no!"

"She—and my daughter died in childbirth last winter," he tells me, resting a hand on my shoulder. "So you see none of us are exempt from grief."

"I am sorry, Master Dane. With all my heart I am sorry," I tell him, reaching out to wipe away a tear that has strayed onto his cheek. I draw in a breath. "Sorrow runs high at this court of Henry VIII, it seems," I add, my voice tinged with bitterness. "And your boys? Who is caring for them?" I ask then.

"My sister in Cornwall," he says. "I want them as far away from here as possible. It is no life for children."

"I'm not certain if it is a life for anyone," I admit.

"From the lips of a professional courtier," he says. He wraps his arm about my shoulders and I do not pull away. It is highly improper being alone with this man, both of us widowed; not to mention that we are touching. But I no longer care for what's proper, for what's right. I have just been asked to help lead an innocent girl into betraying the most dangerous man in the land. Why should I bother with proprieties now?

I turn to him. He reaches out, tracing the bruises forming on my neck. "Lady Richmond, tell me who did this to you. I will kill him . . ." His voice is filled with venom. "I will *kill* him."

"And you would die," I tell him. Tears clutch my throat, a sensation so familiar that I marvel at the rare times it is absent. "I cannot lose you, too, Master Dane." I allow the tears to pour onto my cheeks. There is no point in hiding them, no point in playing games. With Cedric I do not have to be a courtier. I can just be a woman. "Please, whatever your suspicions, promise me you will not act on them."

He pauses, considering. "And what will happen to you? Will I learn of your death one of these days? Or your disappearance from court? Will your name just be phased out as so many others are? *Where's Mary Richmond? Oh, I don't know. Last I heard she retired to Kenninghall* when really you're . . . you're . . ." Tears stream down his face. "Is there no one to champion you, my lady?" His voice bursts forth in a tortured whisper.

"I have only had one champion my whole life," I tell him. "One champion and one enemy. And they are the same man."

His face goes slack in horror. He cups my face in his hands. "My lady—you must leave this court. I have watched you over the years. I have seen your joy sapped from you, your innocence stolen. I have seen you grow serious and old before your time. Get away from here. Get away from *him*."

I shake my head. "Wherever I go he will find me. Oh, now and then he forgets about me. For a time." I shrug, helpless, then meet his eyes, knowing mine are hard green mirrors that reflect nothing but his face. I know it as surely as if I were looking into them myself. "But he always remembers. Please." I reach up, resting my hands over his that still cup my face. "Leave this alone, Master Dane."

His face is soft. He draws in a breath. "Must we continue with these ridiculous formalities?" he asks, dropping his hands. "My name is Cedric."

I pause a long moment. If I allow this . . . if I allow this . . . I look him square in the face. "And I am Mary."

"Mary," he whispers, as though it is forbidden, the name of a goddess. I shiver.

Cedric takes me in his arms. For the second time in my life I am kissed. But there is no guilt now. There is no one alive to betray, no one around to care. Our spouses are with the Lord, leaving us to struggle alone and eke out what little happiness we can find. My father is off betraying his king and I am here.

I am with Cedric.

There is no one else.

Together we sink onto the floor beside the blazing fire. I am swept away on a new current, beyond infantile desire and courtly lust. This is not a game of flirtation. Perhaps it is not love, either. But it is a comfort of sorts, a wild sort of comfort. There is urgency, yes, and something more. Passion, pain, pleasure. We merge and meld into one being; his limbs, fingers, lips no longer separate from my own. We are perfectly, irrevocably entwined. I am enveloped in him and him in me.

It is that night I taste love's sweet bliss at last.

I cannot think of my night with Cedric. I cannot allow myself to go back there. I do not know if it will happen again. Do I want it to? A part of me yearns for him every moment—for his arms, his kisses, his warm flesh pressed to mine. . . . Another part of me cringes in horror. What am I? A harlot? What have all my religious pursuits brought me to? What must God think of me now?

Cat Parr sees the difference. She reaches out to me the next afternoon as the two of us stroll the gardens. I hear Kitty playing badminton with a group of courtiers, boys against girls. Thomas Culpepper is on the boys' team. He is laughing and teasing her. I shiver.

"What is it, Lady Mary?" Cat asks me, rubbing my upper arm. Though she is not much older than I she is so motherly that she has even been called to pacify King Henry's bouts of temper when his leg is giving him a particularly bad time. There is no doubt of her ability to comfort and soothe.

I cannot keep it from her. If I do not tell her I will collapse in upon myself. "I have been wicked," I tell her.

"Wicked?" She laughs. "You?"

I pause. "I have . . . I have known . . . I—"

"Lady Mary," Cat says, taking my hands. "Whatever you have done, be assured I will not judge you. Does not our Lord command it? 'Judge not lest ye be judged'? Come now. You may tell me, dearest, and if there is anything I can do to help, you must know I will do so. And if I cannot, you can take solace in the fact that I am your sympathetic friend who loves you."

I sigh in relief. I should have known I could trust faithful Cat.

"There is a gentleman," I begin. "I—I—that is to say, we—"

Cat nods in understanding. "If you are wicked then I am damned," she tells me. She purses her lips. "I tell you this because I consider you a very dear friend and know I can trust you. If you are wicked for trying to steal a little happiness for yourself then we are wicked together, for I too have sought out my heart's desire."

"Seymour?" I ask her.

She nods, smiling.

I sigh. "Oh, my lady, but I have made a promise . . . a promise I cannot seem to keep." Through a veil of tears, I tell her of my promise to Harry.

"But you have not broken your promise at all," she points out. "You have found love. Didn't he want you to find love?" she asks. "You are not married. You are not even betrothed. So you took what is owed you, what you deserve. Yes, it may not be the most prudent thing in God's eyes, but I cannot imagine He wouldn't understand. He is merciful to those who love Him. And your Harry . . . he wants you to be happy. When you are with this gentleman are you happy, Lady Mary?"

"I do not know," I answer. "Emotions run high when we are together. There is so much intensity . . ." I shake my head. "I am not *un*happy in his presence. He—he is very kind. It is odd. We have been virtual strangers since I was eleven or so, exchanging a few words here and there, and yet I think he knows me better than anyone."

"Then delight in him, Lady Mary," Cat tells me. "Happiness is too seldom found in this life. Take hold of it while you can."

"Yes," I say. "Yes. That is what I shall do."

While we are sitting there a messenger comes to me with a gilt box. Thrilled, I open it to find a pretty emerald and diamond bracelet set in gold to look like ivy.

"Is that from him?" Cat asks as she lays the bracelet across her wrist to admire it.

I read the note in the bottom of the box.

> *Mary,*
> *If you are willing and obedient you shall eat the*
> *good of the land. Isaiah 1:19.*
> *Your loving father,*
> *Thomas Howard, Duke of Norfolk*

Cat has read the note over my shoulder. "Oh, for God's sake," she mutters. "Why on earth wouldn't he just leave it at 'your loving father'? As though you don't know who he is?" She takes the note and rereads it, wrinkling her nose. "What does it mean, anyway?"

I sigh. "He does that from time to time," I tell her. "To inspire me."

She puts the note back in the box. "It's a pretty bracelet. Shall I clasp it on you?"

"No," I tell her, placing it back in the box. "Thank you." I lean over and kiss her cheek. "You're a good friend, my lady," I say. "Thank you."

"As you are to me, Lady Mary." She reaches out and squeezes my hand.

I leave the gardens, walking past Kitty and her games.

I go to Norfolk's apartments. He is not there. I set the box on his desk and leave a note of my own.

My lord Thomas Howard, Duke of Norfolk,
But you have become cruel to me; with the strength of
your hand you oppose me. Job 30:21.
Your loving daughter,
Mary Fitzroy
Duchess of Richmond and Somerset, Countess of
Nottingham

Whatever this earns me, I am smiling at the boldness of my move.

Let that inspire him.

Our personal intrigues are distracted when the king takes ill with a fever. Kitty is sent away for her protection—in case she carries an heir, no doubt—and takes a small handful of ladies, including Lady Rochford.

At night I pray for the king's demise. It is a terrible thing, a treasonous thing, to pray for the death of a king, but I cannot help myself. Perhaps he will die and free my Kitty. How wonderful her life could be then! She would live as queen dowager, free to surround herself with whatever and whomever she wants. If she wants to marry Culpepper she can marry Culpepper. Oh, if only . . .

But it is not to be. The king, whose will is still strong enough to command his failing body, recovers and Kitty is called back to court. She is glowing, her cheeks rosy with happiness. Any fool can see she runs mad with love sickness, and anyone with a beating heart knows to fear for her, for this love that causes her to giggle and skip and dance about is not for His Majesty.

Again she suspects she is with child. The king is delighted at the prospect and dotes on his rose like an idiot, promising her a grand coronation at York Minster if her pregnancy proves true. My stomach churns. But I am so immersed in my own newfound happiness that all of my energy is no longer expended in fretting over the royal couple.

Cedric and I see each other as often as possible. Together we play music and share our compositions; we read our poetry along with other courtiers' works, such as those of Thomas Wyatt and my brother. Cedric causes my cheeks to flush when he says that Surrey is all flowers and no real substance. He prefers Wyatt's more honest style of writing. I of course defend my brother out of familial loyalty.

"I don't think there exists a more loyal daughter and sister in the entire realm," says Cedric one day as we snuggle before the fire. "I hope they appreciate it."

I wave a dismissive hand. "I don't care if they do or not. I don't want to think about them or anything outside of us."

Cedric pulls me in his arms and I stifle giggles of delight.

"Are you going with us on progress, Cedric?" I ask him as I kiss his neck.

"I wouldn't miss it," he says, stroking my hair. "I couldn't, anyway. The king has commanded my presence. It will be a merry progress, Mary. We will have a lot of freedom. . . ." He winks.

My cheeks burn. I feel as naughty as Kitty. "I cannot wait, my dearest."

The progress through the North is a merry journey. We tour different cities and accept the hospitality of local nobles. Everywhere we go we are feasted and celebrated. A court on progress lacks the structure of a mobilized court within the confines of palace life, and everyone behaves like children freed of their studies. We romp and play and I cannot think of a time when I have been happier.

Kitty and Culpepper seek each other out under Jane Boleyn's watch, and I ignore it. I immerse myself in Cedric and my own intrigues. We find each other at every opportunity and, with as much subtlety as possible, conduct our affair. I do not think of Norfolk or his reaction, should he learn of what he would perceive to be my wantonness; I do not think of Surrey. I think of myself. For once in my life I think about me.

When we return to Hampton Court and Kitty is not with child, I begin to face the situation's gravity at last. She has been married over a year now. Enemies are circling, eager to see the rose wither. Old "friends" from Lambeth are given positions in her household, the ancient exchange of glory for silence. One is Francis Dereham, a rakishly handsome courtier with black hair and intense features whose hungry eyes follow Kitty with the possessiveness of a man whose blood is running hot with desire. He has been appointed her personal secretary.

"We meant something to each other once," she tells me, her expression dreamy, as I question the wisdom of having him so close. "Poor chap believed we were married." Her eyes are wide. "Of course we weren't," she whispers. "I don't know why he insists it was so. I always thought it was sort of a game between us; calling each other 'husband' and 'wife,' you know?"

"When you played at husband and wife," I begin in hushed tones, "did—did you do everything a husband and wife would do?"

"Well, yes," Kitty says, lowering her eyes. My heart begins to pound. Does Norfolk know? Would he have pushed her this far if he knew? Oh, God, save Her precious Majesty . . . "That's why he was so put out when I corrected him. But I think we have an understanding now. He is happy as my secretary and is quite over it all, I am certain."

"*Are* you certain, Your Majesty?" I ask her. "He doesn't resent you for . . . anything?"

She shakes her head. "Why would he? He left me for a year while he became a pirate or some stupid thing like that. What did he expect me to do? Wait for him after I thought he was dead?" She shrugs. "I think he's more realistic than that. He realizes life just went on and accepts it."

"Does he know about . . . about Culpepper?"

"What do you mean?" Her blue eyes flash in petulant anger. "What are you suggesting?"

I kneel before her. "Your Majesty, I . . . I know about your goings on. And I fear for you. His Majesty is—oh, Kitty, *please* be careful!"

Kitty's face softens and she reaches forward, removing my hood.

She sets it in her lap, then leans forward to cup my face between her slim hands.

"You mustn't worry. I am sure to keep His Majesty happy," she assures me. "I keep everyone happy."

I want to believe her. How much I do want to believe her!

❧ 18 ❧

Thorns

The happiness Kitty promises is short-lived, as I knew it would be. When a man named John Lascelles learns of Kitty's past with Dereham through his sister Mary Hall, a chambermaid at Norfolk House, he runs with it. It is his moral responsibility, he feels, as he is a reformer against the Catholic faction (in short, the Howards) and takes it upon himself to seek out Archbishop Cranmer, informing him that Kitty had a precontract in marriage to Francis Dereham.

On November 2 at the Mass for All Souls' Day, Cranmer passes His Majesty a note with the charges. It is kept private at first. I suspect nothing till the king leaves the palace on the fifth.

I keep close to Kitty and the other ladies. Kitty is unaware that anything is amiss, as is most of the court. We make merry in her rooms, dancing and giggling as we always do in her presence, when the archbishop enters, his face somber.

"Your Majesty," he says, bowing. He sighs. "We have learned the truth about you and Francis Dereham."

The room is silent. I begin to tremble. My stomach aches. My eyes stray to Kitty's white throat.

"What?" Kitty asks, smiling. "What truth?"

"That you were precontracted in marriage, that you are lovers."

Kitty's little mouth is agape. "It is a lie!" she cries. "I . . . I want to see the king! I shall explain everything to the king! He will understand. Please, take me to His Majesty."

The archbishop shakes his head. His eyes fill with pity. "His Majesty has retired to Oatlands Palace, brokenhearted." He pauses, approaching Kitty, who is trembling. "You must confess, Your Grace. Confess your sins and you may be spared."

"Spared?" she breathes. "Spared what?" She draws in a breath. "Spared *what?*" Her blue eyes are wide with terror. "Archbishop?"

The archbishop closes his eyes. All of us know what she may be spared from. Nobody wants to hear her confession. I place a hand on my churning stomach. I want to run to Kitty, take her in my arms and comfort her.

Her face has gone white. "If I confess I will be saved? I will not go to the scaffold if I confess, is that right?"

"That is possible, Your Grace," says Cranmer.

Kitty lowers her eyes. And confesses. She tells him everything that happened at Lambeth with Dereham, how he took her both clothed and unclothed, how they played at being married. Her words, as strange as they are, are so childish and fraught with innocence that I cannot imagine how a man of the archbishop's years and experience cannot dismiss them as anything but a childish mistake. Kitty could not have been more than thirteen at the time the incident in question transpired.

"I didn't even know the king then." Kitty is sobbing. "What difference does it make if I didn't even know him?"

Cranmer nods. "That is what we will try to tell him. That because it is a precontract it invalidates your marriage. That if, technically, you are not married now, no further accusations can be made against you."

"Further accusations?" She sniffles.

"I must go to the king," he says in gentle tones. "You are not to leave these rooms." He pauses near the doors. "I will pray for you, Queen Catherine."

When he leaves we gather around her, patting her shaking shoulders and stroking her auburn hair. Her pretty hair . . .

"I have to see the king," she sobs. "I have to see him. He cannot resist me. He loves me so much. Once he sees me I can make him understand. Isn't he the smartest man in the land? That is why God made him king? If he is so smart, he will understand. Won't he?" She is near hysteria. "Won't he?"

"Oh, Kitty," I whisper, pulling her in my arms, rocking back and forth.

She tilts her face up to me. "Uncle Thomas. Uncle Thomas will help me, won't he? Will you get him?" She sits up, brightening. "Uncle Thomas loves me well. He protects me and calls me his little kitten. He will help me. Won't he, Mary?"

I begin to sob.

When I am able to leave the queen, I seek out Norfolk.

"What are we going to do?" I cry. "How are we going to help her? Dereham has been arrested. He has confessed to everything, under torture. Some of the servants have also betrayed her."

"Do you think you're telling me something I do not already know?" asks Norfolk in his cool tones.

I pace before his desk in agitation. "We must do something. We must help her. She believes you can rescue her somehow. She has so much faith in you. You must do something."

Norfolk shrugs. "I think we're a little beyond that, Mary. It's over." He sighs and rubs his face. "Two nieces. Two of the stupidest girls to ever be spawned from Howard loins. For God's sake."

"My lord!" I sob. "What are we going to do? We have to help her! We have to stand by her!"

Norfolk shakes his head. "There is no help for her now, Mary. You know it as well as I." He ponders me. "Do you know what he said when he found out, Mary? He requested a sword, that he might run the girl through himself." He shakes his head, a wry smile twisting his lips. "It's over, Mary. She's done."

I cover my face with my hands and run back to my little queen.

I stay with Kitty, offering what little comfort I can. The archbishop hounds her daily with interrogations. She has no idea how to answer his questions and sobs, begging for His Majesty, till

Cranmer gets so frustrated with her that he has to excuse himself. Why he should expect more from a terrified sixteen-year-old girl is beyond me.

At one point, little Kitty throws open the doors and runs from the room down the gallery, screaming, "Henry! Henry! Save me! Henry, save me!"

The guards seize her, dragging her back to the room. She throws herself onto her bed, sobbing herself sick.

"Henry . . ." she sobs. "I did love him, for as much as I could." She gasps and gulps like the child she is. "I didn't mean to hurt him. If we could just talk it over. He would understand. I know he would understand."

Unfortunately her estimation of her husband is greatly miscalculated, but no one tells her that. No one can bear to tell her anything.

"What of Uncle Thomas?" she asks me, wiping her red, puffy eyes. "Is he going to help me?"

I shake my head. "I don't know, Kitty," I say, abandoning protocol.

"Will someone send for him?" she asks, her eyes directed at me. "Will someone send for my uncle Thomas?"

No one moves.

She begins to sob harder. "I want my uncle Thomas! Please! Send for him!"

Still, no one moves.

Kitty is removed, with a handful of ladies, to Syon Abbey for more questioning. As she begins her imprisonment, Margaret Douglas is released for her own crime of loving a Howard. She is to retire at Kenninghall for a time.

I request to go with her. I can do nothing for Kitty now, and I do not want to remain at this cursed court.

Norfolk grants the request and accompanies us to my childhood home. I say good-bye to no one; not Cat Parr, not the friends I have acquired during Kitty's brief reign, not even my Cedric. I cannot bear to see anyone.

Bess waits for us there, beautiful and well looked after. Living as first lady of Kenninghall agrees with her, it seems. I want to embrace her, but wait until Norfolk takes to his bed. I am relieved to be in her arms again after all these years. At once tears begin to slide down my cheeks. Bess rubs my back as she calls for supper to be sent.

Margaret settles in her rooms.

Still I sob.

At supper we update Bess on the court and Queen Catherine. Her eyes mist over with pity.

"And your father? How is he faring?"

I shake my head. He is still in bed, thank God, and I do not want to think about him. "I do not know," I tell her. *I do not care*, I want to add, but dare not. Despite everything, I cannot voice what is undoubtedly everyone's disrespect for the man.

"Well, have a rest here," she says. "We are glad of the company, in any event."

"Rest," I say, my voice wrought with weariness. "Yes. It seems I haven't rested in . . . so very long."

Norfolk keeps to himself for the duration of his stay and I do not make any attempts at seeking him out. True respite is found when he returns to court. Margaret and I relish our friendship, and though she is in exile, I cannot imagine she would want to be anywhere else during these dark times. The news from court is not good. Culpepper has been arrested along with another young man from Kitty's Lambeth days, a music master named Henry Manox, who tried to trifle with the affectionate Kitty when she was but ten years old. How anyone could fault her for anything in this instance is something I cannot comprehend, but they do. They fault her for everything.

All of the men confess. Their judge—Norfolk, of course—announces the verdict. Guilty. They are sentenced to death accordingly. Because of Culpepper's rank as gentleman of the king's privy chamber, he is spared hanging and quartering and is beheaded at Tower Hill.

Few are spared. Even my step-grandmother is brought from her sickbed to be questioned in the Tower.

Jane Boleyn is arrested as well, for helping the queen betray her husband. As much as I try, I cannot summon any pity for her. She knew the risks. After everything she has lived through, she knew well the risks. It is no surprise that she confesses all of Kitty's misdeeds. I cannot help but hope Lady Jane dies. As evil as it may make me, she is a vile woman, a madwoman, as mad as the king ever was, and hers will be no loss.

I wait at Kenninghall, my stomach aching, my head throbbing, as I fret over Kitty's fate.

And then one February day the message comes.

I have been invited to my cousin's execution.

After all the questioning, after all the misery and pain, Kitty is not given a trial of her own. There is more than enough evidence to convict her and an act of attainder is passed against her.

My father is the one who tells her of her sentence. He convinces her to sign a statement admitting her sins and asking for forgiveness, then has guards drag her screaming and kicking onto the barge that traverses her to the Tower.

He has the grace to seem moderately troubled by this when I see him the night before her death.

"Fool to the end," he says as he stacks some papers on his desk. "She just didn't understand what was happening. No matter how many times I explained it, she just didn't understand. She thought I was there to help her, for God's sake. Fool."

"She is sixteen," I tell him. "How can you expect her to understand anything?" I swallow tears. "How can you expect her to think you would turn away from her?"

He shakes his head and turns toward the window. "You know what she said to me as they took her away? She said, 'Why don't you love me anymore, Uncle Thomas?' " He pauses. " 'Why don't you love me anymore?' " he repeats in soft tones, his voice catching. He shakes his head again. "What could I say to that?" he asks. "Fool. Such a fool . . ." He draws in a breath. "Well. I'm off."

"Off? What do you mean, *off?*" I demand.

"To Kenninghall," he answers, quite recovered. "Put a little distance between this unfortunate event and my good name. I have written the king informing him that I have taken no part in my niece's disappointing fall and beseeching his gentle heart to remember the loyalty of his friend, who has, through it all, had only his best interests at heart."

I am stunned. I wonder if he composed the letter before or after Kitty's death sentence. I shake my head, swallowing my revulsion. "But you can't just leave her. Not now."

"Do you honestly think she will derive any comfort from my presence?" he asks.

I shake my head. Words stick in my throat, words I dare not utter. There is no point.

I curtsy. "Safe journey, then, my lord," I tell him, and the insincerity of my statement causes me to cringe.

It is February 13. She has been practicing with the block, I am told. She was always the nervous type, afraid of faltering before a crowd. This is one event she wanted to perform with grace and composure.

She is led by her ladies to the platform, appearing so tiny and childlike, all curves lost in the face of her anxiety. Her chest is as flat as the child she is. She is sobbing. When she parts her lips to speak, they are trembling.

She beseeches the crowd to pray for her soul; she begs mercy for her family—the family that betrayed her, I think to myself, tears streaming down my cheeks as I clutch my brother Surrey's hand. It seems he is always present for the executions. His face is somber, however. I can at least credit him for having the courage to be here, unlike Norfolk—Norfolk, who walked away without looking back and now "rests" at Kenninghall. Then there is the king, absent once again from another of his wives' deaths. He is probably even now scouring the world for his next victim.

Kitty's ladies are holding her elbows. She can barely stand as she surveys the crowds with her wide blue eyes. She draws in a shuddering breath, finishing her speech with, "I die a queen but would rather have died the wife of Thomas Culpepper." She looks around one last time, then looks up at the sky. It is raining. She blinks against the sprinkling, then kneels in the straw, placing her tiny head on the block. "I commend my soul to God," she whispers.

And then . . .

I squeeze my eyes shut as I hear the stroke of the axe.

She is gone. Another Howard girl gone.

She is buried at the chapel of St. Peter ad Vincula in an unmarked grave, near our other ill-fated cousin, Anne.

The only justice that is served is that Jane Boleyn's execution immediately follows. Her speech is rambling and she is clearly mad, but she does confess to betraying George.

"God has permitted me to suffer this shameful doom as punishment for having contributed to my husband's death," she says, her eyes wild. "I accused him of loving in an incestuous manner his sister, Queen Anne Boleyn. For this I deserve to die."

I cannot help it. I cry for her. I hate her but I cry for her. No more do I want her to die. I do not want anyone else to die. Why can't it stop? Why can't it all just end?

Another stroke of the axe. Another life is over.

I cannot tear my eyes from the blood-soaked straw.

Surrey leads me away. "Come, now. We will go. We will go home."

I cannot hear him. I can hear nothing but the whir of the axe slashing through the air, then slicing through the bone and gristle of my Kitty. The blood . . . there is so much blood.

"I want to die, Henry," I tell him.

"No, you don't. Don't be silly," he says, dragging me away.

"I want to die," I repeat over and over again.

❧ 19 ❧

A Poet's Heart

Because there is no longer a queen, there is no longer a call for ladies-in-waiting. The court is vacant, empty. No longer does Kitty's girlish laughter flit through the halls. Now all that remains of her is an echo of a desperate scream as she ran through the gallery begging for her husband to save her.

Cedric confronts me before I retreat to Kenninghall, pulling me into our usual meeting place, the practice room.

"What is the meaning of avoiding me these past months?" he demands.

I stare at him as though he is a stranger. His handsome features and startling violet eyes do little to affect me now. I am numb. I can only see *her*. Her little head on the block . . . her pretty little mouth moving in prayer . . . I see Anne, her swanlike throat cut through with a French sword. I see nothing beyond this.

I heave a deep sigh. "What do you expect from me?" I ask in weary tones.

He grips my upper arms; his touch is gentle, however—not filled with the cruel urgency of Norfolk's. "I could have helped you," he says in soft tones, tears lighting his eyes.

I shake my head. "How on earth do you think you could have helped me? You, a lowly musician? What do you propose you could have done?"

He drops his hands, staring at me, his eyes soft with pity. "Mary, do you think I meant something political?" He shakes his head. "I know I'm nothing but a 'lowly musician' and glad am I of it, considering the luck 'better' men than I have run into at this court." He draws in a shaky breath. "I am not talking strategy or politics or manipulation. I am talking as a man to a maid. I could have been there for you to . . . to talk to, to lean on . . . Mary, why didn't you come to me?"

I shake my head again. "I am too tired for this. I am going home. There is no need of me anymore, thank God, and now I am leaving."

"You will go to him?" he asks, his voice taut with resentment. "You will exchange one cursed place for another?" Again he reaches for me, pulling me into his arms. I do not resist. "Don't go back there." He kisses the top of my head, then my cheek. His breath is hot in my ear as he whispers, "Come away with me, Mary. Marry me. We will be a family. I will give you children. Yes, it will be a far humbler existence than what you're accustomed to but—"

I pull away, gazing up into his dark face. Tears stream unchecked down my cheeks. "You know it is not possible, not as long as my lord lives."

He purses his lips. It is clear to see he has a remedy for that obstacle but is far too respectful to suggest it.

I go on. "He would see to it that you and I are made to suffer no matter where we might go; his vengeful pursuit of me would only cause you to hate me as well." I lower my eyes.

"So you will remain his." His voice is low, bearing a dangerous edge. I shiver.

"I wish you wouldn't say *his*," I say, annoyed. "You twist everything up. You rearrange my words. I am not *his*. I can belong to no one. I made a promise once, a long time ago, to my Harry. I am free to love you, Cedric, but never can I marry."

"It makes no sense!" Cedric cries, running a hand through his black curls in frustration. "Why on earth would you hold yourself to a promise you made when you were seventeen? You had no idea what you would encounter then, what you would be made to endure. If Harry had any notion—"

"Harry did have a notion," I correct him, my tone firm. "He knew far more than I ever did. He knew my lord, what he would do if he were not given control of my match."

"Still, you give him control by not making a match of your choosing," Cedric points out.

"No." I shake my head with vehemence. "Don't you see? He has control regardless. He would find ways to make me pay for my disobedience should I give myself over to you or anyone else. He would—" I cannot go on. Tears clutch my throat. "There is nothing to be done. If you do not want me, then go. Do not see me again. I do not hold you to any pledges said or unsaid." I pause, swallowing several times. "But if you do desire to see me I am receptive to it, now and again. I will be at Kenninghall. There are ways we can achieve happiness without wedding rings."

Cedric's shoulders slump. "You have had a tremendous shock in your cousin's death. You are not in your right mind. We will address this topic again when you are yourself. Good day, Lady Richmond."

With a stiff bow he retreats, leaving me alone with silent instruments, beckoning to be touched, to be made to sing.

I sit on the bench behind the virginals and sob.

I return to Kenninghall where waits a household scrambling to recreate a semblance of normalcy in the aftermath of our great family tragedy. It consists of Surrey's increasing brood, Frances de Vere, Margaret Douglas, and Bess. Of course Norfolk cannot be included in this group, though he is here. His reflections on the situation are kept to himself, and if there is any remorse or regret we will never know of it.

When not sequestered in his study, absorbed in affairs of state or whatever new scheme he is undoubtedly concocting to return to royal favor, he takes long walks or sits in the gardens, feeding the swans in the pond. He does not associate with us for the most part, though now and then he and Bess can be seen leaving each other's rooms.

Two people have taken a keen interest in Norfolk. They are Surrey's boys, Little Thomas, age six, and Little Henry, a big boy of two. In their innocence they have chosen my father as a sort of idol, and follow him about wherever he goes. Little Thomas plagues him with questions about knights and battle. Norfolk is pleased to oblige him with swashbuckling tales of glory on the field and tiltyard (stories that always include him as the hero), while Little Henry sits on his knee and repeats a word here and there.

The other children, Jane and Catherine—yes, another Catherine Howard—are as pleased to stay away from him as I am, for he criticizes them for everything from their table manners to their hair to proper facial expressions. Once I heard Jane pull her sister aside and confide that she hated her grandfather and couldn't wait for him to return to court.

Little Margaret, a babe of two months, is far too young to receive any criticisms, and remains in the care of her nurse or, whenever I can, myself. As fertile as my sister-in-law Frances has proven herself to be, she is not very maternal and is more content to gossip with Margaret than attend to her children, leaving the blessed duty of coddling my nieces and nephews to me.

At Kenninghall I also find time to write. Margaret Douglas and I pass the spring and summer composing verse. Whenever Surrey is home he finds the time to join us and at last we find some merriment. To my annoyance, he still finds ways to jab my writing style at every turn.

"I don't know why you don't say something to him," Margaret says one afternoon as we throw breadcrumbs into the pond for the swans. "He is needlessly cruel to you with his unnecessary criticisms."

I shrug. "Margaret, you know as well as I what we have suffered. I have seen my three beloved cousins beheaded. I have lost my husband. I have fought and won my meager inheritance after a great deal of grief. After all that, allowing my brother's words to bother me would be petty and vain."

"You've a better heart than I." Margaret laughs.

Whatever resentment I may feel for Surrey is replaced with pity when after returning to court, he is promptly sent to Windsor as punishment for hitting a man named John Leigh. What they disagreed about, I can only imagine. Surrey's temper is so hot it could have been over something as silly as insulting the feather in his hat.

At supper that evening Frances is in a state. "I don't know why he has to be so thoroughly disagreeable and showy," she laments. "It will bring him nothing but trouble. The king is amused by him, thank God—sees something of himself in him, he's said. But that won't last. King Henry's affections are fickle, as well we Howards know." She glares at my father.

Norfolk, who is holding Little Henry, glares back. "That will do, Lady Frances," he says in his soft tone, bouncing the toddler a bit.

"I don't know why you insist on bringing him to table, either," she continues, narrowing her eyes at Little Henry. "He should take his supper in the nursery. I'm certain you didn't allow your children to eat at table till they were at least three or four."

"Lady Frances, I said that will do." Norfolk's voice bears an edge to it, a warning Frances should heed. He takes in a breath. "My son is a smart lad, an accomplished lad. He has a bit more growing up to do, that is all. Has to rein in that—what did you call it?—*showy* side of his nature. I assure you we will have words on the subject. For now, however, it is best not to discuss his situation in front of the children."

"Yes, you certainly know what's best," says Frances. "Your *wisdom* has carried us all so far!"

The table is stunned silent. The rest of the children's heads are bowed, though Little Thomas stares at his grandfather through thick dark lashes.

"Lady Frances!" Norfolk barks. Little Henry jumps in his arms. "Excuse yourself. Your spirit is vexed and I believe you have not made a full recovery from Margaret's birth."

Frances rises with such abruptness the bench we are seated on wobbles. "Yes, I must be sure to recover! I shall recover, Lord Thomas. I will be a good wife to my celebrated husband, who comes home just long enough to make certain to get more babes on me, then leaves to cause a ruckus somewhere and land himself in detainment! Yes, I shall recover, my dear 'Father,' if only so that I might spit out more precious Howard brats to carry on this cursed line!"

In a whirl of red skirts, Frances runs from the room, sobbing.

Little Henry sniffles. "Are we cursed?"

Norfolk laughs, squeezing him to his breast. "Us?" he asks as though this is the most ridiculous assumption one could make. "Come now, everyone finish supper. We shall be merry tonight. Let's have a contest. Which lad can finish his supper first? Whoever wins shall get a prize."

Little Thomas cries, "I shall win! I am bigger than Little Henry. I shall win for certain!" He commences to shovel his supper into his mouth as though he hadn't seen food for a week. The little girls watch, appalled, knowing should they attempt the same thing Norfolk would scold them for being piggish.

After a brief silence Margaret Douglas laughs. "You know what I heard? That grandfathers are better to their grandchildren than they ever are to their own brood. It's sort of a second chance. Do you find it to be true, Lord Thomas?"

Norfolk smiles at the king's pretty niece. "I don't know about that. I've always delighted in my children."

"Have you?" she asks, tilting a brow.

I bow my head. I can still feel his hand on my neck, his belt on my back. Still my temple throbs from his fist all those years ago.

I raise my head, meeting his black eyes. "Yes, it's quite true," I tell her. "He has certainly taken a great measure of delight in me."

Margaret leans back, her expression smug.

That autumn Surrey joins my father against the Scots, who are advancing south to personally reject King Henry's invitation that King James V cast aside the Catholic faith and join the Church of England.

The day my father leaves, Little Thomas mans his own training short sword and follows him through the great hall.

"And where do you think you are going, lad?" Norfolk asks him, his tone so solicitous one would not believe he could summon it forth.

"I'm coming with you," Little Thomas informs him, his wide brown eyes earnest.

"You don't believe you're a little young for such an expedition?" Norfolk's tone is conspiratorial as he gets down on one knee, placing his hands on the child's shoulders.

Little Thomas offers a grave shake of the head. "I have to protect you, my lord."

Norfolk's lips twitch. "And why is that?"

Little Thomas pauses. "Well, sir . . . because you are quite advanced in years."

Norfolk erupts into laughter. "Yes, I suppose so. But still you cannot come along, I'm afraid, though I've no doubt you would make an excellent soldier." He casts his eyes toward the rest of us, who linger by the table. "I will give you your own mission, my dear Lord Thomas. I order you to watch over my estate while I am gone fighting the Scots. Watch after the fair ladies living here, and your little brother. Be diligent in your studies, for a good soldier must also be a learned scholar. Can you do that for me?"

Tears light the large brown eyes. "Yes, my lord. You can trust me with this task."

"Good lad," says Norfolk, ruffling the black curls and rising.

Long after his departure, Little Thomas clings to his short sword, standing outside the manor watching for intruders, and nothing we can say will coax him indoors.

During his grandfather's absence Little Thomas stands guard, circling the manor every day, short sword in hand, waiting for news from the North.

It comes soon enough.

Norfolk proves successful in the beginning, razing the borderlands with little resistance, but retreats before the battle of Solway Moss, the decisive encounter that grants England her smug victory over the Scots.

Little Thomas believes Norfolk had a part in the victory, however small, and tells him so. Coming from anyone else, these words would be interpreted as an insult, but Norfolk embraces the boy and tells him he is a very wise lad and will be a credit to the Howard name.

"I am proud to be a Howard," Little Thomas tells his idol.

"As well you should be," says Norfolk, but he is looking at me.

Norfolk returns to court for a while, which grants us a measure of peace until the spring of 1543, when he comes home with the news that the king will take a new bride, the newly widowed Catherine Parr.

I ache for my friend whose heart belongs to Tom Seymour. As misguided as that may be, he is far more preferable a pick than Henry VIII. I can only imagine how it must have been, accepting his proposal. One does not say no to a king unless it is with the express purpose of eventually saying yes, as it was for my Anne and Jane Seymour.

How she must have lamented over being free at last to marry Seymour, only to be betrothed to the portly, beady-eyed, rotting king!

It is no surprise that the king chose Catherine to be his next wife. She is comely, learned, calm, and very maternal. She will make a wonderful stepmother, and, if God grants it, mother to more bonny princes. She tolerates the king's tempers and has even tended his leg as far back as his marriage to Kitty.

The couple is married in June, and once again I am at court, attending another queen—not as lady-in-waiting, but as a friend. I pray this queen meets a better fate than her predecessors.

If she is as terrified as everyone else, she hides it well. Her face is the quintessence of composure. She dotes on her husband even as she dares to challenge him about religious reform.

As is the case with all of his brides in the beginning, His Majesty is smitten. Cat is showered with jewels and gifts.

"I do wonder if the king ever thinks it's a little eerie," says pretty Kate Brandon, the young second wife to the aged Duke of Suffolk, Charles Brandon, and close friend to the queen.

I arch a questioning brow.

"Well," she continues. "Her Majesty has received nothing but dead women's jewels." She shrugs. "With the exception of Anne of Cleves's, I suppose. Still . . . it is rather tasteless, is it not?"

I nod. I know Kate well enough to realize that despite her husband's relationship with King Henry, she can keep a confidence. I've always sympathized with Kate Brandon. She is the daughter of Maria de Salinas—honored friend and lady-in-waiting to Catherine of Aragon—and Baron Willoughby. Upon Willoughby's death, she was brought up in the Brandon household since the age of seven and betrothed to the duke's son, Henry. But when Charles Brandon's wife Mary Tudor passed, the old buzzard married her himself. He was short of funds and not only is Kate beautiful and witty, with curves to spare, she is one of the wealthiest heiresses in England. It is a move so cold and calculated I wonder if he is part Howard.

Kate knows what it is like to be trapped in a loveless marriage to an old man, and it is this, along with their shared reformist convictions, that forges her strong bond with Cat Parr.

I think of every queen I have been both cursed and pleased to serve, even my Anne and my Kitty, I find serving Cat the most rewarding. At last my dreams of serving an intelligent woman, who encourages religious debates and devotions, are realized. For hours we sit in her apartments or the gardens and discuss church reform.

She is not dramatic or flirtatious, and though she holds her own religious convictions she is not overbearing. She is most regal, and as strange as it is for a woman common born, her manner and deportment suggest she was never meant to be anything but queen.

"Look at those diamonds," says Kate, drawing me forth from my reverie.

I glance at Cat's lovely throat and shiver. I cannot seem to look at anyone's neck without an accompanying sense of dread.

"Do you remember those?" she asks me. "You should. They belonged to your cousin . . . this last one, not the first one."

I avert my eyes. My stomach churns.

Kate shivers beside me. "I know. Positively eerie."

I rise from the window seat where we were to be busy at sewing shirts for the poor, and curtsy low before the queen.

"May I be excused?" I ask.

"You're looking pale, Lady Mary," she says in a voice soothing as honey, rising to rest a hand beneath my chin and tilting my face up toward her gentle one. "I hope you are well."

"Yes, Your Grace," I answer. "Just tired."

Cat nods. "You may be dismissed, Lady Mary. Rest, my dear."

I offer another curtsy and quit the apartments, trying to stave off dark visions of little Kitty's neck encircled with diamonds, her pretty neck . . .

I am obliged to walk past the musicians' practice chambers on my way to my own rooms and stop just short of the door. I want to go in. I want to see if *he* is there. My hand trembles, then closes in a fist, ready to knock. I close my eyes and drop my arm, deciding that as Duchess of Richmond I do not have to knock. I shall walk in. If he is not happy to see me again then . . .

I do not find him behind the virginals, however. No one is here.

No one but His Majesty. His bulk is seated on the bench, the stink of his rotting leg filling the chambers with the sickeningly sweet stench of dead flesh left too long unattended. My stomach lurches. His fat bejeweled fingers are busy on the keys, plunking out a lively melody. He is a competent musician. I cannot say I have not enjoyed his compositions at times. However, his estimation of his musical talents is, like everything else he views himself accomplished at, inflated.

I begin to tremble at the sight of this large, fearsome man I can only compare to a beast. If there is anyone under God's sun I fear more than my father, it is he, this Henry VIII, this tyrant king of England.

"I—I beg your pardon, Your Majesty," I stammer, sinking into the deepest of curtsies. "I was—I was—I do not know—"

His Majesty stops playing, resting his hands on his fat thighs, the hose stretching so taut over them the material seems as though it will rip at any moment. The face he turns toward me bears a jolly expression; his smile is broad. If one did not know what he is capable of one would think him a merry old man, not a savage thing swinging on the pendulum of madness.

"Lady Richmond," he says. "Rise, dear child. Come here—

don't be shy. You are not bothering us. Come." He pats his leg and I inch forward. There is no room on the bench, and if he tries some lecherous move like pulling me onto his lap I'll run screaming to the axman for my salvation.

"We have wanted to have words with you for quite some time," he tells me in his gruff voice. "All those years ago when we had that bit of nastiness over your inheritance . . . well, you must know it was political. It had nothing to do with you personally. We always were quite fond of you and wanted to see justice served."

Justice! Now I know I am talking to a madman, as if there was ever any doubt. Justice! Justice . . . a *bit of nastiness!* If it would have served His Majesty politically to starve me to death in the Tower, in the Tower I would have starved. Justice. My head is tingling with anger.

I curtsy once more. "I—I am obliged, Your Majesty," I say in tremulous tones.

"We have always enjoyed your brother, hotheaded lad that he is," he goes on as he places his hands on the keyboard again and begins to play. "His wit and poetry amuse us mightily. How many children does he have now?"

My heart stirs at the thought of my treasured nieces and nephews. "Five, Your Majesty. Three girls and two bonny boys."

"Children are a blessing, aren't they?"

This coming from a man who declared his two daughters bastards.

"Indeed, Sire," I concur.

"A blessing you have been denied far too long," he tells me. "You should marry again, Lady Richmond. Perhaps your father and I can come up with a new match. You're a beautiful young woman." This statement is accompanied by his eyes roving my body up and down. "A beautiful and no doubt fertile young woman."

I shiver. "Th—thank you?"

He laughs. "I remember your own talent at poetry. Can you sing as well?"

I offer a slow, frightened nod.

"Then sing for me while I play," he says.

I obey, sweating and trembling and wanting this moment to end. If it were ten years ago I would have been thrilled to be in His Majesty's presence accompanying him with my voice. But then ten years ago Anne was alive. She would have been singing, too, singing and laughing and dancing. Life would have been merry. That was long before the shadow of the axe fell on the Howards.

Now I derive no joy from singing with my father-in-law, the king. I want to run. I want to be anywhere but here. As I am singing I hear the creak of the door. His Majesty stops playing and laughs.

"Ah, Cedric, my lad!" he cries as Cedric doffs his cap and offers a deep bow. "We suppose it is prudent to leave the music to the musicians. We are weary." He rises, leaning heavily on the virginals. If he collapses, the beautiful instrument is a goner. "This cursed leg . . . I must find my Cat. She will know what to do."

I curtsy.

He smiles at me, resting a heavy hand on my head. "And we have enjoyed your company immensely, little girl. We should like to be entertained by you more often."

I swallow the rising bile in my throat as His Majesty calls forth his guards, who help him from the room, staggering under his heavy frame.

When I am certain he is gone my shoulders slump as I sit on the bench, which is wet with the king's sweat. I wipe my hands on my gown in disgust.

"Well," says Cedric, his tone cool. "At last I am not looking at you across a crowded room."

I turn toward him. "I'm sorry I have not sought you out sooner."

Cedric sighs. "How are you, Mary?"

"Right now?" I ask with a nervous laugh. "Right now I am longing to bathe. Between the stink of His Majesty's leg and the fact that I've just sat on a sweat-drenched bench . . ."

" 'Sweat-drenched bench' . . . I like that," Cedric says, but he is not smiling. He takes my hand and pulls me to my feet. "Mary, I've missed you. How long has it been?"

"Well over a year now," I tell him.

He reaches out, stroking my cheek. I flinch at his gentleness. "Our parting was not a merry one," he tells me, his voice soft.

"No, it wasn't," I agree.

"Perhaps our reunion can be different," he whispers, pulling me into his arms and pressing his soft warm lips to mine. I yield to his kiss.

When we part I say, "Nothing changes for us. No matter how much time passes, nothing changes."

"No." He reaches out, stroking my hair. "It will never change." He pulls my head to his chest, wrapping his arms tight around me. I revel in the embrace. "Mary, I won't pressure you into marriage for now. I won't ask anything more of you than what you are willing to give."

"Thank you, Cedric," I whisper against his chest. "Thank you, my love."

"For now," he stipulates. "Just for now."

That is good enough for me. All I live for is now.

Cedric and I meet whenever possible. They are not the love-crazed meetings we knew when we were on progress with King Henry and Kitty. Our encounters are calmer; we share the comfort and familiarity of old friends coupled with the passion of young lovers. We talk about religion and art and poetry. We compose music. There are three things I have forbade him to discuss: marriage, politics, and Norfolk. So far he is happy to oblige.

These are happy days. What's more, they are peaceful days.

But in the summer of 1543 my father, in an attempt to stir up royal favor, declares war on England's on-again-off-again rival, France, in King Henry's name. It is around this time that I learn of the death of my cousin Mary Carey, now Stafford. She was not yet forty. I recall the last time I saw her, how she vowed that she would be the only Howard to know true happiness despite poverty and exile. I hope with all my heart that she did so.

"All of them are gone now," I lament to Norfolk one night.

He is staring at a map of France splayed out on his desk, marking it here and there, completely uninterested in my commentary.

"Anne, George." My throat catches. "And now poor Mary."

"Yes, now I suppose they hold a merry little court in Hell," quips Norfolk as he draws another line on the map. "And Jane Boleyn is probably there, too, circling about in a frenzy of lust-fueled jealousy."

I stare at him in awe, though why comments such as these coming from him should continue to surprise me I have no idea.

He sits back in his chair, waving the quill between thumb and forefinger so fast that he creates the illusion of its bending in the air.

"Still, I suppose she was the best of them," he says in soft tones. "She was very honest." He offers his bitter laugh. "King Henry's honest mistress." He pauses, staring at the quill he now holds still before him. "Fools, all of them," he says, then returns to his maps.

I blink back tears and rise, dipping into a curtsy. It is not the Anne years or the Kitty years, so there is nothing to report, no orders to carry out. There is only but to excuse myself.

"Good night, my lord," I say in weary tones.

He does not look up from his maps. I swear his shoulders are shaking in excitement over his new mission.

As I turn to leave he says, "Mary."

I turn my head toward his voice.

"Remember. We move forward. We are Howards."

"Yes," I say. "We shall always be that."

As I depart I can think of nothing that means less to me than being a Howard.

Norfolk is given the rank of lieutenant-general of the army and makes ready his campaign. By the spring of 1544 he is ready to cross the Channel.

"I wish you wouldn't go," I find myself lamenting as I behold him standing smart in his military regalia, waiting to board the ship. "War should be left to younger men."

"War is left to younger men," he says. "But it is the older men who must arrange things." His lips curve into the smile I know so well, that sardonic, lifeless smile. "Tell me you are not worried I shall meet with a cruel end in the fields of France," he says, his tone dripping with sarcasm. "No fretting, daughter. I am in finer form than most men half my age—indeed, than most men in general. I will return no worse for wear."

Though he is inarguably in fine form for a man of his years I cannot, despite everything, fight the tears filling my eyes. "Be safe," I whisper as I embrace him.

His arms remain at his sides. He reaches up and pats my back in an impatient gesture and I pull away. I remember the time Kitty threw herself in his arms in a hug of complete adulation, how unaware she was of his response. I recall how she looked up at him, how she told him she loved him, how her eyes were lit with such innocent affection. Never at any time had the thought entered her pretty head that this man she loved would be her ultimate betrayer. No, he was her uncle and she loved him. She told him she loved him so he must love her in return.

I know better than this. I have learned.

Norfolk goes to sea and I am left behind.

The tears dissipate. With Norfolk gone, I will be afforded very little supervision . . .

From May to July, Cedric and I are free to do as we please. We are subtle, we are inconspicuous, but we are together. Almost every night we find time to meet and be merry. I am lighthearted. I am, I tell him, at my personal best.

But in July the king announces he will go to lay siege on Boulogne himself and calls Cedric to be at his side.

"Why on earth do they need a musician in battle?" I cry in rage. "So that you might sing his praises while he is running Frenchmen through?"

Cedric laughs. "I suppose so. You know I am not only an amusing and handsome court musician," he says, "but a historian of sorts. You see, no matter the end result of this battle, it is my duty to make King Henry sound noble and heroic—even if he does not return home victorious. A bard can make anyone a hero. And that is what I must do."

"It is bloody ridiculous," I curse, tears warming my eyes. "I do not understand. Everything King Henry touches he taints, just like his rotten leg. He taints love, his perception of love, and in his misery taints others' happiness as well. He has taken everyone I have ever loved away from me. And if he takes you . . ." Though my tone sounds threatening there is obviously nothing I can do about it. But there is some measure of satisfaction to be found in unleashing my venom.

I take Cedric in my arms. "You must be safe. You must promise not to get too close to . . . anything. Promise you'll return to me!"

He nods. "I will return to you, Mary," he vows, his tone grave. "I will always return to you."

My heart is racing. I feel as Harry must have when extracting his promise from me. I pray that it is not so difficult a thing for Cedric to uphold.

My father takes Montreuil, desperately short of munitions and provisions. I expect he does not even know what the king wants him to do next. While I await news of his and the king's success or failure on the battlefield, I think about Her Majesty, who has been appointed queen regent in King Henry's absence, an honor she is proving most capable of. She signs proclamations, manages the Scottish threat, and oversees the finances of the king's campaign. She hears petitions, devotes time to charitable works, and, in what I believe to be most important to her, offers her heart to her step-children.

She takes the time to acquaint herself better with her step-daughters, both of whom she brings to court from time to time. Her gentle mother's heart influences the king to at last show his girl children the favor they long for, and despite the fact that Lady Mary is very unlikely to swerve from Catholicism, she seems to respect her reformist stepmother very much.

In the nursery I see my cousin Elizabeth, who bears my Anne's sharp black eyes and keen wit, along with the Tudor red hair and hot temper. I am delighted. She is a beautiful little girl I cannot restrain from embracing upon seeing her again.

"Oh, my dearest cousin!" I cry when I am allowed into her presence at last.

She pulls away, assessing me with those grave dark eyes, wary. "You are Lady Richmond?"

I nod. "Oh, my lady, I am so pleased to see you again."

"Your father is the Duke of Norfolk," she comments, her tone laced with disgust. "He saw my mother to the sword."

I am stunned by the words. I cannot deny it. I will not defend him. I blink several times. I can only imagine the wicked tales this poor girl has heard, and perhaps has been forced to hear, about her mother. That Norfolk should be counted as one of her enemies is not something undeserved.

"You must excuse me if I am not beset with joy at acquainting myself with your branch of the family," she says. Her tone rings of one years older than her eleven. I hear she is so advanced in her studies, with her affinity for languages and keen comprehension of logic, that her tutors are constantly looking for new ways to challenge her.

I do not know what to say for a moment. My eyes stray to her hands. They are white, dainty as lilies, her fingers slim and tapering. The hands of a young lady. "You have the Howard hands," I begin feebly. I do not know if it is wise to stay this course, but do. "Your mother . . . she also had fine hands. Everyone admired them."

Lady Elizabeth seems to be torn between offering up something sarcastic in reply or deigning to kindness. Her face softens. "Did you know my mother very well?" she asks, and her voice is sweeter, more childlike.

I nod. It is a relief to be able to talk about Anne with the king away. "I loved her very well," I tell her. I swallow several times. "Oh, my lady, there's so much I want to say to you. So much about your mother . . . how she could come into a room and light it up with her smile . . . how the moonlight could catch her hair through a window and make it shimmer almost blue." Tears clutch my throat. "She always knew just what to say. She could charm anyone. Nothing sordid, my lady, but disarming. She could be sweet but fiery. She was the most determined woman I have ever known." My words are coming out in a rush, as though I fear the king will burst through the door of the nursery any moment and imprison me in the Tower for daring to speak favorably of the witch. "Her views about religion were similar to those of Her

Majesty, your stepmother. In fact, your stepmother even served her at one time."

"She mentioned that," Lady Elizabeth says. She smiles. It is her mother's smile, a smile possessing its own radiance, a smile to melt a heart. "She is not afraid to talk about her to me, either. She always tells me whatever she can. But she did not know her as you did." Tears fill her eyes but she blinks them away with ferocity, determined to maintain her composure. There is no doubt that this ability to summon hardness is a trait attributed to both the Howards and the Tudors. "I am disposed to like you, cousin Mary. We shall meet from time to time and discuss my mother or whatever else strikes my fancy. I have been told you are most learned as well. I should like to have discourse with you on many subjects, if you are keen for such a thing."

I nod, impressed with the child's regal bearing and mastery of emotion.

"Her Majesty will convince the king to reinstate me as princess," she continues. "I will reclaim my birthright."

Again I nod but cannot contain a laugh. "Indeed, you are a Howard, my lady."

Lady Elizabeth joins me with a girlish giggle of her own. "I am not certain that is a name I should associate myself with too closely."

I shake my head. "Oh, no, my lady. Once a Howard, always a Howard."

She regards me with Anne's eyes. "You are wrong, Lady Mary. There is only one name that matters in this world. Let all the Howards, the Brandons, the Seymours, let them all fall by the wayside with their beloved names. In the end only one name matters." She pauses. "'Your Majesty.' It is a name I shall endeavor to attain."

I sink into a curtsy, taking one of her pretty hands in my own.

At this moment there is nothing in my life I am more certain of than the fact that someday, somehow, this child before me with Anne Boleyn's eyes *will* attain that name.

This girl will show us all. She, the witch's daughter; she, a

Howard girl. She will be queen; what's more, she will hold her throne.

My heart surges with triumph, as though I have been allowed a glimpse into the eternal. It is a glimpse that affords me hope in a world where hope seems so very out of reach.

While the men are away I occupy myself with writing verse.

It is then that at last I unlock my little silver casket of treasures and pull out the unfinished "O Happy Dames."

As I ponder it I think of Cedric—he and any man who has left a maid yearning for his arms. I think of the sea. I think of longing. I think of the fruitlessness of ambition and war. I think of the Howards, of poor Margaret Douglas, of the king's wronged queens, of Norfolk's strange ménage with my mother and Bess, of Cedric. Of me. Emotions capture me, swirling about my mind and heart like the currents of the Channel. I take up the quill.

And I write. One word, then another, till the phrases flow with the urgent determination of a river's unswerving course. I write and write . . .

When it is done I lock it away in the little casket. I have vowed not to read it over, not even once, until he comes home. Until he returns to me, as promised.

With instruction from the king being vague at best, Norfolk is left in Montreuil, his resources dwindling and the overall morale low. Eventually the siege is raised and once Boulogne is garrisoned, he retreats to Calais. Word has it that the king was ill-pleased with my lord and I can only imagine the shameless groveling Norfolk reduced himself to in order to remain in favor.

Norfolk, to his credit, has the presence of mind to realize what is attainable in this battle. He knows, just as I do, that England is not capable of holding a city such as Boulogne for very long.

In October they return home, two old men weary of war and disappointment.

I do not embrace Norfolk when I see him. I can no longer bear the feel of his rigid body, a body so abhorrent of any physical demonstrations of love, in my arms. Instead I remain cool and composed, offering a perfect curtsy.

"My lord," I say in smooth tones. "I am pleased to see you home and safe."

He nods, then smiles as though pleased with my formal greeting. "It was a farce, Mary," he tells me. "But we will not speak of it. The topic disgusts me." He proffers his arm and I take it; together we proceed into Hampton Court. Despite his loss, his manner is light. Indeed, he is as close to cheerful as I have ever seen him.

The king, conversely, is not light of manner. Instead of praising his worthy queen for her competent management of his kingdom in his absence, he accuses her of trying to usurp the throne, and this because she dared don a purple cloak!

Our Catherine Parr is a clever one, however; as much as I love her, it is still a bit begrudgingly that I admit she is far cleverer than my Anne. She soothes the snarling lion, placing his putrid leg on her lap, changing his soiled linens and massaging ointment into the oozing sore with her own hands. He moans and cries when she rubs his leg while speaking sweet and low, telling him what he most wants to hear, that he is the most glorious king to ever sit the throne of England and no one could dare replace him, least of all her, lowly woman that she is. She only did as her master and sovereign bid her; guarded his kingdom with her heart, relying on the support of her regency council and the earls of Hertford and Shrewsbury to guide her so that she could make decisions that may best please her good husband. She tells him of his accomplished children, the studious Mary, the vivacious and intelligent Elizabeth, and fiery young Edward.

They are the right words, the right things.

For the first time, England may have a queen who can manage Henry VIII.

When the king is settled he orders an entertainment. Perhaps wine and song will help blot out the French failure. The king, once such a lively dancer, sits at the high table beside the queen, resting his leg in her lap. She is a master of composure. How she can resist the urge to vomit right there is a feat which should earn her some kind of additional title.

She sits, a font of dignity, rubbing her husband's leg while he devours every delicacy in sight. I watch him stuff food into his doughy face. Crumbs gather at the corners of his mouth, wine spills from his cup down his chin as he gulps it. Remnants of food remain on his face while he converses with courtiers too terrorized to point out any flaw of His Majesty's countenance to him.

I avert my eyes from the high table to the group of musicians, hoping to find Cedric among them. I have not seen him since the army's return.

I do not know who to ask. Should I inquire of Norfolk he would scoff at me, then suspect my fallen virtue and do God knows what. There is only one person to approach. As much as I detest the thought I advance to the high table, offering a curtsy to Their Majesties.

The stench of his leg assaults my nostrils and I make a strident but subtle effort to breathe through my mouth, though I swear I can almost taste that sickeningly sweet smell. It catches in my throat and I swallow the urge to gag.

If I still believed in saints I should count Queen Catherine Parr among them.

"Lady Richmond." The king's voice is merry. His cheeks and nose are red. His eyes, once one of his comeliest features, are little blue beads bugging out of his fat. "And fairer than ever. Look at her, Cat—is she not fair?"

Cat offers her gentle smile. "That she is, Your Majesty," she agrees, her voice like warm butter.

"I am so grateful Your Majesty has returned home safe to the kingdom that loves him," I tell him, forcing sincerity into my tone.

"Bless you, child," he says.

He has not bidden me to rise so I remain almost on one knee. "Your Majesty," I begin. "I . . . was wondering if I might make an inquiry."

"Speak, child," he says, gesturing with his plump hand for me to go on.

"I . . ." I draw in a breath. My cheeks are hot. I cast my eyes to my silver slippers, hoping that I appear modest. "The musician . . . Master Dane . . . he accompanied you to France." I dare look up.

His Majesty is taking in a long draught of his wine. I continue. "I was wondering, Sire, did Master Dane return to Cornwall to see his children after your return? I have not seen him at court."

King Henry's face is drawn. "Yes, Master Dane. Good musician." He clears his throat. "A fine lad." He breaks off a piece of cheese and begins to nibble as he speaks. "No, my dear lady, he is not in Cornwall. Master Dane took ill on the voyage home." Cheese is spewing forth as he talks. A piece lands on my pearl-encrusted bodice. I stare down at it, my gut churning. I cannot hear what His Majesty is saying. All I see are the specks of cheese landing on my pretty dress . . . "cast into the Channel . . ." he is saying.

Cast into the Channel.

He is not saying it. He did not say it. He is making a royal pig of himself, spitting and spewing. He is not talking about death. He did not say the body of his treasured musician was thrown into the sea like a sack of rotted apples.

I rise from my curtsy. Like a fool, I stand before him. My head is tingling. The color has drained from Cat's face as she regards me, her eyes filled with tears. Her hand has ceased its tender ministrations on the royal leg.

"I beg your pardon, Your Majesty." My voice is drawn forth in a tremulous whisper. "I did not hear you, I think."

He nods as though repeating himself is not a problem. "Yes, he took quite ill. An imbalance of the humors of the bowels. He was cast into the sea." He sighs. "Such a loss. The lad was a wonderful lute player. Quite able at the virginals as well. And his voice! Ah, he is no doubt a credit to the angelic choir."

I curtsy, bowing my head. I cannot look at his massive countenance, nor Cat's pity-filled eyes. "I thank you, Sire."

I must leave. I will not remain at court. Cat is sympathetic. She will dismiss me. I will go to Kenninghall. I will help Frances with the children. Yes, that is what I will do. For how is it to remain where *we* have been? Everything at this palace calls to mind his image. And now . . . now . . .

I must leave this room. One foot, then the other. I can walk. I can walk . . .

I turn but am stopped by the king's thunderous voice.

"Lady Richmond, I do not recall—are you a dancer?" he asks.

Am I a dancer . . . My love is dead . . . Am I a dancer? I will never see him again. Never hear him sing or strum his lute. Never hear him play a new composition on the virginals. Never hear him laugh. Never be challenged by him. I will never kiss him, never hold him, never . . . He is gone . . . cast into the sea. The sea . . .

My hands have gone numb. My face is numb. "Wh—what?" I breathe.

"Look how flustered she is!" he cries in delight. "We asked, do you dance?"

I stand before him. I cannot move. Can I dance? Have I ever danced?

I shake my head. "I do not know if my dancing will please you, Sire," I manage to say.

"Let us be the judge of that. Do a pretty turn for me now, will you?" he urges.

I remain rooted in place. I stare at him as though he is some creature from a faerie tale, some ogre . . . He will eat me or kill me and there is nothing I can do about it.

"Your Majesty," Cat says in her sweet tone, "if I may beg your indulgence. Poor Lady Richmond complained of a headache earlier this evening and hoped to take to her bed. Perhaps she can dance for Your Grace on another occasion?"

The king's eyes take me in, assessing me from the tips of my slippers to the hood on my head. "All right, then, another time." He grunts in disappointment. "How old are you now, Lady Mary?"

"Twenty-five, Sire," I answer. Twenty-five years behind me and God knows how many left. How much more must I endure now, now that I am completely and utterly alone?

"Twenty-five," he says. "A good age. Past the age of being silly . . . A woman's twenties are her prime, wouldn't you say, Cat?"

Cat nods. "Indeed, Sire."

He strokes his crumb-ridden beard. "We will continue to consider a match."

I curtsy. I must not look at him. If I keep looking at him I will vomit.

"You are dismissed, Lady Richmond," he says. "Do feel better. We will expect that dance."

I flee his presence, brushing past Norfolk, who tries to seize hold of my arm. I wrest free of his grasp and run to my rooms, where I throw myself on my bed, my lonely bed, and sob.

He would have taken me away, he said. He would have taken me away. But me, foolish me . . .

I sob until my throat is raw.

In the morning I am summoned to Norfolk's privy chamber. He is holding a wooden box with intricate carvings of roses on it.

I am so overwrought from sobbing that every move is sluggish. It is as if I am wading through water, pulled down by my heavy skirts. If I wade deep enough the water will take me to its breast where waits my love . . .

I curtsy, resisting the urge to sink to the floor and remain there in a defeated heap.

"In the event of Cedric Dane's death," he begins, causing my heart to leap, "an event that apparently has transpired, it was his express wish that you have this."

I rise, accepting the box with trembling hands. I do not think to ask how he came about acquiring it.

"I took the liberty of going through it," he tells me. "To make certain it contained nothing harmful to your reputation."

I open it, taking in a breath. It is a necklace, the pendant of which bears the perfect likeness of his face. The signature of the artist is tiny but decipherable. Hans Holbein. I close my eyes a moment, warding off fresh tears for kind Master Holbein, also in the next world, almost two years dead of the plague.

Holbein, whom I always felt a special rapport with, saw beauty in my Cedric. Indeed it is his eyes that are most pronounced in the miniature, those startling violet eyes that behold me even now with an expression of the utmost compassion and love.

At last I allow my tears to stream down my cheeks unchecked. "Where did you get this?" I breathe.

"Intercepted the messenger," he confesses.

"W—was there anything else?" I ask. "Anything at all?"

He shakes his head as I look at the empty box as though if I squint hard enough something will appear.

"You tell me the truth, my lord?" I ask him.

"I tell you the truth, Mary," he says. What is it I detect in his voice? Is it, could it be, that there is a note of gentleness there? Sympathy?

"You knew," I state in awe.

He nods.

"And yet you did nothing." I clutch the miniature. "Why?"

"It could come to nothing," he says.

His one gift to me, then. A season of happiness.

I regard the miniature a long moment, memorizing every feature of Cedric's likeness, wishing that somehow it would spring forth into life. I hold it up to the light; the chain twirls about a moment, and something catches my eye. Three words, not in Holbein's hand, are painted on the back:

Sing. Write. Pray.

I clutch the pendant to my breast. All those years ago, after the loss of my Anne, when I had to hide my grief, he told me . . . he told me . . .

I begin to sob.

Norfolk wraps his arm about my shoulders and ushers me to the window.

"Look outside, Mary," he says in his soft voice. "Look out at the beautiful new day."

I cannot see through the tears.

"Look, Mary," Norfolk urges. "It is misting today. Look, child. Do you see it? Look to the river. Do you see the rainbow touching the water?"

I blink away my tears. Indeed, a rainbow, vibrant in its color, stretches down from the heavens to greet her soul's mate, the water, the river . . . the river that leads to the sea.

It is both of them, then. Harry and Cedric together, guiding me, blessing me . . .

I lean my head on Norfolk's shoulder and watch it fade into the mist.

*   *   *

He never asks, not once, about Cedric, though he does deny my request to leave court. I do not fight him. It takes too much energy. Instead I drift through the days in a sort of altered state. The queen, in her unending capacity for understanding, lets me be. She asks for nothing. She makes no demands of me. She is surrounded by her own circle of devoted ladies, Kate Brandon being a favorite of both Majesties, and they provide all the entertainment and stimulation she needs. I am content to circle on the fringes.

I am not suited to this life anymore.

While the world presses on about me I am still, suspended in reverie. I think of Cedric, of what was and what can never be. I think of his children. Do any of them have violet eyes? Do they sing and play the lute? Do they know what a wonderful man their father was?

I would not know how to find them. The Danes of Cornwall are as the magical island of Avalon, hidden by an enchanted mist. I have no access to their world.

Tears stain my pillow every night. Pain grips my belly. He is gone. I am empty. He is gone.

And yet, I think to myself, I would not have married him. He would have returned and still I would have adhered to my convictions. I would never have thought that I would have to live without him completely . . . I believed he would always be there. I am a fool and curse myself for mourning my foolishness as much as I mourn Cedric.

Cat and Kate Brandon discuss religious reforms, hoping to arouse some sort of response from me, but all I can do is smile and add a few comments here and there. Though I am still passionate about the topic, I am too numb to be an enthusiastic contributor. It takes too much effort to offer an opinion on anything; regardless of my thoughts the world will go on, and all will occur as God ordains, whether He be Catholic or Protestant. I imagine our battle over the issue is very minute to Him.

Christmastide comes and goes and there is little joy to be found, both because of the great French failure and, for me, my personal loss. It is a bitter winter. I spend many a night snuggled deep in my blankets, blowing on my fingers to keep warm.

Lent arrives, and we pass our guilt-ridden days of deprivation until at last it yields itself to Easter, and Easter to spring. A year ago Cedric and I were making merry at this court. We had no life plan; we lived for the present, and how we enjoyed every moment! Now that present is swallowed by the past, and I cannot wrench free of it.

A strange distraction arrives in the form of Anne Ayscough, a young reformer who has more courage than I could ever hope to possess. Not only has she defied her husband by not taking on his surname when they married, but she has dared preach against transubstantiation, the idea that the Host transforms into the Body of Christ during the sacrament of Holy Communion. It is a belief I happen to agree with, but unfortunately am not brave enough to discuss. Anne has even distributed banned Protestant books, which gets her arrested, to my queen's regret. Upon Her Majesty's intervention she is released, only to be arrested later that year for her passionate Protestant sermons.

This time there is no mercy. Sir Kingston, the same constable of the Tower of London who observed my Anne in her last days, is ordered to put the girl on the rack. Though he obeys, her courage and eloquence under duress touch him so that he cannot continue torturing her, leaving Lord Chancellor Wriothesley, a ruthless man who hides behind a handsome façade and dear friend of my father, to proceed in his stead. The girl is tortured until she is so crippled she is without use of her limbs. I am certain they hoped she would name more Protestants, perhaps even people such as the queen, Kate Brandon, maybe even me. But this Anne is stubborn, as devout as any martyr, and implicates no one.

The court follows the saga on tenterhooks. Indeed, we had all known Anne. She was an intimate of Cat, and though I sometimes feared her fervor, I admired her. But now is not the time to be sympathetic to those who are considered heretics. Gardiner is far too eager to have any and all arrested for daring to disagree with the king. There does not seem to be a day that goes by when we do not hear of so-and-so burned at the stake or hanged or beheaded for some unfathomably inane crime. Even Archbishop Cranmer is not exempt. To his great fortune the king gave him his signet ring to safeguard him should such an instance arise, and it was that which saved him from the stake when his reformist sympathies were called into question.

The king's insatiable thirst for blood causes my belly to churn and ache in despair.

I take pleasure in neither court life nor the passing holidays and feast days, nor do I delight in the entertainments and the tourneys. The small things, all the small things that Harry told me to derive joy in, are too far out of reach at this place where fear and distrust reign supreme.

I begin to fret for the queen. It is no secret that Cat leans toward the New Faith; she is even authoring a book some could call heretical, though in my mind I can see nothing about the devotional that does not support Scriptures. In any event, she is brave to compose such a thing; I cannot imagine how she can continue to hold herself with such an extreme measure of composure.

It is now summer, 1546. Cedric has been gone almost two years, and yet every day I expect to see him among the musicians, strumming his lute or playing the virginals. I walk past the practice room, that room so filled with bittersweet memories, that room I have dared not enter, not once, since his death; and still, still I hope to hear his voice on the other side of the door.

It is more than I can bear.

What I need, I decide at last, is a visit to Mother. She may not be the warmest of women but she is wise. Perhaps she can offer me some respite. And if she cannot, there is always Bess, sweet Bess.

When I approach Norfolk with the request I find he is not alone. Bishop Gardiner is there, seated at his breakfast table eating comfits. He is an altogether unattractive man, his features so non-descript I could not tell anyone what he looked like had I seen him but a minute ago. He is not as fat as the king, but round enough to huff about and look uncomfortable wherever he is.

The two men seem to be involved in an intense conversation. Norfolk is leaning forward, elbows on the table, hands folded in front of his mouth as he watches Gardiner touch almost every dessert on the plate before choosing one.

Fear grips me. Gardiner is one of the men to evoke the most anxiety about the court, so eager is he to catch someone in a heretical moment.

"You must leave this to me," Norfolk is telling him in low tones. "You must trust that I know how to handle the delicacy of this matter."

I offer a deep curtsy, deciding it best to speak before learning whatever dark task Norfolk is handling now. "The guards did not tell me you were entertaining, my lord," I say, forcing a smile. "I shall come back—"

Gardiner shifts his weight, leaning back in his chair, licking his fingers and smiling. "No, no. Not at all, my dear. Won't you sit with us?"

I inch forward and sit in the chair the bishop has pulled out for me.

"There's a good girl," says Gardiner. "Tell us how you are faring, Lady Richmond."

"Well, Your Grace," I answer, casting my eyes to my folded hands.

"You attend Her Majesty?" he asks me.

"Yes, sir," I answer.

"And how find you the queen?"

What is he asking? If he means *is she with child?* I can assure him the answer is no. If he is asking how I like her I can assure him I like her well. I love her well. Somehow, with gut-churning certainty, I know he is not asking me either of these questions.

I offer a little laugh and a shrug, which appears girlish and silly. "She is very fine, sir," I tell him. A diplomatic response, I think.

Gardiner smiles. "And you enjoy court life?"

"It is a busy place, my lord," I say.

"Your father tells me you are a most learned girl," Gardiner continues. "He says you are a pretty dancer and gifted poet and musician as well."

Why would Norfolk discuss me with Gardiner? To what purpose? My heart is pounding. I turn my eyes to Norfolk, who is staring at the plate of comfits. He swallows and reaches out, suspending his hand over one, then another, until settling on a sugared almond. He stares at it a moment, as though pondering the possible consequences of ingesting something Gardiner has touched with his slick fingertips, then shrugs and pops it in his mouth. He chews thoughtfully, avoiding my eyes the entire time.

"I thank my father for his gracious compliments," I say, returning my eyes to the bishop.

Gardiner rises. "Well, I suppose," he says, nodding to Norfolk, "I best leave you with your daughter. We shall continue our discussion later."

Norfolk has risen as well. He bows. "Indeed, I shall look forward to it. Good day."

Gardiner bows to me, taking my hand and offering upon it a slimy kiss. "You have a most beautiful daughter, Thomas," he tells him.

I shudder.

"Yes," says Norfolk in affable tones. "I am quite aware."

When Gardiner takes his leave I wipe my hand unceremoniously on my gown.

"I was hoping for a word, my lord," I begin.

"Let's have something to eat," Norfolk suggests, his tone as sugared as the comfits. I look about the room to see if there is still someone present he is trying to impress. There is no one. "I, for one, am ravenous. What shall we have?" He strolls to the window. "I shall have something brought up. Anything you like."

He returns to the table and sits, leaning his hands on his thighs so his elbows jut out in opposite directions. "Well, what will it be?"

I blink back a strange onset of tears. I do not know from where this kindness comes, but am grateful for it. I am too tired for suspicion and resentment. I welcome his attentions. "Whatever you like, my lord," I say with a small smile.

Norfolk steps out of the room to exchange a few words with a servant, then returns to sit beside me. He stares at the sweets. "The man ruined it for me. Touched them all."

I laugh. "It is tasteless, my lord," I say. "But I am sure they are fine."

Norfolk pushes the plate away. "Now." He leans forward. "What did you want to discuss with me?"

As he is in such a rare mood of amicability I am loathe to bring up anything that will upset him. I proceed with caution. "I . . . I was hoping to visit"—I swallow—"I was hoping to visit Mother. I have not seen her in . . . many years."

Norfolk waves a hand. "No. There is too much at hand here."

"If I may ask, my lord, why am I needed? I hold no office; I am of very little import to anyone. Why may I not be allowed a brief sabbatical?" I implore.

Norfolk pauses. "You are of more import than you realize," he says, then slaps a hand on the table. "Now! Closed subject. Moving on." He rises and removes my hood, running a hand through my hair. "Still a mess, I see," he says. "That will have to change. You must attend yourself better, Mary, for God's sake." He rounds the chair, standing above me, placing his fingers beneath my chin and tilting my face up toward his. It is amazing how well preserved the man is; he appears the same to me now as he did when I was but three. "Still, I must say, you are rather attractive." He taps my nose. "Though you have my nose." He laughs, and I recall that it is one of the first observations Anne made when I joined her court sixteen years and a lifetime ago. I swallow tears. "You and your brother both. Not quite as comely on a girl, however, but I wouldn't say it detracts."

He pulls me up by the hands, holding them as he surveys me from head to foot. "And you are of fine figure." He nods as though concurring with some ghostly counterpart. "Perhaps not as . . . rounded as Kate Brandon, but a fine figure, nonetheless."

I do not know what to say. I have no idea what the aim of his assessment is.

"You're every bit as intelligent as Lady Suffolk," he says, referring to Kate by her title. "Tell me, Mary, do you have any sort of"—he cocks his head as he searches for the words—"any sort of sense of humor?"

I am taken aback by the unusual question. Not only because it is strange a man such as Norfolk should concern himself with anything humorous, but because . . . because if one knows someone as he should his own child, he would never have to ask such a thing.

I furrow my brow, annoyed by the question. "I suppose so, though I can't imagine I can conjure up a sample of it at this precise moment."

Norfolk erupts into laughter at this, as though this statement in itself is all the sample he needs.

He drops my hands when the food arrives and watches the servant lay the table; set forth are trays of brawn, eels, cheese, bread, and tarts. Norfolk pulls my chair out and I sit. He follows suit and folds his hands, bowing his head.

"Lord, bless this bounty for that which we are about to receive," he says. "Bless my king and country, my family"—he raises his eyes—"my Mary. In Lord Jesus's holy name I pray, amen."

I am startled by the prayer, not so much by the incongruity of Norfolk communing with God; though he is a convinced Catholic and author of a great many religious papers, I still cannot consider him a devout man. No, it is that today his praying flows forth in such a relaxed manner that I am taken aback by its . . . *normalcy*. It may be the most ordinary few moments of my life, and that in itself is of the highest irregularity.

Norfolk begins to eat with an enthusiasm he has never shown for food before, at least not in my presence. As far as memory stretches he has been a man of moderation, never taking more than what he needed. Now he is helping himself to generous portions of our little feast.

"I am thinking," he says. "It is time you had some new gowns." He studies me a moment. "How is it you never have new gowns made for yourself?" He breaks off a piece of bread and sops it up in some juice from the boar. "We shall have made for you a gown of Tudor green. How would that be? Green to bring out your eyes. They will shine like emeralds."

The knot in my chest, the knot that has strangled me for almost two years, begins to relax as I search his black eyes. They seem a little less hard, a little less calculating. I want so to believe this is our new start, that in his old age he is becoming more . . . what is the word? Mellow.

I take a tentative bite of some bread, the thing least likely to upset my stomach. "Yes," I say. "I would love some new gowns."

"New hoods, too," he says, reaching out to catch my chin between thumb and forefinger. "And slippers—whatever you need." He strokes my chin a moment before dropping his hand. "It's time you were made merry. Far past time."

I stare at him in awe. I cannot believe what I am hearing. Can it be Norfolk has the desire to see me happy just for the sake of seeing me happy? My heart pounds. No. He wants something; he has to want something. Nothing can ever be this simple; nothing can ever be without some kind of attached expectation.

But I want to believe it. I want to believe it so badly I am willing to smother memories of my Anne before the swordsman and sweet Kitty at the block, memories of Norfolk's hand in their deaths and in my life. I will smother the memories like a fire; they will be snuffed out of my mind.

I will not think of the state of this mad court, of the word *heresy*, nor of the countless burnings and murders. I will instead yield to the innocence I yearn for, the thought that Norfolk is my loving father and wants to see me happy at last; the thought that he is sorry, that he is making up for our tumultuous past. The thought that he loves me.

I slide from my chair to the floor, kneeling before him and taking his hands. "Oh, my dearest lord," I whisper through tears. I lean up and wrap my arms about his neck. "Whatever has come before, know I love you so."

Norfolk detangles my arms from him, taking my hands. "Now, now. Eat. It will get cold."

I swallow my humiliation. I should have known. How could I not have known that he is incapable of expressing tenderness? As I gaze at him I wonder how he interacts with Bess. Is she alone the woman he has reserved the softer part of himself for? Has he ever told her he loves her?

Has he ever told anyone?

I sit, focusing on our little midday feast, and choose to revel in what is unsaid. I willingly suspend my disbelief. For now there are no ulterior motives or deceit. There is just us. For now that must be enough.

It is all I have.

As promised the dressmakers visit me and I am measured for five new gowns; one is Tudor green with resplendent sleeves, though not as long as was in fashion in Anne's day. These sleeves are slashed, revealing ivory lace beneath. The bodice is a richer shade of green velvet and the kirtle is ivory lace to match the undersleeves. The other gowns are of my choosing; one is a summery orange, another is yellow with white lace accents, yet another is a sweet shade of pale blue. The last gown is pink, my favorite as it reminds me of my youth, and it, too, has slashed sleeves, revealing fitted sleeves beneath. Each gown comes with matching slippers and hoods, and when they are finished I cannot contain a little squeal of delight as I finger the beautiful materials.

Norfolk actually seeks me out to visit me. He seats me next to him at entertainments, and dances with me before Their Majesties. The skirts of my Tudor green gown swirl about my ankles, creating a pleasant breeze at my feet.

"At last, Lady Richmond dances!" cries His Majesty, resting his putrid leg on his wife's lap. She is rubbing it idly, her brow furrowed. I wonder if she is stifling a gag or if I have displeased her somehow.

The king leans forward, resting an elbow on his swollen knee, stroking his graying beard with his fingers. I almost pity the man—once the consummate athlete, now reduced to being carted about in a wheeled chair. I am even told he has a special mechanism that hoists him in and out of bed. I shiver as I think of his bed and of poor Cat, who has to share it with him.

"We recall dancing with my lady at your wedding," the king says. "Do you remember, Norfolk?"

Norfolk nods. I note he is trembling. Perhaps at his age dancing tires him.

"She is far lovelier now than then, twirling about in her pretty green gown," observes His Majesty. "Wouldn't you agree, Cat?"

"Lady Richmond is a beautiful young woman," says the queen. "And a lady of high morals."

"A trait to be admired," says the king. "That and prudent silence," he adds gruffly.

As I do not know to what he is referring I offer a feeble smile.

"Do dance some more, Lady Richmond," the king orders. "It brings this old soul pleasure."

I stare at Norfolk. He nods and I do a few turns by myself, recalling all of the days spent in Anne's apartments, practicing our steps. She was an incomparable dancer. Never before or since have I seen one to match her abilities.

I am light on my feet, however, and lose myself in the fast-paced music—until, that is, an image of Cedric floats before me. He stares at me from some other plane, his expression somber. I stumble a bit, then cease dancing altogether, blinking the image away. What was it I saw in his eyes? Warning? Disappointment? Both? I begin to tremble uncontrollably.

The queen laughs. "Your Majesty, you must realize Lady Richmond is a modest girl. I am certain your attentions frighten her."

The king leans forward. "Is that right?" He laughs. "Do we frighten you?" His beady eyes sparkle as though he is delighted at the prospect. If such a thing excites him it would please him to know the whole of England sits in terror of him.

Flustered, I blink and nod, then shake my head, dipping into a curtsy. "I apologize, Your Majesty. It's just that I do not dance very much anymore."

He leans back, roaring with laughter. "You are a splendid little dancer. Next time you dance for us, you must do so as though no one is watching."

"Yes, Your Majesty." I curtsy again.

Norfolk catches my arm and smiles at the king, then escorts me away from the royal couple.

"Interesting," he says. "I did not give you enough credit. You are a smart girl, Mary." He squeezes my arm. "Faltering in your steps has endeared you to him more than perfection."

My heart begins to pound. No . . . no . . .

I will not believe it. I will not believe it. Norfolk is just surprised at the king's reaction, that is all. He is glad the king did not chastise me.

That is what I will believe. It is nice, living like this, believing what I tell myself to believe. I can convince myself that I am almost stupid, and there is a certain amount of contentment to be found in stupidity.

The next day I receive a collar of sapphires from His Majesty's messenger. My hands are trembling so that I can barely grasp the thing. I stare at the messenger, wondering if he can read my terror. What do I do? Give them back? I cannot return a gift from the king. Anne did that. Jane did that. And that piqued his interest.

"You may . . . you may thank His Majesty for the lovely gift," I tell the messenger. He lingers a moment, as though I should add something more. When it is at last clear that I will not, he departs.

The newly widowed Kate Brandon is with me when I receive the present and she laughs.

"We are a sorry lot, Lady Mary," she tells me. "He sent me some of Queen Catherine—Catherine Howard's jewels as well. It seems we are rivals."

"You can have him," I say before I have the presence of mind to contain myself; then, knowing the words to be treasonous, clamp my mouth shut, unable to keep my tears at bay. They pave slick trails down my cheeks.

Kate rushes toward me and takes my upper arms, squeezing gently. "Not to worry, Lady Mary. We are together on this. If you think I would betray my queen and give myself to that—that—" She shrugs. "I will tell you this much: I have been married to one old man. I will not give myself to another, least of all . . ." She trails off, knowing that I am well aware of the thought's direction.

"What do we do, Lady Suffolk?" I ask her.

"Devise some sort of escape plan," she advises. "Meantime, wait and see what develops. The king loves Queen Catherine. This may well be one of his phases."

Long after Kate takes her leave I stand alone by the window, staring at the necklace, trembling.

I cannot do this. I cannot wait around to see what develops. I will not be wife number seven to that monster, a man who was once my own father-in-law!

I crumple the necklace in my hand. My knuckles are white.

It is so clear to me now; yet was it not always clear to me? But I, foolish, foolish Mary, did not want to believe it. I almost would rather have died than believe it . . .

I draw myself up, squaring my shoulders as I saw my Anne do on so many occasions when she herself battled the one who raised her up and helped cast her down, the one who is always behind everything.

Norfolk.

Gardiner is with him again, but smiles and excuses himself when I enter.

I stare at Norfolk; his expression is arranged into one of calculated patience, as though I am an annoyance to be tolerated a little bit more . . . a little bit more until, to his relief, I will go away. Then he can relax his face and assume the same disinterested expression he has worn as long as memory serves.

I throw the sapphires on his desk. "A gift from the king," I spit. I remind myself to remain calm. I will not yield to the hysterics of years past. The more composed I am the better I will translate.

Norfolk lays the necklace across one exquisite hand and ogles them. "How lovely of His Majesty to think of you," he says in an offhand manner.

"Indeed?" I retort. "This man who has in effect killed all of his wives in one way or another, save Her current Majesty." My face is burning. "This man who was my *father-in-law*—and to think Harry and I had to get a dispensation for consanguinity!—this man who sees fit to torture and murder and make miserable all who dare to love him . . . yes, this man holds me in some esteem now and you say it is 'lovely.' "

Norfolk draws in a breath. He sets the jewels aside. "Yes, I say it is lovely. And you would be a fool to think otherwise. Think, Mary, think! For God's sake, the king is not a well man . . . you have only but to seize your opportunity, wait a bit longer, and then—then—" His black eyes sparkle with excitement.

The whole sordid plot is sickeningly clear. I am trembling. My temple is throbbing. I shake my head in horror.

"Mary, you must realize how vital it is for us to uphold the tenets of His Majesty's faith," he tells me. "Once little Edward is on the throne, the Seymours will try to sway the country to the New Faith. It is our responsibility to see that that does not happen."

"And if I—say I became queen—support the Seymours and their New Faith?" I seethe. "Then what will you do? Find a way to dispose of me, no doubt—that is, if King Henry does not do so first!" I cover my mouth with my hand, shaking my head again. "You do not care about upholding any sort of faith. I know well you would have the country Catholic again and allied with the pope as well. His Majesty's reforms, aside from granting you the lands from the monasteries he destroyed, mean almost less to you than I do."

Norfolk has the grace to flinch at this.

"This, my dear *Norfolk,* is about you," I hiss. "Like everything else. You didn't gain enough from your nieces' unfortunate reigns—have we but to imagine what is in store for you should your own daughter sit the throne!"

He emits a frustrated sigh. "How else are the Howards to rise again? From whom else are we to gain back our right?"

I back away from him in sheer horror. "Our . . . right?" I breathe. "Our right? Since when has the throne been *our right?*" For the first time in my life I have the pleasure of looking at him as he has always looked at me; as though he is a fool. "When did you actually decide we had a *right* to the throne? Long before little Kitty stumbled to the block, I am sure. And long before you sentenced our Anne to her death. How quick you were to betray them when the king decided the throne was no longer the Howards' *right!*" I shake my head in a frenzy. "The throne will belong to a

Howard someday, I promise you, but not the one you think. No. It will belong to the greatest of us, the greatest Howard to ever live. Lady Elizabeth." I force my voice to simulate calmness as Norfolk waves away the mention of the king's younger daughter's possible rise to power as sheer fantasy. "Put your store in her," I urge. "Toss aside whatever ill-fated scheme you are concocting. Attempting to seize your *right* will only lead to your downfall and I assure you I will have nothing to do with it."

I tilt my head back, revealing my white throat. "Where does the axe fall? Here?" I take Norfolk's hand, placing it on the back of my neck. "It comes through about here, wouldn't you say?" I bring his hand around to the front, making sure that he feels the strong pulse. I swallow a painful lump. "What will you do then, my lord? Will you retreat to the country for my execution? Or will you stand there and watch, as you did Anne?" At last I allow my tears to fall. "Can you tell me truly that you wish to see me in my cousin's place, after all we have seen?" I shake my head. "If so, then mark my words, my lord: I would rather slit my own throat than take part in such villainy!"

Norfolk wrenches his hand free. "Really?" he asks, his voice calm.

"Yes," I answer, matching his composure. "Really."

"All right, then." In his abrupt manner, Norfolk retrieves his dagger from its sheath and throws it at my feet. "Do it."

In an instant I have lost complete control over this conversation. Once again, perhaps as it has always been, it is all in Norfolk's masterful hands. Nothing I have said has had any effect on him. How could I have dared hope to reach him? I am nothing to him; I have always been nothing to him. Nothing but a means to his glorious end.

I stare at the little instrument of death for a long moment, making no move to retrieve it. Surely even Norfolk does not expect that I would dare take my life out of God's hands, and in front of him.

My heart leaps when, with a sound between growl and agonized cry, Norfolk takes hold of my shoulders and throws me to the floor, using his own weight to pin me down. He is a slight man but I am smaller yet, and am crushed beneath him. I cannot breathe. I gasp in terror. One hand grips my chin, the tips of his fingers bearing into my flesh so hard I know they will leave bruises. His face is inches from mine. I hear the whir of metal slice through air, feel the cool point of his dagger at my throat.

"Do it, Mary," he tells me. "You would rather slit your own throat than be queen of England? Then do it. Right now."

I blink several times. I must keep my wits. I must stay calm. With great effort I force my breathing to become regular.

His breath is hot on my face. *"Do it."*

I squeeze my eyes shut a long moment, reopening them in the vain hope that the scene has changed, that this is not real. But the horrifying reality is staring me in the face, large black eyes narrowed, nostrils flaring.

I make no move toward the dagger. I cannot. As much as I may want to, I cannot end my life. I do not know if this makes me a coward. I do not know what distinguishes bravery from cowardice any longer. I have not known for a very long time.

"What's this—you cannot do it?" he taunts. "You cannot do it, Mary?"

"No!" I cry. "I cannot do it!"

He presses the dagger hard against my throat. It bites into my flesh like the prick of a thick needle. I am too horrified to gasp.

"Then I shall!" Norfolk hisses. "Do you think I cannot?" he asks me. "I am a soldier, Mary. I have lived by executing orders that would turn your insides out. Do you know what I have done in my life? I have raped women, then run them through after taking my pleasure. I savored every execution after the Pilgrimage of Grace; in fact I mourned that I could not kill more of the bastard rebels! I have burned down houses with entire families inside. The screams of the children, Mary, still ring in my ears." His voice has lost its calm. For the first time he registers real emotion. He speaks in a frenzied rush, his words tumbling out in an agitated tangent. "And, yes, I looked into Anne Boleyn's eyes as I pronounced her death sentence. I watched the soldiers drag sweet little Kitty away to the Tower, screaming and writhing in their arms. I watched all this and *I have no regrets*. I do my duty by king, country—but first, always, by the Howards—by me." He offers up a strangled laugh. "When it is no longer prudent to ally myself to one, I ally myself to another. I have ended more lives with my sword and my word than I can even count. One more, especially one as insignificant as yours, will make no difference to me."

I swallow my tears of horror as I listen to his list of evils. I keep my eyes focused on his face, his tormented face. His chest is heaving as he draws his tears inward, just as I have for the entirety of my life. I take a breath, daring to bring my trembling hand to his cheek where a tear has managed to escape. I wipe it away with my thumb. I stroke his hair. I trace his jawline, then run my fingers across his trembling lips. I do not understand either of us at this moment. We have been swallowed up in wickedness and deceit for so long that neither of us knows who we are, what to do. Like hawks freed from their mews we soar, viewing a ravaged land without boundaries. Love is twisted. It is as though the insanity of King Henry has seeped into our minds and souls like water from a poisoned well.

I pull him to me, pressing my lips to his in what I wish to convey as . . . what? A kiss of forgiveness? Or is it that I am grasping vainly for one moment of love between us, any kind of love? I try to convey chastity, holiness. But we are as far from those two things as people can be. The kiss translates nothing but our mutual urgency and confusion.

I pull away. Tears pave icy trails down my temples, pooling on his priceless rug. "Do your duty, then," I tell him, keeping my voice soft and low. As I speak I continue to trace his face, every feature; memorizing the man who is both my mortal enemy and greatest love. "And I will watch you," I whisper. Each word is deliberate. "I will not close my eyes, nor utter a sound. I will watch you, my father, run me through. As my life ebbs away I will gaze into your face until at last I am swallowed up in the blackness of your eyes, those eyes I first looked into with so much trust when you held me aloft as a wee babe. And when I am dead, then you will close them." I draw in a shuddering breath. "I forgive you and pray for your vexed soul. You are a tortured creature and I pity you. But you are my father and have all of my respect." I pause, waiting for him to move or speak. "You may commence," I say at last.

Norfolk presses the blade to my neck. Then, with a slight whimper, throws it from him. It lands on the other side of the room with a clank. He collapses on top of me, emitting wracking, broken sobs. Whether it is because he has failed in carrying out something he has said he would do without compunction, or because he actually regrets his actions, I do not know. I will never know.

I wrap my arms about him, drawing in a deep breath. His heart races against mine.

And I am alive.

True to my word, I have disengaged myself from any plot concerning the removal of our current queen. If Norfolk bears any regret over our last encounter, he shows it in his avoidance of me. No more am I sought out at meals and entertainments. No more does he parade me before His Majesty. No more does he see me alone.

It seems I may have won this battle.

I am not fool enough to believe he and Gardiner have ceased in their plotting altogether, however; if a woman cannot be procured to take Cat's place, they will find another way to undo her, and that way is so easy for them that it is a marvel they even bothered with me at all.

For that way is heresy.

I hear them, Gardiner and Norfolk, discussing it in his privy chamber one late night when I thought I might reach out to him, but prudently decided against it in favor of eavesdropping. The guards do not suspect me, little Mary Fitzroy, to be anything but his stupid, devoted daughter, waiting in his presence chamber for a word. It is so easy it frightens me; indeed, I am unaccustomed to things going so well.

It only takes two words, threaded together with Gardiner's malicious chuckle: "Queen Catherine . . . heretic."

It is enough for me. I excuse myself, telling the guards I will come back another time as the hour is late and I am tired.

There is no chance I will find sleep. I lie awake until the next day, when I take it upon myself to warn Her Majesty about it as we are reading in her apartments. Her household has dwindled somewhat, I have noticed. Not as many ladies flock to her as they used to. The silence of her apartments echoes of unhappy times when other queens were abandoned at the end of their reigns. I shiver at the memories.

"Your Majesty, may I see you in private?" I ask, a strange sense of panic gripping me at once.

Noting the urgency in my tone, the queen rises, setting her book aside and ushering me into her adjoining bedchamber.

"What is it, Lady Richmond?" Her tone is guarded. She does not trust me anymore, I realize. But then to trust a Howard is a foolish thing and this Queen Catherine is far from foolish.

I swallow tears. "You must know, Your Majesty . . . you must know—" I wring my hands. "A plot is being wrought against you. I do not know the exact nature of it except to say that I believe they hope to have you arrested for heresy."

Cat laughs. "Of course they do," she says. "It was only a matter of time. It is Gardiner, of course."

I nod. "Yes."

"And Norfolk?"

I hesitate. My heart is pounding. I want to—God knows I want to—but I will not. I will not implicate him. "No . . . I do not believe he is involved."

Cat cups my cheek with her hand. "God bless your devotion, child, misguided though it may be. You are still loyal enough to me to be worthy of my regard." Tears light her eyes. "I was certain . . ." She averts her head.

"Your Majesty?"

She sighs. "You know, Lady Mary, when I watched you dance that night in your beautiful green gown I thought . . ." She returns her eyes to me. "I thought I was looking upon the next queen of England."

I shiver. "Never, Your Majesty," I reassure her with vehemence, clasping her hands in mine. "Never."

Cat draws me into an embrace. "God bless you, little Mary," she whispers.

I cannot thank her. I cannot speak past the tears rising in my throat.

Wasn't it my Anne who always called me little Mary?

My brother Henry, Lord Surrey, has returned to court after a visit to France. He is in fine form, as outspoken as ever, but this is a trait I decide to excuse, knowing we are all lacking in one way or another and are very unlikely to change. Instead I find I am thrilled to see him, and exchange with him a long embrace, hoping that despite our past, relations might be mended between us.

Surrey does not seem to hold any grudges. It is a happy reunion. In his presence I forget for the briefest of moments the tension of this court, the fear I have on my queen's behalf, the regret that twists my gut whenever I think of my father. Now there is only my dear brother, and I concentrate on him. He updates me on Frances and the children and entertains me with his poetry, inquiring as to whether I have composed any.

"There is one," I tell him. My heart is pounding. It is a poem I thought never to share with another soul. But this man, this great poet, my lord brother, is of my blood. Perhaps in finding one person to share my innermost being with, I will begin to heal from what has seemed to be a wound as persistent and festering as the king's rotting leg.

Surrey and I sit alone in the gardens. I have retrieved my little silver casket of treasures, reading him one poem, then another, till at last I arrive at my opus. Surrey wraps his arm about me in a manner so casual and filled with familiarity that tears sting my eyes.

I lean my head on his shoulder and begin to read "O Happy Dames." As I read I think of my Cedric, how much he loved the first verse, how he was denied hearing the rest. How it was one of his only requests that I finish that poem. I think of the melody he set to it. I think of the sea, my love's watery grave . . .

"O happy dames that may embrace
The fruit of your delight;
Help to bewail the woeful case,
And eke the heavy plight,
Of me, that wonted to rejoice
The fortune of my pleasant choice:
Good ladies! help me to fill my mourning voice.

"In ship freight with remembrance
Of thoughts and pleasures past,
He sails that hath in governance
My life while it will last;
With scalding sighs, for lack of gale,
Furthering his hope, that is his sail,
Toward me, the sweet port of his avail.

"Alas! How oft in dreams I see
Those eyes that were my food;
Which sometime so delighted me,
That yet they do me good:
Wherewith I wake with his return,
Whose absent flame did make me burn:
But when I find the lack, Lord! How I mourn.

"When other lovers in arms across,
Rejoice their chief delight;
Drowned in tears, to mourn my loss,
I stand the bitter night
In my window, where I may see
Before the winds how the clouds flee:
Lo! What a mariner love hath made of me.

"And in green waves when the salt flood
Doth rise by rage of wind;
A thousand fancies in that mood
Assail my restless mind.

Alas! Now drencheth my sweet foe,
That with the spoil of my heart did go,
And left me; but, alas! why did he so?

"And when the seas wax calm again,
To chase from me annoy,
My doubtful hope doth cause me plain;
So dread cuts off my joy.
Thus is my wealth mingled with woe:
And of each thought a doubt doth grow;
Now he comes! Will he come? alas! No, no!"

At the poem's conclusion we sit in silence. Tears stream unchecked down my cheeks. I had never read the poem after its completion. I was unaware at the time I had written it that I had all but prophesied such things as Cedric's death before, or perhaps, as it was occurring. I am stunned.

Surrey takes the poem from my limp hands and reads it over to himself. He then places it in the little casket and wraps his arm about me again, holding me tight.

We say nothing. There is nothing to be said. Somehow I know that I have impressed Surrey, that at long last he finds me a worthy peer, and that is enough for me.

I do not realize until the middle of the night that when Surrey and I parted company I had left the casket behind. Oh, well. Not to worry. I am certain he has not forgotten it.

Indeed, he has not forgotten it. When I overhear courtiers discussing Surrey's haunting and tragic new poem, "Complaint of the Absence of Her Lover Being Upon the Sea" I begin to tremble with rage.

"Have you heard the poem?" I ask Kate Brandon, my face burning.

"What poem?" Kate asks. "Oh, yes, your brother's. I think I did."

"How does it begin, do you recall?" I ask, trying to remain calm.

Kate shrugs. " 'O happy dames . . .' " She cocks her pretty head.

"Really, I don't excel at memorizing poetry. But it is quite good if one can't find enough things to be depressed about at this court."

O happy dames . . . O happy dames . . . I choke back a sob and excuse myself.

What is there to be done now? Everyone knows Surrey is The Poet; King Henry designated the epithet upon him himself. He is so proficient and skilled in it that there is no doubt it is his calling. I am an amateur, a dabbler at best. No one would believe that it was I, not Surrey, who composed it.

No one would believe now that the renamed "O Happy Dames" is something that I wrote with passion, love, and longing. That "O Happy Dames" was my heart's pride.

I seek out Surrey in despair. I may have lost all credibility, but I will not lose out on the chance to confront my brother.

He is found in the gardens, arguing with another courtier about something. I do not pay heed. I seize his arm.

"My lord! I will have words with you," I say in firm tones.

Surrey laughs. "Excuse me," he tells the receptacle of his tirade. "My sister sees fit to be rude."

The other man is thrilled to escape Surrey and bows toward me with a smile before making quick strides in the opposite direction.

I have not relinquished his arm. "My lord," I ask, only now allowing tears to fill my voice. "How could you?"

"To what do you refer?" he asks me, brown eyes wide with feigned innocence.

I shake my head. "Oh, you are Norfolk's son," I breathe in horror. "My silver casket, the casket with the poems you stole. If I cannot have the credit for my work, at least return me my property."

"Oh, that," he says. "I'm sorry, Mare," he says. "Really, I am. It's just that you forgot the casket and I was reading it over again when someone asked what it was and . . . well, they assumed it was one of my compositions. I would have said something, but once they started attributing it to me, well, it sort of took on a life of its own. And you must admit, the writing is rather like mine. You must admire my style," he adds with a smile that is meant, I am sure, to disarm me.

I do not acknowledge the last statement. "Yes, it must have been an extremely difficult situation to extricate yourself from," I say, my tone oozing with the famous Howard sarcasm. "How do you bear it?" I shake my head. "Take the poem. God knows I have lost everything else. I give it to you, Surrey. I did not write it for the world; I do not write for any praise or adulation. I write for myself. The poem will bear your name but I know the truth. I will always know the truth. And you cannot take that away from me."

"Mary, listen. I'll tell them—I'll tell them—"

"It doesn't matter what you tell them," I spit. "The damage is done. Take it. It is my gift to you, dear brother. But the rest, the casket. I want it back."

"It will be returned, my lady," he replies, his tone thick with an emotion I do not care to analyze.

Later that evening, as I am preparing for bed, a messenger delivers my little silver casket.

Everything is there.

Everything but "O Happy Dames."

The court is rife with too many other intrigues for me to remain caught up in my own petty resentments. So I let it go. I let go of "O Happy Dames." I let go of my anger toward Surrey, and with it all feeling toward him as well. If I cannot extricate myself in full from Norfolk, at least I can from my brother, whose impact on my life is far more peripheral.

Now is no time to think of anyone but the queen.

Queen Catherine proves herself to be cleverer than anyone has ever given her credit for. She soothes His Majesty's suspicions with a word; all of her religious debates, she tells him, indeed anything she may have said or did to upset him, why, it was all to serve as a distraction from his bothersome leg. He rewards her with his signet ring, the ring he had given Cranmer to save him if he were unable to.

It is on 13 July when they come for her. She is sitting in the gardens with His Majesty, quite reconciled, when Lord Chancellor Wriothesley and forty guards throw open the gates to arrest her.

King Henry struggles to his feet, crying, "Knave! Knave, beast, and fool!"

Poor Wriothesley, as much as I detest him, must have been scared witless. I am certain it was prearranged that Her Majesty was to be arrested for heresy while taking her leisure with the king in the gardens, but King Henry, ever the role player, wanted to act the part of hero and neglected to tell his lord chancellor that plans had changed.

And so, upon the presentation of His Majesty's signet ring and a strident objection from the king against Queen Catherine's arrest, she is saved.

Saved!

I can breathe.

But only for three days. Only until Anne Ayscough and John Lascelles, the man who accused poor Kitty of her adulteries at Lambeth, are burned at the stake at Smithfield. Anne was so weak and crippled from her months of torture that she had to be carried to the stake and chained to it in order to keep her body upright.

I pray that her death was quick. Even Master Lascelles did not deserve such a death, whatever hand he may have had in Kitty's fate. No man is fit to judge another, and as much as I mourn my little cousin I cannot harden my heart against this tragedy.

No, there is no breathing at this court of Henry VIII. There is nothing to be done but count the heads that roll, sift through the ashes at Smithfield . . . oh, God, this is madness. Truly Hell cannot be much worse.

I will flee. I will go anywhere, I decide. I will do anything it takes, if only to get away. *Self-preservation, Mary* . . . Mother's words, uttered to me a lifetime ago when I could not comprehend their meaning. Now I know too well the significance of this advice and I will adhere to it.

To my surprise it is Norfolk who proposes to me my way out.

It is the first time I have been summoned to his apartments since the night I dared go against his wishes. Now, with both plots to seize power having failed, Norfolk sits behind his desk, his face drawn with weariness. He appears as any ordinary old man, an old man who stayed too long at the feast and longs for nothing more than to take to his bed.

"Sit, Mary," he says in a soft voice.

I do so without a word.

He removes his cap. His hair, once black as ravens' wings, is now streaked with silver. He leans forward, folding his arms on the desk.

"The Seymours will be in power before long," he tells me, as though this is something I have not known all along. "I am certain Edward, Queen Jane's brother, will be named regent once the little prince . . . once he . . ." He trails off. He cannot seem to finish the sentence. "In any event, it has become prudent to ally ourselves to the Seymours."

If it is no longer prudent to ally myself to one, I ally myself to another . . .

I nod, indicating for him to continue.

"We have worked out an agreement, a sort of triple alliance," he says. "Hertford and I." He refers to Edward Seymour's title. "Two of his children are to be wed to two of your brother Henry's. And you—you marry Thomas Seymour."

Tom Seymour! Tom Seymour, the supposed rapist. Tom Seymour, Cat's true love . . .

Yet was it not Surrey who told me of Seymour's dark past? I am no longer as willing to believe a word that comes out of Surrey's mouth. But, whether Seymour is a rapist or not, to marry him is to wed the man my dear friend loves. How can I do that to her?

Yet . . . yet . . . Cat married another. I cannot think of her. I cannot think of anyone else right now. It may be wise to accept the offer. Tom Seymour is good-looking, not that that should be my chief concern, but it would be nice to be married to a good-looking man. And he is a reformist . . . There could be advantages.

"Does Surrey know?" I ask.

Norfolk shakes his head. "Not yet. You are the first." He says this as though I should feel privileged.

I do not take much time to think about it. Maybe Tom Seymour will allow me to live at Sudeley Castle, away from court. I could have children of my own. The little prince is bound to come into power soon. And I do not believe the Seymours will continue King Henry's reign of terror, which is another mark in their favor.

I cannot afford to look at the matter as a girl avowed to a promise made at seventeen. I am getting older, twenty-seven already. I cannot live like this much longer. I do not want to be alone. It will not be a love match, but few matches are.

"Yes, my lord," I say, my tone hard. "I am agreeable. Tell Lord Hertford to recommence preparations for my wedding to Lord Sudeley."

Norfolk closes his eyes and draws in a deep breath, expelling it slowly. "Good girl," he says, reaching out to take my hands in his. "Good girl."

Surrey does not take the news as well as I did. Indeed he is enraged that all the arrangements were made in his absence from court, a fact I did not realize, but should have, since Norfolk's ability to juggle various plots is unrivaled.

In the long gallery at Westminster, before the whole of the court, Surrey approaches me, seizing my arms.

"Plan on marrying Seymour, do you?" he seethes. "Didn't I warn you years ago of what you'd be getting yourself into should you get into bed with that upstart?" He shakes me slightly. All eyes are upon us. "Despite this, you still contemplate marrying into that clan? You want power that badly, do you?"

"Henry—please—" In vain I try to wrest myself from his clutches.

"Whore yourself out to whom you please, Mary, but I'll be damned if any of *my* children marry into that lot!" He releases me. I have lost my balance and stumble a bit, staring at Surrey in horror. "You know," he says as he turns to walk away, "if you want power so badly, you should aim a little higher. I'm sure the king isn't abhorrent to the idea of taking on a new mistress!" He collects himself, as though taking a liking to his suggestion. "Let him congratulate you on your betrothal to Seymour and while he's at it, charm him with those feminine wiles of yours—"

"Lord Surrey!" I cry, scandalized; not only because he is speaking the words aloud and in front of the entire court, but because I barely escaped becoming the very thing he suggested.

In those few moments, with those few words, Surrey has destroyed any chance at a Howard-Seymour alliance. It is over. All over. The dreams I dared seize are gone.

I stand alone and dejected amidst a court that laughs and whispers behind their hands, all playing at being appalled, when in truth they cannot recall a humiliation so delightful in years.

❧ 20 ❧

A True Howard

There is naught to do after Surrey's outburst but keep to ourselves. I do not seek out Her Majesty, too ashamed am I now for having considered marrying the man she loves, and Norfolk avoids court altogether. I return to Kenninghall, to my mother, returned of late from Redbourne, and Bess, and try in vain to seek peace.

Peace is not ours to hold; it eludes us with the grace and speed of a butterfly.

In December we are awoken by thunderous knocking on the door. They have come for us . . . it is over. They have come for us. Visions of the block swirl before me. I blink the disturbing image away as I scramble out of bed, dressing hurriedly as the soldiers advance into the house. Before going down, Bess and Mother—my strong, certain mother—congregate with me in the hall outside my chambers.

"An unlikely faction of allies we have become," says Mother as she squeezes both Bess's and my hands. "Whatever happens, save yourselves. Remember, there comes a time when it is us or them."

Us or them. Norfolk's words. When did he say them? Was it after betraying Anne, or Kitty? Anne. Yes, it was Anne. Oh, God, I am losing my mind . . .

I choke back a sob as I take in her words. *Save myself.* Save myself for what?

We descend to the dining chambers, where wait our "guests."

They are familiar faces, all courtiers led by the strong, well-muscled John Gates, and Sir Wymond Carew.

I am trembling with fear. Bile rises in my throat.

They inform us, as they gaze around our luxurious surroundings with hunger in their eyes, that Surrey and Norfolk have been arrested. From what I am able to gather, Surrey had bragged to his friend George Blagge that no one but Norfolk was fit to serve as regent to the little prince when he came to power; a family without establishment, riding on their late sister's glory, has nothing on the Howards, whose great line can be traced back hundreds of years. Not only did Surrey brag about all that the Howards would achieve once ruling through little Edward, but it was rumored Surrey had quartered his arms with those of St. Edward the Confessor, a right reserved only for kings.

Blagge knew treason when he heard it, and presented Edward Seymour, Lord Hertford, with the information. Hertford ran with it and when the report was laid upon the royal ear in November he threw in the rumor that Surrey was also planning on kidnapping little Prince Edward until after the king's death, which would ensure the Howards' management of him when he took the throne.

Norfolk, who I can only imagine was in a panic, composed letter after letter, begging every friend he had at court for information regarding Surrey's behavior. The letters, each and every one, were intercepted.

On 1 December Surrey was arrested and detained at Lord Chancellor Wriothesley's town mansion. It must be awkward, I find myself thinking in spite of everything, for Wriothesley to detain the son of his good friend.

He did not keep him long. On 12 December Surrey was marched through the streets to the Tower of London. Some jeered him, they are happy to report, but I imagine that others with any heart watched in sadness as another of the king's victims went to meet his fate.

And Norfolk, my Norfolk, was stripped of his titles and honors that same Sunday. His golden chain signifying his rank as Knight of the Garter was seized along with his staffs of office. Gates smiles as he tells me Norfolk had the audacity to claim himself the most loyal servant the king ever had and proclaim complete mystification over his arrest. I am certain he is convinced of every word. My cheeks burn in shame for him.

After this statement, my lord was escorted to the Tower, that horrific place to where he has condemned so many himself.

I take in this information, tears of despair filling my eyes as my mind scrambles for the best way to approach this situation while keeping my own head intact. I sink to the floor on my knees, not only out of feigned respect, but because if I stand any longer I believe I will swoon.

"My good lords, I . . ." My voice catches. I swallow, keeping my head bowed. "I am constrained to love my father and brother . . . but my lord Surrey is a rash man. I will conceal nothing, but declare in writing all I can remember."

Gates spreads the parchment on the table. "Be frank, my lady, and truthful. Leave nothing out; we will know." His voice takes on a gentler tone. "And do not despair. Nothing has been decided yet."

I stare at him. Both of us know everything has long been decided. This is just a formality before they commence going through Kenninghall, seizing up whatever they can to fatten the Crown's coffers.

I hesitate. Anything I say can send Surrey to his death. Yet to lie or cover for him in any way could mean the signing of my own death warrant.

Save myself . . .

I think of my brother. Perhaps the king will be lenient toward him. King Henry loved Surrey; whenever he saw him he'd ruffle his hair and exclaim over his poetry or military prowess.

If there is anything nostalgic about the king, perhaps he will also remember that my brother was the companion of his son, my

Harry, all those years ago. How well they loved each other! How could he bear to hurt the best-loved friend of his son?

If I had the heart I would laugh at my own naïveté. This is a man who has murdered more people he claimed to love than can be counted. Why I would think he might spare Surrey, for some pretty words and a bit of sentimentality toward an illegitimate child long dead, is nothing short of ridiculous.

I can only pray. Please, God, whatever love has been lost between Surrey and me . . . Please, please spare him . . .

With a trembling hand I begin to write out my statement, prompted by Gates's persistent leading questions. Every petty incident between Surrey and me, save "O Happy Dames," is recounted, including what occurred in the long gallery when he suggested I become the king's whore. I make certain to repeat the strident sentiment that I would rather slit my throat than take part in such villainy, though I do not confess the origins of the proclamation. I will tell no one of that terrible night, not ever.

My evidence cannot have amounted to much, I am certain. After all, I didn't know much about the quartering of his arms with Edward the Confessor's. I'd never seen it personally. I am certain I came across as vindictive and paltry, but in truth I am hoping my vagueness on the matters at hand will help save both my brother and father from harm. There is nothing to be said regarding Norfolk's involvement in the "plot." All he was doing was seeking information regarding his son's arrogant and impulsive behavior. Surely he cannot be condemned for that.

Mother's testimony does little to help clear Norfolk of suspicion. She is all too happy to fling open the floodgates of dark secrets long kept hidden.

My heart swells in admiration as I watch her.

With a small smile she reveals every horrific evil.

"He can dissemble with the best of them," she says as she writes her account. "He is as amicable to a friend as he is to an enemy. A more self-serving, driven man you will not find. Nor will you ever encounter a more brutal one."

It is then she reveals Norfolk's cruel side. The beatings administered by both him and his servants, endured all these years, are brought to light at last. It is now that I learn the circumstances of my birth; that he had dragged my mother through the house by the hair while she labored with me, all this before an assemblage of servants who did nothing to save her.

His ruthlessness knows no bounds. And despite this, despite all of this, I tremble in fear for him. Despite all of this, I do not want him to come to harm.

Bess does not testify to physical violence, but reveals incriminating statements Norfolk made in the past: that my father often confided that the king was not bound to live much longer.

As we all know that statement in itself is treasonous.

We have all, it seems, stayed true to ourselves first, betraying lover, son, brother, husband, and father.

Us or them.

Bess's lands and jewelry are seized. Kenninghall is stripped of anything considered valuable, but so happy are we to have our heads that no one protests. Mother expresses little emotion one way or the other concerning the turn of events.

And I wait.

I wait out the absolute worst Christmastide of my life, as the fates of my brother and father are decided, all the while reviewing my testimony. I told them the silly names Surrey had called me in every trivial fight we ever had. I told them . . . I told them . . . What did I tell them? Oh, God . . . what is going to happen to them?

I spend the majority of the Christmas season rocking back and forth wherever I am, fretting. I interact with no one. I wait.

It is a new year: 1547. New years are when we are supposed to be filled with hope for brighter times ahead. How many New Year's Eves have I passed, wishing for that, in vain?

I am not so foolish as to wish for a bright new start now. There are none to be had for the Howards.

In the first few weeks of that year I sit in the very hall where my cousins Anne and George were condemned to their deaths. There, despite Surrey's eloquent arguments, his sentence is pronounced: he is to be hanged, drawn, and quartered at Tyburn. My brother, the brother I used to hold hands with as a child, the brother I lived with and played with and fought with, is to die.

Frances de Vere has arrived from the country for the sentencing. When it is pronounced, she screams. I clutch her hand, squeezing it hard to silence her.

"Make no sound, lest you implicate yourself as well," I tell her.

She turns helpless eyes toward me. "It's all over, isn't it?"

I nod, wrapping my arms about her, allowing her to sob against my chest.

On 19 January the court assembles at Tower Hill rather than Tyburn. The king is feeling merciful. He has decided to spare my brother the sentence in favor of a quicker death by axe.

The wind is bitter, whipping against my chapped face. My eyes are swollen and puffy from sobbing and it is an effort to keep them open. I struggle for composure as I try to catch Surrey's eye in the hopes of conveying my remorse for my part in his death. My part in his death . . . yes, in whatever small way, I have played a part in it. I have that to ponder for the rest of my life. I suppress the urge to emit a laugh as edgy and maniacal as Anne's. All my life I condemned Norfolk for playing the betrayer, and here I am, my father's daughter after all.

I stand with Frances now. At the other executions—imagine I can say that, as I have attended so many now!—I would bury my head in Surrey's shoulder and clutch his hand as I heard that sound, that sound that never really evacuates the consciousness, steel cutting through flesh and bone and muscle. Now I must be here for his wife; I must be the strong one.

I look to the Tower and wonder where Norfolk is being held. Is he watching his son draw in his last breaths? What is he thinking? Is he even now scrawling his last desperate appeals to the king to save his own skin, while cursing Surrey for bringing us to this dark place? Or does he weep for the little baby he held in his arms, now a twenty-nine-year-old man standing on a platform awaiting the fall of the axe, a young man whose only crime was being too proud, just as he was taught to be.

Surrey meets my gaze and holds it, offering a sad little smile. What is in it? Apology? Regret? I search for hatred, for anger and bitterness. There is none. I remind myself to breathe.

He kneels on the platform, placing his head on the block. I find myself wondering if it is the same block George and Kitty . . . no, I do not want to think about that.

He spreads out his arms in a gesture of supplication, commending his soul to God. I keep my eyes on the block. The axe swishes through the air, meeting with my brother's neck . . . my brother's neck . . .

I do not flinch or blink. I watch as his head is slashed from the bloody trunk and tumbles into the straw.

It is over. I draw in a shuddering breath. It is over.

Frances clings to me, burying her head in my shoulder.

"There, there," I coo in a tone so calm it is as though Norfolk is speaking through me. "We must be brave," I say. "We are Howards."

The king is failing fast, but will pull down with him as many as he can before leaving this world. No mercy is shown. On 27 January an act of attainder is passed against my father.

Norfolk is to die.

They will not let me see him . . . they will not let me say goodbye . . .

I cannot leave my bed. I lay curled up, sobbing. I have put him in this place; he is innocent, but I have betrayed him. Oh, I tried to save him but he will never see it that way. I bore witness and that is enough.

I have become everything I loathe. I killed my brother and now my father . . . my father . . .

Yet wouldn't he betray me were he in my place? There is no doubt of it. He came close to killing me once; I am certain betrayal would have been nothing to him.

But it is something to me.

I am a betrayer. I will live with this sin the rest of my life. There is no expiation for it. There is no absolution to be found.

I am a betrayer.

A true Howard.

❧ 21 ❧

Long Live the King!

He is dead! On 28 January in the year of our Lord 1547, the king, that rotting, vile, putrid mass, succumbs to his mortality at last!

The news is not announced for three days. When the bells at last begin to toll, the palace of Whitehall is in an uproar. It is real. The rumors are true. The king is dead.

I cannot imagine that many tears are shed over the loss of His Majesty. I wonder if anyone has told Norfolk and, if so, how he reacted to the news. Is he saddened at all over the loss of the man whose life was so inexorably tied to his own?

No tears are shed here. Indeed, I could dance for joy. I would congratulate Cat Parr for outliving him if I were brave enough, but refrain. Outlasting Henry VIII is such a victory that the observation is too obvious to require reiteration.

The little prince, nine-year-old Edward, is now King of England. The streets are lined with merrymakers cheering the accession of the little boy now to reign over us all.

"Long live the king!" they cry, their voices raised in jubilant chorus. "God bless and keep His little Majesty!"

Indeed, this little boy is a king who, I pray, will reign a good long time. He is a sweet child, not much loved by his father. He was so coddled, for fear some harm would come to him, that he was never allowed to prove his athletic abilities to old King Henry, which created a chasm between them. But that is in the past; the king left Edward a throne, and no more will anyone have to fret about the production of heirs, at least not for quite some time. In this regard, the king saved one last act of kindness before passing. He reinstated his daughters as princesses and placed them back in the succession. Should, God forbid, something happen to little Edward before he had children of his own, Mary would take the throne, and then my cousin Elizabeth.

It seems at last everyone has what they want. Everyone but the Howards, who have been left to scramble about on the periphery.

I wait for news of my father. Have they murdered him in secret, as went one rumor? If so, then what did they do with him? Is there no one to care for his body, to take him home and lay him to rest? Desperation seizes my heart. I am drowning in helplessness.

Edward Seymour is named lord protector of England. Called to mind are images of Surrey, insisting there would be no regent other than the great Duke of Norfolk when little Edward came to power. Oh, foolish Surrey. Would he have kept silent had he known his words would not only implicate himself as a traitor but send his beloved duke to the Tower as well?

There is no use going back. No use trying to warn a dead man of his fate. Instead I wait, as it seems I have spent the majority of my life doing.

At last, the same week the nation learns of Henry VIII's passing, I am informed that Norfolk has been spared. Tears stream down my cheeks as I thank God for allowing one member of my family to escape the executioner's axe, even if it may be the one person most deserving of it.

"We will not begin our reign with bloodshed," the little king informs me in his shrill voice. "He will remain in the Tower, as is our pleasure."

I dip into a deep curtsy before my young brother-in-law. As I regard him, I search for Henry VIII. Is there any sign of his ruthless, paranoid nature in his son? As yet I see no trace of madness in the gentle brown eyes. In fact, I like to think I see a bit of his half brother, my Harry, in him.

"Your Majesty is most merciful. Thank you and God bless you, dear Sire," I say, careful to keep my head bowed.

The king nods. I am impressed by his regal bearing. Between the queen's loving influence and the masterful governance of the Seymours, King Edward VI shows a great deal of promise.

"You are dismissed, Lady Richmond," he tells me. "And may God keep you."

I retreat from the throne room of my new sovereign and, upon leaving him, depart the life of a courtier as well.

It is a life I am most content not to return to.

Most of Norfolk's lands are seized by the Crown. He had willed them to his godson, King Edward, but his wishes were not carried out, and many of our manors are divvied up between the Seymours and other favorites in their faction. I can only imagine what Surrey would have made of that.

It does not matter so much to me. As long as I am left with some living family members I care not for landholdings.

I am certain Norfolk would not agree. Most of his lands were gained from the dissolution of monasteries or granted from the elevation of his two nieces, my beautiful cousins, to the English throne. To lose them signifies how low he has truly fallen in the eyes of the Crown.

I am sure it is this that he ponders most while sitting in the Tower. The loss of the lands, the grand manors, the *things*. I wonder, does he ever once think about the people?

In February I am permitted a visit.

I do not know how to describe walking through the Tower, that place that held captive so many members of my family. As I am led to his cell I recall the fate of my uncle Thomas, who wasted away behind these cold stone walls for the simple crime of loving Margaret Douglas. Will that be Norfolk's fate as well?

I am so nauseated I have to keep swallowing back burning bile as I look about this dismal place. I have been inside the Tower before, on numerous occasions. But I have never seen this; I saw only the grandeur of Anne's lovely remodeled apartments when she prepared for her coronation in the years of my innocence.

There is no grandeur or luxury to be found in these damp and darkened halls that carry the echoes of screaming prisoners all too well.

Before entering Norfolk's cell, the lieutenant offers me his arm. "Are you quite well, madam?" he asks in solicitous tones.

I can only stare at him. Tears strangle me. I must gather control. Norfolk would not like to see me this way. It would only annoy him. I nod. He opens the door.

The room is barren of any comforts. No wall hangings or tapestries warm the damp stone walls. There are no books to entertain my lord, not even so much as a blanket for his bed. There is nothing but a little window to let in the light.

He must have hours to spend in introspection; hours to go over a long list of what I hope to be regrets.

Norfolk's back is to me. He is staring out the window. It affords nothing but a view of a gray sky and the moat below.

I clasp my hands together in a moment of uncertainty. "My lord . . ."

No response. He does not turn toward me.

My lips quiver. There is naught to do but run to him as I always have. I embrace him from behind and lean my head on his back, sobbing. "Oh, my lord, my lord . . . what have we come to!"

He emits something like a laugh.

I pull away, turning him about by the upper arms so that he might face me at last. He stares at some fixed point above my head.

I reach up, cupping his face between my hands. "You . . . know about Henry, Lord Surrey, my lord?"

At last his eyes travel downward to meet mine. He takes my hands, lowering them from his face and placing them at my sides before taking a few steps backward.

"Yes," he says. He draws in a shuddering breath. "You know, it is strange. When I was married to the Lady Anne Plantagenet and we had our first boy . . ." His black eyes gaze beyond me into the distant planes of the past. A trace of a smile curves his lips. His eyes sparkle. "I was in my twenties, optimistic about life, as most young men that age are. My boy was my pride. He was so filled with promise, my first little Thomas. Next came Henry, the first Henry . . . I held him aloft like so." He holds out one arm, fingers splayed as though supporting a baby's fragile head. "And, you know, Mary, I just loved to look at him. He had blond hair—the softest hair, like down. His eyes were so clear, and when he looked at me . . . he would study me. Anne used to laugh at me, holding him like that, the two of us staring each other down for hours at a time." He laughs but there is no joy in it. "He was so dear." He squints at his arm as though any moment the baby will appear on it. "All I could say to Anne was, 'Look at those little feet.' " He drops his arm. His Adam's apple bobs several times before he continues. "Those . . . perfect little feet. Such an insignificant thing." He turns to the window once more. "When he died I would sit and hold his shoes and just stare at them, those . . . empty little shoes." He squares his shoulders. "Then came William. Such a solid little lad. Surely"—his voice catches—"surely nothing would happen to him. But then—then—suddenly there I was again, left with another pair of little shoes." He shakes his head in a moment of frustrated disbelief. "But I still had my little Thomas. He was thriving. We—Anne and I—we explained things as best we could. His brothers were in Heaven, you see. That was when I believed in such nonsense." He turns to regard me, his eyes hard as onyx. "Little Maggie was born, then. I didn't mind so much that she was a girl. She brought Anne delight and was a lusty little thing. But she died in my arms when she was six. They had to wrest her away from me. I . . . couldn't . . . let . . . her . . . go . . . ." His shoulders heave as he chokes back a sob.

Tears stream down my cheeks unchecked. What can I say to all this? How can I begin to grapple with the profundity of his losses?

Collecting himself, he continues. "Then little Thomas . . . oh, God, little Thomas. He followed not a year later. All of my babies—all four of them, gone by my thirty-fifth birthday. And what do I have to account for them? Little pairs of shoes.

"When Thomas went I could not stop screaming. I screamed

and screamed till my throat bled. The servants had to hold me down and force a sleeping posset down my throat." He laughs his bitter laugh. "When I awoke, he was still gone, Anne not long in following." He draws in a breath. "So you see, that is why this should be so easy for me.

"Except for one thing . . ." His face is void of calculation. It is open, bewildered as a child's; the complete picture of vulnerability. "I am thinking, despite it all, Mary, can you believe it? I am not thinking about your brother's valor on the battle field or of his poetry. I'm not thinking about Tower Hill. I am not even thinking about the stupidity and recklessness that brought me here." For a moment he opens his mouth. No words come forth. And then in a strangled voice he says, "I—I am thinking about his little baby feet." He covers his face with his hands.

"Oh, Father," I say, knowing any words uttered now are feeble at best. "Would that I could have saved you both. . . . I—I didn't know what to do. I had no counsel. I did what I thought was right. I tried to save you . . ."

He says nothing as he removes his hands, revealing a calm, cool countenance.

My shoulders slump. "There was no saving my lord Surrey. But God has seen fit to spare you, and I swear by all that's sacred I will try to get you out. I shall petition His Majesty and the Council—whomever I have to in order to secure your release." I reach out to him again, taking his cold hands in my own. He is shivering. "Oh, my dear lord, you are so cold . . ." I lead him to his bed, where we sit. I wrap my arms about him and rock back and forth, but the movement does nothing to soothe either of us. It is wrought with sorrow.

Norfolk reaches up and holds my wrist. I lean my head on his shoulder and sob. I sob for Surrey, for all of my brothers and sisters who went before, for my cousins, for the Howards' ill-fated ambition. I sob for Norfolk and all the empty pairs of shoes.

The lieutenant knocks on the door to signal that my time has expired.

I rise. Norfolk has not released my wrist.

I whisper, "I will come back to you. I will get you out. You have but to wait."

His hand slips from my wrist to my hand. He squeezes it.

I squeeze his in turn. "I—I would stay with you if I could," I tell him in vain.

His mouth twists into that bitter smile I know so well.

The lieutenant enters, offering his arm.

One last look at Norfolk and then the door is shut. I am led away.

The lieutenant sighs. "You know," he says, "I think I believe you, Lady Richmond."

"I beg your pardon?" My voice is tremulous with tears.

"You really would stay with him, wouldn't you?" He stares at me in befuddled admiration.

I blink back tears. "Yes," I tell him. Where else would I be?

"You've a great deal of heart, my lady," says the lieutenant as he shows me out.

I quit the Tower and commence to my London home, Mount-joy House, one of the few Norfolk holdings allotted us, where I proceed with the first of my petitions appealing for the freedom of Thomas Howard.

I have betrayed my family once. I must find a way to mend what can be mended.

I will not be remembered as a Jane Boleyn.

I will not be remembered as a Thomas Howard, for that matter.

I want to be remembered as the woman who with all her heart tried to hold her fragmented family together. That has to count for something.

In March my father is granted clothing and appurtenances befitting his station. Still viewed as too much of a threat to be freed, it is clear that the Seymours and their like plan on his being a long-term resident of the Tower, and it hurts no one to make him a little comfortable.

In May, with a mixture of delight and apprehension, I learn that Cat Parr has married her longtime love, the man I twice rejected,

Tom Seymour. Delight because for so long this was all she ever wanted. Delight because maybe now she can have the normal life Henry VIII denied her. Apprehension because despite Tom Seymour's looks and charm there is something about him, something shady and restless. Old rumors echo in my mind; old questions are raised. Was he a rapist?

It occurs to me that I do not want to know. My days at court have provided me with a lifetime of horrific memories, and I am more than pleased to be excluded from everyone's dark secrets.

I want to be happy for Cat. I admire her so. She has no care of the scandal she has created in marrying so soon after the king's death, halfhearted scandal though it is. Anyone surviving marriage to Henry VIII should be immediately elevated to sainthood and be privy to whatever happiness that is to be found. No, Cat's marriage is just another episode to provide the court with further gossip, and as Norfolk so accurately said, gossip is the court's sustenance.

I find myself envying Cat. She has no one to be beholden to— no parents, no overbearing siblings, no children. She controls her own fate. Perhaps it was her life my Harry wished for me, a kind of independence he could never have predicted would be so difficult in attaining.

I send her a little note of congratulations but hear nothing back. I suppose it is prudent for her not to associate with me any longer, with our history, yet I am saddened just the same. I never set out to be her rival. God above knows I never wanted the king. I never really wanted Tom, for that matter.

All I've ever wanted was a little normalcy.

Cat has been given charge of my cousin Elizabeth. Perhaps in the future I will be permitted a visit to my little princess. Cat and I will have a long talk, then. Time will have passed and put any residual tension behind us. She will have babies to show me and we will discuss the New Faith just like we used to. She will show me the book she is writing.

We will discuss common things; wonderful, common things.

Yes, someday that is how it will be. In the meantime, I will pray for her happiness and that of my dear cousin, the Princess Elizabeth. Perhaps Cat and Tom Seymour can give the child the family she was denied for so long.

That same spring Mother arrives from the country for a visit to Norfolk.

"We shall go to the Tower together," she tells me.

I stare at her in shock. At fifty she has never looked better, dressed in her deep red velvet gown, brown curls framing her strong jawline, her blue eyes fierce and alert. She is in fine figure as well, and could pass without effort for a woman ten years her junior.

I lay a hand on her arm. "Mother, with all due respect, what would make you want to see him?"

She offers her wry little smile. "There is much to be said."

It is not too often anymore that I find myself beset with curiosity, but when I accompany Mother to the Tower that day I am fidgety with it.

When the lieutenant, John Markham, shows us in, Mother maintains a cool countenance. Her back is straight, her shoulders are square, her head is held high. She is the quintessential noblewoman.

The lieutenant permits her entrance, maintaining a discreet distance since he must be present for any and all of Norfolk's conversations, lest the duke take up his habitual plotting again.

"I buried our child," she tells him. "At Framlingham."

I close my eyes as an image of the children sobbing before Surrey's tomb swims before me. Frances stands hopeless before the cold effigy of my brother, laying her hand upon its face. So much does the vision disturb me that I am swept up in a spell of dizziness. I lose my footing over nothing.

The lieutenant reaches for my arm, squeezing my elbow. "Madam?"

"I'm quite well," I assure him in hushed tones.

Norfolk stares at Mother, his expression cool as moonlight. "Well, where else would you have buried him?" His voice is thin with impatience.

As I watch him now I cannot believe he is the same man who

months ago allowed me the briefest glimpse of humanity. Watching him I wonder if I imagined the entire exchange.

Mother purses her lips. "I wanted to tell you . . ." Her blue eyes are dancing. My heart begins to pound. She clears her throat. "I wanted to tell you, my lord, that Elizabeth Holland—you remember her, I see—it seems she is to be married to a Henry Reppes."

Norfolk's face offers nothing.

My heart skips in a moment of terror, but the presence of the lieutenant assures me that no beatings will take place today. I try to contain a smile. Bess to be married! At last some joy will be afforded her after twenty years of near indenture!

"How many months have you been imprisoned, my lord?" Mother asks, her tone light with conversational amicability. "Six, is it?" She smiles. "Yes, six. Mistress Holland wastes no time."

She surveys the room: the second-rate tapestries, the sparse furnishings. "Are you quite comfortable here, my lord?" She strolls to the window, casting her eyes to the moat below. "I see you have a view. It is good to have a view. Reminds you there is still a world out there." She turns around, laying a hand on his arm. "All my prayers and sympathies are yours, my lord. Was a time I recall being locked in a tower myself, with none of the proper accoutrements. It is a most difficult adjustment. But you're a Howard. I believe you will be quite capable of adapting to any living conditions."

If I were watching from a place where they were not permitted to see my reaction, a place such as the faerie country perhaps, I believe I would have danced a little jig. Despite my love for both parents, the taste of my mother's small victory over Norfolk after his years of cruelty is indeed very sweet.

"While it has been a pleasure to have this lovely discourse with you, my lady, I am certain we all have more pressing matters to attend to," says Norfolk in response.

"Do we?" She turns to me. "Do you have anything to attend to, Mary? I certainly do not. I had hoped to spend as much time as possible with my lord, reassuring him of his family's loving support during his travails. Unless of course you were implying that—oh, how foolish of me—you must have been implying that *you* have something to attend to. What is it, my lord? You must tell me if I can be of any assistance."

"No." Norfolk clears his throat. "You have done quite enough, thank you."

"Well, then, perhaps you are right. Perhaps we should be off." She takes in a breath. "It is such a lovely day. Would that you could join us outside." She feigns a most convincing pout. "But then of course you can't go outside, not even to take in a little exercise. Such a pity."

To my complete surprise Norfolk laughs. He reaches out, taking her hand. "Ah, Elizabeth . . ." His voice is beset with a mixture of amusement and despair. "Take your delight, my dear. Take your delight while you can."

Mother cocks her head, gazing at him a long moment. She steps forward, laying a hand on his chest, running it up his shoulder then down his arm. "You're still in fine form, Thomas Howard," she says, and I swear there is affection in her tone. She leans up, bestowing the gentlest of kisses on his mouth.

Norfolk stares at her, amazed. If she had hit him he would not be more shocked.

"Good-bye," he says in soft tones.

She nods, then turns.

I offer a curtsy but my lord has already turned to the window, to his view of the big world outside.

The year 1548 offers little progress in my efforts to obtain Norfolk's release, but it does bring about a unique development regarding my late brother's children. It has been decided by good King Edward and his Council that they shall be warded to me, so that they might begin their education.

"We can think of no better place for their virtuous education," the king said, to my delight, "than with their honored aunt."

Before the Privy Council arrived at this conclusion, twelve-year-old Little Thomas had spent a lonely year in the care of Sir John Williams, treasurer of the Court of Augmentations, and was left to grieve the death of his father alone at Rycote while Sir John occupied himself in London. His sisters and brother, eight-year-old Henry, were taken into the custody of Lord Wentworth, a man who, while kind, does not have the time for four young children.

I am beset with joy. They are good children. I feel it in my soul. I look at each of them, searching for traces of my own family in them. Young Jane has my mother's fierce blue eyes and set jawline. Catherine, much like my own sister, is a beauty as most Catherines seem destined to be, with her sun-kissed blond hair and hazel eyes. Baby Margaret, a wee girl of five, is a chubby cherub with round, inquisitive brown eyes and an eager smile. Henry, sweet little Henry, is the picture of his father, with brown hair curling about his ears—so soft that I must refrain from reaching out to finger its silkiness. His sleepy brown eyes are soft and gentle but filled with awareness.

Little Thomas is the prize, however. He is the most beautiful child I have ever beheld, with his curling black hair and intense obsidian eyes, fringed with thick long lashes. His set mouth is full and rosy, his skin light olive like a little gypsy. At twelve he already boasts a fine form, and I am certain he will make some young lady a good husband.

God has placed these children in my care. By His grace there is nothing in this world I want more than to do right by them. They will learn the best of everything—everything! Latin, Greek, all the useful languages. They shall learn music and dancing. I will share with them their father's poetry and tales of his valor. I will tell them all the good things about the Howards, the good things about their cousins Anne Boleyn and Kitty Howard . . . all the good things about their illustrious grandfather, the Duke of Norfolk.

Only good things.

They are brought to my London home, Mountjoy House; a home no longer to be condemned to loneliness and isolation. And though they are acquainted with me, the move has been unsettling. They long for their mother, I imagine, and do not understand why they must be fostered out. In truth it is a fact I never agreed with either, but I do not question it.

"I am not your mother," I tell them their first night. "I will never try to replace her. But I am your aunt and your friend. I will guide you and be kind to you always. In turn I require respect and obedience. If you can adhere to these two requests I believe we shall get on quite well together."

It seems these are requests that are not too difficult for them to follow and I am treated with courtesy and, after a while, affection, which is returned in full.

At Lord Wentworth's advice I send for a former fellow of Magdalen College at Oxford, a man named John Foxe, whom I had heard of from Cat. He made quite the scandal when in 1545 he resigned his post at the college for not adhering to their strict guidelines of taking holy orders within seven years of their election; chapel attendance; and enforced celibacy. Indeed, Master Foxe even took a wife, Agnes Randall, stunning them all.

His Protestant convictions, coupled with his audacity and courage, are enough to win my admiration and I follow Wentworth's suggestion. I offer him a position as tutor for Surrey's children. I am eager to have discourse with such a learned man as he, and hope he will be a merry addition to the household.

To my delight Master Foxe accepts the position. He is an earnest man, self-contained, a picture of discipline and reserve, but despite this is quite easy to talk to. His wife, Agnes, however, is silent and difficult to engage in conversation, though I do try. When confronted with people such as her I grow intimidated and pull back, and to my dismay Agnes does not seem to mind at all. She keeps her distance, taking up residence in the apartments they have been allotted, where she sets up her home and is seen as often as a mouse in hiding. Master Foxe assures me that she is not unkind; she is just terribly frightened of meeting people and must adjust to the new living situation in her own time.

With Agnes segregating herself to the periphery, I am given more time to observe my investment. Master Foxe is as intelligent as was reputed, winning the children's respect and admiration within the first week of lessons. His soft, unassuming manner can be made firm and uncompromising, teaching them that he is not a man to be pushed or made fool of. Nothing escapes him.

The children discover they do not want to pull any pranks on him, that indeed they like him too well. Thomas adores Master Foxe and develops an excellent rapport with him; they spend hours in good-natured debate and intense philosophical discussions. Foxe enjoys introducing the children to great philosophers such as modern-day Erasmus, ancient Plato and Socrates. Under his guidance, they translate Greek and Latin; they read plays, some of which have been written by the master himself. They are taught their arithmetic and literature, military strategy and history, and as I watch their progress I find myself most pleased.

I introduce him to John Bale, a controversial allegorical playwright who sought me out upon learning of my support of the Protestant cause. The two men strike up an instant friendship and exchange their manuscripts along with other writings, and we spend many a jolly evening discussing the strides of the reformed church.

Master Foxe and I speak of many things: the children—who are the most studious, whose antics are the most amusing, another's keenness for Latin or proficiency in mathematics. We talk of religion, by and large our favorite subject. We read together. His gentle, nonjudgmental nature makes him an easy confidante.

To my dismay, Master Foxe is a handsome man, tall and lean, with wavy blond hair that falls to his shoulders in layers, and a beard to match. His eyes are blue as cornflowers and manage to convey alertness and sweetness at once. I had hoped to be above noticing such things and pray not to be swayed by it too much. Instead, I endeavor to concentrate on the beauty of his soul.

It is he who first helps me grapple with the intensity of my guilt for having sent Norfolk to the Tower and my brother to his death.

We are alone in the parlor one evening. Agnes has taken to their apartments and the children have long since dispersed, their merry voices echoing through the halls as they ready for bed.

"For one, my lady, you did not send either of them to their fates," he tells me, and though this is something I have oft heard, it does little to reassure me at first. "That was a decision made by the government of King Henry. You told the truth as you are sworn by God to do. You did nothing wrong, Lady Richmond. I pray God allows you to see that." His voice is thick with emotion, his eyes are alight with compassion. A vision of Cedric is called to mind as I gaze at him. I squeeze my eyes shut in an attempt to will it away. "God teaches us that in order to attain forgiveness we must first forgive others. Do you understand?"

"No," I tell him, feeling ignorant and helpless as a child.

"Lady Richmond, God forgives. All those who seek Him through His son, our Lord Jesus Christ, find mercy and forgiveness. He does not discriminate or exclude anyone from His grace. If God the Almighty can forgive your father for his sins, if He can forgive your brother, and even King Henry if he sought it, then he certainly can forgive you of any sin, real or imagined. Not to forgive is to insult God and hold yourself above Him. My lady, you must draw from yourself the strength to forgive."

"But I do!" I cry. "My whole life all I have ever done is forgive!"

"Indeed," says Master Foxe. "You have. You have forgiven everyone. Everyone but yourself." He reaches out, taking my hand. I study it a moment; it is strong and slim-fingered, not at all the hand I would imagine a scholar to have. It is the hand of a warrior. "Please, my lady, please forgive yourself. In truth you are the least offensive personage to be found."

I blink back tears. He averts his head, staring at the fire burning low in the hearth, disengaging his hand and moving on to other more comfortable subjects.

He is reverent of those he considers martyrs, calling to mind the tragedy of Anne Ayscough and others who have perished at the stakes of Smithfield. His intention is to write a comprehensive book on the subject, including any martyr he can think of who suffered for our Lord's sake.

"There are living martyrs as well," he tells me. "Those who go about their existence in a constant state of sacrifice without bitterness or complaint." He is silent a long moment. "Those like you, Lady Richmond."

I bow my head. He rises. "I hope you come to realize how good a woman you are, my lady," he tells me.

I blink back another onset of tears. "I thank you for your generous words," I tell him huskily. "Good night, Master Foxe."

"My lady," he says as he departs for his wife and his bed.

I sit alone, thinking of the compassion in his blue eyes.

❧ 22 ❧

The Reigate Years

To my delight, we have been invited to remove to Reigate, my uncle William's estate in Surrey, beautiful Surrey! I believe the country air will be better for the children. As it is, London bears so many memories for all of us that I am most eager for a change of scene. And so the household commences its passage to the south.

Never have I taken a more wonderful journey. Here we are, a train of loud, happy Howards. I am as excited as the children and find myself alive with animated conversation. I promise my nieces pretty new gowns, and to the boys new ponies and trips to the sea where we might play and watch the waves roll in.

We arrive at the bustling manor of Reigate, the most beautiful place I have ever seen, with its gardens and endless paths, its ponds and rolling green vistas. And the people! There are people everywhere! Servants with happy countenances go about their work as though they are actually pleased to be in their occupations. Animals—cats, dogs, and livestock—roam about as though they have as much claim to the place as their masters. Everything has an aura of welcome and I cannot help but embrace myself as I step out of the litter and gaze about.

The first person to greet us is my aunt Margaret. She is a sturdy young woman with rosy cheeks and sparkling blue eyes, her sleek flaxen hair escaping from its plait as she runs to us. She is barefoot, dressed in a simple brown gown with few adornments. She embraces the children first, fussing over each of them, though she does not extract hugs from the boys, who are far too grown-up to be mollycoddled.

When she comes to me she takes me in her arms, squeezing me as though I am a long lost sister. "Well, here we are. I'm four years your senior and yet you're to call me 'aunt'!" This is followed by an easy laugh. "A title I do hope you will dispense with!"

I laugh in turn, immediately put at ease by her outgoing nature. "I shall. I thank you for your hospitality, Aun—Margaret."

"Peggy, please," she corrects. "I do hate to be called Madge or any of those other epithets that sound so old."

Madge brings to mind my cousin Madge Shelton. A pity I do not even know what became of her. She faded away, hopefully to seek out a life that brought her more happiness than court life ever could.

I blink away unpleasant thoughts of court to smile at Peggy. "Unfortunately I have nothing to go by," I tell her. "Mary is about as plain a name as one can get."

"I'm sure we'll come up with something." She laughs again. "Nobody can escape being called some silly pet name or another here."

At which point she introduces me to her children, who are by now engaged in enthusiastic converse with their cousins.

"Hold still, will you, and try to be polite for one moment!" cries Peggy as she ushers them forward. "Charles, this is your cousin Mary. You are to be tutored with her nephews, your cousins Thomas and Henry. I do believe Tommy and Charlie are about the same age."

"Two years difference," says Charlie proudly. "I'm two years older."

Thomas does not seem to resent this much. He looks at his new cousin with adoration.

"This is Agnes, but we call her Anne," says Peggy. "Really no one should be named Agnes." At this I cast my eyes about to see if

Agnes Foxe has heard the comment, but fortunately she is nowhere in sight.

Presently, the lithe eighteen-year-old girl presented before me bows her head, but is hiding a smile. It seems she is not offended by her mother's observation but is amused.

"This is our little Mary," says Peggy, patting the head of a sturdy six-year-old girl who seems to be herself in miniature. I laugh out loud at the resemblance. "We call her Mare-Bear. And this"— she stoops down to retrieve the most delicate little creature I have ever seen—"this is our baby." Peggy's face softens as she kisses the plump cheek of her three-year-old daughter. "Our little Douglas."

I reach out, taking Douglas's hand in mine. She calls to mind an image of the dainty Kitty Howard, and as I look at her I wonder if she will resemble the late queen of England as she grows. "Douglas," I repeat, my heart swelling with such emotion I cannot speak.

Combined with my cousins there will be nine children about. Nine little voices, nine different laughs to memorize. Nine pairs of eyes and little button noses. Nine beautiful children to love . . .

"Who's that out there? Who's here?" a stern male voice calls from indoors. My heart begins to pound.

At once he appears. My jaw goes slack. He is the image of Norfolk, a young Norfolk, his black hair swept back in a ribbon, his large black eyes lit with that same fierce determination. This man wears a close-cut beard, however, which would be quite fetching were his features not arranged in a scowl.

I begin to shake.

The man is approaching me, his steps brisk and purposeful. His hands, the lovely Howard hands, are clenched at his sides. He stands before me, looking me up and down.

Tears fill my eyes.

And then the strangest thing. He bursts into laughter. "What's this? Tears?" He takes me in his arms. "Come now, I didn't scare you, did I?" He holds me tight. "I was jesting, poor dear. You've no need to fear your uncle Will," he assures me, pulling away, keeping his arms about me in the same comfortable manner his wife bears. He is a man used to doling out hugs, I realize as I look at him. Indeed, from his bright, warm smile and gentle eyes I can see that the resemblance with his oldest brother is only skin deep.

At once I begin to sob with abandon.

"I'm so sorry, my lord," I gulp. "It's just that I've never been so happy . . ."

"Look here, Peggy, and we haven't even gotten her inside yet," says Uncle Will. He taps my nose. "I think you're going to be easy to please."

I nod. "Oh, yes, my lord, I am most easy to please," I tell him. "I will be no trouble. We are so happy that you have extended your generous hospitality to us."

He hugs me again. "Now, now, we're family. And none of that 'my lord' business. It's Uncle Will to you—or, if you please, just plain Will."

"And I am Mary," I tell him. "Just plain Mary."

Just plain Mary. Right now it is the perfect thing to be.

It is endless summer at Reigate. These are the days of long walks through the gardens barefoot with Peggy, talking for hours about nothing. These are the days of riding horses with the children, watching them grow in their equestrian skills, watching them grow confident and happy. These are the days of picnics, of lying on the grass amid the daffodils and hollyhocks, staring up at the stars while Uncle Will tells stories around a little fire he has made in a stone pit that he calls a "campfire." The children roast small game upon it that they have caught hunting that day and we all take of it, exclaiming that not even at court are the pickings so good. These are the days of berries and cream, of long baths in lavender and rose water, of children's sticky hands and easy laughter.

These are the days of sitting by the pond feeding the swans, watching the sun set upon the water, thinking not of the past but of the beautiful present God has blessed me with.

These are the days of respite and growth.

* * *

Henry has received his first suit of armor. It dominates his tiny frame and the older boys tease him, but good-natured Uncle Will takes them in hand with gentleness and humor, reminding them they were all quite the same upon receiving their first suits of armor and there'll be no putting on airs at Reigate.

"Why, they say your own grandfather was so little that his first suit of armor nearly brought him to his knees, and look what a fine soldier he became!" Uncle Will tells Henry.

"He may be a fine soldier," says Little Thomas gravely, "but he still landed in the Tower."

Uncle Will does not know what to say to this. "Well, many a fellow has a turn there," he replies with a slight laugh; for indeed, what can he say? He narrowly escaped the same fate when he was accused of abetting Kitty Howard. Fortunately he was rescued by a pardon from the king. "The point is, Thomas, that what makes a man is bravery and heart, not size."

This seems to satisfy Thomas for now, and they show a little more charity toward Henry.

While the boys are coached in the arts of fencing and jousting, the girls are instructed in music, dance, embroidery, and the other feminine arts. Master Foxe maintains his position as tutor and allows the magic of Reigate to take hold of him as well. He and Agnes have been given a little cottage with a garden, and she can be seen tarrying in it every day.

She has warmed somewhat toward me. Now and then she will approach Peggy and me with a gift of flowers or vegetables from her little garden, accompanied by a shy smile.

"Perhaps she isn't as nasty as was my first impression," Peggy comments one day. Indeed, we had many chats regarding the introverted and almost snobbish nature of Agnes Foxe.

"I think she is just quite reserved," I say.

"We'll coax her into the thick of things." Peggy laughs. "No one is left behind at Reigate."

Indeed, if anyone can make her feel welcome, it is Peggy and Will Howard.

* * *

Uncle Will has built a pleasant set of swings, the seats of which are woven from strong rope and padded with thick velvet cushions. From a series of trees are suspended nine different swings for all the children, though Thomas and Charles believe swinging to be quite foppish and will take no part in it.

For Peggy and me, he has constructed a large hammock that is strung between the willows by the pond, and there he is content to lie in the grass, his head supported by a plush cushion while he pushes us for hours. The children run and play about while we lounge after supper, talking of this and that.

One evening as dusk is settling on the garden, illuminating the flowers and shrubs with its magical purple hue, Uncle Will informs us of news from court.

"It seems Tom Seymour, that rake, has been caught trifling with the Princess Elizabeth," says Uncle Will.

My heart begins to pound. "What happened?" I breathe. Elizabeth is but a fifteen-year-old girl, and though I am certain her beauty and intelligence surpass many her age, she is still fifteen, with the heart and mind of a child. No amount of intellect can compensate for the virtues of experience and maturity. A child that age is easily manipulated, and if what is rumored about Tom Seymour is true then . . . oh, God . . .

"He had the audacity to ask her for her hand in marriage before asking the queen," says Uncle Will. "You know that, don't you?"

"I'd heard that," says Peggy offhandedly.

"He did not ask permission of the king or the Regency Council or anyone. He went straight to the little princess, thinking he could cajole her into marrying him, to secure a place in the succession, no doubt."

Upstart.

I cannot breathe for anxiety as I wait for him to go on.

"But our little Elizabeth is a clever one, is she." Uncle Will's voice is filled with pride. "She is every bit her mother and father's child. She refused his offer. So Tom went to the next best thing, I suppose."

The next best thing being my poor Cat, who put so much store in Tom's affections. The next best thing is a woman who loved this selfish, driven man with all her heart, only to have it thrown back at her.

"So upon marrying the queen dowager, Seymour had access to the princess," Uncle Will continues. "Word has it he would sneak into her bedroom for a tickle now and then. The queen caught them in their flirtation and Seymour is reputed to have been most apologetic. Indeed, he claimed that it was a silly game, that the girl had an innocent fascination with him that he indulged for her sake. The queen is said to have gone along with that; she even took part in holding down Elizabeth while Seymour slashed up her pretty black mourning gown in the gardens one day. Why she did that, I have no idea. They say they were all having a bit of a romp that day. I wasn't there so am not fit to judge, I suppose."

"That sounds so unlike Cat," I say, baffled. Perhaps the situation has caused her to go a bit out of her mind. After surviving her ordeal with King Henry, only to marry a man almost as despicable, must have filled her with a terrible sense of disillusionment. I do not know how I would cope with it. Perhaps she feels Elizabeth, though an innocent young girl, is partially to blame, being that she is so lovely and witty. Perhaps she is projecting Seymour's responsibility in the unfortunate event onto the princess; far easier to believe it is all the girl's fault. Far easier to suspend one's disbelief in order to retain that brief sense of happiness just a little longer.

"What happens now?" asks Peggy, rising from our comfortable spot to stretch and pace about. Her manner is relaxed, however, as though while the story is interesting, it does not really touch her here at this place, this wondrous place of Reigate.

"Elizabeth was packed off to Cheshunt in a hurry," Uncle Will responds, continuing to rock me in the hammock. "What was the poor lady to do? Being that she's with child—"

"With child?" I interpose, excitement filling my voice. "Why, that's wonderful! Once the baby's born perhaps Seymour will put behind this foolishness and they can concentrate on being happy."

Uncle Will laughs; for the first time it is bitter, an echo of Norfolk's famous almost laugh. "Children don't solve everything. Not everyone is as easily contented as you, my dear. No, what Seymour wants is power. He wants governorship over the king's person, anything. Anything to spite his older brother for being named lord protector instead of him. No one can tell me he didn't marry the poor queen dowager as strategy and nothing more."

I didn't want to think it. But I knew. Too many years of living with the Master Strategist has shown me that men seldom are motivated by anything but ambition.

My heart aches for Cat and Elizabeth, each isolated in her own way, denied a family she could have enjoyed if only Tom Seymour had any sense of decency.

"It would be nice to think the baby could bring her a little happiness," I say wistfully.

Uncle Will laughs. "Yes," he says. "Let's pray it offers the poor lady some comfort."

Peggy clicks her tongue at the inherent tragedy of the situation and folds her arms across her ample bosom. "Well, I think I shall take to the indoors. The fresh air has exhausted me."

Uncle Will scrambles to his feet. "Coming, Mary?"

I shake my head. I am content to lie on the hammock and gaze up at the stars. I am content to thank God that I am neither Cat nor Elizabeth.

As they walk away I hear Peggy whisper to my uncle, "Really, Will, you should stay with the poor thing. She needs affection as a starving hound needs a scrap of meat. Certainly being the duke's daughter hasn't done her any favors."

My heart sinks. I do not want to be viewed as pathetic. I do not think Peggy meant anything malicious by the observation, but I am embarrassed nonetheless. Most of all because she is right.

I hear Uncle Will's footfalls as he heads toward me. The hammock sinks as his weight descends upon it, but since he bears the slight Howard frame it does not impact it much.

"Room enough for me?" he asks, merriment in his tone. There is nothing forced or sordid in it; he is as natural and easygoing around me as he is with his other children, though he is far too young to be my father.

He slides his arm beneath my neck, drawing my head toward

the crook of his shoulder, keeping one foot on the ground so that he might continue the soothing rocking motion.

"Put all the sad thoughts out of your head," he tells me. "I know our princess. She is as keen as they come. She will prevail. And the queen dowager will survive this as well. She survived Henry, didn't she?"

I nod. "Why is it that everything is to be survived and endured?" I ask, tears filling my voice. "Sometimes it seems life is nothing but a chore."

"Life," says Uncle Will, "is a chore. Our daily chore for God. As a reward we are given the joy of celebrating our victories over what we survive and endure." He holds me tight against him. "So, when performing this chore of living, do so with a light heart. There is so much joy to be found, if you look."

"Joy in the small things," I say, thinking of Harry and Cedric, of the children, of this happy place, of the pleasure I take in the learned Master Foxe and the delight I take in my uncle and aunt.

"That's right. Joy in the small things."

We are silent a long while until, very softly, he begins to sing. I join him. Our voices lift into the night.

"You sing like a little bird," he tells me. "There's your pet name. Bird."

I giggle. I have never had a pet name before.

We lie in the hammock, talking and singing.

Never before has the chore of living seemed so easy to commence.

My joy is interrupted, however, when I learn of the death of the queen dowager, my one time friend, Catherine Parr. After the birth of her daughter, Mary, on August 30 she took ill with the dreaded childbed fever, perishing on 5 September.

Cat died betrayed and brokenhearted, disillusioned and despondent.

I was never able to make things right between us. I was never able to reassure her that I had no designs on her husband. Never will we have that long talk now. Like so many things that have come to pass, there just wasn't enough time.

And what is worse—to think there can be worse—I learn that same autumn that Bess, dear Bess, has succumbed to the same fate.

Peggy shakes her head upon learning this. "It's a dangerous thing to bring a child into this world," she says in soft tones. "Not everyone is made for it."

As she says this I take measure of my nonexistent hips with my hands, recalling Norfolk's words that I was far too small to have children when I so longed to start my family. Was he right in preventing me? Would I have met with the same fate that Jane Seymour, Cat Parr, and now my dear Bess have encountered? I shiver at the thought.

There is naught to do now but to journey to the Tower, where I have decided to impart the news of Bess's death to my father in person.

By now he is allowed to walk the gallery and garden with the lieutenant, and when I arrive he has finished taking in some exercise and is lying down.

He arises upon my entrance, shaking off sleep as though ashamed to have been caught in a moment of idleness.

"Have you made any progress?" he asks me in reference to my petitions for his freedom.

I shake my head. "We must not give up hope, my lord."

He huffs in impatience.

I approach him, leading him to his bed. We sit.

"There is news," I tell him. I draw in a wavering breath, blinking back tears.

"Out with it, girl," he urges, resting his hands on his knees. I study them a moment; they have grown thinner, along with the rest of him, accentuating the delicacy of his bone structure.

I cover one hand with my own. "It is Bess Holland—Reppes, my lord," I say, forcing myself to remain calm. I concentrate on our joined hands. "She has been called to the Lord . . . after—after dying in childbirth."

Norfolk's expression is stony. He averts his head, expelling a sigh. "I don't know why she thought she was young enough to have a child to begin with," he spits.

I squeeze his hand. "She meant a great deal to you. *Please* don't pretend she didn't. She was with you for twenty years."

"She didn't hesitate to bear witness against me when called," Norfolk observes in cool tones. "I believe they even rewarded her for it, after a while. She was restored her lands and jewels, was she not?"

Frustration causes me to tremble. Here I have just informed him of the death of the one woman I believed he loved, and all he can think about is her possessions.

"I would think she took her cues from you, my lord," I tell him, disregarding the vulgar comment about her properties. "Were not we all taught by your example that it is far better to betray those closest to you when the axe is in question?"

Norfolk grunts, "Yes, you would see it like that."

I am seized by a moment of sheer rage. "After all that you have done, after all of the people you have abandoned and destroyed, you are going to begrudge her for saving herself? Do you begrudge me as well? Do you begrudge Mother?" I laugh. The sound mirrors his own; it is harsh with bitterness. "I do not need to ask that, I suppose. Your treatment of her all these years reflects your vast regard for her. My God, man, is there not one person on this earth that you love?"

Norfolk rises, crossing to the window. "Lieutenant," he says, his voice soft. "Please escort my daughter out now."

"Father—" My voice catches in my throat. I so want to know. Called to mind are images of little Kitty, who in her bewilderment beseeched my father, asking him if he loved her anymore. *Don't you love me anymore, Uncle Thomas?* Now I find myself wondering if he has ever loved me; indeed, if he has loved anyone to begin with, or if the loss of his first family served to harden his heart forever. But if it did, why would he have bothered with taking Bess on as mistress, if not for some undeniable affection? Why, if he cannot love, would he have grieved for Surrey?

No, I will not believe he is incapable of love. There is only one person I knew completely unable to love in any normal capacity, and to my eternal relief he rots beside Jane Seymour, the mother of our King Edward and the only woman he in the end considered to be his "true wife." No, King Henry was the antithesis of love.

But not Norfolk.

I swallow tears as I approach him. Gone is my desire to interrogate him about his innermost feelings; gone is my fear that he has none. I have assured myself, as I always have, that things are exactly as I imagine them to be.

"I have said what is needed to be said," I begin, "and will let you sort it out in a manner that suits you." I touch his arm. "I will leave you now, my lord"—I lean up to kiss his cheek—"but my heart will remain."

Norfolk swallows several times but does not respond.

"Come, madam," says the gentle lieutenant, taking my arm. "Come; let me take you away from this place."

Yes, away. I shall go away, back to Reigate, back to my respite, where people are not afraid to love.

In January 1549 the Act of Uniformity is passed, making the celebration of the Catholic Mass illegal. Archbishop Cranmer's *The Book of Common Prayer* replaces the Catholic liturgy at church, and England is a reformist country at last. Now perhaps the fires of Smithfield will burn out; perhaps the dreaded word "heretic" will lose its power to send fear into the hearts of the devoted.

It is a victory I celebrate with all my heart. I am thrilled not to have to fear for my views any longer. I know it is a stride that would have brought much satisfaction to Cat Parr.

Cat is brought to mind even more, however, when that same month her widower, Tom Seymour, is arrested and becomes my father's neighbor in the Tower of London. He has been plotting an uprising against his brother the lord protector, and was caught breaking into the king's bedchamber with the purpose of kidnapping him, no doubt to coerce him into endowing him with more power over His Majesty's little person.

On March 20 he is beheaded at that evil place, that place where were slaughtered my cousins and brother, Tower Hill.

"I am glad Cat did not live to see this," I tell Peggy in strangled tones. "It would have killed her all over again."

"To be sure," Peggy agrees. She casts a pointed glance at me.

"You can thank the Lord above that you never married the man either. He would have brought you nothing but heartache."

I nod. Indeed, I am most fortunate in that regard. Still, I find myself mourning for the misguided man, who has in his thirst for power left his daughter an orphan. Luckily Kate Brandon has taken charge of the baby girl and will no doubt provide for her a life of love and devotion to Cat's New Faith. Kate proved herself a dear friend to Cat in the end, even funding the publication of her book, *The Lamentations of a Sinner*, a triumphant legacy she can share with little Mary Seymour. I pray Kate will share all of Cat's triumphs, that she will make known how clever and noble a queen Cat was, and how kindhearted and courageous a woman.

The sigh I expel is heavy with sadness. Mary will never really know. The glories and traits of an absent parent are abstract, faraway, and almost meaningless. Indeed, Surrey's children, save the older ones, have nearly forgotten him already, and he has been gone but two years.

No, she will know little of her mother. Yet I'm certain everyone will be all too happy to share with her the scandal of her degenerate father. I tremble for her as I think of how merciless the court can be, and pray she will live out her life in some quiet place, some obscure place, a place where cruelty and duplicity have no weight.

A place like Reigate.

I press on. The tragedy of Tom Seymour and Cat Parr is added to the others I have witnessed in my life, but in true Howard form, I am not seen dwelling upon it. There are children to attend to, distractions I am more grateful for than I can ever express.

In early summer Jane Howard, Surrey's eldest, asks me to promenade with her in the gardens. She is a bright, animated young woman with a great deal of her father in her. She is creative and hot tempered, given to heated debates without—in my and Master Foxe's opinions—enough information to support the point she is usually defending. Despite this, she is an endearing young woman of great beauty and humor.

I am pleased young Jane has sought me out, as I always am.

Where she resembles Surrey in temperament, she resembles my
Anne in looks, and being with her calls to mind those happy days
of my youth when I sat at the feet of my queen while she toyed
with my hair and spoke of her hopes for the future.

Jane is much the same, always looking ahead, and as we walk
that day she shares with me her wishes for marriage and children. I
pray that her dreams, unlike the cousin she so resembles, are not
so cruelly denied her.

We walk through the gardens, Jane exclaiming over this flower
and that, until at last she tires. It wasn't much of a walk, I think,
and tell her so as she leads me by the hand into the house.

At once my heart begins to pound. What is she about? Has
something terrible happened where she needed to distract me in
order to spare me from some new drama?

As I am led into the great hall, a great chorus of voices rises up
to cry, "Happy birthday, Mary!"

My face flushes deep crimson. Tears fill my eyes as I scan the
room, finding all of the children, Peggy, Uncle Will, and the Foxes
standing before a magnificent feast laid out in my honor.

I place my hands on my cheeks, taking in a breath.

"There's presents, too," says little Douglas, running forward to
tug my skirt. "I made you a—"

"Douglas!" cries my niece Margaret. "You're not supposed to
tell her!"

"Thank you all so much," I say through tears as I take my place
at the table. After a prayer led by Master Foxe, in which he thanks
God for my patronage, we feast upon stuffed capons, lamb, cheese,
fresh warm bread, tarts, comfits, and puddings.

"When is she going to get to open her presents?" asks Douglas.

"She isn't opening yours first," says my Henry. "She will open
mine because I'm her favorite."

"You are not her favorite," says Thomas. "I am!"

"Hush, now, children." Uncle Will laughs. "Lady Mary's heart
is bigger than anyone we know. She has room enough in it for all of
you and then some. She will open presents from oldest to
youngest, and as *I* am the oldest, her first present will be from
me! Ha!"

There are a few pouts and comments made under the breath, but the children accept Uncle Will's ruling and finish their supper. After which we retire to the parlor where are laid out a pile of presents the like of which I have not seen since Christmas.

"These are all for me?" I breathe in surprise, trying to swallow another onset of tears.

"What are birthdays for?" asks Uncle Will, wrapping an arm about my shoulders. "We are celebrating you today, Mary. Now, remember: oldest to youngest. Open mine first!"

I kneel before the gifts, as excited as a child but trying to maintain the dignity of the thirty-year-old woman I have become. I select the package from Uncle Will and pull away the wrappings with care. Each movement is deliberate; I want the joy of this moment to last.

I cry out in delight when the wrappings reveal a lute. It is the most unusual lute I have ever seen, painted red and decorated with ornate little flowers, ivy, and hummingbirds.

"Oh, Uncle Will!" I shake my head as I run my hand across the beautiful instrument. "It's so unique. I've never seen the like."

"That is because I painted it myself," he tells me. "Much to everyone's displeasure," he says, shooting a playful glance at Peggy. "Peggy thought I'd ruin it if I painted it."

"No . . . oh, no," I assure him as I gaze at the instrument in reverence. "Oh, Uncle Will, it is so beautiful. I never knew you painted."

"I thought my bird needed a lute of her own on which to accompany herself when singing to me," he tells me, his voice soft with affection. "So you see, it is a gift with a selfish motive!"

"On to mine," cries Peggy.

"No," says Master Foxe in a tone matching the jocularity of the room. "I believe I am next—I was born in 1516."

"Master Foxe!" cries Peggy in teasing tones. "You are not supposed to draw attention to a woman's age!"

Master Foxe retrieves my package himself, handing it to me with a smile in his eyes. I open it to find a copy of Catherine Parr's *Lamentations of a Sinner.*

"Master Foxe . . ." I breathe. "Oh, my dear friend Cat."

"I didn't know if you owned a copy yet but . . ." His voice is soft. "I do hope I am not being too forward in giving you one."

"Of course not," I tell him. "I shall cherish it."

"Oh, these men," says Peggy to Agnes Foxe. "They are bent on outdoing us."

Agnes offers a shy little laugh. She retrieves a package and hands it to me.

"Dear Agnes," I tell her, "you did not have to get me anything."

"Were not for you we'd be near starvation," she says in her quiet voice.

I open the package wherein lie five beautiful linen handker-chiefs sewn with her own hands, embroidered with my initials. I reach out and embrace her. "Thank you, Agnes. They are lovely."

She bows her head as though she cannot accept a moment's at-tention, retreating to her husband's side, hiding slightly behind him so as not to be noticed.

"Now, me, thank you very much!" cries Peggy as she hands me her package. "It is in truth from me and the older girls—Jane, Anne, Catherine, and Margaret. We worked on it together."

I open the heavy package to expose a large soft quilt.

"Spread it out and look at it," says Jane.

I do so and take in a breath. It is a patchwork of material from gowns the girls have grown out of, gowns I remember them wear-ing at one time or another.

"See our names?" Catherine asks me.

I run my hand over my family's names, embroidered expertly into the quilt by Peggy. All of them are there, from little Douglas to Jane, to Uncle Will and Peggy. She has even included the Nor-folk branch of the family, embroidering the names of my mother, father, and siblings into the quilt.

"That's to remind you of all the people whose lives you have touched, all of the people who love you," Peggy tells me in a soft voice. "If ever your memory lapses, look at this, the Howard quilt, and know how loved you are."

"Oh, Peggy," I cry, running to her to embrace her. "I'll never be able to thank you enough for this, for all of this."

She holds me tight.

"Is she ever going to open ours?" cries Douglas.

"Yes, yes, now she can open yours," says Uncle Will, clearing his throat. "Children, present arms!" he teases as the boys retrieve their gifts.

From Charles I receive a woven leather bracelet he made himself. From Thomas, a necklace to match with a little cross carved from a smooth pink stone.

"Oh, boys, they're lovely," I tell them as I put the gifts on.

The little girls, Mare-Bear and Douglas, have made me a wreath of dried flowers and herbs to hang on the door of my bedchamber.

"I shall hang it wherever I go," I tell them.

It is Henry whose gift converts my sentimental tears to laughter as he pulls a frog out of his pocket. "I didn't know what to get you," he tells me. "I remember you said you liked how they sang, so I thought you could keep him in your room at night so you could listen to him."

"You must help me build the proper home for him," I tell him as I take the wriggling creature from his hands and cradle him to my breast. "He is a most handsome frog, Henry."

"Thank you," says Henry in earnest tones.

"Thank you," I reply with a chuckle, handing him the frog for safekeeping as I rise to address my family. "Thank you all for your thoughtful gifts and for giving me the most wonderful birthday party of my life."

Hugs are exchanged. I cannot contain myself from crying as I embrace Uncle Will and Master Foxe.

"Are you happy, Lady Richmond?" Master Foxe whispers as he pulls away.

"Yes," I tell him. "I am happy. At long last."

That night as I lay in my bed under my new quilt I think back on the day's wonderful events and thank God for my good fortune.

I do not think about being childless and unmarried at the great age of thirty. For the first night since we came to Reigate I do not think of Norfolk in the Tower or of Surrey's death. I think of today, of my first birthday party. My first and my best.

Strange, when I awoke that day I did not even realize it was my birthday.

* * *

Rumor has reached the manor about a strange cult that has gathered about a shrine dedicated to the Virgin Mary, where many claim miracles and healings take place. Master Foxe is on top of it and puts a stop to the gatherings immediately. The Reformed Church does not venerate the Virgin as the Catholics do and puts no store in such relics as saints' bones or so-called healing locales. He does not want people to lay all their hopes in a lifeless statue, and I am filled with relief when I learn he has taken care of the problem. I do not need the children exposed to such idiocy. They have been exposed to far too much as it is.

Otherwise the year is passed with my surrogate family in peace, each night taking supper together as a merry household, where we discuss the ups and downs of our days. Agnes Foxe, to my delight, has warmed to us at last, and now takes evening walks with Peggy and me through the gardens, or lies with us in the hammock while Master Foxe or Uncle Will pushes us.

The children take their lessons, progressing and growing into beautiful young ladies and gentlemen. I report their progress with pride to their grandfather in the Tower, but he scoffs at their radical teacher, Master Foxe.

"I do not approve, Mary," he tells me again and again.

So relaxed have I become that I fail to care whether he approves or not, and simply say in soothing tones, "I know," while inside I think that there is not much Norfolk can do about it so will allow him his tirades. I am certain they make him feel alive.

On Christmas Eve 1549 I send the bishops of Lincoln, Rochester, and St. David's to attend him. If Norfolk has remained as intelligent as I suspect, he will pick up on why they are there. If it is seen by the Seymours that he has converted to the New Faith, then perhaps they will release him. Of course I do not really care if Norfolk's heart is sincere or not; I know my father and know his capacity for sincerity is limited at best, but I also know how convincing Norfolk can appear at times when it is expedient for him. If he can convince them . . .

To my astonishment, Norfolk does nothing of the kind. He is unresponsive and annoyed by their visit. When in January I bring him belated Christmas presents of new clothing sewn by his granddaughters and me, along with a plate of cheese, meats, and comfits from Reigate, he scowls.

"Keep your holy men to yourself, Mary," he tells me before I am able to offer so much as a greeting. "So. You are proving to be quite the reformer, keeping company with the likes of that John Bale and John Foxe," he goes on. "You are not a good influence on those children. I can only imagine what ideas are being formed in their impressionable minds under your care."

"I can tell you what they are not learning," I say, forcing lightness into my tone. "They are not learning how to betray or abandon. They are not learning how to scheme or plot or connive. They are learning to play and work and love. Their minds and hearts are open and honest. They are sweet, good Christians, and if you knew them you would be most proud of them."

Norfolk shakes his head in disgust, unaffected by my words. "You think you're doing right, Mary, I know," he says, his voice thick with disappointment. "You always have. But you have the habit of walking into one blunder after another."

I open my mouth to defend myself, but he holds up a silencing hand. Like the child I always become when around him, I snap my mouth shut.

"You are too naïve," he says. "It frightens me to think of you alone out there without my protection. You are led by these so-called pundits into God knows what. You trust everyone."

"I trusted you most," I whisper, too worn down to rally against his latest insult.

"A good thing, too," says Norfolk, "because I have served as your protector as long as I have been able. Everything I have ever done has been for you."

I cannot help it. I emit that bitter, mirthless sound that is more cry than laugh.

Norfolk rises from where he was seated on his bed and approaches me. Though he is not much taller than I am, he has the same effect as he did when I was a child—the effect of towering above me, his stern black eyes staring down with their ever-present light of displeasure.

"You think I have always been against you," he says, his voice strained with something akin to sadness. "You think I kept you from Fitzroy because I wanted you to be unhappy, because I didn't want you to have a family of your own."

My heart lurches in anguish at the mention of Harry. To think after all these years it still hurts.

He wraps his arms about me, pulling me close, not in an embrace, but to ensure the lieutenant does not hear what he says next. "Mary, I kept you apart because I got wind of a plot," he whispers. "King Henry—he became threatened by his son's presence. He was afraid that Harry would rise against him and wrest the crown from his potential children with Queen Jane. He . . . he had him poisoned, Mary. He killed him. Do you understand? He killed him."

"Why are you telling me this?" I breathe in despair. It is not true. Not even King Henry could have killed his own child. No. Norfolk just wants to hurt me, just as he always has. "How dare you say such things?"

"Come now, Mary," Norfolk says, annoyed. "Why do you think the king wanted his son's body encased in lead and buried in secrecy? So no one could perform an autopsy—so no attention would be drawn to his death. You recall the boy's illness. A little sudden, think you not?"

I am trembling with so many emotions I know not what to do. Rage, agony, sorrow, fear, confusion . . . I am dizzy. I want to faint. I want to run. Anything to escape this new horror.

"So you see, you believe me to be your great enemy when, were it not for me, you might have ingested whatever it was that killed your husband," he says as though quite proud of himself.

"Yes, you saved me," I tell him, pulling away from him. "You saved me for more years of heartache and sorrow. You saved me for Henry VIII. You, who knew all of this, would not have hesitated to give me to him as his bride. It was expedient for you to risk my life then."

"You would not have come to harm," Norfolk tells me.

"Like Anne and Kitty, I would not have come to harm!" I cry.

"Let us dispense with this, Mary," he says with a wave of his elegant hand, as though the gesture had the power to banish the past from our minds. If it were that simple . . . "We cannot go back. We have only the present and that is my concern now," Norfolk continues, his voice calm and cool, "because presently you keep company with fools. You offer your heart and mind to people unworthy of it; you are every bit the child you were when married to Fitzroy, and in your naïveté expose my grandchildren to heresy."

"It isn't heresy now," I say feebly.

Norfolk shakes his head. "It taxes me, conversing with you," he tells me. "You are dismissed, Mary. And, remember, no more bishops."

"Have no fear of that," I seethe as I allow the lieutenant to escort me from his room and into the world, my heretic world that I love so well.

This new knowledge of the circumstances surrounding my Harry's death haunts me day and night, and even after spring yields to the ripeness of summer, I find I am less able to lose myself in the enchanted realm of Reigate.

Master Foxe inquires after the source of my melancholy as we are taking an evening stroll through the gardens.

I purse my lips. I am so weary of tears that it is an effort to shed them. I draw in a breath. "For so many years, Master Foxe, I was a person of great optimism. Some could call me an idealist. Most, my father especially, would call me naïve." I swallow. "I retained a great deal of that optimism even after the deaths of my cousins George and Queen Anne." Now the tears come—how easily they spill forth, beckoned by my sweet cousins' names, just as they always are. "Then my husband, my Lord Richmond, followed her. Still—" I hold out my hand, gazing at my longtime reminder of hope, the fiery opal ring Norfolk gave me an eternity ago. "Still I lived in almost . . . almost a dream. I always believed that things would get better. I would just have to keep praying, keeping hanging on, keep fighting. And so I did. I won my inheritance through years of struggle and tears. The future seemed bright when the king married his German Anne. Even when they divorced, I remained hopeful. At least he spared her." I bite my quivering lip.

"Then came little Kitty. Oh, Master Foxe, you may have thought her a silly, errant child, and that is what she was. A child. A child sorely in need of love, not the twisted imitation granted by His Majesty." I dab at the tears coursing down my cheeks with one of my new handkerchiefs from Agnes. "She was so beautiful, Master Foxe. So lively and energetic. So young." My voice softens as an image of Kitty conjures itself before my mind's eye. She is twirling about in a new orange gown, covered in jewels, wrapped in a sable. Her blue eyes sparkle with youth and mischief. And life . . . "I believe it was when she died that it began, this cessation of hope. Then my brother followed . . . oh, Master Foxe . . . Now my father stews in the Tower, taking his pleasure in tormenting me with the sins of the past." My voice grows hard. "We have wrought our own fates by deception and betrayal. And now I have charge of these innocent children; it is my responsibility to ensure that they do not turn out like us." The last word is uttered in horror. "You will defend me, I know, and I thank you, dear Master Foxe. But I have been an accomplice to all that has occurred, no different than my father. In my complicity. In my cooperation. In my . . . my malleability."

I sit on one of the garden benches, resting my elbows on my knees and my forehead in my hands. "As I watch the children play, do you know what I think about? I wonder, while searching their little faces, which one will be the deceiver? Which one will be the most manipulative? Who will betray whom? I wonder . . ." I can barely speak through my gulping sobs. "Which . . . one . . . will . . . lose . . . their . . . heads?"

"My dear lady," coos Master Foxe, his tone soft.

The gentleness in his voice causes me to sob harder.

He is at a loss. I am ashamed of my tears but cannot hide them.

Master Foxe reaches over, taking my hand in his. "My lady, you must recall God's words from Romans chapter five, verse five. 'Now hope does not disappoint, because the love of God has been poured into our hearts by the Holy Spirit who was given to us.' You speak of the cessation of hope in your heart, yet you have not yet said it has been extinguished. Whatever hope resides there, smoldering like the dying embers, it has only to be rekindled. *Hope does not disappoint,* my lady. You lost your husband but you did regain your inheritance. You lost many members of your family, an undisputed tragedy, but God has given you charge of your brother's children so that you might be a guiding force in their formative years, a force they are not like to forget." He reaches up to trace my cheek with trembling fingers. "My lady, do not search for what is not yet there, for what might never be. Live in the now. In the Song of Solomon, we are told, 'For lo, the winter is past. The rain is over and gone.' "

"But, Master Foxe," I whisper through tears. "The rain always returns."

Tears fill his eyes. He cups my face in his hands. " 'It shall be, when I bring a cloud over the earth, that the rainbow shall be seen in the cloud.' "

The verse from the ninth chapter of Genesis causes my memory to stir. I see the beach of Calais. I see Harry and Cedric. I see Norfolk . . .

And now, before me, I see Master Foxe. His hands warm my face, his thumbs stroke my tears away. My heart begins to pound. It has changed. Something has changed.

He blinks, withdrawing his hands. He knows.

We sit a moment, regarding each other in silence.

There is nothing to be done. We must return to the manor. We must not think on it.

I must live in the now. The rain is gone. I must look to the clouds; I must look to the rainbow.

Master Foxe and I do not avoid each other, but we no longer keep company alone. We remain amicable. I try to ward off fantasies as we dine together with the children, that he is my husband and they are our children. When I catch myself in these flights of fancy I distract myself with fervent prayers that God will forgive me and take these torturous thoughts away.

"Do you ever think of marrying again, Mary?" asks Peggy one evening as we lie in the hammock. "You would make such a wonderful mother."

I shake my head. "I have seen none too happy a marriage in my day, Peggy. I know what I am missing but, strangely, I am content."

"God bless you," she says, patting my hand.

Indeed, it is this brief conversation that brings about the epiphany that I *am* content.

I begin to let go of my infatuation with Master Foxe and after a while we are able to keep company without discomfort.

For the first time in my life, I realize that it is all right to be alone.

❧ 23 ❧

Rainy Days

In 1552 my sweet Uncle Will is called to Calais, where he has been named lord deputy and governor. We send him off with a feast and he and Peggy vacate the manor with their children, leaving behind a void no one can fill. But I still have "my children," as I often refer to my nieces and nephews, and we adhere to our routine. Master Foxe, now an ordained deacon, remains with us and Agnes and I have grown closer.

But it is quieter. I miss singing with my uncle and chatting with the gregarious Peggy. I miss our long evenings in the gardens together.

Nothing stays the same.

My petitions for Norfolk's release fall on deaf ears. Now and then John Dudley, the Duke of Northumberland, responds that he is, in so many words, entertaining the notion of letting him free.

But he never does.

The year 1553 brings home my uncle Will, and I am thrilled he is once again at Reigate. Peggy and I cry tears of joy for hours. Though she enjoyed Calais, she informs me that she "detests French people!"

I recall my Anne and her adoration for all things French. I smile at Peggy. She is too earthy to hold fast to their love of the superficial. Indeed, it must have been an uncomfortable year for her.

To Uncle Will's delight he has been named lord high admiral, a position my father once held, and though we are pleased, it will take him away from us all too often. But I take pleasure in the fact that at least Peggy and the other children will remain. My nieces and nephews enjoy a happy reunion with their cousins and the house is made merry again.

Until July when, to our horror, the bells toll again, that same old mourning song.

Master Foxe finds me in the gardens without Peggy and Agnes. He seizes my hand. "The young king is dead, Lady Richmond." He draws in a wavering breath. "God save the king."

I shake my head as I recall the kindness in my brother-in-law's eyes when years ago he awarded me guardianship of the children. "He was but sixteen," I breathe in saddened awe.

Almost the same age as his half brother when he passed.

"Oh, dear God, how did it happen?" I whisper as I sink onto the garden bench.

"They say it was the consumption," he tells me.

Consumption. The same supposed fate my Harry succumbed to. Was that it, then? Or was his death, like his brother's, wrought by much darker forces?

"What happens now?" Agnes asks. "What will this mean for the church? Once the Catholic takes the throne it is all over for us."

I shiver as I think of Princess Mary, who is indeed so ardently Catholic that there is no doubt any strides we have made in reform will be put asunder by her and her supporters.

Master Foxe reaches out to his wife, taking her hand, letting go of mine. "We must wait and see. Nothing has been decided."

"But King Henry's will . . ." I say. "It has named her as successor to Edward." My voice catches when saying his name. "Who will dispute it?"

"The Dudleys, another group of upstarts," says Peggy, utilizing my least favorite word. "We shall see what happens."

And so we wait.

True to form, there are few transitions of power that can ever go smoothly. It seems King Edward signed a document on his deathbed in the presence of the Duke of Northumberland naming the Lady Jane Grey his successor, claiming she has more a right to the throne through her Tudor-Brandon connection than his sister, who is little more than a bastard. Of course anyone with cognizance knows Northumberland is behind the entire scheme. Jane is his daughter-in-law, having married his son Guildford by force. He probably guided the king's failing hand in the signing of the document himself.

Another Norfolk.

On 10 July Lady Jane is proclaimed Queen of England. I can only imagine what she is feeling right now. I remember her in the days of Cat's reign, serving as her little maid. She was sweet and intelligent and keen on the ideas of reform.

We listen to the unfolding of the events from our safe vantage point at Reigate, each of us unsure as to what our hopes are for the outcome of the situation.

"I, for one, wish they'd dispense with all of this nonsense and name Princess Elizabeth queen," mumbles Uncle Will.

Peggy shushes him. Now are not the days for free opinion. We do not know what is coming. Oh, to fear those dark days of Henry VIII come to life again . . .

We wait.

We do not have to wait long.

On 19 July Princess Mary wins the day, dispersing Lord Suffolk's army that was sent to detain her, with her own loyal troops and imprisoning poor, used Queen Jane and her pitiful husband in the Tower of London. There is little doubt who the next ruler of England is to be.

I fret for poor Lady Jane, nine days a queen, and wonder how she will be punished. Surely Queen Mary will be merciful; surely she will realize that the girl was a tool of men's ambitions, men who hoped to rule through her just as Norfolk hoped to rule through me. Oh, God . . . please let her be merciful . . .

When Queen Mary enters London in early August, my mother is pleased to come from Kenninghall to attend the daughter of her beloved Queen Catherine of Aragon. Touched by the longstanding loyalty, the queen decides it is now expedient to release from the

Tower the high-profile prisoners incarcerated during the reign of her late brother.

At long last Norfolk is free.

I am in London when he is released along with Stephen Gardiner, that man I so detest. They kneel before her, the picture of humility, while she exclaims, her voice filled with tears, "These are my men!"

She rests her hands on my father's shoulders, smiling down at him while he lifts his face to her as though staring at the Blessed Virgin herself.

He will forget—no doubt he will forget—my years of petitioning the Crown. All will be lost in the light that surrounds the daughter of his Catherine of Aragon like a holy aura.

Despite my resentment I find myself running to him, as I always do. I think of all the wonderful liberties he will now be able to indulge. At last he can ride without an escort. He can come home to Kenninghall and hunt, visit whomever he pleases, and enjoy the remainder of his life, *free*.

I look to the Tower, that dreaded place, and think of little Lady Jane, wondering if she will ever enjoy her freedom again. I force her from my mind. As cold as it sounds, it is not my worry.

Now I must attend Norfolk. I throw my arms about his shoulders, our tears mingling against each other's cheeks.

"You are free!" I cry. "My dearest lord, you are free!"

He pulls away, offering a rueful smile. *"Gracia Dei sum quod sum,"* he says. His voice is filled with energy. "There is much to be done. Meet me at Mountjoy House."

Much to be done. Not a day of freedom without moving on to his favorite pastime: plotting.

Gracia Dei sum quod sum. By the grace of God, I am what I am.

At Mountjoy I arrange a small supper, my father's first as a free man. I make sure all of his favorite things are served. He eats little. He is so thin now that it must be difficult for him to consume much.

"Mary, I am being reinstated to the Privy Council. As many of my lands are to be restored to me as possible, along with my titles.

We are in the ascendant once more." His eyes are alive with that old sparkle and I admit being caught up in it.

I reach out, taking his hands in my own. "I am so glad, Father."

"You must realize that your days of playing the reformer are over," he says then.

My heart sinks. I begin to tremble.

"This is a Catholic court now. Queen Mary plans on restoring England to the True Faith once more," he tells me. "I am telling you this because I do not want you to come to harm. Your views could compromise you if you are too vociferous."

"I appreciate your concern," I tell him.

"Do you understand what I am saying, Mary?" he asks, leaning forward. "I am telling you that there are going to be some changes." He draws in a breath. "I have taken it upon myself to dismiss your friend Foxe. I will be taking the children in hand now."

My heart has stopped. I swear it has stopped. I cannot breathe. For a moment I think I have gone blind. The world is black. My gut lurches violently. I blink several times, trying to restore my senses.

"I do not think you understand . . ." I begin. "You cannot understand. I have engaged the best tutor possible for the children. They—they have flourished under his instruction."

"I will not have them partaking of this radical education any longer," he says, his soft voice firm. "I will do nothing to offend Her Majesty. I am free now and I will remain so. Thomas, as my heir, must receive only the best, and I am instructing Frances to send the others here to Mountjoy House."

"But they love Reigate," I whisper, too stunned to say anything else. "That is their home. The city is not good for them. The air carries too many illnesses. They need to stay at Reigate. They need to stay with me!"

"Mary—" Norfolk's voice is almost gentle. "You are not their mother. Frances deserves to be with her children. It is time."

At once I am filled with rage. "As if that means anything to you at all! You, who will tear families apart as soon as create them! No, this is all about pleasing the queen. It is all about proving how

Catholic the Howards have remained. Well, I will tell you, you can play the devout Catholic all you like, but nothing will change who I am and what I believe. Nothing will sway me from my faith!"

Norfolk rises, the movement swift and sure, filled with the confidence he has always demonstrated with such ease. He seizes both of my wrists, pinning them to the table.

"Believe whatever you please!" he cries. "Just take care you don't burn for it!"

The lieutenant is no longer here. There is no one to protect me now. I have forgotten. For so long I have been able to be free in my speech without fear of repercussions, but now, with Norfolk's face inches from mine, every violent exchange that has ever occurred between us is recalled. My temple begins to throb.

"Whatever your faith, you are no longer to be an influence on my grandchildren," he continues in his calm voice. "They are to be returned to me if I have to seize them by force. And believe me, I can do that."

There is no doubt of it. There is no doubt at all.

My shoulders slump in defeat. All the years of work, all the years of striving to be the best example I could be, dashed by a restored duke and a Catholic queen.

I gaze into my lord's face. I cannot cry. The tears have been sapped from me. They are in the clouds.

"They shall be returned," I tell him, my voice very soft. "But you must promise me you will not upset them by seizing them by force. Let me bring them to you." My voice is a pathetic plea and I am ashamed of the desperation in it. "Because I loved them, my lord. They were my joy for . . . some time."

Norfolk releases my wrists, cupping my cheek with his hand. "A wise choice, my lady," he says, sitting back down.

He returns to his supper.

He eats a little better now, it seems.

I return to Reigate while Norfolk commences to do what he does best—wreak havoc. He presides over the trial of John Dudley, Duke of Northumberland, on 18 August, where his old enemy is convicted of treason for his part in the Jane Grey calamity and, I am certain, attends his execution with a light heart four days later. I am sure he does not even look at the Tower as he watches Dudley's head roll.

Norfolk presses on.

Pressing on is not as easy for me. I am beleaguered by terrible stomach pain that causes me to walk hunched over at times as I ready the children for their trip to London. The younger ones are excited to return to the bustling city. They do not understand. Perhaps it is better, this shroud of innocence. It will be shed soon enough. Let them be happy, let them anticipate their new life with joy and not dread.

Frances says that I might stay on with them, but I know I cannot. My views are too well known to remain too close to this new court. And if Queen Mary has retained any of her father's traits, then this is a dangerous court and I am through with dangerous courts.

Master Foxe, famed for his Protestant views, decides it is unsafe to remain in England any longer.

"I have more to think of than myself," he tells me as he draws Agnes near. "We are expecting a blessing of our own. It must be safeguarded."

I embrace him and Agnes. "God bless you and keep you. May He watch over you wherever you go."

They hold me tight.

Master Foxe assists Agnes into the coach then returns to me a moment, taking my hands in his. "I love you, Mary," he says simply. He drops my hands. And is gone.

I will never see him again.

"There will be a lot of changes," I tell the children, echoing my father's words on the day we make for London. I am unable to hide the tears from my voice. I give them a piece of advice that I received years ago. "You must pray as they pray, believe as they believe, but only outwardly. They do not own your hearts or minds. There you are beholden only to God. It is not cowardly to hide your true beliefs in order to preserve your life, no matter how much we all admire the martyrs. Please. Remember, self-preservation is the means to survival. Always." I draw in a breath, clutching my stomach, doubling over a moment. Catherine clutches my arm, her hazel eyes lit with concern. I right myself, offering a quick smile of reassurance. "I cannot stay with you, but I beg you to remember that these past years I have endeavored to do right by you. I believe in each and every one of you and your capacity to do good. *I love you all.*"

The children surround me in the gardens and we embrace; they envelop me in their warmth and love. In one another's arms we draw strength from our present, hoping it will accompany us into the uncertainty of the future.

The journey to London, so unlike that first journey to Reigate all those years ago, is not filled with anticipation or eagerness. I imagine the children are nervous, wondering what kind of world they will find. Thomas asks me questions about his grandfather and I am not inclined to answer him honestly.

I want to make things sound as positive as possible.

We arrive at Mountjoy House, where Norfolk awaits to collect Thomas. He makes a show of exclamations over all of the children; how they have grown, how lovely the girls are, how strong and sure young Thomas seems. He promises them that life will be wonderful here; indeed, if they are only obedient they shall be much favored by Her Majesty . . .

I do not listen after this point. I have heard it all before.

When it comes time to take my leave, young Thomas embraces me.

"I will never forget you, Aunt Mary," he says. "I will never forget your grace or your wisdom. I will never forget your love for us."

"My dear lord," I tell him, holding him to me. "Never have I been so proud of anyone."

We disengage.

I do not speak to Norfolk. I do not trust myself, and as I want to avoid violence in front of the children, find it is best to quit Mountjoy House, quit London.

Indeed, quit it all.

*   *   *

I hear tales of Norfolk and the family through Frances. She writes of the beautiful coronation banquet my father supervised for Her Majesty. She writes of young Thomas being the youngest ever to be created Knight of the Bath the day before, and how fine he looked in his regalia.

Through her I learn that Thomas serves Gardiner—vile Gardiner, now named lord chancellor—as his page, while Henry continues his education under the supervision of a stern priest named John White.

Disgusted, I toss the letter aside and lie under my quilt at Reigate, tracing the children's names, thinking, as I should not, of the past . . . the magical past . . .

In October Queen Mary presides over Parliament with the proposal that the marriage between her parents be legitimized. It all seems rather pointless to me, but I am not there and I suppose it is too trying to care.

To my relief, however, I learn that Lady Jane Grey is to be pardoned. At least the queen has some heart. She must see that the girl was a pawn, as most women are. I hope the girl will be released soon and allowed to live out her life in some semblance of peace.

But when the queen pardons Lord Suffolk, the duke proves himself to be as dense as they come, and proclaims his daughter Jane queen again, rallying an army led by Thomas Wyatt to support the claim. It is his hope that the country will support Jane in favor of the "Spanish-loving" Mary, who signed a marriage treaty with Philip of Spain on 12 January.

I retch when I hear of another father's thoughtlessness toward his daughter. How can he be so foolish? Now there is no hope . . .

Norfolk is named lieutenant-general of the army sent to disperse Wyatt's insurgents at Rochester on 22 January—Norfolk, who is eighty-one years old. I cannot believe the queen sees fit to send him, out of all the able-bodied men at her disposal. In Norfolk's triumphant letter to me, he tells me that no one is quite as capable in the area of military strategy, which is why she favored him with this responsibility.

Norfolk cannot predict that at Rochester Bridge some of his own forces would decide to switch sides and join up with the charismatic Wyatt. Norfolk could not seem to contrive of a strategy to combat that one, and retreats, retiring to Kenninghall, humiliated.

The queen's forces prove victorious on 7 February, however, when Wyatt surrenders. If Norfolk could have held out a little longer, perhaps he would have been able to credit himself with the triumph. But it was not to be.

On 12 February, while I lie under my quilt and watch the snow fly, Lady Jane and her husband are executed for high treason, though her only crime was being born to the worst of people.

Again, all I can do is thank God I am not present to see more lives submitted to the axe.

Jane's father is executed on 23 February.

So this is how Queen Mary's reign begins—with death.

In March I learn the worst, the news that sends me again to my bed, where I will find no comfort. Princess Elizabeth, my clever, beautiful, black-eyed cousin, has been sent to the Tower, where so many Howards before her have suffered. She is suspected of participating in the Wyatt rebellion.

I remember my impression of the young woman with the beautiful Howard hands. The young woman I was so certain would be queen of England in her time. I was convinced it was ordained by God.

"What does it all mean?" I cry to Peggy, who holds my hand as I retch into a basin. All I can see is Princess Elizabeth, a tawny-haired babe in my arms. Her little hand curls about my finger . . . "God, what is it all for? Is she to follow her mother to the block? Oh, Anne, my beautiful Anne, were I but stronger I would have seen you spared!"

Uncle Will sits at my bedside, swabbing my fevered brow with a cool cloth. "Please, my little bird, please. You are mad with grief." His eyes seek out his wife. "Should I write the duke?"

Peggy glares. "So he can finish her?" She shakes her head, drawing in a wavering breath. Her voice is soft, speculative. "My lord, how many heartbreaks can one person take, d'you believe?"

Uncle Will does not respond. He gathers me in his arms, commencing to rock, singing gently. I lose myself in his voice.

* * *

April brings about Wyatt's execution—ah, Mary is her father's child!—but Elizabeth, to my eternal relief, is spared and transferred to Woodstock, where she shall live in isolation. As she always has.

I give thanks to God. He is sparing her for her own reign. I know; somehow I have been given the knowledge that she will endure. She will be what her mother and cousin could not. She will be queen. Someday. In her time.

It occurs to me in the wake of these events that I no longer want to hear anything more about court, not even about the tragedies and triumphs of my own family. Indeed, I do not think I can bear it.

Norfolk sends me letters. Where am I? he is wondering. Why am I not with him at Kenninghall? I am overdue a visit.

Peggy and I watch the letters burn in the hearth; the parchment curls up and blackens. My father's hurried scrawl is obliterated in the flames.

I do not write him back. I lie under my quilt, my Howard quilt, and think of the people who loved me.

❧ 24 ❧

Norfolk and Me

I receive the news in August.

He is dying. I repeat the phrase to myself over and over. *He is dying.* Somehow it doesn't seem possible that he should die. He has outlasted them all; five of Henry's queens, Henry himself, Wolsey, Cromwell, Surrey, Bess, King Edward, Henry Fitzroy . . . Harry . . .

Now he will join them, wherever they have gone—if indeed we go anywhere at all. A wry smile curves my lips; years ago I would have chastised myself for the thought. Now I do not shut out what is real. Reality has always pursued me. So I yield to it. In this perhaps Reality and I will make our peace.

I arrive at Kenninghall—running to him again—and draw in a breath as I enter the chambers. I have imagined this scene before many times; a strange and reluctant morbid fantasy. In a dynamic confrontation, Norfolk lies dying, beseeching me for forgiveness; I grant it with a heart as pure as a prayer, rising above my base instincts so that he may be afforded peace.

It will not play out that way, I am certain.

He is in bed, that much is a given—a great mahogany four-poster with a beautiful blue velvet canopy. He looks tiny. It occurs to me for the first time how much this small man has done, how many lives he has raised high, how many lives he has shattered. To think what one small man might achieve . . .

I approach and curtsy. He is dying, after all. I must try to be gracious.

He gestures for me to sit beside him. I remain standing. Years of experience have taught me not to get too close to Norfolk. I do not know how much strength he has left in him, but I am certain there is enough to strike out at me like a coiled snake.

He purses his lips and eases himself up into a sitting position. "I think you have been avoiding me," he says with his almost laugh.

I say nothing.

"I'll be leaving you, it seems." He averts his head to look out the window, out at the world. "You will be free."

I close my eyes. Anger hot as wine surges through my veins.

"Free?" I breathe, incredulous. This will not do, I tell myself. I am supposed to exemplify grace and composure. But the words come, pulled forth by a force greater than I am. "I can never be free. You have made sure of that. All my life . . ." Tears clutch my throat. I allow them to stream down my cheeks unchecked. "You have taken away everyone and everything that has ever meant a thing to me. Mother, Harry, Anne, George, Kitty, Surrey, Master Foxe . . ." I shake my head. I still can't believe the length of the list, even after all this time. "And the children, my beloved children . . ." My shoulders quake with sobs. "Now you dare say I am free." I offer a bitter smile. "Free to do what? Marry? Marry whom? I am thirty-five years old and in poor health. I am known forever as the woman who condemned her brother to death and her father to prison. I am regarded as little better than Jane Boleyn."

He says nothing. His black eyes are alert; indeed, he does not look like he is dying. His expression bears the same calm indifference it always did; his lips twist into that same sardonic half smile. The only indication that he is unwell lies in the fact that he is abed in his nightclothes. He would never have presented himself before anyone thus when he enjoyed good health.

"So you do hate me, then," he says, his voice soft, almost as though he is hoping to satisfy a point of curiosity.

"I should," I tell him. "But no. Stripping me of everyone deserving of my love ensured that I would always need you, that I would always be yours. You were the only man, the only *being* I was ever permitted to love." I pause, allowing him to appreciate the profundity of the statement. "So I did love you, with all my *soul* I loved you. So much so that I blinded myself to your savagery and indifference. What I allowed myself to see was justified or, at the very least, explained. And now, now when I can hate you, when indeed I *yearn* to hate you, I cannot. Too much has come to pass between us—a lifetime of fear and awe and the love that you took and twisted."

He flinches at this. His head lolls to the side. He closes his eyes. For one panicked moment I fear my outburst has been too much for him and this will be my last memory of this man—this man who, despite everything, I still love.

"My lord?" No response. "Father!" I cry in fear.

His eyes flutter open. He draws in a sigh. "It was not your fault, you know."

"What?" I ask, sitting beside him now. I take his thin hand in my own, recalling how I used to fear its power while marveling at its perfection. Now it is a gnarled patchwork of veins and wrinkles and age spots. An old man's hand.

"Surrey." He regards me. Tears stand bright in his eyes; they are like liquid onyx. "The trial. My imprisonment. It was not your fault."

I am unable to mask my bitterness. "You tell me this now? Is this a recent epiphany or did you enjoy my years of guilt?"

He emits a heavy sigh, ignoring the question, just as I expect. "My drawer . . . in the desk over there. There is something I want you to have."

I rise and make way to the desk, opening the drawer. My manner is distracted and angry. I pull it harder than I should and it slides out so far it gets caught. I cannot push it back in.

"Never mind that," says Norfolk, his tone weary. "Look inside."

I look. Tears form a lump in my throat. I reach down to finger the circlet, the little silver circlet with the seed pearls that he presented me when I was eleven years old, the circlet I had thrown at him in anger on my wedding night.

"You kept it," I murmur.

"I carried it into battle with me," he tells me, coughing. He taps his chest with a slim finger. "I placed it under my armor."

I sit beside him again, fingering the circlet, so dainty, so perfect for a maiden. Norfolk takes it from me, admiring it a moment himself. He reaches out, cupping my cheek, wiping away tears with his thumb before slowly removing my hood. When my hair is exposed he runs his fingers through it. "That hair of yours," he says in an absent way, a half smile playing on his lips. I try to laugh but it catches in my throat. Norfolk places the circlet on my head, keeping his warm hands on either side of my face.

"Mary," he says, his voice thick with emotion. "It was always you. Only you."

It is a love I do not understand. Nor do I understand my reciprocation of it.

So I do not try. I crawl into bed beside him, resting my head on his chest, wrapping my arm about his middle. He draws me close, holding me a long while. It is our first true embrace. There is nothing expected from it. No more is anyone being manipulated; no more is power being sought; no more is ambition fueling Norfolk's every breath. There are no more dreams or hopes. All these years of pain and struggling and fighting have brought us to this: a list of fruitless no mores.

We hold each other a long while. I find myself enveloped in death's mantle; I cannot shrug it off.

When I leave him, my anger faded to a numbness some may call peace, I know I will not see my lord Norfolk again. It does not matter so much. Wherever he goes I will soon follow.

So it has always been with Norfolk and me.

❧ EPILOGUE ❧

Elizabeth Stafford Howard

December 1555

A year later my daughter Mary, Duchess of Richmond, joined her father in death. Her appetite dwindled; her stomach was relentlessly upset; pain stalked her in her waking hours and she found little relief. It was as though she lived for the challenges he presented her with; so accustomed was she to strife that when freed of it at last, she did not know how to thrive. So she did not. Like a Tudor rose, she withered and died.

She rests beside her husband, her Harry. I do not know if she would have rather been beside Norfolk, but I could not have suffered it. Her entire life belonged to him. Perhaps the solace that forever evaded her will at last be found lying beside the man who would have loved her, had fate been a little kinder.

I bury her with four jewels: her wedding ring, a little opal ring, a miniature bearing the face of a violet-eyed man, and, upon her golden head, a little silver circlet inlaid with seed pearls.

How young she looked in her casket. No, I will not think of it.

So here I am. I outlived them all—a goal one should not strive for, I have learned. I buried three of my four children, my husband (what a relief!)—even my rival, poor Bess Holland. I suppose I loved them. If I could not show it, it was only because I was not able; my own suffering eclipsed everything else, depriving my family and me of the opportunity to know my true self. I don't know. I miss little Mary, though; her sweet unassuming ways, her understated courage, her beliefs that, despite everything, remained uncompromising. I miss what was. I miss what will never be.

Sometimes I wonder if I could have saved her. No doubt I could not. There is naught to be done for a woman but to await the Lord's embrace.

No one will remember her. The annals of history will record her thus: Mary Howard Fitzroy, Duchess of Richmond; wife of Henry Fitzroy, illegitimate son of Henry VIII; daughter of Thomas Howard, third Duke of Norfolk.

They will not remember that she narrowly escaped being the seventh bride of mad King Henry. Too many others take precedence; their portraits line the halls of the palaces, faces staring out with flat, lifeless eyes. Anne, Catherine, even Norfolk . . . images to haunt the mind for centuries to come. But like Holbein's drawing, Mary's life is sketchy.

I stand at St. Michael's Church, Framlingham, my daughter's resting place. It is the strangest thing. Whenever I am here I see a rainbow. It arches over the tomb, a myriad of colors stretching down for an embrace, like God's great arms. I squint. It is fading— just one more glimpse . . .

So brief is its beauty; now it is gone.

SECRETS OF THE TUDOR COURT

D. L. Bogdan

ABOUT THIS GUIDE

The suggested questions are included to
enhance your group's reading of D. L. Bogdan's
Secrets of the Tudor Court!

DISCUSSION QUESTIONS

1. Discuss how Mary's character changes throughout the novel.

2. Who were Mary's biggest influences?

3. How did Mary's regard for the king change throughout the novel?

4. Discuss Mary's fascination with Norfolk's hands.

5. How do you think Norfolk regards Mary? What were the major contributors to his persona?

6. What were, in your opinion, the three biggest turning points in the novel?

7. Analyze The Kiss.

8. Compare and contrast Mary's relationships with Harry, Cedric, and Master Foxe. Of these three, who would you consider "the love of her life"?

9. Did your opinion of Mary's mother change throughout the novel? If so, how?

10. Why do you think the novel was told in the first person, present tense? Is this a writing style you like?

11. Why does Mary refer to her father as "Norfolk" throughout the novel? How does this affect her view of him?

12. Three themes are present in the novel: self-preservation, the rainbow, and the circlet. What is the relevance of these three themes to the story? Why do you think I chose to expound on them?